WHITE
VILLA

Emily Hourican is a journalist and author. She grew up in Brussels, where she went to the European School and learned how to fake it as a Eurobrat, and now lives in Dublin with her family. She has written features for the *Sunday Independent* for ten years, as well as for *Image* magazine, *Condé Nast Traveler* and *Woman and Home*. She was also editor of *The Dubliner Magazine*.

www.emilyhourican.com
@EmilyH71

Also by Emily Hourican

Fiction
The Privileged

Non-Fiction
How to (Really) be a Mother

EMILY HOURICAN

WHITE VILLA

HACHETTE
BOOKS
IRELAND

First published in Ireland in 2017 by
HACHETTE BOOKS IRELAND

1

Cataloguing in Publication Data is available from the British Library

ISBN 978 1 4736 2826 7

Typeset in Garamond by redrattledesign.com

Printed and bound in Great Britain by Clays Ltd, St Ives plc

Hachette Books Ireland policy is to use papers that are natural, renewable and
recyclable products and made from wood grown in sustainable forests. The logging and
manufacturing processes are expected to conform to the environmental regulations of
the country of origin.

Hachette Books Ireland
8 Castlecourt Centre
Castleknock
Dublin 15, Ireland

A division of Hachette UK Ltd
Carmelite House, 50 Victoria Embankment, EC4Y 0DZ

www.hachettebooksireland.ie

For all the usual suspects – the people I love

PART ONE

CHAPTER 1

The house felt emptier of more than just the people who had passed through in the days around the funeral, as if they had taken their good wishes away with them, along with their subdued voices and chilly hands.

It didn't matter where Natasha went because all the rooms were the same. For all their lofty ceilings and deliberately sparse furnishings, they felt mean; crouched, dispirited, like dogs waiting for their master's voice. Natasha, who knew that voice would never come again, pitied them. She wondered would the house ever respond to her, then decided it wouldn't.

She knew how the house felt, as she wandered through its rooms, looking for something that wasn't there. Someone who would never, now, be there. All that was left was the knowledge that there would never be anyone else for whom she was the most important person in the world.

As much as she looked for him, she also looked for the loss of him. Her own feelings of grief and pain, so raw in the few days after his death, were distanced from her now, a distance she couldn't bridge, so that even though she could see her grief, could have spelled it out, she couldn't feel it.

There was a thick layer of something heavy and congealed between her and it, something that subdued the edges not just of grief, but of everything. And so Natasha went in search of something that would trigger the storm of weeping that rose up inside her but would not break, except in dreams.

Since his death, she had dreamed, night after night, of being able to cry. In sleep, she found a release that was denied to her when awake. She dreamed of great tearing sobs that came, one hard upon the other, until she was, at last, thrown up, beached upon the shore of her own distress, brought through the storm and now calm, emptied, if only temporarily, of the pain of his loss.

But that was only in dreams. Waking, she had a split-second where her mind searched itself, feeling gently, the way she had often felt a bruised leg or ankle, to find out how bad the hurt was. Then it found the bruise, the break, and memory came rushing back – he was gone – and with it came the same feeling of cold lard settling upon her.

Having toured the house – in search of what she did not know . . . perhaps nothing more than the proof of its emptiness – Natasha went looking for some kind of sharpened stick, something to goad her beyond the place she was, where she felt as stuck as an insect in amber.

The sitting room at the back was the least cheerless spot she could find, although rain spat at its windows, and the garden beyond was huddled into a wet heap beneath the blanket of soggy grass and flattened flowers. It had been raining steadily since her father's death, over a week earlier, and Natasha felt a savage satisfaction in nature's recognition of an abomination.

The fire was lit, and Natasha momentarily admired her mother's instinct towards comfort, her attempts to hold back the abyss that trailed at their feet with soup and freshly made pastries and warm fires. Natasha had a similar instinct, the opposite to her sister Nancy, who was more likely to tear off her clothes and run into the storm than she was to make herself a seawall of comfort.

Natasha went to the bookshelf with the photo albums – the work of one long summer when she was a teenager, but still a child too; beset by the confusions and uncertainties of her age, she had looked for order here, and imposed it as she had seen fit: carefully cataloguing the jumbled mess of family holidays, memories, changing haircuts and seasons, by name, by date, by place. Imposing order on chaos. Nancy, gnawed at by the same uncertainties and confusions, had turned her need for order inwards, divorcing herself from her body and accepting food under some peculiar system known only to her.

Natasha looked at photos of herself on a white-sand beach, skin coloured golden by the sun, her long dark hair lit up with reddish strands beneath a yellow sun hat. Behind her, the sky was blue velvet. 'Nerja 1996' was written in careful letters at the bottom of the page, which would mean she was then about ten years old. Beneath were more photos – of her in the water, Nancy in a hole dug up to her neck, both of them on a blanket eating slices of watermelon. In the first photo, her father in a khaki green T-shirt sat beside Natasha with a newspaper folded across his knees. The masthead said *El País* in assured letters.

Natasha looked hard at the photo, trying, not to recapture the moment, which was gone from her entirely, so much as to feel again in her imagination the warmth of his arm close to hers, the solid reassurance of his body beside her. She stared hard, without blinking, as if the intensity of her effort could melt the barriers in her mind. Light from the fire flickered across the photo behind its plastic sheet, so that it seemed as if the sun of that day burned still.

She couldn't see who she was behind the wide grin, and wondered if the man beside her had known, or had he only seen what he had wanted to see – a child he believed to be in his own image: bright and fearless.

Her mother walked in then, looked at Natasha curled up on a high-backed leather armchair with the photo album on her lap and came over to her.

Natasha turned the pages. Together they watched as the past flickered by in a series of bright images, no more real than advertising posters. Any one of them could have been used to sell washing powder, Natasha thought. Or cheese, or breakfast cereal. They spoke of effort and contrivance, posed photos tending all towards the same result: perfection. Where are the out-takes? Natasha wondered. The bloopers. Anything to give a dose of reality to the sterile images in front of her. Were all family photos like that? Lies. Or was it just theirs?

'Look.' Her mother stopped the flick of pages, the stop-motion animation of time passing, bringing a finger down heavily on a picture of Natasha and her father in a convertible sports car. The car was lean and camel-coloured, like the filter of a cigarette, Natasha remembered thinking. She was older in this photo, maybe fourteen, hair piled on top of her head in an obvious bid for sophistication, wearing a pink cardigan over a white summer dress. Her mother's finger, with its carmine nail, rested in the space between Natasha and her father.

The car had been lent, along with a house in the south of France, for a few weeks by friends. Her father had found it in an old stone shed and had driven it round to the front of the house where Natasha, her mother and Nancy had been unloading cases from their own navy Ford.

'Who wants to come for a drive?' he had called, tooting the horn and laughing so that they'd all dropped their boxes and run to him. 'So, who's coming?' he'd said. 'Natasha?'

'Yes, please!' She'd reached for the door handle, but Nancy's voice, plaintive, held her back.

'I want to come too.'

'I can only take one,' their father had said. 'It's a two-seater.'

'Why does Natasha get to go?' Nancy had been shrill, building to a scene. 'I want to.' There was silence then, and it had swirled around them like a dust storm.

'Because she's the eldest?' Her mother had said it helplessly, an interrogation, not a statement.

'She's not. You are, Mum. So why don't you go?' Nancy had been triumphant, thinking her blow unanswerable. And it was, Natasha knew, the perfect solution for Nancy. As long as Natasha didn't get singled out, she was happy. Natasha had waited for her parents to respond but there was only more silence. She'd watched her mother look at her father – another interrogation – and had seen her father close himself to it.

'I can only take one,' he'd repeated. 'Natasha's coming.'

She had considered ceding her place but knew it was too late, so she'd slid into the car instead, leather seats already warm from the sun, like melting caramel, and watched as Nancy and her mother grew small behind them.

She wondered now was her mother remembering the same scene. The finger with its carmine nail moved to flick a grain of something from the page.

'The car of envy,' her mother said, and Natasha knew that she too had played out the scene in her mind, but with who knew what extra shading and detail. Even after all these years, the inflections of the land of her mother's birth were still obvious.

'I'm hungry,' Natasha said, shutting the photo album.

'Good.' Her mother said it mechanically. 'You should eat.'

It's what they had said to each other since his death: *You need to rest. You should eat. You ought to get out.* The currency of their interactions was ambiguous – careful stepping-stones made up of trite reminders, the kind that could have covered a depth of concern and kindness. Or could simply have been all that they felt able to say to one another.

They went into the kitchen together and Natasha ate the ham and rocket sandwich her mother made, slumped on one elbow at the table. The effort of sitting straight was too much for her, the weight of grief too heavy.

'I know what you have lost,' her mother said suddenly, an attempt at sympathy.

'What we all have lost.' Natasha tried to be fair.

'Most of all you. What I lost, I lost a long time ago.'

Natasha felt this was true but couldn't work out exactly why, or whether that gave her mother more or less of a claim to misery than her. Because of how much the answer to that mattered, she closed down the conversation, the better to think about it at another time.

'What will you do next?' she asked.

'I have many things. I need to clear the house.'

'Will Nancy help you?'

'I don't know. She didn't say when she'll be back from London. Maybe you will help me?'

'I can't. I can't go through his things. I can't look at them and decide what they are without him. Which have value and which don't. Either they all do or none does.' She shrugged off the impossibility of explaining further. 'I don't understand how you can.' The accusation stood between them, an invitation. But her mother refused it.

'Someone has to', was all she said.

Knowing she would scream if she sat there any longer, Natasha finished the sandwich and stood up.

'I'm going to rest,' she said.

'Good.' Her mother watched her go, and Natasha tried to force herself to catch her mother's eye at the door and smile, but she couldn't.

Up in her room, staring out into the darkening sky, hoping for one late gleam of light before the day collapsed in on itself, Natasha thought about what her mother had said, *I know what you have lost*, and wondered why she had restrained herself from screaming, 'Everything! I have lost everything!'

Why had she not said it? Was it because she suspected her mother wouldn't understand? Or because her mother might resent this declaration of absolutism, a declaration that should surely have been hers?

She wished Nancy were there. That they could have patrolled the house together, searching its corners and crevices, looking for proof of what they had all been. Except she knew Nancy wouldn't see what she saw, or even seek what she sought. Instead, Nancy would have looked for confirmation of what she suspected: that her own loss, like their mother's, was different. Second best.

Natasha wished there could have been a unity of purpose between them in death. For a few days she had even pretended it was so, until Nancy's determined rejection of her efforts forced her to withdraw. Even choosing the readings for the funeral hadn't brought them together in the way she had hoped.

'Choose what you want,' Nancy had said when Natasha had suggested 'The souls of the righteous are in the hand of God'.

'Well, do you think 'The just man, though he die early, shall be at rest' would be better?' Natasha had persisted.

'Honestly, Natasha, you choose. You know I don't think it matters what we read over a dead body. You could read the shipping forecast and he wouldn't know or care.'

Natasha had flinched from the hardness of the words.

At the funeral itself she had tried to stay close to Nancy, in the belief that they needed to be together. But Nancy had eluded her, slipping off after the mass to stand with John and a knot of his friends, so that Natasha had been left with the long line of people who stood, one behind another, shuffling forward to clutch her hand

and whisper their regrets. 'A good man,' they had said. 'A brilliant man. A loss to us all.' Natasha had wondered at their idiocy in trying to put their pain on a par with her own. Her mother had stood beside her, taking refuge in her foreignness and saying little.

'You won't always feel like this.' The woman who had said it was, Natasha thought, a work colleague of her father's. She had said it urgently, intimately, as if the delivering of this message were a sacred charge. *You won't always feel like this*. It was the only thing that had made sense to Natasha that day, the hope she continued to cling to.

'Natasha.' Her mother tapped at the bedroom door, startling her. 'Nancy is on the phone. She wants to speak to you.'

'Nancy!' Natasha opened the door and grabbed the phone. 'When are you coming back?'

'Not for a while,' Nancy said, distant, evasive. 'I'm staying here for a bit longer, then I might go to France for a few days, or Italy. It depends.'

'On what?' Natasha demanded, wishing that Nancy would say, 'Come too. Meet me there. Let's do something – just the two of us.'

But Nancy didn't say that.

'A few different things. John, for one. But I'll let you know when I have a plan.'

'OK.' Pride would not allow Natasha to say anything else.

'Look after her.' Nancy coolly delegated what had always been her role.

Natasha gave the phone back to her mother, who stood, awkward, in the corridor so that Natasha had to say, 'Why don't we watch that detective thing I recorded? I'll be down in a minute.'

'OK,' her mother said. 'I will make mint tea.'

She went down the broad staircase of polished wood, back straight, hand drifting lightly along the bannister, and Natasha envied her a poise she believed came from birth and upbringing, although it could just as easily have been learned the hard way, through years of humiliation.

Evenings like this one stretched in front of her. Nights in front of the TV with her mother. Dinners in the kitchen while the rain hurled itself in derision against the windows, and the offers of help, of company and sympathy, dried up from underuse.

Her phone beeped. A message from Jennifer: *Do come. It'll do u good.*

CHAPTER 2

Jennifer stretched out on her sun lounger, saw Natasha smile at her and smiled back automatically. She wished she hadn't invited Natasha. She had thought long and hard before doing so, had decided not to, then found the words falling out of her mouth, blurted in a moment of pity for the misery writ so plain on Natasha's face. 'Why don't you come with us?' she had said, uneasy even as she spoke. 'It'll be fun. They're a nice group, and they'd love you to come.'

It hadn't been true even as she said it. If anything, the rest of the gang was used to regarding Natasha with a hint of suspicion. She moved in different circles in college – an older group, scholars and tutors as well as students, known to be smart and sometimes rude. Natasha always seemed entirely at home with them, something to do with her upbringing as a diplomat's child, Jennifer had decided; an ability to fit in, blend, to always find something to say that reflected well on her and moved the conversation along.

Sometimes she appeared in photographs on the back pages of fashion magazines, on the social pages, at gallery openings and book launches, perhaps with a glass of wine held lightly in one hand; often with the author or painter at her side. So the group hadn't been happy when Jennifer had announced, 'I've asked Natasha to come. She needs a break.'

They had grumbled, pointing out that the villa was full, they'd have to hire another car, skirting round the main objection until Julie, always the least tactful, dumped it unceremoniously. 'She'll be a total downer. She's grieving, and we're all off to get loaded and have fun. It's just a mismatch.'

'She has a point,' Jennifer's boyfriend, Todd, had said. 'This is a holiday, it's not a Vincent de Paul volunteer day out to the seaside.'

Sometimes, Jennifer found his hard arrogance a turn-on. At other times, like then, she worried that it wasn't just an attitude – it was actually him.

She had persuaded them, finally, by saying, 'Well, it's too late now anyway because I asked her and she's coming. Unless any of you wants to tell her she can't?'

None of them did. So here they were, embarking on a holiday that reached out into their wide-open futures. And Natasha was with them, for better or for worse.

Villa Blanca – White Villa – was even more lovely than the website had suggested. The photos, although pretty, had not been able to capture the lazy charm of its L-shaped embrace, the way it arranged itself around the bright-blue pool that tipped into infinity at one end. The riot of honeysuckle that climbed across the walls spilled towards the water in sweet-smelling fronds. Below them, the sea stretched to an unbroken horizon in many undulations of blue. It was, Jennifer thought, as much like paradise as anywhere she had seen.

Julie was out of the taxi and into the villa faster than anyone, leaving Paul to get her bags, knowing he would. Her speed had a purpose: she had bagged the best bedroom and pronounced herself satisfied, almost before the rest of them had got their bearings.

'Well done, Jennifer,' she said. 'This is very nice.'

'Of course it's nice,' Jennifer said. 'It's Ibiza!' But inwardly she felt relief then delight as the exclamations kept coming. 'Look at this amazing balcony. You can see right down to the sea!' That was Katherine – prepared to be pleased almost before she set foot in the place. 'Five bathrooms – practically one each. What luxury!' 'Look at this,' Martin called from outside. 'There's a pizza oven built into the wall of the terrace.'

As the only couple, Jennifer and Todd took the biggest room – Julie had passed it over on her predatory tour because it was on the ground floor – but Jennifer made sure Natasha was installed in one of the prettiest. She watched, amused, as Martin, who had entered the room first, insisted that no, Natasha must have it, and the way Natasha seemed genuine in her refusal, saying she really didn't mind where she slept, until she gave in at last and thanked Martin so warmly that he blushed.

But such was the obvious potential of the vine-covered terrace with its barbeque and outdoor oven, pool and sun-drenched surrounds, that everyone was prepared to be pleased.

Even Dermot declared he didn't mind at all when he got the worst bedroom, small, airless and too close to the kitchen, because he was a single man and because he moved more slowly than Paul, who was quick to grab the room beside Julie's. 'We're not here to sleep,' Dermot said cheerfully. 'A broom cupboard would do me.'

And he was right, of course. That evening, as the sun set before them, the delicate translucent pink of the lip of a seashell, they pledged again their troth: No sleeping! No complaining about hangovers! No wimping out!

The villa had worried Jennifer – what if it was horrible? Or didn't exist and she had been conned? But Natasha had worried her even more. What would they do if Natasha stood aloof, made them all feel small and silly by refusing to join in? But that first night, Natasha had promised as enthusiastically as any of them to throw herself into the aggressive hedonism of the holiday. And she had. In fact, Jennifer noticed, everyone had very much come round to Natasha. More than come round, in fact. They were all a bit charmed by her. Even Todd. Especially Todd, she knew. She had caught him staring, too often to be simply an accident, and she noticed that he made sure to manoeuvre his way beside Natasha as they set out on their reckless careering journeys across the island, often wasted, nearly always half drunk. They hadn't got another car in the end, they'd simply opted to squash everyone into the one, and Todd was careful to try and squash in beside Natasha, rammed close inside, on the sticky leather, her bare brown leg and arm pressed close against him. Jennifer, who got car sick, hadn't been able to do anything but take her allotted place in front with the driver, usually Martin, and pretend to ignore what was so very visible.

'You tan so easily,' Todd said on the third day, running a finger lightly along Natasha's arm, and indeed she had adapted to the heat quickly, voluptuously, unlike the rest of them. She didn't seem to burn or get strange rashes and patches of redness brought on by the alternation of heat and salt water and compounded by insufficient sleep and too much booze. Her skin soaked up the sun, giving it back in a smooth glow, even except for a faint smattering of freckles across her nose – small, dainty ones, Jennifer noticed, not the big splodgy ones she herself produced.

'I'm lucky,' Natasha responded, smiling up at Todd. 'I never really burn. It must be such a pain to have to go through an entire paint-and-prep session before leaving the house.'

Had Natasha, Jennifer wondered, cast a sly look in her direction as she said it? Maybe not, but Todd had turned and looked openly at Jennifer, even then applying more Factor 50 to her red nose, and smirked.

The flirting had intensified over the next few days, deepening over the silly green and blue cocktails they all knocked back and through the long nights out. And because they had all chosen the holiday precisely because they wanted to behave carelessly, Jennifer didn't know what she could say, what curtailment she could ask for. She and Todd shared a room, in which they crashed out at different times, depending on who was the more smashed and exhausted. They'd had sex just once since arriving five days earlier, a hurried, almost absent-minded shag, in which he had stared over her shoulder as she sat astride him, moving his hips in time with her but seeming distant, preoccupied. Since then, for all the eroticism of the island – the light, the warmth, the smells – they had avoided each other subtly but neatly.

It was easily done – they were all bent on partying, forever coming up with novel ways to get trashed, whether shots of something small and strong, or a hollowed-out melon, filled with vodka and left to ferment for hours before they consumed it, eating the mushy strips of booze-soaked fruit, laughing and grimacing because it didn't taste terribly nice – gone off really, too potent – but insisting that 'it does the job'. The comings and goings were so frequent that the house was in constant motion – smaller groups were forever setting off on trips, to shops, the beach, a new bar someone had told them about at the club the night before, or coming back from somewhere. At first, Jennifer thought she must be mistaken about Todd avoiding her – surely it was simply that he was caught up in the merry ebb and flow? – but then she realised that he wasn't so caught up that he didn't make sure to be always where Natasha was. And Natasha, who probably did not seek him out, kept no distance between them, smiled invitingly when she saw him approach. In the haze of heat, hangover and lack of sleep that surrounded them all, Jennifer thought she could see the desire ripple in the air between them, hotter even than the sun that beat down in seeming approval of excess.

As she sat by the pool she remembered the first time she had met Natasha, over two years earlier. Natasha had fallen down the stairs of the bus, right in front of Jennifer, landing hard.

'Are you alright?' Jennifer asked.

'I'm fine,' the girl replied, cheeks burning hot with mortification. Jennifer would rarely see her so discomfited again.

As they got off the bus, Jennifer noticed that the girl was limping. 'You sure you're OK?'

'Actually, I seem to have buggered my ankle.' The girl grimaced. 'But it'll be fine.'

'Let me carry your bag at least,' Jennifer insisted.

They walked up to college together, with the tight, clear smell of autumn around them and a showy display of reds, yellows and soft, squirrelly browns on all the trees.

'The only time this place looks nice is now,' the girl said. 'In summer it's so dry and dead, and in winter it's bare and dead. Only autumn works for it.'

'What's your name?' Jennifer asked, feeling silly because it was such a dull question, wishing she could have said something wonderful in response to her comment.

'Natasha,' the girl said, pronouncing the second 'a' hard so that it came out 'Nataasha', in a way that was faintly familiar. Where have I heard that name before? Jennifer wondered.

They discovered they were both taking first-year English, but that Natasha had combined it with history and politics, whereas Jennifer was doing Spanish and Italian. Natasha was far more critical in her appraisal of the course and lecturers than Jennifer, to whom everything was still so new, so exciting, that she couldn't see that there were separations and joins beneath the shining mass of it all;

bits that were less good than other bits. To her, it was still all of a piece. Later, she realised that Natasha's analysis had been correct, her dismissal of one lecturer as 'a day-tripper; he goes round and round the point and never gets to it' was cruel but accurate.

She found that she was quite shy of Natasha, who seemed far more autonomous, more self-possessed, than anyone else she knew of their age, but she was determined to befriend her. After all, she had come to college to meet new and unusual people, not just the same sort of girls she had shared years of hockey practice and schoolyard chat with. The fever that burned in her to get out, get more, grasp the world, was too strong to trick with what she had always known. Natasha was interesting, she decided, and so she made plans to meet her for coffee after their next lecture.

Friendship with Natasha wasn't easy. She was reserved and avoided intimacy, skipping away from it like a stone skipping across the surface of a lake. She was better in a group, where her wit and gift for mimicry thrust her into the centre, but when they were alone, Jennifer often struggled for conversation, embarrassed by the silences that fell between them in a way that Natasha wasn't.

'Where did you go to school?' Jennifer asked over their first cup of coffee together in the canteen. It was morning and the place was empty and smelled of vinegar. The sun lit up the grimy streaks on the large windows. She knew her question was gauche, but it was what they all still asked each other, that first year, because they had so little else within the frame of their reference to talk about. She didn't dare, yet, ask Natasha about the things she really wanted to know: *How come you're so poised? Where did you learn to analyse books like that? How is your hair always so perfect and glossy?*

'I didn't much,' Natasha replied. 'I went to boarding school for a while, in France. A few months in a place called Mary Immaculate, not far from here. Mostly I was schooled at home, by my dad.'

'Mary Immaculate! Miss Mary's,' Jennifer said in excitement. 'Me too! How amazing.' Then, as the scenery of her mind shifted, the painted backdrops shuffling apart so that she could see into the further reaches, said. 'Wait! *Nataasha* . . . I think I remember you! You were in our class, but only for a while, not quite a year, and then you left, and for ages I wondered what happened to you!'

'Oh, right.' Natasha seemed far less excited, with no answering gleam of recollection on her face.

'I was a boarder, you were a day pupil. In fifth class, right? We were all so curious about you. You sat beside Sarah McGovern.'

It was all coming back to her. The new girl, who had arrived midway through the year, turning up one Monday morning without the uniform; a navy skirt and neat white shirt with rounded collar, in the sea of rust-brown. The next day, she was in the proper uniform, but something about her had still stood out.

'This is Natasha,' Sister Margaret had said. 'She will be joining us.' But she never really did. She had done lessons and played hockey and gone to the swimming pool and church with them, but had never seemed to sink into their world. She'd remained on the surface, polite but unenthusiastic; oil on water.

At first, the bitchier girls had been inclined to look for a weakness, imitating her quaint accent, a jumble of Irish and Spanish that had come out as almost English, and the way she'd stood, shoulders down and back rigidly straight. She had been taller than most of the girls in the year, with a style that had clearly irritated them. Dark, neat hair, brown eyes and golden skin, a nose that was too big for her face and very little inclination to be liked. The bitchy girls had mocked the few things she'd said, but Natasha had seemed so indifferent, they had given up. After that, one or two had tried to be friends, but she'd been indifferent to that too.

Natasha had spoken to Sarah McGovern, a sweet girl with terrible warts on her hands, like a series of tiny, gnarled mountain ranges, whom Jennifer had always felt guilty for avoiding. Natasha had seemed not to mind the warts, or even notice them much, taking Sarah's hand when required – crossing to and from church, on the rare outings to town – without the shiver of repulsion that Jennifer was sure would cross her own face.

There had been talk at one stage that Natasha would become a boarder, staying on when her parents left the country, and Jennifer remembered wondering would this deliver Natasha to them at last. Surely she couldn't remain so aloof when all she had was school? But instead she had left, walking out of their lives neatly and completely.

'Did you stay in touch with Sarah?' Jennifer asked, recalling how Sarah seemed bereft to be friendless again, going everywhere alone after the short respite of being two.

'No. I've never been very good at staying in touch,' Natasha said. 'We moved so often.'

She didn't say she remembered Jennifer or ask anything about those days, so Jennifer dropped it. But she liked the feeling that they had history together, that there was more between them than a chance meeting on the steps of a bus.

'So wasn't it lonely, being home-schooled?' she asked.

'Not so much lonely as hard!' Natasha said. 'My father's idea of a well-rounded education was pretty intense. All the academic stuff, like Latin and poetry and history, but also the way I sat and ate and walked. He tried to get my mother to teach me deportment – she has wonderful posture – but we fought too much. Sitting at tables while she tugged at my shoulders . . .' She laughed.

'Why did he want you to learn all that?'

'He thought it was important. I guess it was. I went to lots of things with him, formal dinners and receptions, that sort of thing, and he wanted me to be able to behave properly, you know, sit still and not fidget.'

'Did your mother go too?'

'Not much. I think she found all of that difficult.' She didn't say in what way her mother found it difficult, and Jennifer didn't ask.

'Didn't *you* find it difficult?' Jennifer thought how much she would have hated it.

'No, I quite liked it. Even though everyone else was very old. But they were kind and liked talking to me – I think because I wasn't as old as them! Anyway, it was a relief after boarding school. Those French girls were dull. And mean. I liked being with my dad. And my sister was there.'

'Oh, wow, I didn't know you had a sister.' Jennifer cringed at the note of gush in her voice. As if she was saying, '*Oh wow, I didn't know you had a giraffe*'. 'What's her name?'

'Nancy.'

'Nancy and Natasha. Are you twins?'

'No . . . although almost, Irish twins. Thirteen months between us, so we did the same lessons. Nancy's very bright.'

'Did she go to the receptions and things like you?' Jennifer was curious about this sister, the very mention of whom seemed to light up Natasha's face and voice.

'Sometimes, but Nancy is very fidgety, so my father didn't like taking her. He said he always had to bring her home early, before she exploded or tipped over the table or something. And Nancy began to refuse to go, as soon as she was old enough. She said she felt she was on show and didn't like it.'

'But you didn't mind?'

'No. Nancy always made more of a fuss about stuff than I did. Anyway, it was time with my dad, and that was the main thing.'

'So how did it work, the schooling?'

'We had tutors sometimes, depending on where my dad was posted and how long we stayed there, and my dad did the rest. We worked odd hours, early in the morning and in the evenings.'

'Did they divide up the subjects, your dad and the tutors?' Jennifer was fascinated by the mechanics of a situation so far from anything she'd known.

'Well, it was more that they divided up the pupils.' Natasha said. 'I mostly worked with my dad and Nancy with the tutor, when we had one.'

'Why?' Jennifer knew she should stop, but couldn't. Not yet.

'He was impatient, and she was, well, reluctant I guess . . .'

'And where was Nancy when you were in Miss Mary's?'

'Still at home. They didn't want to send her then. Maybe if we'd stayed, she would have gone, but we didn't.' Talking about her sister seemed to loosen up Natasha a bit: her face relaxed its stiffness and she smiled more.

'Is she in college too?'

'No, she's taking a year off, but she'll probably come next year.'

'That'll be nice.'

'It will,' Natasha agreed – but Nancy didn't come the next year, although she often joined Natasha for parties and trips to the pub, giving her opinion on the books and plays they talked about with as much confidence as if she had been the year above them. She even came to lectures with them, on the basis that she was 'trying things out'. She would take notes and prepare for the lectures, often far more diligently than Jennifer did.

A loud scream and splash jerked Jennifer back to the present. Paul, Dermot and Katherine were playing water polo and a particularly violent slam-dunk had sent up a sheet of water, drenching Julie.

'Be more careful,' she snapped.

Natasha, Jennifer noticed, although also wet, seemed to have barely registered the intrusion. She was engrossed in a fat paperback, lying on her stomach, legs kicking lazily in the air behind her. As

Jennifer watched, she picked up a corner of the blue-and-white striped towel on which she lay and wiped her face, all without lifting her eyes from the page in front of her.

'Un-put-downable?' Todd called across to Natasha from beside Jennifer. 'Or are you just imperturbable?' He has clearly been watching her, Jennifer thought, then realised how they all seemed to be waiting for an answer, a response, from Natasha. The game of water polo had been suspended and Julie, sitting now, had stopped her ostentatious wiping of self and sun lounger.

'What?' Natasha looked up, although she clearly hadn't heard the question.

'The book,' Todd said. 'It must be enthralling?' The inevitable edge of mockery was fainter than usual.

'It's not. It's awful.' Natasha laughed. 'I picked it up inside. Some previous inhabitant of the villa must have left it behind. '"A story of love and loss across three generations in the Indian Raj . . ."' she read out for effect. 'Dreadful stuff.'

Jennifer, who knew the book belonged to Julie because Julie had told her how wonderful it was and that she really must read it, looked to see how she would greet this. To her surprise, Julie said nothing, just lay back down on her sun lounger. The way Todd laughed made her suspect he too knew the book was Julie's, but he said nothing either.

Water polo resumed and Martin came out to suggest barbequed prawns for lunch. Natasha went back to the awful book, and Jennifer wondered if she knew well that it was Julie's. She thought about what it would be like to be Natasha's sister. Thought about the way in which Natasha was protective and Nancy competitive, and how suddenly both could lurch into something else.

She remembered the first time she had met Nancy, early in that first year at college, the night a famously controversial author had visited to give a guest lecture on the futility of literary criticism. Nancy had been tall, taller than Natasha, and so slender she had seemed to sway. She had Natasha's wide mouth and glowing complexion, but in a more fragile version so that where Natasha had seemed vivid, capable, Nancy was more delicate, Jennifer had suspected, noticing the dark shadows under her eyes, the nervous flutter of her pale hands.

Natasha asked a question after the lecture – something Jennifer would never have dared to do – and sounded cool, intelligent while doing so. Afterwards, Jennifer saw the controversial author make a beeline for the sisters, and he remained talking to them for as long as the bad wine reception had lasted. Then they all left in a group, with a couple of the smartest professors, the ones who wrote important books and could be heard on the radio on Sunday mornings talking about the 'state of the nation'. Jennifer was very impressed with the way both girls put on their coats – slowly, without hurry, certain that these erudite men would wait for them.

When she asked Natasha about the night later, she just shrugged and said, 'It was fun, although all that controversy is such a put-on. He's as eager to please as anyone underneath the showing-off about writing with the penis and the spleen.'

Jennifer wanted to giggle at the word 'penis', a kind of shocked reaction to hearing it said so casually and without warning, but restrained herself. Be more grown-up, she thought sternly. Determined to cement the friendship, she instead asked Natasha to a party that weekend, but Natasha said she couldn't make it; she had things to do.

Together, Nancy and Natasha seemed to speak in a private code, a shorthand accessible only to them, made up of half-sentences, allusions and private jokes they could never explain. They called their parents by their first names – Vincent and Maria – or simply 'she' and 'he', but with a particular kind of inflexion, so that the words came out weighted down with things Jennifer didn't understand and they didn't explain.

So much of their conversation seemed tied to the magic of 'do you remember?', punctuated with the triumph of coaxing from each other missing pieces of various jigsaws. Or maybe it was all just one giant, sprawling jigsaw.

'Remember that funny American girl we met in Greece? The one who lived with her parents in the caravan? What was her name?'

'Eloise?'

'That's right! *She* said the parents were hippies and hated them, and *he* said they were non-conformists, which was "different and perfectly honourable".' Natasha mimicked her father at his driest.

'And Eloise practically moved in with us for a few weeks, in the Grande Bretagne Hotel, which was fine, until Maria found her teaching you how to French kiss during our siesta hour.'

'That's right.' Natasha made a face. 'I got such a fright. I only asked what French kissing was, and the next thing her tongue was darting around in my mouth like a fish.' They both dissolved into giggles.

'We're like a lost Amazonian tribe,' Natasha said when Jennifer asked about the funny way she and Nancy spoke to one another. 'We spent far too much time on our own together as kids. We evolved in such splendid isolation that the only people who really get either of us is each other.' She said this like there was nothing she wanted to change about it, which made Jennifer seek her friendship all the more.

'But why does Nancy bother coming to lectures and stuff, but won't join properly?' Nancy seemed odd to Jennifer, a precocious child rather than an adult.

'Lots of reasons. Partly because she really hasn't decided what she wants to do, and she doesn't want to make a mistake. Partly she's bored. And partly she's used to following me around.' Natasha laughed. 'I used to joke that she was my shadow when we were younger, because every time I turned round she was there.'

'Was that not annoying?'

'It was, but it was sweet too. And the times she wasn't there, I would be devastated. I remember we once went to stay with friends of my parents who had older daughters, and they decided that Nancy was really cute and they were going to dress her up like a doll, and they took her off with them, and I was heartbroken, because she went so easily. And because I was all on my own. Being with Nancy made me brave, because she was so shy. I had to be the one who spoke up for both of us, and I got used to it. Sometimes, now, I still think I need to speak for her, and that makes her furious.'

But for all that Jennifer could see what Natasha meant when she said Nancy was brilliant – she had flashes of insight, or made connections across time and genre which were inspired – nothing was sustained. She changed tack too often, and seemed strangely uncertain of any of her decisions.

'She hasn't found the right thing,' Natasha said, but, to Jennifer, Nancy's inability to commit seemed more than excitement and indecision.

'Doesn't she need to settle down to something?' she asked, feeling that she sounded like her own mother, and wondering how much she liked that feeling.

'I don't see why,' Natasha said. 'You say that because you were brought up to think that you have to finish everything you start, even if it's a terrible book or a disgusting bowl of soup. It's all those years on the hockey pitch, playing teams whom you can't beat, in the driving wind and rain, and having to battle to the bitter end with no hope of victory. Sometimes it's OK to say you're out. That the thing isn't worth finishing.'

To Jennifer, that sounded like sacrilege – or an excuse that Natasha hoped was true.

The pair bickered too, in a way that Jennifer, who had no sisters, found fascinating. Squabbling over dates and places with ferocity.

'It was Italy, not Spain,' Natasha asserted, about some restaurant.

'No, you're wrong.' Nancy sounded desperate to be right.

'It was. I know it was, because everyone said "Ciao, bella," not "Hola, guappa."'

'And of course with you it's all about how gorgeous everyone thinks you are,' Nancy said furiously.

'That's not what I mean.' Natasha was shocked. 'It's not. I just meant that's how I know, because I remember the different sounds on the street.'

'Yeah, right.'

The resentment in Nancy's tone was so deep that Jennifer was embarrassed to be a witness to it. And astonished when, minutes later, Natasha said, 'Are you trying to pretend that no one ever pinched your bum on the street?' And Nancy answered with a laugh, 'Of course they did. But not as much as they pinched yours. And' – reprovingly – 'I don't make such a big deal of it as you do.'

But they could fight in earnest too, mainly when it came to antagonistic recollections of their parents. Their versions of the past could be shockingly different when it came to the motivations of these parents, about whom they could be cruel, but also possessive, a battling for supremacy of affection that Jennifer, who made sure to love her parents equally, and who had never felt they were anything but entirely fair to herself and her brother, was astonished by.

'They were the gods of our world,' Natasha tried to explain it to Jennifer. 'More so, I think, than is even normal for kids. Again, because of moving so much, being always only us, with no cousins or close neighbours or family friends that we saw often, we were too isolated, and everything that happened in the family was too intense, with repercussions that rippled everywhere. When mys parent fought – which they did often – it was like the thunder gods throwing rocks at each other or something. Terrifying.'

'Why did they fight?'

'All sorts of reasons. I think they aren't terribly suited to each other. *She's* annoying and *he's* irritable?' She shrugged. 'I don't know. Nancy says one's as bad as the other, but it always seemed to me that *she* started things. She complained a lot. About food, the weather, the places we lived in. Lots of moaning. It annoyed him, and then he'd shout.'

'But they never divorced?'

'No.'

To Jennifer, whose parents agreed on nearly everything, who worked in tandem, with decisions taken jointly, harmoniously, this background of discord seemed exciting, and Natasha a new friend to be proud of.

She smiled to think of this now, watching Natasha bent over the book, oblivious of everyone.

Martin emerged wearing a white apron to say that the prawns were ready.

'I'll get some white wine,' Julie said, then looked cross when Todd called over, 'Get beers too.'

'I'll help you.' Paul leapt up, eager as ever to earn himself any kind of bond with Julie.

They moved over to the table in the thick shade of the corner terrace, where Martin had laid out platters of prawns, barbequed black and pink, with bowls of salad and loaves of bread. Katherine and Dermot were first and squeezed into the coolest corner, squashing up together under the pretence of leaving plenty of room for the others.

Julie, brandishing two ice-cold bottles of white wine, and Paul, laden with beers, were next, so that by the time Natasha got to the table, there were no seats left. Jennifer, already moving to make space for her, was forestalled by a chorus of voices – 'Sit here, Natasha'; 'There's room here'; 'Take my seat' – so that Natasha smiled charmingly and said she was spoiled for choice, before squeezing into the space Todd had made for her.

And Jennifer, who had the soul of a romantic, who believed she was part of a potentially neat quartet of lovers, like at the end of a Shakespeare play, paused. She had expected to see the obvious attraction between Katherine and Dermot catch fire, Julie succumb to Paul's desire, had even hoped that Natasha might be brought to see Martin as *she* saw him – the person who lay beyond the white aprons – but suddenly wondered if she had called it wrong. Was the pattern, so clear and desirable to her, not the right one after all?

CHAPTER 3

Natasha woke from another of her crying dreams, disoriented and sodden with the depths of slumber she had been dragged down to. Unable at first to recognise the room with its white curtains blowing gently in the morning breeze and rotating ceiling fan, she sat up in a panic, ready to bolt for the door, then remembered where she was. She sank back on the pillows, unwilling, yet, to face the day.

In her dream, she had been crying with abandon, an ocean of tears to drown a mouse, she thought, remembering *Alice in Wonderland*, but when she put her hand to her face, it was dry. The tears would still only come as part of whatever life she led at night, in sleep. By day, the fire blanket settled on her once more, deadening and muffling the feelings of grief.

She wondered how her mother was getting on, squashing down the guilt she felt at leaving her alone, telling herself that it had been Nancy who left her first.

She remembered her mother's response when she had told her she would be leaving – 'I won't stand in your way' – and felt again the irritation of that moment. In what way? Natasha had wondered in silent fury. In the way of what? What did her mother think she wanted to do?

She could hear voices on the terrace outside, and began to try and haul herself into the person she needed to be to go outside and face them all, amazed that any were even up yet.

She got coffee first and grabbed a book from the dim-lit sitting room, shutters pulled down against the growing heat. Something about the Raj and three generations of love. It looked suitably trashy for a day by the pool, she decided, and might act as armour against the well-meaning questions and comments of the others as she went through the daily process of reorienting herself.

'You won't always feel like this . . .'

The morning was clear and beautiful. The kind of day on which God had made the world. Natasha uttered a series of cheery comments – 'Good morning', 'Isn't it beautiful?', 'How did you sleep?' – then settled herself on a sun lounger and lay back, listening to the bird song she knew would cease as the day got hotter, and the drone of bees which would intensify.

She wished Nancy were there. Wondered where she was and what she was doing. Why she wouldn't be reached, couldn't be reached. She had pulled away so successfully that she could have been one of the people who had said politely, idiotically, 'a loss to us all', as if Natasha's father were not also *her* father. As if her loss was something only she could know. She had been distant and unforgiving, with John beside her even stiffer than she was, his smooth and blandly uniform features betraying resentment at the effort it had taken for Nancy to speak her few words. Nancy, who had taken their shared past, their one set of memories, and ripped it apart, tearing her own roots out of the tangle of Natasha's so that what was left behind lay exposed and bare without the kind earth of their shared everything to cover them and give them decency.

31

And so here she was, in the hot brightness of the island sun, with these friends who didn't know what to say to comfort her, with whom she didn't know how to communicate what she needed. Because she had no idea. And so she clung to the one thing she had: '*You won't always feel like this*'.

She looked at them – at Jennifer and Julie, at Martin, trying so hard to find a place for himself amongst them. At Todd, aloof but vigilant, watchful as a man on a roof, with that slight squint that said how far below him they all were, dots to be made out.

'*You won't always feel like this.*' She wondered what she might feel instead, but could come up with no answer. Certainly not as she had felt before the death, that almost-luxurious sense of sadness in the imperfection of the world, which had brought as much enjoyment as it had sorrow. That, she saw now, was only posturing. When the world had revealed itself to be actually even more sad, more crudely tragic, than she had thought, she knew she had to fling her weight the other way, to redress the balance, lest she capsize and they all capsize. So she became cheerful, bright – outwardly at least. She threw off expressions of sympathy with energy – 'You're so kind. Thank you. It's very sad, but what can you do? These things happen' – and then changed the subject, to the relief of the sympathiser, and herself.

It was, she told herself when she felt increasingly imprisoned behind her veneer of ease, only good manners. After all, she had more or less crashed this holiday. The others had probably not welcomed the news of her coming, conveyed by Jennifer, who, Natasha knew, had invited her in the days after the death out of pity and awkwardness, and who had seemed disconcerted herself when Natasha had accepted. But having once crashed, she was determined to be, if not the life and soul, at the very least a merry and willing participant. After all, who came to Ibiza for mournful recollections and miserable communion with another broken soul?

And it was a better place to be than back home. The brightness of the blue, the heavy seduction of the heat were a help; the unfamiliarity of it all a boon.

Beside her, the infinity pool stretched and then dropped away, while, behind it, a line of sea did exactly the same thing, reaching hard for the horizon, then falling into nothing where it met the different blue of the sky. They swapped colours, the sky and sea, Natasha had noticed, ceding place to each other on the spectrum, now darker, now lighter, always different, so that it was possible to spot the line of divide, no matter how faint. Heat shimmered over everything, sinking into Natasha's bones, creating a welcome layer between her outer self and the inner layer of grief – not enough to melt it, but enough to distance her for a while from its stiff and ugly touch. She yawned and straightened her legs on the sun lounger, looking up to where Jennifer sat on another sun lounger.

Jennifer, with her cloud of red curls that seemed to carry the heat of glowing coals so that Natasha had once joked they could walk across them. Thin and pale, with limbs that looked feeble in their gangliness until you saw her chase a hockey ball or stand on her hands. Who claimed she was 'never' sick, but who had nose bleeds, great gushes of blood like oil from a well that soaked her face and clothes and left her weak and dizzy. Jennifer, who sent her personality before her like a dancing flame to find more people and places to explore.

She was, thought Natasha, *nice*. But in a way that made 'nice' something almost exciting. Nice, Natasha knew, was so often a veiled insult, a compliment that came complete with sting so that it pricked you even as it pretended to caress, like a dressmaker's pin hidden in the lining of something pretty. But Jennifer made 'nice' into something stronger, more admirable, so that it was with a tiny bit of regret that Natasha realised how little anyone would think to say it about her.

Jennifer did that with people too, she knew. Made them something other than what they had been until then. Took them, with all their failures of daring, their hesitancies and blurred lines, and gave them a more definite shape. Sometimes, she invented little things for them, personality quirks and traits – 'Martin is so demanding', she might say, when they all knew that Martin had never demanded anything of any of them. And as she said it, it became true, for those moments at least, and, sometimes, in curious ways that left marks on them all.

Natasha had once watched in astonishment as Jennifer skilfully created a whole persona for Helen, a quiet girl in their English tutorial, based around Helen's few thin, stammered questions. 'That was very bold of you,' Jennifer had said to Helen afterwards with a smile as they walked away from the study room. 'Poor Mr Keane was getting quite agitated by the end, because he couldn't give a good enough answer. And every time he tried to change the subject, you just came back at him from another angle. He must have felt he was fighting a hydra.'

Helen had looked embarrassed, but delighted. She had mumbled something about 'I didn't mean . . .' and almost ran away. But, there-after, Natasha had noticed that she asked far more questions, even at lectures sometimes, and with an arch tone of voice that said she had taken Jennifer's vision of her and decided to own it.

'Are you just making it up as you go along?' she had asked Jennifer later.

'Making what up?'

'All that stuff about Helen being bold and chasing Keane down with tough questions?'

'Not at all,' Jennifer had insisted. 'Didn't you see how relentless she was?'

'No.' Natasha had laughed. 'I really, really didn't. She strung two boring points together and stuck a question mark at the end; that's all I saw.'

'Relentless,' Jennifer had insisted.

Remembering the conversation now, Natasha looked over at Jennifer on another lounger, curled up with her back to the sun. As Natasha watched, she sat up, stretched and, seemingly infected with the sheer glory of the day, called 'watch this' over to Natasha. She pattered on bare feet over to the deep end of the pool and dived in, a perfect swan dive, arms held gracefully out behind her, and swam the length of the pool under water, emerging dripping at the other end.

'Very good!' Natasha said, clapping her hands. 'What's for encore?'

'No encores,' Jennifer said, walking over to her as she dried her face. 'Once is enough in this heat. I know it's just a pleasant sunny morning to you, but to the rest of us, it's an inferno already, and it's only going to get worse. I need to conserve my energies.' She flopped back down on her lounger and closed her eyes, 'I'm going into lizard-mode.'

CHAPTER 4

'I'm going to walk down the road, to the café,' Natasha said. Lunch was finished, the barbequed prawns and salad demolished, despite various protestations that it was 'too hot to eat'.

'Why on earth?' Julie asked. 'It's a dingy little place, full of flies and stale bread. We'll all go out later, to the bar that does those mad cocktails.'

'I like flyblown little Spanish cafés,' Natasha said. 'Even if the bread is stale, the coffee is always amazing.'

Martin looked as if he was about to offer to go with her, but Natasha forestalled him – on purpose, Jennifer suspected – by grabbing a straw hat and her bag and saying firmly, 'Don't anyone feel they have to come. Stay here and I'll see you all later.'

She was gone so fast that Jennifer understood she had been building up to this all day, to the time when she could be alone and unaccountable, without their questions and eager stares around her. She knew the effort it must be taking for Natasha to live in two such incompatible worlds – of grief and giddiness – and she admired her for succeeding so well, even as she wondered again just why Natasha had said yes to joining them.

It was Julie who broke the silence, as Jennifer had known she would.

'So, is it not a bit weird that she's here?'

'How do you mean?' Jennifer asked.

'Well, so soon after the funeral. You'd think she'd be at home, with her mother, and there's a sister, right?'

'Yes. Nancy.'

'Right, so why isn't she with *them*?'

The others gathered round, interested as they now were in everything to do with Natasha. Todd was indoors somewhere, but Katherine dragged a chair closer and made space on it for Dermot. Paul and Martin stopped flicking water at each other and leaned over the edge of the pool, the better to hear.

Jennifer wondered briefly if she was being disloyal, but was too interested in teasing out an answer herself to hold back.

'Well, I asked her, because I knew how miserable she was. I was surprised when she said yes but, then, when I thought about it, I could understand a bit better. She was really mad about her dad, I mean more so than even most people are. He was a diplomat, sort of famous, because he put together a really important treaty. Something European . . .' Natasha had explained to her what exactly he had done, but Jennifer hadn't really taken it in. It had been complicated, with many negotiating parties, and over something Jennifer hadn't properly understood – not land or water or borders or anything concrete. 'The funeral was huge. I went to it. There were hundreds of people, and Natasha stood for ages, shaking hands and having little words with people. I felt so sorry for her. She looked so stiff and cold, like she would shatter if you bumped into her, and when she wasn't shaking hands, she sort of cradled her arms together as if they ached, but she stayed and stayed until everyone was done.'

'Where was her mother?' Martin asked.

'She was there, but she didn't seem to be saying anything to anyone. She just shook hands and then turned away from that person to the next.'

'And the sister?'

'Nancy was there too, but she didn't do any of that stuff. After the mass, she kept to the back and looked as if she was trying to avoid being noticed. Outside the church, when everyone was milling around and talking to one another, she sort of tucked herself into a corner. I went over to say how sorry I was, but she saw me coming and turned away to the guy she was with – her boyfriend, I think – so I didn't, because I could see she didn't want me to.'

'So she's at home now, with the mother?' That was Julie again, as ever, wanting precise distributions of fact.

'Actually no, she's away too. France or somewhere. With friends.'

'Weird,' Julie said with satisfaction. 'You'd think they'd stick together.'

'Maybe they just have different ways of doing things,' Martin said and Jennifer smiled at his fair-mindedness.

'What's their house like?' Paul asked, clearly more curious than concerned.

'I've only been once,' Jennifer said.

'Once! I thought you and Natasha were such friends.' That was Katherine, genuinely astonished.

'We are, but she's funny like that. Very private in lots of ways. Certainly when it comes to her family.'

'Well, what's it like?' Julie asked.

'It's a beautiful house. One of those Georgian ones near the canal, with nearly all its original features.' She had been going to say more, about how empty the house felt, cold, although there had been fires lit, and more like a collection of beautiful rooms than anything coherent, like a home. But Julie interrupted with a story about a friend of hers whose parents had bought just such a house, and the trouble they had had renovating it, so that Jennifer found herself silently recalling her one visit to Natasha's family, and how self-conscious she had felt, terrified that she would do or say something wrong, until she had realised that they were all far more caught up in whatever lay between them than in anything she could say or do.

All their words seemed to count so much, she had realised. Like everything had a meaning beyond what it seemed to have. At first, admiring the flash of conversation between Natasha and her father, Jennifer had been wistful, thinking how brilliant and witty they both were, considering her own father and his gentle enquiries about her health, her happiness, and finding them dull in comparison.

But gradually Jennifer had realised how little a part Natasha's mother seemed to play in the back-and-forth between her daughter and husband, how she had seemed to almost physically extract herself from their conversation, sitting rigidly against the back of her chair while the two of them had leaned forwards, elbows on the table, talking animatedly but never appealing to her for any additions or corroboration.

Perhaps if Nancy had been there, she had thought, the balance might have seemed more even. But Nancy hadn't appeared until much later, even though a place had been set for her, the empty chair beside Maria's only emphasising the thicket of silence around her.

For Jennifer, whose mother's voice was heard as though it were a church bell, ringing clear, sweet notes over everything that happened in their house, Maria's silence had been strange and a little pitiful.

The shadows on the terrace had deepened and lengthened now, from silver to charcoal, and Jennifer was about to suggest a game of draughts using the giant outdoor pieces, when Todd yelled for her from their ground-floor bedroom.

'I'm coming,' she yelled back, ignoring Julie's smirk as she crossed to the back door of the villa.

In their room, Todd had already bolted the shutters to the outside. No sooner had she shut the door than his arms were around her, backing her against the door as he kissed her. He was bare-chested, and sticky with sweat, so that Jennifer instinctively pushed him away.

'Let me have a shower,' she said, 'it's too hot.' She hoped he would have one as well, both because it would slow him down, enabling her to catch up with the intensity of his arousal, and wash the sheen of sweat that covered him.

'Never mind that,' he said, his voice with that thick, blurred note that lust gave to it. He guided her by the shoulders towards their bed, pulling down the straps of her swimming costume, then yanking the whole thing down to her knees as he pushed her back onto the bed.

Jennifer, knowing she must smell and taste of chlorine from the swimming pool, struggled to fast-forward herself into arousal, but he was moving too quickly.

'Todd, slow down,' she muttered, highly conscious of the rest of the gang so close, separated from them by a wooden shutter. She hoped they would have had the discretion to move down to the other end of the pool, could imagine the glee with which Julie might have suggested such a thing.

Todd, far from slowing down, thrust straight into her and carried on thrusting, hard, while Jennifer rather mechanically submitted to his rhythm. He came, with a loud grunt, and collapsed, sweatier than ever, with his face buried in her neck. Jennifer gave a few moans and pretended to come too. It was easier that way, she decided. She'd make up for it next time. And of course, she reminded herself, it was flattering that he should want her so badly. As much as she wanted him.

Where Natasha seemed older, Todd actually *was* older. He was in college after a couple of years 'trying his luck' in the world, as he put it, insisting that his luck had been good – he had worked in finance in London, had left because 'it wasn't going anywhere' and because he had realised how much better it would be if he 'did the degree thing and got it out of the way'. Todd was ambitious, beyond anyone else Jennifer knew. Where her other friends talked vaguely, earnestly, of doing 'something interesting', 'something worthwhile', Todd talked in specifics. He talked of starting his own company, in a field that was new and exciting: 'So that I'm at the forefront of it, ahead of everyone else. I don't want law or architecture or anything where the discoveries have been made and claims staked. I want what's new, what can be made and proven by me, because I'll get there first, faster than anyone else.' She'd once asked him if it was money that he wanted, to which he had said, 'Of course. I want plenty of it, but it's not just that. I want to make something that no one else has ever made.'

She liked this in him. It made him different from the boys she had known growing up, from the private schools and teenage socials that provided the careful opportunities for interaction allowed to girls like her.

Tall and so obviously handsome that he turned heads at times, causing girls and boys alike to swivel automatically in his direction as he passed, Todd was so perfect that Jennifer never understood what he saw in her. Surely he could have had anyone, so why her? She knew she was striking; 'You look like an oak forest in autumn', her mother used to say when she was younger and lamenting her thick handfuls of reddish-gold hair, the way it wouldn't lie down flat and smooth like her friends', her pale skin and freckles. She'd eventually grown to appreciate the difference of her looks, even if hot summers were a flustered round of knowing that she was too pink, that her face clashed with her hair, and her freckles were multiplying so fast that she worried she would be entirely covered in them, a kind of mask behind which the subtleties and nuances of her expressions would be lost. But she had always felt she understood her market, the niche quality of her appeal, until Todd, who should have dated one of the beautiful, high-maintenance girls Jennifer saw getting in and out of dinky cars, hair swishing behind them and an expression of faint astonishment on their faces – astonishment, she had always thought, at being surrounded by so many ugly, dumpy people – instead had chosen her. Or, if she was absolutely honest, had allowed her to choose him.

The funny thing was how alike she and Todd looked. He had the same red-gold hair, the same colour and profusion of freckles, although he translated better to the sun, taking on a warm glow that accentuated the blond of his hair over the strawberry. His beauty was blurred and softened around the edges so that, she thought, he was like someone seen constantly through the haze of nostalgia. Even close up he was like a faded Polaroid picture, a lost youth from a golden age.

Until he opened his mouth, and said something that was funny but rude and hurtful too, something that made you want to stay close and hear more.

His was a kind of charm she hadn't come across before. Certainly it was not the kind she had been brought up with, where respect, deference to elders and consideration for the feelings of others had to take precedence over everything. You could never be funny at the expense of being kind, she had been taught. Never mocking or cruel, even when witty. But Todd did all those things, and got away with them. His kind of charm was based, not on being nice, but on being nasty. At first she had said, 'You can't say things like that', in shock, before realising that, actually, you could. *He* could. That people flocked to him. Not just for his looks, but for his power to insult them, tease them, make them laugh, occasionally to flatter them with observations that weighed twice what anyone else's did.

So much of what he said was a provocation, a gauntlet thrown down again and again so that being with him was stimulating, and then exhausting. It wasn't even the provocation itself, as much as the driving sincerity behind it, a sincerity that seemed absolute, until it was abandoned in an instant.

'So speaks the underprivileged private schoolboy,' he had said mockingly to one of Jennifer's friends who had ventured a moan about the ease with which 'scholarship students have it, all that hand-holding and extra tutorials.' 'What bit of their lives are you so resentful of? The crap schools or the fact that they are probably the first person in their families to get a decent education?' Then Todd pursued his point, needling and cross-questioning as if determined to get to the truth or die, until the friend had reached the end of his intellectual resources in defence of his comment, was ready to capitulate and admit that he hadn't thought through any of his beliefs, whereupon Todd had suddenly lost interest entirely and dropped the conversation like a stone. The clouds that had covered his face, making it sombre and analytical, had cleared suddenly and he had switched, with bewildering rapidity, to another topic entirely, a song he liked that he'd heard on the radio that morning.

More even than what he said was the way he said it. Jennifer could have listened to him forever, that low voice, like the reassuring purr of a car engine ticking over on a cold morning, had the power to mesmerise her, hold her still until he stopped speaking and released her.

He was the only person she knew who didn't need context. Put him anywhere and he thrived. She knew that without her gang, her friends, the people who knew and liked her, who got her jokes and expected to find her sweet and entertaining, she wasn't much. Stripped of any shared history, up against new people, she mostly made a pretty poor showing. Natasha had a touch of what Todd had too, Jennifer thought. That chameleon quality that was actually the opposite; that consisted of remaining herself, rather than absorbing someone else, but had an identical effect, drawing new people to her as effectively as Jennifer drew old friends.

Which bit of it is true? Jennifer often wondered about Todd. The sincere provocation or the sudden switch-off? There was something in his eyes at times, a look of such profound disgust that it made her both desperate to find out what caused it, and terrified of the answer. Was it her? College? Her friends? Himself?

That disgust, she presumed, was why he was with her. He'd once said that she was kind: 'So kind that you never will be able to bring yourself to see faults in the people you like.' He'd said it as if it was a wonderful thing, and also something he despised her for. But Jennifer had clung to it. If kindness was what he wanted, needed, then kindness was what she would give him. If that was what was required to make him stay, she would oblige, in endless doses, like a repeat prescription, so that she need never be without him. And so she had tutored herself to remain ever tolerant, even when he sometimes ignored her for days and at other times kept her awake far later than she wished. Smoking, talking, drinking cups of coffee late into the night when she secretly wished he would have some hot milk and go to bed.

She had tried stocking up on soothing herbal teas, stuffing the tiny kitchen of her flat with things called 'Good Night-time' and 'Sleep Easy', but he ignored them, reaching instead for the coffee tin, kettle ever on the boil; he was too big for the kitchen, like a grown-up in a playhouse. He's tortured, she told herself, liking the intensity of the word, the idea, and the possibilities of her role as the one to calm him. But sometimes she felt like she was the one being tortured: deprived of sleep – he clearly didn't need much, was powered by something more primal – ranted at, and with sex always and only when *he* wanted it.

He would go through intense lustful periods, when he reached for her several times a night, often without preamble or foreplay of any kind, thrusting hard and fast, determined to come as quickly as possible, face knotted in concentration above her, breath coming in heavy gasps. Sometimes, she woke to find him already inside her or fumbling with the waist of her pyjamas from behind, his dick already rock hard, and so much determination in him that she would find herself caught up in it, fired momentarily by the same urgency, until he came moments later, and fell asleep, leaving her wide awake and still humming with desire that had been woken and then ignored. Those times, she would finish the job herself, by hand, wondering if he would wake and be turned on by the sight of her masturbating. But the only time he had ever let on to being woken up, he had just grinned at her and said 'good for you', before turning over and going back to sleep, so that instead of feeling sexy and wildly desirable, Jennifer had felt like an idiot.

His lust seemed curiously unrelated to her, more the product of whatever drove him than anything she did or said or wore. She got used to being rejected at the times when he lost interest in sex. No matter what she did, no matter what combinations of lace and satin she put on, no matter how drunk he got, there were times when he couldn't be roused, seemed indeed to look through her rather than at her.

She wondered was he on drugs, more drugs than the rest of them took casually on nights out, but she dismissed the idea. She would have seen, would have known. And, anyway, she dimly knew there was more to the rough awkwardness of his character than just a few too many pills or lines.

His company was exhausting in a way Jennifer hadn't experienced before, leaving her so drained at times that she felt muffled, removed from the world, but the way he looked at her, the times when he wanted her, that was so hot, so wild, that it made her squirm with excitement. He might not have been a great lover – far too self-absorbed, his mind ever reaching forward to the next thing – but he could still turn her weak with longing.

But being there with him, on this hot bright island, was different to being in her flat at home or in his place, the few times he had allowed her to see him there. So far away from the familiar, she felt less herself in his company, more like a shadow that his brightness could disperse.

CHAPTER 5

The following morning, Natasha lay in the sun by the pool, alone. By the time she had returned from her trip to the café the previous evening, the others were drinking in earnest, cocktails made with some kind of blue liquor Paul had found in the supermarket and mixed with fresh lime juice and soda water. Before Natasha had even sat down, one had been shoved into her hand with the order, 'Drink up, you're way behind.'

There had been questions about the café – 'Was the coffee really good?'; 'Was anyone there?' – but no one had listened to the answers. Julie and Katherine were dancing to the Black-Eyed Peas' 'Where is the Love?', which was blaring from the sitting room, egged on by Paul, who, Natasha decided, must have sampled several of his cocktails in the making of them, given that he was clearly more drunk than the rest.

She had abandoned any attempt to tell them about the café – the old men playing cards and drinking bitter, black coffees, chased down with small glasses of something clear and potent – and joined in, knocking back a couple of the blue drinks fast so as to hit the same high as the rest of them.

They had talked about going out, quarrelling enthusiastically about the merits of various bars and clubs they had been told about, but had ended by staying put, unable to agree on anything except the desirability of another drink. They had danced and laughed and played silly games that had ended with more drinking. Julie and Katherine had taken their tops off in the pool, calling to Natasha and Jennifer to join them, to feel how gorgeous the water was on their half-naked bodies, but shrieking when Dermot and Paul had tried to get in with them.

'You know what it's like already,' Katherine had said sternly. 'You never have to wear tops. This is for girls only. Come on, Natasha!'

But Natasha had laughed and said she wasn't drunk enough yet to feel their recklessness, conscious too of Todd's gaze upon her and what it might mean.

He had drawn near to her at one stage, sitting close by her at the edge of the pool where she dangled her legs in the water and offering her a cigarette. Natasha, who didn't smoke much, had taken one, for the pleasure of sharing something with him, of leaning towards him for a light, then settling back on the same exhale.

'Did you finish the awful book?' he'd asked, voice low, deliberately pitched beneath the music and yelling.

'God, no, it's unreadable.' She'd laughed.

'You know Julie brought it?'

'What? No!' Natasha had made a face of mock-horror. 'Oh Lord. I had no idea . . . She must hate me!'

'I doubt she would have liked you very much anyway,' he'd said.

'But why?' Natasha had pretended to be surprised. She knew very well that Julie was not disposed to like her. Knew, too, that she could have made her, but was unwilling to do what was required, to show Julie the level of deference she wanted. 'I think I'm quite a nice person.'

'I don't know if "nice" is the word,' he had said, considering, 'but you are . . . different.'

'I am?'

'Yes. You aren't what I expected.'

Natasha, with a faint thrill of excitement at the knowledge that he had thought about her, had expected something of her, was about to ask more, when Jennifer had interrupted them – 'Come and dance, Natasha, quick' – dragging her up from where she sat. There had been no more intimacies with Todd, indeed, he had seemed almost to avoid her, but Natasha was aware that something, perhaps, had happened.

Watching them all dance and drink and flirt around her and with her, Natasha had felt she understood something important about these people – about what they wanted, how they saw themselves – that was relevant to her, but now, in the light of the next day, with a headache and tired eyes, she couldn't remember what it was.

She shifted on her lounger, following the sun as it nudged its way across the blank blue slate of the sky.

'Coffee?' Jennifer asked her. She was wearing a wide-brimmed straw hat with olivey-green ribbons trailing from it and a long cream-coloured dress. She looked, Natasha thought, like a medieval angel, something by Hans Memling.

'Iced, if there is any,' Natasha answered. 'You look as if you were about to announce the birth of Christ.'

'Huh?' Jennifer looked confused, then glanced down at her dress and smiled. 'Oh, right.'

The others were beginning to emerge, in various states of hungover-ness, clutching cups and glasses of things, ready to discuss the events of the night before, a quiet one by the standards of the holiday.

'Bed before the sun came up. I think that's pretty respectable,' said Julie.

'Given that you started drinking at midday, I'm not sure I agree,' said Paul. His interest in Julie had taken the unfortunate but typical form of endless slagging, Natasha had noticed. He was unable to make a clear declaration of his desire or to engage her in reasonable conversation, and so he teased her instead. 'You're great craic, I'll say that for you', was as close as he got to a compliment, and even that came out of the side of his mouth with no eye contact, just a sort of bluff squint. It didn't seem to be working. Julie paid him no attention except to slag back, almost absentmindedly.

'I'll go and get some buns,' said Martin, ever helpful and eager to make sure everyone was happy and entertained.

'Tasha, you disappeared early.' That was Julie, always the one to notice, to comment, sometimes openly, sometimes slyly. Pert and smiley, with light-blonde hair cut in a pageboy style and round blue eyes, she behaved like the baby of the group, a kind of indulged *enfant terrible*, Natasha had decided, but underneath the childish pouting and wriggling were plenty of barbs.

'Hardly early!' Natasha laughed. 'Well, past any normal person's bedtime.'

'Yes, but we're on holiday,' said Julie, 'the—

'Holiday of a Lifetime,' they all chorused obligingly. 'Sun, sea and shamelessness' was how Julie had described it, and they had all fallen into line – the others because that was exactly the kind of indolent hedonism they had in mind; Natasha because the belief that she could switch off the misery that surrounded her was vital.

'Well, I'm sure I'll make up for it tonight.' She smiled at Julie, carefully anodyne.

Tonight, they had all agreed, was to be the big one. But first there was the day, to be spent like all the days, in magnificent idleness. By the pool, at the beach, dozing in the shade, swimming lazily, an effort to cool off rather than exercise, eating calamari in the grotty beach shack where everything cost ridiculous prices, which they paid anyway because they were on the Holiday of a Lifetime and didn't want to think about budgets. This is what Natasha was here for really – lazy, golden days, the play of warm shadow on too-hot skin – not the long, hectic nights out, driven, she felt, by the others' determined desire to be, for once, extraordinary; celebrities in their own minds for those ten days, with all the trappings of clothes and shoes and attitude. The white-knuckle ambition they felt to live like the girls they saw in magazines lived, if only for a short time. And so they spent as much time talking about what they would wear and trying on clothes for nights out as if there were hordes of paparazzi outside, and their photos might appear in the 'Spotted!' pages of magazines, rather than simply on their phones and Facebook pages.

To Natasha, that desire, which the group shared, was all the more poignant for its inevitable brevity. They were like mayflies, she thought, shining and flickering desperately, knowing, if only in their hearts, how short was their time – for youth, for beauty, for freedom. She felt she could have mapped the futures of them all with certainty – good jobs in big firms; banking, law, accountancy. Marriage, with children where children were possible, solid houses and irreproachable lives. School mum chats and morning coffee with friends. A bit of charity fund-raising and two-week summer holidays in Portugal. One day they would look back on the holiday of a lifetime with faint bemusement, as if it had happened to someone else and they had only heard the stories.

All except Todd. Todd was different, difficult, his moods hard to follow, his future unclear.

There was still no sign of him. He slept later than the others, surfacing only when the day was well advanced to its hottest point. 'It's good for him,' Jennifer had said. 'He's relaxing. He's such a ball of tension most of the time at home that he's up by dawn most days.'

When Todd did emerge, he looked thunderous.

'Hi, darling,' Jennifer called out. He ignored her. Ignored them all. He crossed the patio wearing just a pair of faded navy togs, and dived into the deep end, sending a sullen splash of water up behind him. He was magnificent-looking, Natasha thought. Tall, bleached blond by the sun with broad, strong shoulders and a narrow waist. But what really attracted her was the abundance of certitude that spilled from him. Beyond question he knew he was magnetic, that everyone had always wanted him. He was the perfect schoolboy hero, like a man dreamed up by an anxious small boy, born out of intense longing.

Todd emerged from the pool after a couple of lengths and lay down, dripping, on a recliner in the shade. Even from a distance, the set of his back was unmistakably irritable. Jennifer went over with a mug of coffee, but stayed only a moment. She came back, rolling her eyes at Natasha.

'He's in a fouler,' she whispered. 'This could go on for the whole day.' She looked miserable.

Natasha knew she was right. Todd's moods had already shaped the holiday, subtly but definitely, causing the others to tread lightly around him, gather silently but protectively close to Jennifer, who felt his remoteness or surliness as a personal failure. When Todd sulked, there was no time limit to it, no natural cut-off point. He was just as capable of pursuing his bad mood to the bitter end, of retiring in a furious cloud for hours, as he was of simply snapping out of it, sneaking up on Jennifer with a laugh and sending a wave of cold water over her, or throwing himself down beside Natasha, asking, 'What are you reading? Sebald. Typical. Don't you ever get tired of being the virtuoso?' but in a laughing way.

'What is it this time?' she asked Jennifer.

'No idea. Could be anything, but he's going to ruin the day if he keeps it up.' She paused, then: 'You're good at getting him out of his bad moods. Go over and chat to him, before he decides to give it free rein.'

'He's not going to want to talk to me.'

'Try. *Please.*'

Conscious that the others were watching her with interest and, in Julie's case, a faintly malicious smile, Natasha went into the kitchen and poured a glass of melon juice into which she squeezed a lime and added ice. She checked her reflection in the mirror and took her hair out of the high ponytail into which she had thrust it earlier. It swung dark and glossy around her shoulders, although the base, where hair met neck, was already damp and sweaty. Her cheeks were pink with the heat, her eyes dreamier than normal. She was wearing a short green-and-white sundress printed with daisies, her feet bare and brown. Taking the drink and a packet of salt with her, she walked over to Todd, still wreathed in the darkness of his mood.

'Here. Salt first, then the drink.' She held the two things out to him. He stared up at her, silent, considering.

'What's that for?' His voice, always low, was scraped hollow by the late morning and the long sleep.

'The heat. It's a trick I learned when we lived in Mauritius. You lick the salt off your hand, then you drink the melon and lime. It's the combination of salt, sour and sweet that works, although in Mauritius we didn't have juice – we just squeezed lime over pieces of melon.'

'When did you live in Mauritius?'

'My dad was posted there for a while. I was young, seven or eight, and we've never been back since, but I remember it as pure heaven.' He moved his legs and she sat on the edge of the recliner beside him, stepping out of the sun and into the rosy shade of a red beach umbrella. 'It felt like being shut out of paradise when we left.'

'Poor you.' He looked as if he meant it, holding her gaze so long that she wondered what, how much, he was commiserating with. None of the group had ever mentioned the death, the funeral, whether by tacit agreement or because Jennifer had told them not to, she didn't know. The first day or so they had been gentle, careful, around her, but that had soon worn off. She had doubted whether they even remembered why she was there, the circumstances that had brought her to them. But perhaps she was wrong; perhaps Todd remembered. 'Will you ever go back?' he asked.

'And try for paradise regained? I don't know. I don't suppose it's as I recall it.'

She remembered stalking lizards with Nancy, trying to sneak up on them as they lay, sun-drugged, in the hottest places they could find, and the spider the colour of a burned almond they had found one day in a web like a tunnel, thick and sticky. 'For who goes up your winding stair can ne'er come down again,' Nancy had said, in a sing-song voice, poking at the tunnel with a stick, tearing bits of it, so that the spider had retreated temporarily in subdued ferocity.

Natasha shook her head slightly then, as if to physically clear the recollections that came too fast, threatening one upon another so that they seemed ready to flood her.

She watched as Todd licked the salt from the back of his hand, pink tongue curling over the brown surface lightly speckled with grains of white. He made a face, then drank half the melon and lime juice. He poured more salt onto the underside of his wrist, and held it out to her.

'Your go.'

He watched as she took hold of his hand, drew it towards her mouth. Her eyes wanted to flicker over to Jennifer who must also be watching, but she kept them steady, held his gaze as she licked up the salt, watched his pupils widen as her tongue touched the soft skin of his wrist. His other hand, when he passed her the juice, shook slightly.

'That seems to be doing the trick.' He smiled at her, then lay back in the recliner. She resisted the urge to curl in beside him, fitting her body to his in the narrow space that remained. She got up.

'I think we're going to the beach soon.'

'Good,' he said.

'He seems to have cheered up a bit,' she said to Jennifer as she went back to her sunny spot.

'Great,' said Jennifer through what might have been gritted teeth. Then she turned towards Julie, 'What beach will we go to today?'

'The one with the sea stacks? It's usually the most lively. Not that things aren't pretty lively here already,' Julie added, with a sly look at Natasha.

Why was she ramping-up the flirting? Natasha wondered, an hour later, as she stuffed spare bikinis, towels, sunscreen and a baseball cap into her beach bag. She had decided she wouldn't, having seen early on in the holiday that she could. Todd had made no secret of his inclination, but she had told herself that she wasn't really interested. That he was too obvious, too masculine, aside, of course, from being Jennifer's. So why was she now tangling her glances with his, allowing him to brush against her, tease her with a quiet intimacy that, by design or not, excluded the others? It wasn't just the way he made her feel, the way she wanted to gasp every time they locked eyes, the way her heart thumped when he touched her. It was to do with Jennifer too, her passivity and silent acquiescence. If she would just assert her claim, warn Natasha off, have a row with Todd and set some kind of limit, Natasha felt that she would be bound by it. But Jennifer didn't. She said nothing, turned away from the increasingly obvious with a mute, humble appeal that Natasha found it strangely pleasant to ignore, as if answering the pain that had come to her own life by parcelling it out to others.

And so Natasha, who was not proof against the spark that flew between herself and Todd, any more than she was proof against the need for someone large and masculine, someone with strong hands and natural authority to care for her, let the tension build, although she continued to tell herself, *Just a little more and then I'll stop.*

No one else did anything either. In fact, it seemed to Natasha that they had drawn away, to the fringes, in a circle, watching and awaiting the outcome, eyes beyond the campfire.

Their friendship hadn't started out like this. If anything, she knew, it was Jennifer who had craved something from her at first. All the points of difference that Natasha had felt, the little things that had acted as barriers between herself and most of the people she'd met in college – her accent, her lack of a fixed background so that when she was asked 'Where are you from?' or 'Where did you go to school?' the answer was always either long and convoluted or, if she shortened it, too abrupt – were things that Jennifer had seized on. The differences between them had excited Jennifer, in a way that Natasha at first had found unconvincing, then faintly annoying, before allowing herself to be beguiled by the enthusiasm that seemed to have no end point, growing neither old nor jaded with exposure.

'You know so many weird things,' Jennifer had said to her one day, after a lecture.

'It comes from too much time with grown-ups,' Natasha said. 'The things I should know, like catch-words from TV shows and chart music, I'm ignorant of, and then I know all sorts of strange facts that don't even join up, just muddle around in my head in isolation and pop out at odd moments.'

'If that's true, it's very convincing,' Jennifer said wistfully. 'You always sound as if you know everything, as if you're only revealing the tip of an iceberg full of knowledge and wisdom.'

'It comes from being brought up like a magpie.' Natasha laughed. 'Wandering around the world, meeting new people all the time, acquiring snippets of this and that, the customs of one country, the manners of another. But none of it adds up. It's just fragmented scraps. That's why I'm here. Trying to learn a solid block of information, something coherent that runs from A to Z and that I can fit the rest of the floating bits and pieces around. Nancy doesn't think that's the way to do it. She thinks you just carry on gathering things that interest you, until eventually you know more than you don't know, if you see what I mean, and it all joins together.'

'I do see,' Jennifer said. 'But I think your way makes more sense. Although I can't believe you've thought about it so much. That it matters so much.'

'Of course it matters,' Natasha said, astonished. 'Why are *you* here?'

'Well, because, I mean, because you just do, right? Finish school, go to college, get a job. Isn't that the way it goes?' She looked uncomfortable, possibly conscious that her reasoning sounded pathetically childish in comparison with Natasha's dedication. 'My parents would have been really disappointed if I hadn't gone to university.' That made her sound even more childish. 'But I'm also here to meet people, different people, not the ones I knew growing up,' she added. 'People like you. Even if you are a bit full of yourself.' She looked momentarily frightened, as if she might have dared too much, but Natasha laughed.

'You're right, I am. I take things too seriously, don't I? Nancy says the same thing.'

In fact, Jennifer was the one to take things too seriously, they both knew. Her friendship with Natasha, her relationship with Todd, her sense of duty towards her group of pre-college friends, all these things pressed far more upon her than essay deadlines or exam revision.

Towards the end of their first year, she insisted on Natasha coming home with her for a weekend, and Natasha agreed without too much reluctance because, in those days, there was time to do everything she wanted, without urgency.

The weekend was scorching, and the bus ride long and sticky, so that Natasha, passing through small grimy towns where everything seemed pebble-dashed, even the few monuments to death and sacrifice, began to regret saying yes.

Jennifer chattered away beside her, stories of Jake, her older brother in London, and what he'd said and done on his last visit home – 'I might go and live with him after college. Do a Masters or something. I certainly want to keep studying, I think now it's what I was born to do' – seeming to find enough encouragement in Natasha's occasional 'umms' and 'uh-uhs' to keep going. She was nervous, Natasha knew, hence the babbling. She also knew that she could relieve Jennifer's nerves, by engaging, listening, responding, seeming open and interested, glad to be where she was. But it was hot, and she didn't feel like it. So she stared out of the window and Jennifer ran on, until eventually she ran herself into silence, sitting still and quiet beside Natasha until finally she said 'We're here', and got up.

The bus stopped at a crossroads on a country road, opposite a church. A woman in a rust-coloured T-shirt and baggy jeans was waiting beside a blue station wagon. Her hair, long and thick and bushy, was like Jennifer's put through a too-hot wash so the colours had faded and the edges frayed. She hugged Jennifer hard the minute she stepped down from the bus, but smiled over her shoulder at Natasha.

'Natasha.' It wasn't a question, but rather a statement, and Natasha momentarily wondered who she might be to this woman behind it. 'I'm Mary,' the woman continued. It was a name Natasha disliked, but she thought it possible that this Mary, with her unrepentant mop of hair, might make a go of it, the way a very plain dress or top could sometimes be the perfect foil for beauty.

'Pleased to meet you,' Natasha said, holding out a hand.

The station wagon was old and dirty and smelled of dog, which Natasha disliked. 'What kind of dog?' she asked with a smile, trying to be relaxed, to be a good sport, indicating the seats covered in white and reddish-brown hair. There was a pause, awkward, pained, then Jennifer turned round from the front seat, eyes brimming with tears. 'A spaniel, Coco, but he's dead. Put down just a few weeks ago.' Her voice wobbled. Natasha smiled sympathetically, trying to find within her anything that would enable her to relate to the small tragedy recalled in front of her. 'I'm sorry,' she managed. 'That must have been very hard.'

'It's the worst thing that has ever happened to me,' Jennifer said, sounding strangled.

'It was the kindest thing,' her mother said, patting Jennifer's hand with the one of hers that wasn't holding the wheel. She didn't sound anything like as choked as Jennifer, Natasha thought. And how could Jennifer possibly have reached college-going age without anything worse than a dead pet occurring? Natasha felt she could name a dozen more devastating episodes in her own life – betrayal by friends, by Nancy, of her own principles in moments of weakness; injustice; moments of shame and rage. But, she reasoned, perhaps she simply didn't understand. She put a hand on Jennifer's shoulder and squeezed gently. Jennifer lifted her own hand, laid it across Natasha's, and squeezed back. In the rear-view mirror, Natasha saw Mary smile momentarily.

The house, when they had arrived, was a solid two-storey farmhouse on the outskirts of exactly the kind of pebble-dashed town they had repeatedly passed through. The kind of house that used to belong to the local doctor, Natasha thought, before remembering that it still did, that Jennifer's father *was* the local doctor. It was comfortable, old-fashioned, a bit shabby. The paintings were heavy oils of sombre landscapes, dusty bits of patterned china were displayed in glass-fronted cabinets and on the floor were thick carpets of indeterminate colour, a kind of brownish-pink or pinkish-brown. The best thing about it was the lake at the back across a field.

'We've got a couple of canoes and a tiny sailboat that's my brother's. We can go out after lunch,' Jennifer said with excitement. And they did, spending the afternoon zipping up and down the lake, pushed forward and goaded on by a wind that had nipped and teased despite the sun, then throwing themselves off the tiny jetty and into the water again and again until Natasha's head buzzed from the glare of light on sharp little waves and the slap of cold water against the top of her head as she dived.

Back at the house, they had dinner in the kitchen – a roast leg of lamb with roast potatoes, roast vegetables and even a potato salad that was really too heavy for the day, but worked because they were hungry and chilled.

'I hope you don't mind not eating in the dining room,' Mary said. 'The kitchen is much cosier.' Natasha, who had seen the dining room, didn't mind at all. The kitchen might have been cluttered – there had seemed to be a huge number of old, clean jamjars with a jumble of pens, rubber bands, bits of old string and stray stamps, stuck into them (one seemed to have a heap of batteries, whether old or new she couldn't tell) – but it was certainly cosy and warm, with the Aga, and, in comparison with the rest of the house, clean and dustless.

They drank wine and Jennifer chattered to her parents, the same mix of enthusiasm, eagerness to please and slightly awkward self-consciousness that she displayed with Natasha, leaping from one subject to the next, determined to cover far more than could really be dealt with. She clearly adored them and, wanting them to think well of her friend, insisted that Natasha be shown in her best light; doing what she did – tailoring a personality for Natasha that was less than the truth.

'Tell them about the time the lecturer asked did anyone disagree with her analysis of Dante, and you were the only one who put up your hand . . .'

'Tell about the time in the bar when that idiot spilled his drink on you and you told him he should pay for the dry cleaning and he actually did . . .'

In fact, Mary and Thomas, Jennifer's dad, asked their own questions, better questions, that enabled Natasha to tell them a little about her life without feeling the need to be, or pretend to be, the person Jennifer pitched her as – someone so assured and competent, so daring and archly challenging, that she was half-tempted to play the role, but realised with a rush of sudden clarity that it could never be sustained. And so she stepped aside from it, kept it close enough not to embarrass Jennifer by disowning it too violently, but remained herself.

'Jennifer tells me you moved around a lot as a child,' Mary said. 'Was that for your father's job?' Her questions were so direct they would have been nosy from anyone else. From her, they seemed simply an effort to impose clarity on what was before her. She was meticulous, Natasha saw, frowning slightly at any exaggerations, even those done for comic effect, as if no comedy could ever outweigh the crime of inaccuracy.

'Yes. He was a diplomat. He's retired now. That's why I was mostly home-schooled. They tried boarding school, because they thought it would be less disruptive, but I was miserable, so they brought me back.'

She remembered the nights in the school in France, near the Belgian border. The layers of brown that she had thought might choke her. Brown walls, brown floors, brown blankets on the narrow beds, brown leaves on the trees outside, a brown smell throughout the old, unloved building, brown meat covered in brown sauce. The way the other girls, daughters of French and Belgian *notaires* and *commerçants*, had stared at her, without rancour, but without interest either. Everything they said had been a criticism or a sly question. Nowhere had she found a spark to warm to. No tiny ray of humour, kindness or familiarity. No Nancy to tell stories to and with, to giggle when things had been unbearable so that they became merely silly or ridiculous, their sting drawn by her absurd, irresistible wit.

'And your mother? Did she work too?' Mary continued, imposing order on Natasha's unruly past, one she rarely laid out in any great detail, because no one ever seemed sufficiently interested. 'Gosh, that's so weird . . .' they would say politely, before changing the subject, moving swiftly on to something more urgent; who had been out last night and what they had done.

'My mother is Spanish. She never worked.' To Natasha, the conjunction of these two statements had always made perfect sense, although she was dimly aware that, to others, they did not necessarily illuminate each other.

'Hence your beautiful hair.' Mary smiled at her.

'You never said your mother was Spanish,' Jennifer burst out excitedly.

'Well, it just never came up,' Natasha said, smiling. 'I wasn't hiding it.'

'But how fascinating!' Jennifer said.

Natasha caught Mary's eye for a second, and both smiled with perhaps a tiny hint, Natasha thought, of indulgence.

'Well, a bit interesting, I suppose . . .' Natasha trailed off.

'She must be so beautiful,' Jennifer gushed.

'Why, because she's Spanish?' Natasha teased.

'No, because you are,' Jennifer said, so that Natasha laughed, pleased but embarrassed too. 'So you must speak Spanish?'

'Actually, I don't.' They all looked surprised at that, so she continued. 'I spoke it until I was about four, quite fluently, I think, because my mother spoke it to both me and Nancy, but then I stopped. I've forgotten most of what I knew, and never learned any more.'

'But why?' Jennifer looked baffled.

'Because my father didn't speak it. He refused to.'

'Why?'

'I don't really know. I think he thought it was up to her to learn English.' Natasha was conscious of how strange this must sound, worried by the disloyalty of implied criticism, and tried to explain further. 'Like, he thought she would inhabit his world better if she cut ties with her own world.' The explanation was hopeless and she knew it, so she tried once more. 'He wasn't very good at languages anyway. He learned French, because he had to, and knew Latin, but it wasn't easy for him. And because he didn't speak it, and she never spoke it when he was around, I just stopped.'

There was a pause then, as she had known there would be.

'Where did they meet?' Mary seemed to have somehow felt the slight catch in Natasha's thoughts, the hesitation within her that had pulled her up suddenly short.

'They met when he was posted over to Madrid. She was very beautiful, but spoke barely any English. They married quickly. Her family were against it. She still doesn't speak great English . . .' The facts were as correct as she assumed Mary could wish for. The bits between those facts – the treacherous colours and indistinct shapes – had not yet formed in a way that she could speak them.

They talked late into the night, with Jennifer thrusting first one subject and then another before them, and Natasha understood that she would never have the other girl's headlong spontaneous enthusiasm or self-generating energy; that she was far more dependent on being asked specific questions in order to reveal herself. And that not everyone would always ask the right questions. The idea troubled her slightly. To those who asked the wrong questions, what, she wondered, would she be?

Going to bed in the spare room, late and slightly drunk, Natasha found a photo of Jennifer, aged maybe twelve, cuddling a liver-and-white spaniel, wearing a white T-shirt too tight for her developing body, but grinning with entirely childish abandon into the camera. The spaniel must be the dead Coco, and Natasha wondered if the photo had been removed deliberately, from downstairs or even from Jennifer's room, as something too painful to be seen.

The room was tidy but cluttered. Too many pictures on walls covered in faded floral paper – badly framed prints of yet more landscapes – and furniture that looked as if it was there more because it had nowhere else to go than because it had any function. Boxes stacked in a corner bore labels: 'Jake, school stuff', 'Jennifer, books', 'Jennifer, toys', and the old-fashioned dressing table had jars and bottles of creams and lotions, all long out of date judging by the smell of wet sheep they gave off when she opened them. A large tortoiseshell butterfly flapped at the window, to Natasha's alarm. She wondered what it was doing there, and would it flap anywhere near her as she slept. She shuddered at the idea of the frantic wings beating against her face or hair, a rhythm of desperation drummed out against an unyielding object. She toyed with the idea of opening the window and letting the butterfly out, but worried that the night air might kill it; that freedom would, in the end, prove the worst of two outcomes. The mattress of the bed sagged badly and gave off a sound of rusty springs from deep within it, but the sheets were clean and made of cool linen. It might be pleasant after all, Natasha thought as she lay down, to have a house that was so obviously a home. A place where all your years had something still to say, a light, loving touch on the present.

She thought of her own house, the lofty ceilings and spare, echoey rooms, where only the objects of her father's collection – strange masks and shields from Africa, ancient Greek vases and amphoras; carefully preserved rare books – told a story older than the day. And that story was their own story, the triumphant story of their making and preserving, not the story of Natasha or her family, who were but episodes in a long career of survival.

The return visit, when it happened, was far less successful. Natasha left it so long that she could tell Jennifer was starting to feel offended, only saying 'Come for dinner on Saturday? With my parents. Come early so we can have a drink beforehand,' when it became obvious that Jennifer was ready to feel thoroughly slighted.

It was a miserable day. Summer in name only. Grey, drizzly, with a blustery wind that had spoken early of autumn. The house, in comparison with Jennifer's, and even to her who was used to it, felt cheerless. Empty and indifferent, the bare floors suddenly cold and glum instead of pared-back and elegant.

Nancy had shrugged when Natasha had told her that Jennifer was coming, had said 'sounds nice', and had then disappeared without saying where she was going, when or whether she would be back. At first Natasha presumed she was behind the curtains, sitting on a radiator reading, the way she did, the way they both used to as children, but as the day wore on it became apparent that she wasn't, and that she would not emerge from behind a great swath of velvet, ready to chat and laugh.

Her father spent the day in his study while her mother fussed over dinner, wondering would she make something traditional and Spanish, or stick to easy, obvious fare.

'Just do a roast,' Natasha said, remembering Jennifer's mother's roast lamb.

'No one would eat a roast in the summer,' her mother said peevishly. Then, 'I wish you could be more helpful, after springing this on me.'

'I didn't spring it. I told you days ago,' Natasha snapped. Then she relented. 'It's just one friend, for a simple dinner. It doesn't need to be a big deal. Make spaghetti bolognese if you like.'

'Oh honestly, Natasha!' Her mother slammed down her mug so that milky coffee leapt over the side and landed on the section of newspaper she had been poring shortsightedly over. 'Even if it is just one person, she is your friend, and the dinner must be nice. It is the same if it is one person or ten people.' She always said this, insisted on it. It was one of the reasons they didn't entertain very often.

'It isn't,' Natasha said through gritted teeth. 'It's just one person. For a simple dinner. I'll cook if you don't want to.'

'No.' Her mother wasn't ready for the giving up of control that this would mean. 'I will make stuffed peppers with tomato.' Now that she had a plan, a menu, her agitation lessened. 'You can make gazpacho.'

Jennifer arrived early, laden with presents – flowers for Natasha's mother, chocolates, a bottle of wine, so that Natasha felt embarrassed, remembering her own empty-handed arrival at Jennifer's.

'Let me show you the house,' she said, knowing that Jennifer's reaction would show it back to her as she had wished It to be: discreet, lovely, filled with precious objects from her parents' travels, and not the rather cheerless place she sometimes feared it was. And indeed Jennifer exclaimed and admired extravagantly.

'It's like a museum,' she said, looking at the African masks. 'You could charge people in, and they'd be happy to pay!'

'Nancy and I used to put them on sometimes.'

'Weren't you frightened of them when you were little?'

'Not really. At one stage, we lived in a house, a rented place, that had heads of animals mounted on the walls. The husband of the woman who owned it had shot them in the Congo. They were really scary. In comparison, these are nothing. I grew up with them I guess. They grinned into my cradle.'

'What animals?'

'I don't really know. They were all so dusty and old and worn that whatever colours they started with, they were just grey by the time I saw them. I know there was a lion, because of the shaggy mane, like thick, knotted cobwebs wrapped around the poor thing's head. And Nancy used to get very upset at one of them, some kind of impala, because she said it was a baby. But the rest all looked like warthogs, even though I think there were zebras and buffalo and things. My dad used to laugh and say he was surprised there wasn't a human head up there too.' Jennifer had looked bewildered. 'Because the husband had been Belgian, and they killed so many Africans in the Congo,' Natasha explained.

'Oh.' Jennifer looked uneasy, as if wondering how that could ever be a joke.

'It's not that he thinks their behaviour was funny,' Natasha said. 'That's just his way.' Jennifer looked, if anything, more uneasy.

Dinner was bad. Jennifer clearly didn't like the stuffed peppers, filled with rice and chopped tomato. She pushed them round on her plate, then partly unstuffed a couple and ate bits of the rice. Her father was twinkly and worldly, very much the retired diplomat. Natasha knew he did it only when he didn't want to be anything more like himself. When he didn't want to bother with the effort of engagement; slipping on the mask as easily as if it had just come down off the wall. It was a way he had learned of keeping his distance, and Natasha had learned it from him – the necessity of having something to slip into, that would carry you through but keep you separate too. A kind of low-maintenance social distance run, was how she thought of it. Energy-conserving but practical.

Conversation had been lumpy, like trying to pour porridge. They couldn't seem to find any common ground that would lift them from platitudes, and short-lived ones at that.

'Is Burroughs still in the English department?' her father asked, even though he knew very well that he was. Had already asked Natasha.

'He is,' Jennifer said.

'Still as pompous and boring as ever?'

Jennifer laughed, but didn't dare agree. She still wasn't used to the idea that lecturers could be judged and criticised like normal people. 'Is it nice being back in Ireland full-time?' she asked.

'Maria enjoys not moving house every few years,' he said, 'but, for the rest of us, stability is a high price to pay for stagnation, isn't it, Tash?'

Natasha laughed and agreed with him, knowing that the sly mockery of his wife must sound bad, but unwilling, unable, not to cheer him on. Jennifer, again, looked uncomfortable. If criticising lecturers was too much for her, what must she make of sneering at wives?

Natasha sighed, wished Nancy were there, with her ability to change the course of conversation with one observation or question; a knack that sometimes made her seem odd, disjointed, but more often rescued them all from something dull and pointless.

Later, she and Jennifer sat in the garden, smoking and watching the uninspiring setting of a pallid sun.

'It looks guilty, doesn't it?' Natasha said, waving a cigarette at the sun, which was slipping without fanfare below the horizon. 'Like someone ducking their head into the collar of their coat, so as not to be noticed.'

'Can't blame it after that crappy day. Twelve hours of rain is nothing to be preening about.' Then, 'Your mother doesn't talk as much as the rest of you.'

'No,' Natasha agreed. 'It would be hard,' she continued, with a laugh.

'So she's the quiet one who does things, and your dad is the one who talks? And you're like your dad?'

Natasha nodded to show that, yes, she was.

'And Nancy?' Jennifer asked.

'She's like him too, I suppose,' Natasha said.

'So no one is like your mother?'

'Not really,' Natasha replied. 'I mean, if you had a choice, who would you rather be like? My dad is the brilliant one. My mother is much more . . . I don't know, ordinary?' Even as she said it, she knew it was entirely the wrong word, but that she didn't have any of the right ones.

'But she must have her strengths too?' Jennifer asked.

Natasha wondered why she must, then agreed. 'She's sort of like a peasant, earthy and coarse, but intuitive.' The clichés horrified her, even as she uttered them. Why were words, so useful when describing things like the location of a pain, or the correct process for applying for an official document, suddenly so hopeless when you applied them to people? To the slidey nuances of their characters and secret selves? But she persisted. 'She's good at figuring things out about you, physical things, like whether you've got your period or you need to drink parsley tea for your kidneys, and she talks about it, casually, even when you don't want her to. When I was a teenager, I hated it. She used to say things like "now you are a woman", and it made me feel sick, because I didn't want to be a woman, not the way she said it, and I didn't feel I was. She tried to make me get into a kind of gang with her, a gang of "women",' Natasha said the word with disgust 'just me and her, as if now we understood each other, and I hated that.'

'At least she talked to you about it,' Jennifer said, laughing. 'My mother never said anything except vague things about me "growing up", and then I got my period and, even though I did really know what it was, I was frightened. I didn't think the blood would look so much like, well, actual blood. And I didn't dare tell her, because she'd never mentioned it properly. And when I did tell her, she just said "oh, you poor thing". I think it's better to be open about these things.'

'Probably,' Natasha agreed. 'But my mother's *too* open. As if everything can be explained by what happens in your body; your hormones and reproductive organs. She's crude. She believes in the most basic motivations for everything – sex, hunger, jealousy, loyalty – like we're all cavemen. And she believes in revenge. An eye for an eye, a tooth for a tooth. Literally, I sometimes think.'

'Well, that makes her a good person to have in your corner, surely?'

'I suppose so.' Natasha sounded begrudging. 'If you ever need someone to commit murder for you, she definitely would. Or help you dispose of a body if you'd done the murder already. But in fact it's pointless, because I would never tell her anything, because I don't believe in revenge the way she does.'

'Even if someone does something awful.'

'No. It's not civilised. There are better ways.'

'She looks like you,' Jennifer continued. 'Less like Nancy, but the same colouring as you, and the same kind of glow.'

Natasha was annoyed. 'I've been told I look very like my father's sister,' she said, face shut.

'By someone who never met your mother,' Jennifer laughed, determined not to give in.

Later, Nancy joined them as they sat in the empty kitchen drinking tea before Jennifer cycled home.

'Where were you?' Natasha asked. She didn't offer Nancy any tea.

'Out.'

'Obviously. But where?'

'Just out.'

'Why?'

'Because I didn't fancy being in.'

'Well, thanks for your help.'

'It was your party. I figured you could handle it.'

'It wasn't a party,' Natasha said tightly. 'And of course I could handle it,' she snapped. 'But I could have done with some help too. You know what they're like.'

'Yes, and I know what you're like too, so I went out.'

'Meaning?'

'Meaning they are perfectly fine until you come along and do your thing.'

What thing? Jennifer looked as if she longed to ask, but didn't dare, because of the choppy waves of anger between them.

'I don't do any *thing*,' Natasha said.

'Oh, yes, you do. You know you do. He encourages you, and you do it. And I wasn't in the mood for it.' Nancy's tone was almost singsong; she skipped through the words like a child playing hopscotch.

'I don't know what you're talking about,' Natasha said.

Jennifer began to rise, muttering something about how she'd 'better be going now', but Natasha put a hand out, held her back.

'Don't go. It's fine. Let's play Scrabble.'

'Good idea. I'll play too,' Nancy said happily. She had helped herself to a slice of bread and blackcurrant jam. The jam made crimson pools around the butter and was sliding off it, onto her fingers. She seemed indifferent to how sticky her hand was, wiping it casually on a linen tea towel, a smear of russet left behind.

They moved into the sitting room beside where they had eaten. The curtains had been drawn; heavy swathes of dusky yellow silk that caught light from the three or four lamps lit on side tables and bookcases, throwing it back so that the curtains looked as if they were moving, swishing and switching.

'You could make a dress out of those,' Jennifer said.

'Natasha probably will,' Nancy said. 'When the family fortunes have failed entirely and she needs to catch a man.'

Natasha laughed then and Jennifer looked astonished at the sudden switch in mood.

They were both much better than her at Scrabble, and both played to win, keeping careful score and using double and triple word squares strategically. But for all the competition between them,

Nancy made up words and Natasha let her. She put 'de' down beside 'clench' and had said, 'Declench. Like the French *'déclencher'*.'

'OK,' Natasha said, 'but only if you have an 'r' and an 'e' for the end – you can have "declencher" as a noun, not a verb.'

'"Declencher" isn't a word,' Jennifer tried to say, but they ignored her.

'I've got an 'r' and an 'e',' Nancy said. She put it down. 'Twenty-eight.' Natasha wrote it down, and Jennifer realised that Natasha, who deferred to no one, deferred to Nancy, either because Nancy truly was as brilliant as she said or because she wanted her to be.

CHAPTER 6

By the time they got to the beach, the day had reached its hottest point and few of them could bear too much exposure. Julie, Martin, Paul and Katherine headed for the beach bar – 'shade and sangria', Julie said, with the put-on imperiousness that seemed to charm Paul so much – Dermot wandered off for a walk, while Jennifer huddled beneath the cover of the big red beach umbrella, the red glow lighting up her hair and face so that she looked as if she was burning with her own internal flames.

'You look like Lady Lazarus in the Sylvia Plath poem,' Natasha called over.

'Which one is that?' Jennifer asked.

'The one who rises out of the ash with red hair . . .' said Natasha.

'And eats men like air,' added Todd, lying still as a salamander on an olive green towel between the two of them. 'Except Jen doesn't eat men, do you, Jen?' He didn't open his eyes as he spoke, remained as still as though he was carved, with only his mouth moving, so that he seemed to Natasha like an effigy, speaking through the frail flesh that contained him from some distant place. 'Jen breathes out life, not death. She creates rather than consumes.'

It was a compliment. Natasha could scarcely think of a lovelier one – to be the source of life – and he delivered it with warmth, but Jennifer looked uncomfortable, as if unsure quite how to interpret his words. She looked over at Natasha, for help, for clarification, but Natasha found that she didn't want to reassure her.

'I'm going to swim,' Natasha said. 'It's far too hot to sit here.'

'I'm coming too.' Todd got up but, when Jennifer made a movement as if she too might stand, he said, 'You stay here. You'll fry in the water, no matter what adamantine coating you have on you. We'll be back in a minute.'

They weren't. They stayed in the water for what felt like hours, swimming lazily, chatting, splashing each other, Natasha marvelling at the layers of sparkle the water contained, from the hard, bright glitter of the surface to the mellow ripples deeper below. 'It's like the sun and water combine to make something almost solid,' she said, trying to describe the feeling it inspired in her. 'As if you could lean against it and feel yourself supported by something a bit rubbery but fundamentally sound.'

'"Fundamentally sound",' he teased. 'You're so pompous.'

'I know I am a bit' – she laughed – 'but I do want to figure it all out. I want to know more, about how the world is made, and why it's made, and what the parts of it are that we can't see and don't understand, but that we know are there. Sometimes I feel like one of the workmen in *A Midsummer Night's Dream*, clumsy and stupid, blundering through the forest, seeing only shade and trees and solid, immovable objects, and all the while the fairies are hidden, laughing at me, because they can see all the things I can't. They can see what I miss, what I walk straight through without noticing, because it's too delicate and insubstantial to register, and probably that's all the important stuff.' She finished in a rush, adding, 'it must be hilarious to be one of the fairies. Like having night-vision goggles and watching someone else trying to navigate a crowded room in the pitch black.' But Todd seemed faintly sneering, unwilling to engage with her, maybe even a bit embarrassed by the fervour with which she had spoken. He looked back towards the beach, at Jennifer under her red umbrella.

'Race you to that lobster pot?' Natasha asked, determined to change the subject before it hung any more awkwardly between them, and set off before he was quite ready, so that she nearly beat him, overtaken only at the end, admiring the way he cut through the water with the kind of rhythmic determination that made it seem as if he had to win, as if other options were out.

He persuaded her to stand on his shoulders and dive off, helping her back on after each go, ducking so that her legs were around his neck, then holding her hands as she clambered up to a standing position. She wondered if Jennifer could see them from the shore, but found that she didn't care, such was the exhilaration of the feel of his hard, wet body against hers. The frictionless contact as she slithered on and off his shoulders, coupled with the dazzle of the water, was hypnotic.

'You're like a seal in that swimsuit,' he said admiringly. Her one-piece was black and shiny, stretched tight across her with no pleating or forgiveness of fabric anywhere. The knowledge that so little separated them from each other, from what she was now sure they both wanted, was exciting, and she found herself smiling deliberately at him.

When they finally came out of the water, the others were back from the bar with pitchers of *tinto de verano* and cold beer.

'You missed the most amazing belly dancer,' said Julie with satisfaction. Julie, Natasha had realised, was one of those girls who loved you to miss things. 'Apparently she does a fire routine as well, just as the sun sets, when it's dark enough. It's supposed to be brilliant. We should come back at night and watch it.'

Looking across at Jennifer, Natasha realised that she was asleep, lying on her stomach, cheek resting on the book she had been reading, and that the sun had crept around the side of the red umbrella and was now shining full upon her head and shoulders.

'Jen, wake up!' She shook her hard. 'You need to get out of the sun.'

Jennifer raised her head, looking bleary. There was a livid mark down the side of her face where she had lain on her book. Her eyes were heavy.

'What?' She sounded confused.

'You're too much in the sun. It's too hot. You need a hat.' Natasha readjusted the umbrella as she spoke so that it cast its kindly shadow over Jennifer.

'Thanks.'

Jennifer still sounded confused, so Natasha said, 'Drink some water.'

'Pity you don't have any of your magic lime and salt drink here,' Julie said maliciously. 'Or maybe that's not for everyone.'

'Don't be silly,' Natasha said. 'I wish I did have some.'

'Well, in the absence of that, there's only beer. Or *tinto de verano*,' said Julie, with amiable indifference.

'That's no good, I'll go to the bar.'

'I'll be fine,' Jennifer said. 'I'll have a swim and cool off. I'm just too hot.' But she didn't sound quite convinced.

'It's OK, I'm going anyway,' Natasha said. 'I fancy a lemonade myself. Beer and watered-down wine aren't right for this heat.'

'We can't all be experts on hot countries,' Julie said with a sneery laugh, turning away to Paul, who sniggered obligingly.

Martin walked to the bar with Natasha, his desire to keep everyone happy causing him to instinctively try and create a link between the different groups. 'I thought the island was supposed to be on some kind of magic ley lines that would make everyone more enlightened,' he said. 'Instead, we're all scrapping with each other.'

'It's just the heat,' Natasha said soothingly, unwilling to let him start fussing. 'It'll be fine. Once the sun goes down and we hit the hotspots!'

At the bar, she asked for lemons, sparkling water and salt, causing Martin to say admiringly, 'How come you speak such good Spanish?'

'I really don't.' She laughed. 'Although I should. I speak decent Italian, and I just use the same words with a different accent. It might sound convincing to you, but half the time no one here knows what I'm talking about,' she laughed. 'Still, it's good enough to order salt, lemons and water.' She squeezed the lemons into the water, then got the barman to give her a twist of tinfoil into which she poured salt. Far from being irritated at the requests, the barman commended her on her good sense and said there was no need to bring back the glass, she could balance it on the nearest bit of wall and he would collect it later.

Back at the towels, she made Jennifer swallow the drink, even though Jennifer said it was disgusting and screwed up her face.

'You'll get sunstroke if you don't,' Natasha said firmly. 'You're already burnt.'

'I put sunscreen on,' Jennifer said, in dazed bewilderment. 'Factor fifty.'

'I think with skin like yours, the only thing is to stay right out of the sun. I'm not sure factor-anything is going to work.' Natasha meant it kindly, but noticed the furious look on Jennifer's face. 'On the upside,' she added, 'you'll have beautiful skin all your life, and won't get all lizardy and wrinkly like the rest of us.'

Jennifer looked slightly mollified, muttering, 'I'd take the wrinkles', as she lay back down in the shade and shut her eyes.

A mist drifted in from the sea, shrouding the hot brightness of the day and diffusing the orange glow of the setting sun, so that it took on a velvety softness. As evening approached, excitement at the night ahead was stirred up among them all: a feeling of skittishness, a nervous tremor that Natasha could feel like butterfly wings under her ribs, and that shone back at her from the eyes of the others.

'Let's go,' said Julie, jumping up. 'It's time to get ready.'

On the way back to the villa, they talked about food – 'Barbeque steaks and jugs of margarita,' said Martin with the authority he assumed in matters of provisions – and what they might wear. Julie described a halterneck dress in yellow and blue with a print from Barbarella on the front, and Katherine said she was going to wear her backless black dress again, but with silver boots and silver jewellery. 'What about you, Natasha?' she asked.

'I'm not sure yet. I don't think I brought anything very fancy. I have a red dress that might do.'

Back at the villa, they played the music loud— Moloko's 'The Time Is Now' blaring— and Jennifer went to lie down. The boys had last swims in the pool and cold beers, and the girls wrestled with the ravages of the beach, transforming wind-whipped, salt-tousled locks into something sleek and careful, a tool for seduction, ready to slip across a face like a satin curtain, or to tumble over bare shoulders and down tanned backs. A deadly weapon, lightly worn.

Martin grilled steaks and baked potatoes in foil in the barbeque embers. Natasha offered to make a salad but he declined, said he'd watched her do it the night before and thought he could manage, wanted to try.

So Natasha went to her room, knocking for Jennifer on the way. Todd was at the pool, lying in the last patch of retreating sun, ignoring the clowning of Paul and Julie as much as Martin's efforts to chat to him.

Jennifer didn't answer so Natasha went on to her own room, to lie down in the quiet darkness. It was the relief she needed from the teeming sociability of the holiday, she who had been used from childhood to the gentle pace of a compact family unit – her parents, who often didn't speak to each other, and the subtle, instinctive understanding between her and Nancy that did not always require words.

She must stop thinking about Nancy, she decided, wondering why it was easier to avoid the buried than the living in her mind.

For the first days of the holiday, the relentless chat and laughter had been a trial. The lack of any moment that was hers alone had jarred.

'*What are you reading?*'

'*Where did you get that hat?*'

'*What do you think we should do tonight?*'

The questions and comments had been launched at her from all sides, no matter what corner of the patio, pool or villa she had retreated into. The production of a book was ignored, even closed eyes were no proof against the bombardment.

'Are you asleep?' someone would ask, not waiting for an answer before launching into the next question or observation, so that Natasha had felt edgy, jangled with the constant exposure. It was as if they couldn't bear even a small, temporary divergence from group consensus. 'Strength in unity,' Natasha had muttered under her breath as she'd been required, yet again, to agree that such-and-such a celebrity looked terrible in her bikini. Only Jennifer had spared her, seemingly content to let Natasha slip away, read quietly or lie drowsily, without feeling the need to intrude in any way, except sometimes to smile over. Julie had been the worst, her questions the most pointless and relentless, sharpened by a thin hostility.

And so Natasha had got into the habit of a pre-dinner half hour of quiet in her room, a pause between the demands of the days and the promises of the evenings. Now, she lay on her bed and watched the ceiling fan whirl around, the blades slicing through the warm air with a throbbing hum, stirring up not cool air, but a faint warm breeze that was pleasant. The lack of air-conditioning in the villa was, for her, a plus, although Julie complained frequently of the heat in her bedroom. Natasha had tried suggesting she sleep with the window open and the blinds up, letting what cold night air there was in, but Julie had refused, horrified, because of 'bugs'.

'There are so many over here, and they are so much more gross,' she had said with a pout. Some of her other gripes were about food – 'Everything is so greasy' – and loo paper – 'Does it have to be so thin and shiny? Martin, see if you can get proper, soft stuff, in the supermarket.' All the differences, the otherness of the island were as nothing to her, just inconveniences to be ignored, or complained about. For Natasha, who loved every bit of it, from the loo paper that was more like tracing paper, to the warm, unwashed smells of the women in the local convenience store, Julie's way was a flat refusal; a door slammed shut in the face of possibility.

'All she wants is sun so she can get a tan,' Todd had said one day to Natasha. 'If she could get decent weather in her back garden, she'd happily stay there. She hasn't the slightest interest in anything else that comes with the country.' He'd said it in his most sneery way so that Natasha had believed he had as low an opinion of Julie as she did. Except that just a few hours later she'd heard him, in a quite different tone, say, 'I admire your energy,' to Julie, who'd seemed to swell visibly at the praise, grow sleeker and smoother under his approving eye.

'I don't see the point of waiting around,' she had said adamantly, determined to prove him perceptive and herself the sort of person not everyone could understand. 'I think if you want something, you should just go after it.' As if this were an attitude both controversial and unexpected.

'I agree.' That had been Jennifer, slowly. 'But it's the knowing what you want that's the hard part.'

'Nonsense,' Julie had said energetically. 'I always know what I want.'

'I bet you do,' Todd had said, the admiring note there again. 'And I'm betting nothing stops you from getting it.' There had been a quiver to his voice which had made Natasha look carefully at him. Was he mocking or did he mean it? Hard to say with Todd. That, of course, was what kept them all dancing around him. And they did all dance around him, to greater and lesser degrees. Jennifer, with the most to lose, also danced the most, raised up or cast low by the balance of Todd's moods. Natasha tried hard not to, but found herself unable to squash the elation she felt when something she did gained his approval. Julie, so much a creature of her own self-regard, wasn't proof either. She had, for the rest of that afternoon, showed herself more energetic and decisive than ever, making choices so fast and insistently that Natasha had rocked with silent laughter at the sight of her slamming down recommendations of where to eat, what to drink, where to sit, like someone playing a game of snap.

Lying there now, sprawled above the white candlewick bedspread, listening to the subdued whump of the ceiling fan, Natasha thought back to the Grande Bretagne hotel in Crete, the weeks spent there when she and Nancy were children, the rhythm the days had fallen into – early starts when the mornings were slow and soft, moving with a quiet hesitancy before picking up speed and certainty with the growing heat. Peach juice and hard, Greek pastries for breakfast, eaten at the end of the pier, legs swinging over the edge as they threw bread for the fish below, she and Nancy competing as to who could stir up the greatest frenzy of fishy activity, glistening silver bodies whipped into a furious knotted ball, turning in on each other and the scraps of bread.

'Would you jump in?' Nancy had asked her one day, pointing down at the fish attacking a crust with fluid savagery.

'I don't know. Would you?'

'If you would,' Nancy had answered. Then: 'Will we?' She'd looked up, scared but determined. Natasha had no doubt that she would leap straight into that writhing mass if the encouragement she looked for were to come.

'Let's not.' Natasha had shuddered. The ball of glittering fish flesh below had made her feel sick, convinced that it was writhing and glistening somewhere within her. 'Let's go.'

The red dress did very well. Fitted, without being excessively tight, it looked, Natasha thought, both stylish and sexy. She wore her dark hair long, with high, strappy sandals.

'You look great,' Katherine said when she walked into the sunken lounge.

'So do you,' Natasha said truthfully. The black dress fitted Katherine well, the silver boots adding length to her tanned legs. Looking like that, Natasha thought, there was no way she wouldn't get together with Dermot, something, Katherine had confided during a sleepy hour by the pool one afternoon, she badly wanted.

'Jennifer still has a headache. She's not coming with us,' Todd announced. 'She said not to look in on her' – this to Natasha – 'she's just going to sleep.'

'What a pity,' Natasha said lightly, knowing she didn't mean it even as she said it. Judging by the look Todd gave her, he didn't think it was a pity either.

They ate fast, drinking faster – beer, wine, margaritas. Around them the night fell as abruptly as a theatre curtain. The sound of cicadas grew, offset by mysterious night-time rustlings from the scrubby hillside, as they talked, laughed, made plans and jokes. Finally, Julie said, 'Let's go. Natasha, will you order taxis?'

The club they had chosen was one of the biggest and brashest. Seven dance floors, terraces and a rooftop bar, gardens and hidden corners, music that ranged from thumping house to hypnotic trance.

Pills were the first step. 'OK, let's separate and see who scores. We meet back here in half an hour.' That was Todd, laying down the law as always, though no one was inclined, at that moment, to disagree with him. They wanted the night to be a success. To be wild, daring, outrageous; a night worthy of the Holiday of a Lifetime.

Natasha headed for the main dance floor, a kind of amphitheatre surrounded by tiered seating on which no one was sitting. The dance floor was full even though it was still, by Ibiza standards, early. The boys wore jeans and T-shirts, shrouded in clouds of cheap aftershave and the brashness of their attitude; the girls wore tiny dresses or tiny shorts and vest tops. Every one of them seemed to be playing a part in their own private version of the Holiday of a Lifetime story.

It didn't take Natasha long. She had worked out that the most baby-faced boy in any club was the one to ask. Why, she had no idea, but as a system, it worked. She soon found a fresh-faced kid pumping his fists in the air exuberantly and jumping up and down as the DJ played something heavy and shout-along. She danced next to him for a while, smiling and mimicking his moves in a more graceful version. Sure enough: 'You're gorgeous,' he said. North of England, she guessed.

'Great night.' She smiled back.

'Bloody right. I'd go anywhere to hear Paul D. Fifth time I've 'eard him, and 'e's better every time.' It was unlikely to be true, Natasha thought, just one of those things they all said to one another in clubs, on nights like these: 'Best DJ ever', 'Best night I've had', 'Best pills you'll find'.

'Do you know where I can score?' she shouted into his ear after a few more moments of dancing and silent, grinning, thumbs-up gestures, like a grotesque parody of some kind of emergency where words were no longer available.

'I'll sort you,' he promised cheerfully. And that was it. There was always a risk that the money would disappear and the drugs would be duds, but it almost never happened. In general, guys like Baby-Face were more interested in a buzz than in ripping people off. They wanted a room full of pretty girls in dancing form more than they wanted cash. Plus, his type fancied themselves as fixers, guys who knew how to get things. Sure enough: 'They're good,' he said, coming back and discreetly handing her the pills. 'The whole place is on them.'

'I'm going to meet my friends. I'll be back. See you later,' she yelled into his ear. She got another thumbs up, before he resumed punching the air and whooping.

Natasha was first back to the rendezvous. She ordered a whiskey and Coke while she waited, enjoying the ripple of irresponsibility that began to run through her, like a small, teasing wind, whipping up excitement and that feeling of butterfly wings under her ribs. Todd was next back. Somehow, she had known he would be. She doubted very much that he had bothered trying to score. Why would he, when those around him would exert themselves on his behalf?

'Well?'

'Sorted.'

'Resourceful, aren't you?' He smiled down at her, then took a strand of her hair that had fallen forward and twisted it round his finger, tugging gently. Natasha found herself staring up at him for a moment in which her insides contracted to make way for this feeling, lust or alarm, she didn't know what to call it, that still confused her.

'Well, you haven't wasted any time.' That was Julie, looking arch.

'What?'

'Scoring. I presume you have scored?' That wasn't what she had meant, Natasha knew, but as always with Julie, there was nothing to pin a confrontation to. Her barbs disappeared like smoke, absorbed back into the air even as you grabbed at them.

'Yes. Pills. He said they were good. Apparently the whole place is on them.' She said it nonchalantly, the way you might talk about any other shopping expedition – 'look at the nice shoes I got' or 'isn't this a handy bag?' – because that's the way they did it, even though she privately thought the studied casualness was ridiculous; a bunch of well-brought-up students pretending to the kind of street smarts they simply didn't have.

'Nice.' Julie nodded her approval. 'I got a wrap of speed. From a Dublin guy. He swore he wouldn't cheat a "fellow citizen". Even though I very much doubt our paths would ever cross back home,' she said in lofty tones. Then she added, 'He's invited us to a party later, a villa on the beach, after the clubs shut.' She looked pleased with herself.

Natasha had noticed how Julie paraded any evidence of her worth: something her lecturer had said about an essay, a drunken pass made by a friend's boyfriend, a compliment from the guy who cleaned the floors in her apartment block – all were shared with the same gleam of satisfaction. Even the ambiguous was twisted around until it became right: a girl didn't like her 'because she's threatened by me'. It should have been motivated by insecurity, Natasha had long thought, but in fact, it seemed to be the opposite. That, instead, it was complacency that drove her to thrust these proofs of herself before them; a shining belief in her own importance that Natasha half-sneered at for its unambitious, easy acceptance, but half-envied too for its absolute certainty. The way Julie produced the most commonplace remarks, banality upon banality, quite as if universal interest in them were assured, astounded Natasha, who had been taught to work hard for originality, for insight, and to stay quiet if she failed to find it.

They waited for the others to return, with the hum of the club growing louder, more intent around them, then they divvied up the pills and made their trips to the loos in pairs and threes to snort the speed. The club had bouncers, thick-set men with shaved heads and black jackets, who didn't seem inclined to pursue those things that happened discreetly.

They took to the dance floor in a group, smiling broadly at one another as they twisted and turned, singing along to the anthems, allowing themselves to be moved this way and that by the music as it rose and fell. Todd, Natasha was interested to see, wasn't much of a dancer. He made fists of his hands and shook them in front of him while swaying, slightly out of time with the throbbing music. His movements were awkward, so at odds with the casual grace he displayed normally that Natasha felt embarrassed for him, and wasn't sorry when he leaned in to her and said, 'Let's go outside.'

She nodded, stepping quickly into the space left when he turned and made for the exit. She put a hand on his back, in case the crowd might thrust them apart. His T-shirt was damp and his back warm beneath her touch. At the door to the garden, they passed Baby-Face. Natasha smiled and gave him a wave. He was leaning back against a wall, his face greasy with sweat and his eyes blank. He stared through Natasha with a bare look – no spark of recognition. Too much, she thought. It was easily done. The extra pill, the one-more line that tipped you over the edge so that the night of magic togetherness, of joyful unity with friends and strangers, became instead something stripped and whittled, bleached like an old bone. She put a hand on Baby-Face's arm as they passed, a brief squeeze that was both reassurance and reminder, to herself, that this, too, was a possibility.

The terrace was lit by a string of lanterns so that round patches of yellow brightness were interspersed with pools of inky black. People flitted in and out of the light like moths, laughing, drinking, flirting. Todd and Natasha wove their way to a quiet corner. Although they were outdoors, and a faint breeze lifted the heavy layers of the hot night, the terrace smelled of dry ice, cigarettes and, again, cheap aftershave. But, underneath it, Natasha thought she could still detect the distinctive scent of the island, of wild herbs and aromatic plants crushed carelessly underfoot.

'You're a great dancer.' Todd offered her a cigarette, leaning against a wall, below which was yet another terrace, filled with yet more drinking, chatting groups. Natasha hoisted herself up to sit on the wall so that she was half a head taller than him.

'Thanks.'

'There's no compliment I can give you that you haven't heard a thousand times before, is there?' He sounded irritable.

'What do you mean?'

'Anything I say – that you're beautiful, sexy, a good swimmer – I bet people have been saying those things to you your whole life.'

'I might have heard a few of them before,' Natasha teased, wondering if it was true. She supposed it was, but the compliments sounded different from Todd. Stronger. She toyed with the idea of saying that, then decided not to. It was still easier to let him make the running and respond, rather than to run herself.

'I'll find something,' he said intently. 'Something no one else has noticed about you.' Just as Natasha was about to respond – she searched in momentary panic for the right kind of thing to say, something witty, light – he changed the subject.

'What will you do when you finish college?'

It was an easier question to answer. The drugs had made her expansive, keen to discourse fluently on her thoughts and expectations, her hopes and fears. And so she began.

'I'll definitely do a post-grad, because I'm not ready to stop studying yet. I think I'd like to specialise in something incredibly niche, like a small aspect of Italian literature. Or maybe art history, and focus on a particular type of vase or pot that no one else has bothered much with, and write detailed books about it that will be read only by other people who care about it . . .' She was babbling merrily, half making-up what she was saying, half-talking herself into it, with the certainty that she could talk herself right out of it and into something else within a moment. 'I'll be the foremost expert on this one, tiny thing—'

'Never mind that,' Todd cut across her abruptly. 'Look at that girl there, she thinks she's in *La Dolce Vita*.'

Natasha, feeling snubbed in the flow of her words and ideas, humiliated at the sudden switch in his attention that proved how lightly it had been anchored, looked to where he was pointing. A girl in a skimpy grey dress, her hair in plaits across the top of her head and fluorescent spirals drawn onto her cheeks, was splashing in the tiny fountain at the centre of the terrace, sending up jets of water with her hands and shrieking at the watching crowd.

'She certainly seems to think she's Anita Ekberg alright,' she said. 'She's going to end up covered in bird poo. I looked into the fountain earlier. It's filthy.'

'Now, what were you saying?' Todd turned back to her with a wide, disarming smile.

'It doesn't matter,' she muttered. 'What about you? What will you do?' She leaned down, closer to him, angling herself in towards him as he began to talk. She barely listened – something about setting up a company and challenging all 'the old fools' who thought they had a monopoly on something or other – just stared at him until the intensity of her gaze seemed to slow the flow of his words and he gazed back, a faint smile on his face. She leaned in closer.

'There you are!' It was Martin behind the hearty shout, delivered from several feet away. He came towards them, looking relieved. 'I can't find anyone. Katherine and Dermot disappeared ages ago, and now Julie and Paul seem to have vanished.' He sounded worried, bothered by the fracturing of the group, that no one had thought to confer with him before disappearing, perhaps bothered that no one had wanted to disappear with him.

There's always one, Natasha thought. One person no one else

wanted. One left over, one spare, because even when the numbers were equal, the ley lines of lust never were. It wasn't as simple as someone for everyone, she thought, an image of herself, Jennifer and Todd on the beach that day forming before her. In their group, it was Martin. His basic decency and solid dependability counted for nothing in the obscure twistings of desire and need. She wondered would it always be like that for Martin, or would his time come later, when he was older. When they were all older.

She leaned away from Todd, turned her head to look over the terrace beneath them, as Todd and Martin chatted beside her. The island smell she thought of as the 'true' one seemed stronger now. She thought she could see Katherine and Dermot, bodies close, in a dark corner down below.

'I'm going to dance,' she said, jumping down from the wall and walking off before either Martin or Todd could think to accompany her. She was still stung by Todd's snub. It changed nothing, she saw that, but she was determined to be, for now anyway, less available.

On her way in, she bumped against the girl in the grey dress, who turned and clutched at her, eyes flickering like a lizard's tongue.

'That DJ is amazing,' she said urgently. 'Amazing. What's he doing to those tunes?'

Natasha, who thought the music was perfectly fine but nothing more than that, nodded soothingly.

The girl put a hand out suddenly, grabbed one of Natasha's, and said, 'You are having a good time, aren't you?'

Her face contorted and she gave Natasha a look of anguish, as though she might cry if Natasha said no. Her hands were damp, and she had flecks of white at the corners of her mouth; dried saliva, Natasha guessed. Looking at her, Natasha was filled with an agitated desire to get to a mirror, check her reflection, in case the drugs had done something similar to her.

'A great time, really great,' she said, disengaging the clutching hand. 'You too, I hope. I can see you are,' she said gaily, heading for the loo.

Her reflection reassured her that she looked good. Very good. Her eyes were huge and shiny, her skin smooth and even, and her hair a dark mass of conker-flecked brown. She stared and stared, and only with an effort managed to drag herself away from herself. The pill was definitely having an effect now. She started to feel shivery, with an edge of anticipation that far outweighed the actual possibilities of those hours of drinking and dancing that lay in front of her. This was why they did the pills – that whisper of wonder, the subliminal flicker of fabulous that edged into the corner of their vision. Often ungraspable, it was still enough to drive them forward, even Natasha, who mistrusted it as much as she pursued it.

The dance floor was moving more slowly now, the music leading them all on a winding kind of road, one where the pace was dreamy, not frantic, promising a subtler kind of oblivion to the pounding search for glory from earlier. Even the podium girls, the ones who were mad to tell you 'yeah, I've got a job – as a dancer, in one of the clubs', whenever you met them on the beach or in a bar, even though the 'job' was paid in drink and pills rather than money, had stepped down the pace of their bump and grind.

Natasha danced along, smiling at those around her, doing what the music told her, trying to lose herself. She thought of the Pied Piper of Hamelin and his cruel revenge on the town that had betrayed him. The deadly road he laid down with his music, and the children who followed him into the mountains. And then a sudden chill shot through her, a cold clutch at her heart and the words, 'What am I doing here?' began to pound inside her head. 'What am I doing here?'

The chill descended on her like a column of cold mist, cutting her off from the revelry around her. Everything that had been rosy and fluid became sharp and grey. This had begun to happen to her since the funeral; without warning, a sudden click that detached her from whatever was going on around her, left her on the outside. It could last for moments or for hours, sometimes days. Each time, she wondered would the click back ever come.

She lost her fluid grace, her movements became jerky, as if an unseen, malicious puppeteer was pulling tiny strings attached to her wrists, elbows, collarbone, tweaking them at intervals with mean-spirited wit. The music came after her like a swarm of angry wasps so that she wanted to lift her arms, protect her face. She stopped dancing, turned, looking for someone she knew, anyone, even Julie, but the dance floor was a mass of alien faces, ugly in their lack of familiarity, shiny with sweat, eyes black and blank, hard reflective surfaces that rejected intimacy. She began to fight her way out of the crowd, to the loos, the bar, outside, anywhere, but, whereas before the waves of people had parted easily, instinctively, as she and Todd had moved through, now it was the opposite. As if sensing her disturbance and terror, the crowd knotted together to impede her, a homogenous mass of writhing flesh.

She recalled the ball of fury, made of fish and bread and want, that she and Nancy had stared at over the edge of the pier in Greece. Nancy saying, 'Would you jump in?' She nearly retched, feeling again the fish twisting inside her. Bodies stepped directly in front of her as she tried to navigate towards a pocket of space she had seen, so that she stumbled, almost fell, bumped into a blond-haired guy who rounded on her and shoved her backwards, out of his way, then carried on dancing. She clutched an arm in time to stop herself from falling, held on, looked for help. A face looked back at her, a girl, haughty, who shook her off with a grimace. Natasha righted herself, just, and stumbled on, lurching from space to space as if each pocket were a stepping stone across a savage river.

She made it, finally, heart pounding, breath coming in ragged gasps. Her hands were shaking and she could barely hold them still enough to get money from her bag. The barman – earlier so attentive, so keen to ask where she was from and was she having fun – ignored her until she thought she would take root, there, beside the bar, arm resting on the countertop, and simply grow into that spot, unable to move forward in the space that had clogged around her.

Finally he looked at her and she was able to croak, 'Whiskey and Coke. Please.' She paid, trying to smile, hands still trembling, but he turned abruptly away. She took a gulp of her drink, wondering would water be better, or coffee; if she should try and vomit. Then she held the glass with two hands, trying to affect nonchalance and ease. I'm just people-watching, she told herself sternly, observing what's going on, amused, detached. Not in a blind panic, not hunched over the question 'What Am I Doing Here?', as it throbs through me like the echoes of a monstrous bell beat hard beside my head. She wished Jennifer were there, had come with them after all. That she had not started to do this thing with Todd that would so hurt her friend.

A skinny guy in a white vest with a gold chain around his neck came over and tried to talk to her: 'Good night, yeah? Where you from?' But Natasha couldn't engage him, could see his eyes glaze and stray from her even as she said, 'Yeah, great. Dublin. You?'

'Yeah,' he said, already moving off. She took another slug of her drink. The whiskey seemed to be working. Her heart stilled a little, left off its urgent pounding, like a broken neon light flickering violently, or something wild caught in a trap, turning madly about. She took a deep breath, held it steady at last and straightened up. She had, she realised, been slumping towards the countertop.

I'll look like Baby-Face in a minute, she told herself, trying for humour, for distance. Trying harder to banish the image of her father's face that now pushed its way up from underneath. I cannot see it here, she thought; I cannot see it now. She feared that the face would be unfamiliar, somehow ghostly or slyly transformed, changed by being so firmly held down and back. Or worse, that it would be the same.

With an effort, she kept the face below the line and away from her. Later, she promised herself. Later, I will think.

'Natasha.' It was Martin, suddenly beside her, although she hadn't seen him arrive. 'Are you OK?' He put out a hand, put it on her arm, where she watched it for a second, his hand holding a bit of her she felt no connection with, the warmth of his grasp telling her that, after all, the arm was hers, dispelling the jumble of frightened images like a strong light dispels shadows. She wondered did her flesh feel cold and hard to him. Scaly. 'Are you OK?' he asked again.

She looked up, searched his face, knowing that what she found there would dictate her response. She found nothing but concern, none of the secret amusement she had feared, and so she said, 'Not really. Sort of. I'll be fine.'

'Do you want to go outside?'

'OK.' She let him lead the way, following on legs that felt shaky, as if she had been ill a long time. With purpose, he lost the bewildered plaintiveness she had seen in him earlier, became more definite. He cleared a way for the two of them to the terrace and found empty chairs to sit on. Natasha took a slug of her whiskey and Coke and wondered what to say.

'Did you take any of the pills?' she asked.

'No. I don't much. A few drinks seem to do me alright.' He sounded embarrassed, knowing well that they were there for the drugs as much as the sea and sun.

'Very wise,' Natasha said through chattering teeth. 'They seem a bit off.'

'Are you cold?'

'A bit. Seems absurd, when it's been so hot, but . . .'

'Let me see if I can find you one of those blanket things. I saw some on the chairs earlier.' He went off, came back with a multicoloured woven throw that he draped around her shoulders.

'Thanks. I guess I look like I could tell your future,' she said, trying to joke.

'Only if it's going to be full of good things.'

'It will be, I'm sure of it. You're going to have a happy life.' She suddenly believed it as she said it. There was something about Martin that convinced her. His fundamental decency would eventually outweigh his lack of dazzle; the way he rested so firmly on the ground would become a thing to be sought-after and rewarded, not the slight drawback it constituted just then, when they were all straining upwards, looking for what bobbed and floated above them, distracted by the shimmy of light in the air.

'I'll cross your palm with gold for that.' He laughed. 'How can you be so sure? Does your mother have gypsy blood?'

'Not a drop,' she said. 'Purest Catalan, all the way through. In fact, her family were horrified when she said she was going to marry my father.' But she realised she didn't want to talk about her father, her family. 'Why are you here?' she asked instead. She had wondered. More and more, he seemed an unlikely companion on the Holiday of a Lifetime. It wasn't really his scene, Natasha knew. At home, he was the healthy, sporty one, who played rugby for the university and spent most afternoons in the gym. Dance floors weren't for him, or clubs in general. Martin was a bad dancer, a clumsy drunk, and where the others' conversation became brittle, witty, outrageous on drugs, his, when he took them, slowed right down, becoming so ponderous that none of them wanted to get stuck with him. 'Did you get on the wrong plane in Dublin?'

'I sometimes think I did,' he said, laughing. 'Jennifer is an old friend. So is Julie, I suppose. Their school mixed with ours, when we were in secondary.'

'Teenage socials – what fun!' She tried to keep the resentment

93

out of her voice. Of course they had known each other forever. Even Martin went way back. 'It must have been a relief, after wall-to-wall boys.'

'I didn't mind that. We all got on quite well.' He wouldn't mind, she thought. Would fit in well to the masculine world of dorms, playing fields and communal showers, the endless slagging and jostling for position. He was strong, sporty, straightforward. He probably thrived in the kind of atmosphere that would have annihilated a more sensitive boy.

'But I missed the company of girls,' he was saying. 'I have a sister, younger than me, but we're close. I missed her at school. Hanging out with Jennifer was a bit like hanging out with her. The same kind of jokes and teasing.'

'Which still doesn't explain why you're here.'

'The funny thing is that when we all came to college, I stopped hanging out with the guys I went to school with, and started seeing more of Jennifer.'

'Are you in love with her?' She liked the idea, the romance of it – Martin, holding a candle all these years for a girl he fell for because she carried with her the familiarity of family and home. And, of course, if Martin and Jennifer could be paired off, and really they were so perfect for each other it was ridiculous, then that would leave Todd free. For all his determined pursuit, she knew that Todd was conscious of Jennifer, of hurting her or not hurting her. But Martin looked astonished.

'No, not at all. It's just that Jennifer was actively doing what I wanted to but she's better at it.'

'Which is?'

'Meeting new people, not staying with the same group. The guys from school, they all go to the same pubs, with the same gang. Anyone new, for them, is hard work and they're always sure the work won't be worth it. They like being with people who remember the time Mr

O'Grady threw Stephen Carroll's book out the window because he wasn't paying attention. Who know that when you mention Carroll's older brother, Paul, the first story that needs to be told is the one about the three tries he scored in the second half of the cup match with St James's, and only then can you talk about the fact that he's just got engaged or landed a job with Bergman Goode or whatever.'

'Fuck, yes, I know those conversations. I've sat through zillions of them since I started college. All the in-jokes and nicknames and everyone knowing everyone and being related by blood and upbringing and expectation, and the hilarious things they did after a bottle of vodka when they were fourteen.' She sounded bitter, and she knew it. 'At first I tried to join in by asking them to explain what they were talking about, but everyone looked so horrified that I gave up. It's like trying to push through a wall that doesn't have any cracks or visible joins, it's just a smooth mass.'

'I can imagine.' He looked struck, shook his head. 'Must be awful. But think what it's like on the inside. Getting out is just as hard as getting in.'

'And, of course, far more urgent. Because if you don't get out . . .' They both laughed.

'You know why they say those schools are full of the cream of the country?' he continued.

'Rich and thick?' She was disappointed. She'd heard that before.

'Worse,' he said. 'Clotted. All churned in on itself in a thick, unappetising lump.'

Natasha laughed again, and realised she was enjoying herself. The shivering had subsided, the cold feeling had receded to the place it waited. She liked that Martin felt the same about the people she privately dubbed the 'boarding-school-bots', although he had none of the edge of exclusion that sharpened her reaction.

'You know it's not personal,' he was saying. 'They just aren't comfortable with anyone who goes off-script. Who won't say the right thing, because they don't know what the right thing is, because they haven't said it a thousand times before.'

'Well, that's reassuring. I thought it was just me.'

'God, no. If they were able to make an exception for anyone, it would be you.' He said it seriously, like he meant it, so that she felt flattered, but without the feeling that he meant her to have.

'But still, why here?'

'Jennifer suggested it. It sounded fun. And then she said you were coming.' He looked shy then and Natasha opened her mouth to ask what he meant, but before she could speak, Todd took hold of her arm.

'There you are!' He smiled down at her. 'I've been looking for you.'

CHAPTER 7

What had Natasha meant by saying she ate men? Jennifer wondered. Was that supposed to be a compliment or a sneer? She didn't eat men; anyone could see that. In fact, if anyone ate men it was Natasha herself, who must know the effect she had, with her smooth, cat-like features and curious self-possession.

So why had she said it? If it was a tease, it was a damned mean one, Jennifer decided, wriggling around in her bed, which felt rough and sore on her burnt skin, as if someone had applied a sticky coating to the sheets, then sprinkled them with powdered glass.

The villa was silent and, even though she had cursed the others earlier as she lay in her darkened room, head throbbing and sharp flashes of light darting in front of her eyes, while their music had blared and their shrieks of laughter had mocked her, the silence, she decided, was worse. She had never been in the villa on her own before, and suddenly she realised that she had no idea where she was, how to get to the nearest town, how far away it was. The holiday had gone past in a dizzy whirl of plans and trips and chatter, and at no point had she thought it necessary to orientate herself. Let the others do that, she had thought. Let Martin work it out.

Her mobile didn't work, there were no neighbours, no plan of action should anything bad happen. But what was likely to happen here? The 'Thing' that *was* happening was happening now, in a club in town, where Natasha might be coiling herself seductively round Todd at that very moment, body turned towards his, head raised to meet the gaze he bent upon her; not here in this silent villa.

Jennifer shifted miserably in bed, trying to get comfortable, get cool, get the image out of her head.

Why was she here? she wondered. Why wasn't she out there, fighting for Todd? Why was she such a baby?

She felt lonely and homesick suddenly, wanting her mother's cool hands on her hot head, her kind smile and loving voice. Her mother, she thought, had liked Natasha. How disappointed she would be if she knew what she was doing. But no. An alternative suggested itself, one she could not ignore – that her mother would be disappointed with her, Jennifer, with the way she had simply bowed out of the fray, leaving the field clear and handing over Todd without a fight.

But I couldn't have gone tonight, she told herself, I've got sunstroke. There's nothing I could have done. Yet she knew there was. That the real reason she was lying there wasn't the sun, her head, the ache behind her eyes. It was fear. The fear of confronting Natasha. Of losing Todd. Of losing them both.

As a child, she had hated winning far more than losing. Had never understood how to be a good winner, gracious yet modest. She understood about being the loser – that was easy. You just had to be cheerful and merry, full of congratulations and adamant that the best person had won. But winning made her uncomfortable. Either she dissembled too much, so that her opponent thought her surly, or she enjoyed the victory too much, so that she seemed to be crowing.

'Jen loves losing,' her brother used to say when they made up teams as kids. 'I'm not playing with her. She couldn't win a race if you gave her a mile head start. She's like the tortoise, except she never actually catches up!'

Jennifer had laughed along with the others, secretly determined to one day show them that she too could win. Except she never did show them.

It was an old agony, but she felt now that resolution might have helped her. Because to keep Todd would be to lose, as much as it would be to win and, anyway, the most humble part of her argued, didn't those two – so much more beautiful and extraordinary, so poised and completely themselves – deserve each other? Maybe she was nothing more than a means to their end, and should now bow discreetly out of both their lives.

She twisted again, found a cool spot and changed her mind. Why should she not get up now, dress, pop some painkillers, down a shot of iced vodka, and go to the club to find them? She saw herself arriving, sweeping into the room, discovering them immediately, while everything was still OK, smiling, taking Natasha's arm and kissing Todd.

'I felt better so I came to find you,' she would say gaily.

'You look better,' Natasha would agree, with that air of serious consideration.

'I'm glad you did,' Todd might add, with his own kind of serious look. Might even pull her towards him and kiss her. She knew he was attracted to Natasha, but believed, too, that he felt the conflict of that attraction, might be relieved to have it resolved for him. That the decision made by her arrival would allow the three of them to finally set aside the awkward undercurrents and whip up the night together, united in the excitement of a new place and a carefree tomorrow.

The series of images moving through Jennifer's head were so beguiling that she got up, went to the dresser and looked at herself in the mirror, expecting to see the figure of her imagination, smile lighting a carefully made-up face. Instead, she saw a creature with fiery cheeks and a blotchy forehead; wild, windswept hair, eyes red-rimmed and a tremulous, pleading, fixed on smile.

So she got back into bed, head throbbing all the more, and lay, miserable and inert. She saw now that she would not get gallantly up and throw herself into battle. She would not set forth her claim – her prior, better claim – discreetly but unmistakably. She would not leap forward in her own life.

It's not fair, she thought, the childish words popping into her head. *It's not fair.* All her life she had wanted a friend like Natasha, someone unusual and sophisticated and polished – all the things Jennifer was not but longed to be – and all her life she had wanted a boyfriend like Todd. The kind of guy other girls noticed, wanted, envied her for. It seemed, though, that she couldn't have them. Or not both. And who would she choose if a choice were offered?

She remembered being with Natasha at her parents' house, diving into the lake again and again until they were both shivering and dizzy, then lying on the little jetty, Natasha talking about Nancy and about John, her unease clear even as she tried to smooth it over.

'He's older, established – a professor. Not one of ours, of course. Very smart. She needs someone like that, someone solid . . .' She had trailed off.

'Why? Is Nancy not very solid herself?' Jennifer had asked. She had a fair idea that Nancy was anything but. Nancy so often seemed skittish, on the point of bolting. It might have been a pose – certainly it suited her height and pallor, the extreme slenderness of her frame and translucent purple circles under her dark eyes – but the way she made the air fizz uneasily around her didn't seem possible from a pose, Jennifer had concluded.

'No,' Natasha had said, 'she's not.' There'd been a pause. The splash of sharp little waves had created sound bubbles in the air, in which other noises lived. The swish of treetops blowing back and forth, the distant hum of traffic, rooks cawing like nails scraping across the blackboard of the sky. 'But sometimes I think he's maybe less solid than I hope. And then she needs,' Natasha had continued.

She had clammed up then, saying, 'It feels disloyal to talk about,' and Jennifer had said, 'Of course,' even though she'd so badly wanted to know everything about Natasha, who was very slow to tell anything much. Jennifer had told everything about herself, about her parents and her brother in London who wrote to her, proper letters, and sent her books he thought she'd like, along with silly things like playing cards with characters from *Alice's Adventures in Wonderland* on them. 'He says I'm like the White Queen – flustered, untidy, but smarter than I seem.' Natasha had smiled at that, seemed to agree, although she hadn't said anything.

Since then, Jennifer knew, things had become more difficult with Nancy or with the boyfriend or between the two of them, but Natasha hadn't said what exactly. Jennifer especially wanted to know about Nancy, because she could tell this was the key to Natasha, because Nancy herself was undoubtedly fascinating if a bit scary, and because, if she was honest, Jennifer was jealous. She would have liked, very much, to have been first with Natasha, but knew she never would or could be.

Jennifer felt like a puppy sometimes, wriggling on her belly in supplication, pleading with Natasha for notice, attention, approval. Making jokes, little observations that she hoped were interesting and original, feeling a wave of gratitude when Natasha laughed or agreed, when her attention was held by something she had said.

With Todd, it was different. Very different. Sometimes, she wanted to hide from the searchlight of his attention, too harsh and too bright. Because she knew that in the glare of that beam, she would falter and stutter, find herself unable to create the kind of coherent arguments Todd admired. The sun of his regard was an uncomfortable place to be, because interest could so quickly be withdrawn or replaced with mockery, like one of those acts conjurers performed, whipping a tablecloth out from under a pile of crockery, unnoticed, without disturbance, but leaving the dishes sitting suddenly on an ugly, bare board.

'You're too eager to please,' he had said to her one day, making a motion as if to brush something clinging off his fingertips, a piece of cobweb or sticky candyfloss. 'You have no courage at all when it comes to defending your point of view. I've seen you tie yourself in knots trying to find a way of agreeing with someone whose opinion I know for a fact you don't support. You're like a spaghetti junction. There's no beginning and no end to your convoluted desire to avoid an argument.' He'd made himself laugh with the description.

'I hate arguments,' she had said. 'I don't see the point. You can't change people's minds, so it just ends up in a lot of yelling and people talking over one another.' She'd known he was right, that she was far too quick to find whatever grain or scrap there existed that she could support in other people's views, honing in on that and making it the focus of her pleasantries, ignoring the wider, contentious discourse. She'd wished she had the ability to confront, to argue, but she disliked people shouting at her, and became too easily flustered to do her opinions justice. So she let them away with it; she knew she did. 'Anyway,' she'd tried to defend herself, 'there are plenty of people to disagree and row about things with. You, for example.' He had looked pleased with that, but it hadn't stopped him from criticising her. 'If you don't take yourself seriously, no one else will,' he'd finished pompously. Jennifer had known he was right, really. But she'd wondered could there be degrees of it or did you have to take yourself as seriously as he did?

'I don't know why you put up with me,' he had said another day. The kind of thing, Jennifer later thought, that should have been motivated by criticism of himself, but wasn't. Because when she protested that she wasn't 'putting up', that she liked being with him, he had said coldly, 'Well, you shouldn't. And the fact that you do, or say you do shows either you're lying or you have no instinct for self-preservation.'

'It's not even self-preservation,' he had continued, warming up, 'it's an instinct for self-respect. You don't have it. You let people behave towards you exactly as they wish, in the moment of their wishing, instead of forcing them to behave in a way that shows you respect.'

'I don't know what you mean,' Jennifer had said. And she really didn't. 'Don't people always behave the way they want to? And anyway' – she had found herself getting het up now – 'my friends behave perfectly well towards me. They're my friends. Of course they respect me.'

'They don't,' he had said with satisfaction, rolling yet another cigarette. It had been long past midnight, and Jennifer had wished he would just go to bed, stop torturing himself. Stop torturing both of them. 'Julie insults you whenever she feels like it. Only the other day she called you a dunce.'

The way he'd said it, Jennifer had wondered was it the supposed insult to her he minded, or had he actually been taking offence through her – that his girlfriend should be so treated? As if the respect he felt due to himself should extend out and into her.

'That's just slagging,' she'd said. 'We've always done it. She doesn't mean it.'

'Well, what about Natasha? You fall forwards on your face for her, and she does nothing in return. She never invites you anywhere, you've only been to her house once. She doesn't even answer your questions if she doesn't feel like it.'

He'd been right. Natasha had a way of falling silent, of drifting out of whatever conversation you thought you were having with her, and leaving you hanging. Sometimes she came back to what was being said with a start. At other times she simply got up and walked away, still preoccupied with the contents of her own mind, unshared, guarded.

That conversation had been before, when Todd hadn't much cared for Natasha. Jennifer wondered what he would say now. Wondered, then, what the two of them might be doing at that moment, until at last she wondered herself into indifference. *What will be, will be*, she decided, incoherent arguments about not being able to own people, and loving them in spite of themselves, bubbling up inside her.

The cool patch of sheet was hot now, and itchy. Jennifer turned to lie flat on her stomach, arms and legs thrust straight out like a starfish. The dead silence of the night was now magical instead of lonely, a glorious settling of layers of quiet, like layers of soft whipped cream on a cake. She lay still and listened hard to nothing, thinking of all the wonderful things she would do with life, and that life would do with her. Places and things and people. Suddenly she understood her mother saying to her just before she started college, 'I envy you,' with a funny look, sad and happy together. 'This is the dawn of everything.'

And it will be, Jennifer swore to herself.

CHAPTER 8

There you are! I've been looking for you.

Todd's face above her, smiling down. So Natasha smiled back, because he expected her to. 'I thought you were on the dance floor,' he said. 'If I'd know you were out here, with Martin, I'd have come out before now.'

'I felt awful,' she said, wondering why she felt the need to explain, to defend. 'We were talking about Martin's school and where he met Jennifer.' She tried to broker a conversation.

'Ah yes,' Todd said. 'The country's finest. And thickest. All cooped up together so they take on enough protective colouring to see them into the "top professions"' – he put his own sneering emphasis on the words – 'and camouflage the fact that they have zero actual ability.'

It was pretty much what Martin had been saying, but sounded different, more vicious, coming from Todd. Natasha wondered had she sounded as bitter. Martin said something about getting a drink and excused himself. Natasha watched the back of him, walking towards the door, then began to try and explain what had happened to her inside the club.

As she described the terrible feeling that had taken hold of her, her voice wobbled, and when Todd put his arms around her, she stepped into them. Pressed against him, she knew she was trembling, and that he must feel it too. His arms closed tighter and she felt a lurch of gratitude that he seemed to understand her, could offer the comfort she needed. She opened her mouth to say something that would express her relief at his silent comprehension, but he beat her to it.

'They're quite a rush those pills, aren't they?' he said with a wink. And Natasha wanted to cry because he hadn't, after all, understood anything.

Julie arrived then, triumphant, with a handsome Italian in tow.

'Where's Paul?' Natasha asked, remembering that Martin had said they'd gone off together.

'No idea,' said Julie pertly. 'I left him in the trance room hours ago. Come on, we need to dance.' They followed her, and gradually collected the group together again, on the dance floor, as the sun came up. Martin, delighted that everyone was together again, danced clumsily but happily, beaming at Natasha every time she caught his eye. Katherine and Dermot held hands or had arms around each other, on her face a look of joy, on his something that could have been awkward determination.

The music ended when the sun outside was bright and already showing teeth. In that hard morning light, the goddesses and starlets of the night before were gone, leaving a sad posse of hopefuls, their clothes looking cheap and bedraggled, make-up sliding down chalky faces, hair knotted by dry ice and sweat. The bouncers set about clearing the club, grumpy now that the end was in sight. Outside, they conferred, surrounded by other groups, all talking, gesticulating wildly, making plans.

'We've been asked back to two house parties. Well, villa parties,' said Julie, as if the invitations were delicate personal compliments rather than random free-for-alls, given as easily as a casual smile, as easily forgotten. 'Or we could go to that open-air club on the beach. It starts now and goes on until the late afternoon.'

'I'm going home,' said Natasha. 'I've had enough.'

'Me too.' That was Martin, who never wanted to be the first to bow out, but mostly took the opportunity to be second.

'And me,' said Todd with a lazy yawn. 'Enough indeed.'

So back they all went, and decided to have 'just one more' by the pool before bed.

Natasha was half asleep in a patch of early-morning sun, her vodka and grapefruit almost untouched beside her and was trying to rouse herself to go to bed when Jennifer came out, looking fresh and pretty in a buttercup-yellow sundress.

Natasha was about to remark on the comparison with her own dishevelled state – the soles of her feet were black from the nightclub – when Jennifer said, 'Guys, there's a motorbike just pulled into the front, with two people on it.'

'Must be tourists. Lost,' said Paul.

'Germans,' said Dermot. 'Only Germans ride motorbikes.'

'I'll go and see,' Jennifer offered. 'You lot don't look up to much.' But she said it kindly, Natasha noticed, not nastily, the way she could have. 'If they are tourists, you'll scare them. They'll think they've wandered into a zombie movie.'

'It's Ibiza,' Katherine said sleepily from within the crook of Dermot's arm. 'Not a family holiday camp.'

But when Jennifer came back, she was accompanied by a tall girl in black leather who stood and surveyed the scene in front of her – bodies sprawled in patches of sun or shade, empty glasses, full glasses, ashtrays and a jug of rapidly melting ice – with amusement.

'Well,' she said, 'I guess I found you.'

'Nancy!' Natasha leapt up and ran to her, hugging her. 'What on earth?'

'Easy!' Nancy laughed, disentangling herself. 'You smell terrible.' Then she leaned in again, wrapped her arms around Natasha and hugged her hard. 'But it's lovely to see you.'

'What are you doing here? I thought you were in France.'

'I was, with John, but some friends were coming here for a few days, and I decided to come with them. John had to go back for work. I'm only here another night. We're on the other side of the island, but I remembered you said you were in Villa Blanca, outside Es Cubells, so I decided to take a chance and see if I could hunt you down. Luckily, there aren't many Villa Blancas. Salvatore said he'd bring me' – she gestured towards her companion, also in black leather – 'and here we are.'

'You're amazing,' Jennifer said. 'I'm going to make coffee. Do you want some? Or a drink?'

'Coffee, please,' Nancy said. 'It's too early and too late to join these guys in drinking.'

Her arrival injected energy into them all, so that bed was forgotten. Paul went to make more vodka and grapefruit juice, on the basis that 'there's no point stopping now', while Natasha said she was going to have a quick shower and would be right back.

By the time she returned, Nancy had peeled off her black leathers and was sitting, smoking, her bare legs up on the table. She was wearing a faded, sleeveless Metallica T-shirt and a pair of denim shorts cut-off high on the thigh. She was still pale enough that the thin blade marks on her arms – the regular, repetitive scours she made in times of distress or anger – weren't so evident. Neither, Natasha noticed instantly, was there anything new there, no red lines among the white. Natasha, who had no real idea what Nancy had been up to since the funeral, bar a few short conversations and shorter texts, was relieved.

'I didn't bring many clothes,' Nancy said, catching Natasha's look of surprise. 'I've been borrowing off Salva and his girlfriend, Nadja.' Natasha looked at Salvatore, thin and blond, with tattoos that twisted up his arms – serpents and dragons, fire-breathing birds. His face, under its plated armour of rings and piercings, was hollow-eyed and gaunt, but beautiful, like a medieval saint or knight. Seeing the way he looked at Nancy, she was surprised to hear he had a girlfriend. She wondered did John know anything about him.

'John and Salva haven't met,' Nancy said with a flash of mischief, exactly as if she had read Natasha's mind. She probably had, Natasha decided – and wanted her to know she had.

Natasha shook her head slightly. Her ears were ringing, as if she'd been underwater too long. 'I see,' she said, but she didn't. The drugs still coursing through her made sure of that. They had all done 'one more line' after coming back to the villa. 'To take the edge off,' Dermot had said knowledgeably. *Edge off what?* Natasha had wondered, but now she understood. There was very definitely something moving in on her. It shimmered at the edge of her vision, waiting for a chance to advance. Presumably it was a thumping headache, a monstrous hangover, but it felt more sinister.

'So,' she said, sitting opposite Nancy, suddenly unsure what else to say. There were so many observers, and Nancy's presence, her sudden arrival, crashing in on Natasha's lingering drunkenness and drug-haze, the lack of sleep that made her feel she was floating a few inches off the ground, borne aloft by a shimmering heat haze, confused her.

It was Jennifer who sprang to her rescue. 'Do you live here?' she asked Salvatore politely, so that he answered in halting English that, no, he lived in Sevilla but spent summers on Ibiza. That he worked on the boats in Ibiza town.

Under cover of his explanations, Natasha studied Nancy. She looked, Natasha decided, delighted with herself, smiling round at them all through a plume of cigarette smoke. 'Nice place,' she now said.

And Natasha, who wanted to say so much – to ask how Nancy was, how she really was, who exactly she was with, why she had come – found herself talking instead about the villa, about the club they had been to last night, the bars they had tried out. And Nancy reciprocated with her own stories of parties, a night at the casino in Cannes, the boat Salvatore was working on and how they had taken it out for a spin the previous day.

Every once in a while she broke off and spoke only to Salvatore, for corroboration or further detail on what she was telling, talking to him fast and fluently in Spanish, laughing at his answers and retaliating with jokes of her own. Natasha gritted her teeth.

Around them, she was conscious of the others watching and listening, of Todd's eyes flicking back and forth between her and Nancy. Only Jennifer and Martin gave them space, chatting to Salvatore about things they should see and do while on the island, asking questions about its history and heritage.

Nancy, as conscious as Natasha was of their audience, played to it, telling stories that were deliberately excessive – a Russian mafioso who had asked her to choose a number for him at roulette, then given her 'hundreds' of chips when her choice, Red 12, had come up – and probably untrue, Natasha decided. She could tell by the way Nancy's eyes flickered constantly, turning up and to the left, that she was creating. Making things up. Lying. Not that it mattered – the effect, Natasha could see, was irresistible.

Judging by the faces of Katherine, Dermot, Paul, even Julie, Nancy could have said anything at all and they would have soaked it up. She looked poised, but Natasha could tell how nervous she was. A pulse in her neck beat steadily so that Natasha could almost hear the thrum of blood running at speed through her veins, and understood the effort it was taking her to sit there so calmly. Under the table, she knew Nancy's foot would be jiggling furiously. If the others hadn't all still been so high they would certainly have noticed.

Todd, she saw, was observing Nancy with a faint smile, but he too was listening intently. And as much as Natasha felt proud of this sister who could produce such an effect, who could swing her black hair and have them all in fits over something a drunken tourist had said to her, Natasha found that she missed the silent child who used to hide behind her so that Natasha did all the talking for them both.

I would have gone with you, she wanted to whisper to her. *If you had let me. It could have been just the two of us.* She imagined sweeping away the whole messy lot of them, even Jennifer, and peopling the white villa with just Nancy and herself, a heap of books, a pot of chorizo and chickpea soup, spending a week trying to chase down their childhood, the father they had both known differently.

Todd looked up then, met Natasha's gaze with what seemed like comprehension, and she stared back at him for a long moment. When she dragged her gaze away, she found that Nancy had stopped talking, and was watching her.

'So,' Nancy said with a sideways look, 'enough about me. Who are you all? Let's start with you.' She flashed a smile at Todd. 'You can't be in college with this lot. You look much too grown-up and un-studenty.' Trust Nancy to insult them all at once, Natasha thought with a flash of inner laughter. A job lot of insults delivered.

But Todd seemed flattered rather than insulted, and began telling Nancy about himself in a deliberately low voice so that she moved her chair closer to him and leaned forward, to catch what he said. Soon they were murmuring and laughing together, excluding the rest.

Natasha felt a wave of exhaustion break over her. It was still early, barely lunchtime, but the day had taken on a shimmering, wavering quality that made her feel sick. She knew she needed to get some sleep.

'I don't remember telling you where we were staying,' she said suddenly to Nancy.

'I doubt you remember very much at the moment.' Nancy laughed, looking at Todd. 'You must have done, though, or how else would I be here?'

'How indeed?' Natasha was confused, too tired to figure it out.

'Perhaps Maria told me,' Nancy said then. 'I don't remember.' She shrugged.

'How is she?' Natasha asked, more quietly, trying to make the conversation just for the two of them. Around the table, everyone except Jennifer was slumped in various states of collapse. 'Have you been talking to her? I sent her a card the first day we arrived, but I haven't called her yet.'

'She's fine,' Nancy said. 'I spoke to her yesterday. And the day before. I ring her every evening.' She didn't bother to hide the accusation in her voice, so that Natasha felt driven to say, 'She said not to keep ringing her, that she hates speaking on the phone.'

'Not if you speak to her in Spanish,' Nancy said.

'I have to go to bed,' Natasha said then. 'I'm so sorry, Nancy, if I'd known you were coming . . .'

'I wanted to surprise you,' Nancy said.

'Well, it's a lovely surprise, but I have to sleep for a few hours or I'm going to pass out. Stay, have a swim in the pool, and we can have a late lunch in the village when I get up.'

'Yes,' the others chorused eagerly, 'stay.' But Nancy said no, she had to go; Salvatore was working later and they had to get back.

'Now that I've seen you, I know where to picture you, and that's all I wanted,' she said. 'Have a wonderful time, all of you,' and soon she was gone, the sound of the motorbike roaring away down the hill, leaving the day humming quietly in response. By the time Natasha returned to the house after waving Nancy off, everyone had slipped off to bed except Jennifer.

'Get some sleep,' Jennifer said to her. 'I'll clear up here.' She gestured towards the terrace with its debris of the night and morning.

'I'll help,' Natasha said.

'You will not. Go to bed. You're dropping.'

'Thanks.' Natasha was profoundly grateful, more for being firmly ordered to bed than for being spared the cleaning up.

CHAPTER 9

It was rather lovely to be alone in the house alone by day, Jennifer decided, or what felt like being alone. The air was peaceful and the villa seemed to rise and fall gently with the breath of all those who were asleep.

She tidied up, even sweeping the terrace clean of crumbs and cigarette ends and scrubbing a sticky patch where a glass had been up-ended, then made herself a salad for lunch and settled down with fresh coffee to mull over the morning. There was a skittish wind, enough to stir the day out of its lethargy but not enough to ruffle the surface of the pool, which continued smooth and silky. At the far end, tiny birds were skimming its surface, dipping and rising as they drank on the wing.

I wanted to surprise you.

The look on Nancy's face when she took off her motorbike helmet came back to Jennifer and she considered it at her leisure. It had been an odd look. That Nancy was keyed up, pulled as tight as a piece of sewing thread, was obvious, but there was something else there too. Triumph, Jennifer decided. Maybe born of the satisfaction of finding them without having had any clear directions? But maybe not. There had been more in the look than that.

And dragging that blond Spanish boy along with her. He had seemed barely to know where he was, although this was supposed to be his island. Perhaps it was the effect Nancy had on him.

It had been, anyway, a pretty aggressive form of surprise, Jennifer decided. So unexpected, so violent in its way, that Jennifer wondered what exactly had been Nancy's purpose in crashing, unannounced, in upon them so early in the morning. She thought back – the others must have got back from the club about 7 am, with their yells and exaggerated shushings. They had put the music on. 'Quietly, so as not to wake Jennifer,' as Katherine had loudly, insistently said. She had given up and gone out to join them by about 8 am, and Nancy had arrived soon after. So she must have left wherever she was staying very early indeed.

All that stuff about Nancy deciding 'to take a chance' and see if she could hunt them down didn't ring true for Jennifer. There had been something far too premeditated about the scene. And who simply wandered over from France to Ibiza with 'friends', then wandered across to the other side of the island on the off chance of finding a white villa?

To Jennifer, it looked very much as if Nancy was checking up on Natasha. The line about wanting to be able to picture Natasha and where she was . . . it was needy and neurotic enough to ring true of Nancy, but there was something more to it, Jennifer thought.

Not that Natasha would ever believe such a thing. Jennifer had seen the look of delight, near incredulity, on her face when Nancy had walked in wearing her motorbike leathers, inky hair snaking down her back, all-too-well aware of the effect she produced.

Natasha had looked at her as if she was something miraculous. And yet she had almost immediately left the terrace, gone to shower and change, Jennifer reflected. She had even stayed to wash her hair, coming back with it wet but smelling of shampoo rather than cigarette smoke and dry ice. So what was going on?

It was like a painting by someone really clever, Jennifer decided. You saw the impression the painter wanted you to have at first, but that might turn out to be something quite different from what he or she was really trying to tell you. That was communicated in a kind of code that only certain people would ever understand – the placing of a globe or a dead hare, the angle of light and the source of it, whether a lamp or a window. Natasha had explained all this to her once, on an afternoon visit to the National Gallery of Ireland, walking her through the crowded rooms, stopping here and there to point things out: a hand, appearing as if from nowhere, the trim on a nobleman's cloak, the way a lantern was held up.

So what had been communicated earlier?

Jennifer had spotted the way Natasha's gaze had dropped to Nancy's arms, and travelled the length of them, before rising to her face, and the way Nancy had watched Natasha doing this. Jennifer had found herself looking at Nancy's arms too, slender and pale, and seeing the delicate lines traced upon them, even more slender and pale, but somehow blurred, like the stripes on a fish seen under water. Later, she had seen Nancy scratching her arm rhythmically, nails moving up and down in a repetitive, almost soothing, motion.

Well, that was no real surprise. She knew Nancy was 'difficult', and could even be 'delicate', so small wonder that she should enact these things upon herself. What did surprise Jennifer was the sleeveless T-shirt. If she, Jennifer, had arms criss-crossed with ghostly reminders of old evils, she would keep them to herself. Nancy had seemed almost to flaunt them.

Not that anyone had noticed. Nancy could have been striped like a zebra from top to toe, Jennifer reckoned, and the others would barely have registered, so dazzled were they by her spiky charisma, so addled with the long night and the lack of sleep. Except maybe Todd, she thought, recalling the way his eyes had darted between Nancy and Natasha, the way he had settled himself apart with Nancy, their murmurings and laughter, but with one eye, she was pretty sure, on Natasha too.

And Natasha hadn't liked that bit, Jennifer realised. That was when she had said 'I don't remember telling you where we were staying', with a flash of hostility. Recalling the evasiveness of Nancy's answer, Jennifer was pretty certain that Natasha had not, in fact, told her.

So how had Nancy known? Maria, Jennifer was pretty certain. After all, that was the way the battle lines were drawn in that family: Maria and Nancy, Natasha and Vincent, the father. Except that wasn't fair anymore, because now Natasha was on her own. And it wasn't quite true either, because of the way Natasha made sure to cross the lines so as to get to Nancy. And Nancy made her own darting forays over to Natasha's side.

How complicated they were. More like a wasp's nest than a family.

Jennifer squinted into the distance. The sun was high and hot, the wind had dropped away to nothing and the heat was building. She dragged her chair farther into the shade, lit a cigarette, then settled down again.

Far sooner than she had expected, Todd was awake. He appeared at the double doors of the house, face creased from whatever way he had slept.

'Goodness, I didn't think I'd see you for hours,' Jennifer said.

'I passed out like a light,' he said, 'then just as abruptly I passed back in again. Must be the drugs. There wasn't any point staying in bed; there's no way I'll get to sleep again. I'll have a nap later, before we go out.'

'Come and sit down. Do you want some salad?'

'God, no. Just coffee.'

'I'll get you some.' Then: 'So what did you think of Nancy?' She sat beside him, delighted he was awake, delighted to have someone to share her impressions with. But Todd wasn't to be drawn.

'She seemed fine. Bit messed up I'd say.'

'The arms?'

'That, and the rolling eyes. Like a terrified horse.'

'What do you make of her turning up like that?'

'Not much. Why wouldn't she, if she's on the same island?'

Jennifer felt exasperated. Men were no good at this sort of thing. Could never see there was anything behind noses on faces. Or did he not just want to get involved?

'But her and Natasha? The way they are together.'

'I'd say they look pretty good together.' He smiled. Jennifer hoped he was joking.

Within the hour, they were all up except Natasha, lying around in the shade in various stages of exhaustion but determined not to miss a thing.

Julie, petulant and kittenish, was insisting that she hadn't wanted to come home at all and had planned to go to a beach club she'd been told about. 'Not like the place we went last night,' she explained to Jennifer. 'Much more stylish. Everyone is really well-dressed and glamorous. Lots of French and Italians', as if that clinched it. 'It goes on all day. When you're hot from dancing, you just dive into the sea and cool down, then go back to the bar.'

'So off you go,' Paul said nastily. Clearly sleep hadn't improved his mood.

'Oh, I will,' Julie promised. 'But I need someone to drive me.'

CHAPTER 10

Natasha surfaced, feeling dizzy from dehydration, and it was obvious immediately that tempers were frayed. There were a variety of plans swirling about, but clearly everyone was too tired and hungover to handle the necessity of choosing, and compromising. Julie was bickering with Paul, Katherine was being evasive – she clearly didn't care where she went as long as Dermot went with her – and Todd was scornfully silent.

Jennifer was making a case for a visit to the old town, the only one of them sufficiently together to make a proper pitch for what she wanted.

'We can't go home without seeing the old Ibiza, the real place, before all the clubs arrived,' she said. 'And it's the perfect time. All the shops will be opening again after the *siesta*.'

Natasha felt she had a point, but was too tired, too spaced-out, to want to go. And, anyway, she didn't want to see too much of Jennifer, who had shot her a shy, almost enquiring, smile. Not yet. Not until she knew what had to happen next.

'I'm going to stay here,' she said, almost apologetically. 'I can't see myself enjoying anywhere much today. I might sleep a bit more, swim in the pool, take it easy.'

'Lightweight,' said Julie, but less crossly than she might, because Jennifer had said they could drop her to the beach club on their way. Paul, Katherine and Dermot decided they were ready to head for the old town too. Todd looked surly.

'I have work to do,' he said. 'And I might go for a run.'

'Are you sure you won't come?' Jennifer asked anxiously, eyes flickering between him and Natasha. She looked distressed. 'Should I stay too?' she asked awkwardly, torn.

'No, no,' Todd said. 'You'll be bored here. And I might join you later. If I get a few things finished. I can take a taxi.'

'That would be lovely.' Her face lit up. 'You could meet us for dinner.'

'I'll try,' Todd said cautiously. 'I'm not promising.' He never promised, Natasha noticed. Didn't seem to ever want to put himself in a situation where he might have to do something he no longer wanted to simply because he had undertaken to.

It took what felt like hours for them all to get ready, to collect cameras, hats, sunglasses, money and then, just as they were on the point of departure, towels and swimsuits 'in case'. Julie, between changing clothes – into a maxi dress printed with scarlet poppies and cornflowers – seemed determined to make a great display of her spirit of adventure.

'You're all so boring,' she kept saying. 'This place is amazing, and you're going to miss it. I don't know why you bother coming on the holiday if you're not going to enjoy yourselves.' Natasha, eating toast and chocolate spread, wished they would hurry up and go. Julie's voice, inclined to a whine at the best of times, was grating severely. But her goading worked on Paul, who changed his mind at the last minute, choosing the beach club over old town, either because the club sounded too good to miss or, thought Natasha, because he couldn't resist one more go at igniting some kind of heat towards him in Julie's heart. Maybe he thought she was so wasted – certainly she was teetering on the edge of what Natasha suspected might be total meltdown – that the opportunity was too good to miss.

At last the villa was quiet, empty except for her and Todd, who sat in the shade with a book. Natasha changed into a slimy-green bikini patterned with some kind of animal print – 'lizard', she said with a laugh when Todd asked what it was – fetched herself more coffee, stretched out on a sun lounger and lay staring up at the sky, giving herself over entirely to the sensuousness of the day, her memories of the night before and thoughts of Nancy's strange early-morning appearance that now seemed far more dream than reality.

Her hangover seemed to remove every physical barrier between herself and the day, so that she felt she blurred into the blue, the shimmer. The heat kneaded her sore muscles, relaxing them, and she lay, sodden with sun, unable to move, poured into the humming, pulsing air around her. The heat soaked through the skimpy bikini bottoms and stroked her with a touch that was light, deft. Just as there was no barrier between herself and the air, there would be, she knew, no barrier between herself and Todd. They would melt into each other, carried along by the same intense, intimate desires. She longed to feel his tongue in her mouth, his hands hard on her breasts, later, his dick inside her, the many ways they would express and release what had built up between them. The sun throbbing from the sky was answered by the throbbing deep inside her, that only sex with Todd could quiet.

She would not, she decided, debate the rights and wrongs of it all, the fact that he was Jennifer's boyfriend and she was Jennifer's friend. She wanted him so badly, and that was enough. Life, she knew now, was short. Who knew where any of them would be this time next year? Who knew if any of this was even worth bothering about? Maybe these friendships were destined not to last anyway. And maybe Jennifer would never know.

The extent of her wanting was so strong that she felt a slump of physical relief when she realised that the battle was over, that she was going to fuck Todd; that it was only a matter of time, of moments perhaps.

She wriggled on her seat, flipped over onto her stomach.

'Will you put lotion on my back? I can't reach, and in this heat, even I'm going to burn,' she called over to Todd. He stood up in one graceful movement, crossed the patio and took the bottle from her, pouring a dollop onto his hand. His fingers were strong and brown, capable-looking. He began rubbing the oily lotion smoothly across her shoulders, fingers pressing deep so that she groaned.

'That's nice,' she said, knowing that every word, every step was a cliché, but indifferent.

'Lower?' he asked. His breathing was becoming ragged.

'Yes.' She decided to spin this bit of it out as long as possible. The better the build-up, the better the fall. And they had hours. The others wouldn't be back till evening. His fingers moved down her back and she reached behind to unclasp the strap of her bikini top, letting it fall to either side. His hands moved across her entire back, at one with the heat. He was breathing heavily now, hands moving more slowly, feeling the way forward for both of them. He reached the base of her back, pressing and kneading the area just above her buttocks, then down a little, slipping past the top of her bikini bottoms, stroking and smoothing. Natasha was so wet by then that she could barely hold back.

'Natasha?' Todd's voice came out as a croak.

'Yes.' It wasn't an interrogation to match his, to further the flow of questions between them. It was a statement, an intent. Yes.

She arched her back up to meet his warm hands, ready to give in. She imagined turning, holding her arms up to him so that he would bend his head to kiss her, at last, then pick her up and carry her into the house, to whatever bed they found first.

As she was about to turn, she felt his hands on her bikini bottoms instead, pulling them down in one swift movement. His free hand pressed hard on the base of her back, holding her to the lounger, a pinned insect, unable to wriggle. The sudden exposure of her bare flesh felt cold. As she turned her head to see what he was doing, he dropped her bikini bottoms – she could see them lying in a green heap, like a dead frog she thought – and put his hand, heavy, on the back of her head where it met her neck so that she couldn't turn around. He knelt between her legs, pushing them roughly apart with his knees and cupped the hand that had been on the base of her back around her waist, pulling her buttocks up towards him. He drove into her, hard. So wet was she with the residual heat of desire that she felt no pain, just a surprising smooth coldness inside her, like a stone. Or a knife. She stayed entirely still, too shocked to understand what she was meant to be doing here. Protesting? Struggling? Thrusting back at him? None of it made sense to her.

He finished fast, half a dozen hard thrusts and he was done, slumped momentarily forward so that his stomach lay across her back, his head close to her head. Was he going to try and kiss her? she wondered. But he didn't. Just got up and walked to the pool, diving straight in.

Natasha lay where she was, bare and exposed. The idea of struggling back into the slimy-green bikini bottoms was impossible. She looked for a towel within reach to cover herself. She didn't have the strength to get up, walk inside. Her legs were trembling. Shock, she thought; it'll pass. She pulled a towel off the lounger beside hers and draped it as best she could over herself with shaking hands. The day was still golden, with a pinkish tinge now to the sky in the west where the sun would eventually set, the hum and drone of insects as heavy as ever, the heat still ready to enfold her. But she herself was sharply separate, no longer part of the communion of light and sound but something spat out, tumbled into an unwanted heap.

She lay and Todd swam, length after length, barely raising his head from the water to breathe, never looking once in her direction. She got up eventually, when her legs had stilled a little at last and, wrapping the towel tight around her, made it into the villa and her bedroom. She shut the door, wondering if there was a way of locking it before realising that the time for that was past. She lay down on her bed, huddled under the covers for the first time since she had arrived on that hot, white island, for what seemed like hours.

She heard the others return, a tap on her door that was probably Jennifer, but stayed silent throughout. They must have decided not to stay out for dinner after all. She didn't sleep, wondered would she ever sleep again, just stared straight up at the ceiling fan that rotated with steadying predictability.

What had that 'Yes' meant to him? What had he asked that she had answered with such certainty? And how had she so misunderstood the asking? Did he know she had misunderstood? Did he care?

She didn't understand what had happened between them, only how she felt about it. Like a fire-eater who has inadvertently swallowed the flaming liquid, she decided. Burnt, scorched down and through. As if she was still burning. Hers wasn't a mind made for ambiguity. If he had been a stranger who had dragged her into a dark alleyway, she felt she could have coped better.

Eventually she got up. The part of herself she relied on to always keep the show on the road, keep things going, took over. Told her she needed to eat, to face the others. She got up and walked to the kitchen, smiled automatically when she was addressed, although her legs still trembled a little, nodding, making noises of agreement when she was spoken to.

Luckily they were all tired from the night before and there was no talk of a repeat bout of mayhem. Instead, they opted to 'cook a nice dinner, drink some wine. Chill.'

Martin took over the barbecuing, delighted to have a mission, a role where he could shine. Over dinner, they exchanged their tales of the afternoon and Natasha sat petrified, willing herself to stay put, not bolt from the table as the others performed their pieces, bringing ever closer the moment when she would have to give an account of her own time. And tell them what? The truth? What was that?

Julie raved about the beach club, Jennifer talked about the beauties of the Old Town, everyone nodded and agreed, keen to retain the harmony of the evening, lacking energy to tease or tussle.

'So what did you guys get up to?' Her turn had come. That was Jennifer, smiling over at her and at Todd, who was seated at the opposite end of the table. Natasha waited, for him to take over so she didn't have to speak, to say something that would deflect the question. That might give her a clue as to what had happened.

'Not a whole lot,' he said on a yawn. 'Natasha wasn't up to much. I did some work, a few laps, finished my book, you guys came back.' He smiled at Jennifer, who smiled back at him, her face lit up with the gratitude of love recognised. Natasha choked on a piece of barbecued corn on the cob.

CHAPTER 11

Next morning, the heat was like a Chinese burn. Natasha was last out to the terrace, although she was certain she had been the first to wake. The light of dawn had found her wide-eyed and stiff with tension, trying to still the nauseating thump of her heart while she plotted what to do next, trying to hang on to each small decision in the chain, lest her present lurch away from her, into a future that didn't exist. Sometimes, she drifted out of herself entirely. From a vantage-point that felt as if it were somewhere up beside the ceiling fan, she watched the figure lying ramrod-straight on the bed, struggling to identify a next step. The part of her that watched from above felt reluctant to get involved, felt indeed inclined to simply drift away from the mess forever. Except where would she go? And what would happen to the bit of her, the body of her, left behind? With an effort, she forced herself back down, and into the stiff lump that was herself.

Her jaw ached, in a way that told her she had been clenching it in her sleep. It was a familiar ache, one that warned her more surely than anything else when she was what her mother would have called 'at a bad way', although that was a phrase she used more often about

Nancy. Recalling that, and the shuttered expression that would cross her mother's face when she said it, Natasha knew she would never tell her what had happened.

She would never tell anyone, she decided. That version of herself, the one who had betrayed Jennifer, who planned to fuck her best friend's boyfriend as casually as if she was ordering a drink, must never be released into the world.

Whatever had happened, the humiliation was hers to keep. No sharing and halving of this burden. She wondered was she pregnant, then chose to believe this was not to be her fate. The act itself had been enough, the shocking intimacy of his naked flesh inside her, the memory of his hand on her neck, holding her down and still. A kitten to be drowned, or a bug carelessly crushed. Even now, she couldn't cry. No tears would come. Funny that tears should belong to a time before real sorrow, she thought. Or perhaps tears, too, were for someone less stained with guilt than her.

She couldn't leave, not just because of the difficulties of changing tickets and organising transport to the airport, but because she couldn't face the questions – the inevitable 'whys?' Could think of no reason to give that would not be questioned and analysed, subject to attempts to change her mind, and she knew that even the weakest effort by the others to quiz her would be enough for whatever story she had concocted to crumble. That under the weight of their well-meaning and curious 'what?'s and 'but if?'s she would have to blurt out everything, except that she had no words for it, no way of describing this thing she didn't understand. She couldn't just say, 'Something happened. Something bad. I have to go' – and so she decided she would have to stay, say nothing at all.

It was early enough that no one would be up yet, so Natasha dared to walk softly through the silent house and out. Maybe the magic of the island would tell her what to do, she thought. Tell her at least what to do now, that minute.

The dawn light was milky and swirled around her, clearing gradually, like the reverse of dropping pastis into water, she thought. The smells of thyme and lavender were heightened by the swiftly evaporating dew. Birds were dropping and swooping, making their soft, morning sounds that were so different from the complacent, boastful chatter of evening. Natasha thought again of Greece, of her mother's silent joy in the early morning that rolled off her as clearly as her more familiar, darker moods rolled at other times. Often the set of her shoulders and slump of her hip at the kitchen counter were enough to tell Natasha what humour she was in, but on those mornings in Greece, Natasha hadn't even needed to look. Her mother's delight was in all the air around her, like a high, clear sound.

She sat, feet tucked under her, on the low wall looking out towards the sea and waited, but the island told her nothing that she didn't already know: that she shouldn't be there. That she should not have stage-managed such a setup. That fault belonged to her, although she didn't know how much. And that she would have to stay, see it out.

There were only a few more days, she reminded herself then, just a few more nights, till she could go home, escape from them and all the shoddy, messy, terrible things they did, that she did with them. 'Weather the storm' was the phrase that repeated in her mind, ringing through in dense layers of sound that built and built inside her head. Weather the storm. She went back to bed.

Later, forced from her room at last by the well-meaning knocks, the questions from Jennifer and Katherine – did she want anything? Coffee? A juice? – and out to the terrace, she sought shelter, choosing a patch of dusty shade that had the virtue of being removed from the group on the sun loungers. Todd was with them, up before her for once, and Natasha made certain to angle her chair so that she couldn't see him, although she remained intensely aware of his exact location, the frantic sensors in her skin alerting her every time he changed position or shifted his place. The heat was too much for her now, no longer a blessing but something that seemed to hound her, drumming out a tattoo of shame on her skin. 'I'm brown enough,' she said when Julie asked her why she was sitting so far away. 'I don't want to look like an elderly American on a cruise,' she added, trying a laugh.

Julie looked struck with this, then annoyed. 'Well, I'm off to Paris next month, and I want my tan to last till then.'

'How was the beach club?' Natasha asked, dimly remembering that they had covered this at dinner the night before, but determined to keep things light, normal, at arm's length.

'Great,' said Julie, but she sounded flatter than usual – surely this was a chance for her to do what she liked most, Natasha thought; persuade them that they had missed something wonderful, because they were 'too boring' or 'wimps' – and Natasha saw her head jerk round for one instant to where Paul was sitting, coffee cup in hand. He smiled when he saw her looking. Julie didn't smile back.

'Why are you going to Paris?' Jennifer, Natasha had noticed, seemed to have a gift for the soothing interjection, the attention-redirecting remark that saved them all from awkwardness time and again. Natasha wondered was it conscious, or simply a small miracle of kindly timing that she possessed, unaware.

'It's for a reunion with the people I worked with in that consultancy company last summer,' Julie said smugly. As far as Natasha knew, the 'work' had been an unpaid internship that had seemed to largely consist of scheduling meetings for the new recruits who perched on the rung above the interns, but Julie wasn't going to admit that.

'I can just imagine it,' Todd said loudly. 'A couple of pompous, idealistic Italians from families so bourgeois they can follow a trail of merchants' bills back to the Renaissance; some superior French kids in well-pressed jeans who speak English as if they went to Oxford, and a Dutch girl who insists this is only temporary and that she really wants to volunteer at a refugee camp. All of you persuading yourselves that a summer spent photocopying and making coffee for last year's graduates means you've taken the first step on a glorious career path.' The laugh behind his words might have been at Julie or with Julie.

'That's not anything like it.' Julie was ready as always to defend her vision of herself, but Todd had had enough.

'Paris is a kip,' he said loftily, heading for the kitchen. 'And it's impossible to get decent coffee there.'

Once the terrace was free of him, Natasha relaxed slightly. She lay back, trying to find comfort in the gentle shade. She remembered Paris from years earlier: a teenager, on the cusp of something that terrified her, that would set her apart from her parents for the first time, so that she thought she saw them with other people's eyes and blushed for them. Later, she had realised that she hadn't seen with the eyes of others, but with the hurt, cruel eyes of adolescence.

They had sat outside a busy café with a large terrace at night, after dinner in a quieter restaurant on a side street nearby. Natasha had felt she looked stupid, that her family looked stupid, and that other people were pointing this out to one another: 'Look at them. Why is he so old and she is dressed in that silly skirt and the girls, *mon Dieu*, such terrible girls . . .'

Nancy had seen with her own eyes still and was apart from Natasha for the first time, so that Natasha had felt not just the disorientation of her new cruelty, but also the loneliness of separation. But she had tried to feel this too with Nancy, essaying little criticisms of their parents. Not the childish 'I hate her, she's so mean, I'm never going to speak to them again' that had until now covered their needs, but a different, slyer kind of criticism. 'Have you noticed the way he waves his arms around when he's calling for the bill? It's embarrassing!' She'd felt like crying with disloyalty as she'd said it, but could not stop herself.

And Nancy had not understood, and had stared in astonishment. 'What way? What do you mean? Why are you saying that?'

So that Natasha had dropped it. 'Nothing. I'm only joking . . .'

They were eating peach melba that night, scoops of vanilla ice cream on top of half-peaches in syrup and a drizzle of raspberry sauce. Her mother nudged her father. They were having one of their good times: smiles and whispered chat instead of shouting or silence. He looked in the direction she was gesturing, and whispered something back to her that made her laugh. Natasha followed the path of their gaze. Two African girls – tall, slender, shiny black like treacle and so beautiful that Natasha could barely look at them – were seated on either side of an older man; fat-ish, white, expansive, full of broad, confident gestures. The girls not only metaphorically hung on his every word, Natasha thought, they seemed actually suspended on the things he said, vibrating as he said them, laughing, patting his thick arm, putting an admiring hand up to his fleshy cheek.

'Professionals,' her mother said, seeing Natasha looking.

Just then a man came up to them and said something about Natasha in French, gesturing at her, and then, extravagantly, at his heart with the palms of his two hands joined. She understood only the words 'rosebud' – *bouton de rose* – and 'pretty' – *jolie*. Her mother smiled, agreeing. Her father looked thunderous and snapped something angry that sent the man recoiling back, arms now in front, waving, trying to demonstrate no offence.

'Why were you so mean to him? He was only being charming,' her mother said.

'Damned . . . maggot,' her father growled. For Natasha, the incident meant only more proof of how much things had changed. A year earlier when strangers had complimented her and Nancy, it was always the two together, as a unit. The compliments had mostly come from women, often old, and her parents had always smiled and thanked them, beaming down at their daughters. Why was everything so different now? she wondered.

'He was complimenting your daughter,' her mother said.

'And who the hell asked him!' Her father slammed the table with the flat of his hand.

'She doesn't belong to you, no matter how much you think she does,' her mother said sharply, and then muttered something in Spanish that made Nancy laugh and reply, also in Spanish.

Natasha, worried that the two would start up a conversation that would carefully, deliberately, exclude her father, tried to think of something to say to switch it, conscious of the way his shoulders were starting to hunch forwards, but nothing came to her and it was Nancy who did that.

'What's a professional?' she asked.

'A hooker,' Natasha answered fiercely. 'A prostitute.'

Nancy looked round-eyed at the women, now laughing hard at something the man had said.

'It's disgusting,' Natasha added.

'It's not as easy as that,' her mother said sternly. Usually, she didn't challenge Natasha on anything more than domestic matters – towels left wet and crumpled on beds, shoes behind the sofa.

'Sex for money,' Natasha said, feeling grown-up, cynical. 'I think that's pretty easy.'

Her mother looked angry. 'You have no idea how a woman can make this decision,' she said. 'You don't understand like you think you understand. It can be many things.'

Natasha was surprised at the passion in her mother's voice, and even more surprised that her father said nothing, seemed even to agree, or at least accept her mother's right to say such things. Maybe it was more complicated than she knew.

Julie was still defending Paris, her 'job' and the various people she had met through it, but no one was listening, except Jennifer who kept up a soothing murmur of 'really?' and 'what fun' that was clearly all the fuel Julie needed.

The day wore on, tedious, harnessed to a pace that seemed sluggish to Natasha, to drag weight behind it, just as she did. Everyone was finding patches of shade now, cast out of the glare of sun by their desire to hide, she imagined. Hide their inadequacies and repeated failures, small and large. She thought this with a violent kind of satisfaction that surprised her.

There in the shade she tried to doze, to cast her mind off, free, from the ugly rope that tethered it, a rope made of her memories of the day before, which wouldn't stay still long enough to allow her to properly parse them. Around her, the others laughed, chatted, came and went. She felt marooned, washed up above the high-tide mark with only these people, forever, for company. It became hard to believe there was anyone else on the island. Or that she would ever escape the clutch of this group, these Calibans and Ariels who alarmed and eluded her. She struggled to breathe, to fill her lungs with enough air to keep the growing dizziness at bay. The limits of her eyeline shimmered on every side so that it seemed as if the horizon was dancing, advancing and retreating in sudden swerves that left her clinging to sun loungers and small terrace tables when she tried to walk to the kitchen for water. Only by sitting still and concentrating on the in-breath, then the out-breath, could she manage. In. Out. Trying to hold the breath on the in so that it didn't escape from her too fast, in the hopes that this would still the lurching. It didn't, but it helped. She needed to speak, she realised. To throw out words, no matter how banal, that would act as tethers, keeping her on the ground and within herself, away from those shimmering distances at the edge of her mind.

'Did anyone see *Hamlet* before we left?' she asked desperately, the question coming out more loudly than she had intended. It landed, unexpected, into the chatter and there was a sudden silence. Todd, she saw, was back outside, head turned towards the sea.

'No,' Julie said indifferently.

'But I plan to,' Jennifer cut in kindly. 'I heard it was very good.'

'Nancy saw it. She said it was a great production.'

'You're always talking about Nancy,' Julie said, the usual tones of faint accusation in her voice. Julie could make 'good morning' into an accusation.

She was right though. Natasha did talk about her a lot. 'My sister reckons . . .', 'My sister says . . .', giving Nancy's views on books, films, people, whenever these came up in conversation, eager to share her brilliance and originality; for others to understand, even at a distance, that delicate, shining mind.

'She's the cleverest person I know,' she said now to Julie. 'And the funniest.'

Julie looked affronted, as if at least one of those titles should have gone to her, even though she didn't, to the best of Natasha's understanding, pride herself on being either of those two things. Maybe she just thought all titles should go to her.

Natasha wondered where Nancy was, and wished she knew how to find her. She hadn't answered her phone since leaving the villa, and Natasha had no idea if she had left, as planned, or maybe stayed. She imagined making Nancy's journey in reverse, setting off for the other side of the island, tracking her down with only Salvatore's name to guide her. She imagined Martin going with her, knew that he would, and all the things Nancy would say to comfort and cheer her.

'What does Nancy actually do, apart from pick numbers for Russian Mafioso in casinos?' Julie liked to know what everyone 'did'.

'She's not in college yet, but I think she might start next year.'

She'd been saying that for two years now, but what else was there to say? That Nancy couldn't decide on anything? Not even between English and biochemistry, which she had suddenly decided might be what she was interested in after all? That she couldn't make plans further ahead than a few days, because the plans began to weigh on her and worry her? That Nancy wouldn't talk to her about their father, so that Natasha now had no one to talk to who had known the man she knew? She couldn't say any of that, so she said what she thought Julie would be content with. 'She has a much older boyfriend. He's a university professor, engineering, though a relatively young one, and they have an amazing flat together. A two-storey Georgian.' Julie looked satisfied with that.

'She probably learns from him,' Katherine said vaguely, pleasantly.

'And from his friends,' Jennifer added eagerly. 'I'm sure they have all sorts of interesting friends. Nancy's so beautiful.' As if being beautiful were enough to ensure just the kind of interesting Bohemian life she had imagined for Nancy.

Natasha wasn't sure they had any friends. Certainly Nancy had never been good at keeping friendships. She seemed to use them up very fast, burning from infatuation to bust-up or indifference, and John seemed happy, or maybe just content, for it to be the two of them. Natasha was never sure whether he didn't wish to share Nancy, or simply didn't trust her in company.

'Nancy doesn't look much like you.' That was Todd, head still turned away, but clearly listening. Natasha jumped, then tried to ignore the feeling it gave her to hear him speak Nancy's name.

'I think she does,' Jennifer said. 'She's thinner, and taller, and she has more exaggerated features, yes, but there's definitely a strong similarity. Like Natasha drawn by Egon Schiele,' she finished, triumphant at finding just the right description.

'That's good, Jennifer!' Natasha said. 'That's pretty much it exactly. Clever you!'

Jennifer smiled at her. It was the first proper, direct look they had exchanged since the evening of the club, and Natasha realised with a relief that made her want to laugh that the kinship she felt with Jennifer was still entirely separate to what had happened with Todd. That Jennifer still had the gift to make everything alright, even if only for the moment of her making. She smiled back.

Todd said nothing, but he turned his head and he too looked at Natasha.

CHAPTER 12

Jennifer knew something had happened, something that had exploded the shapes and colours around her so that they fell back into quite a different pattern, but she didn't know what. Todd was kind, attentive, seeming to depend on her company and sympathy. He looked for her constantly now, seemed restless, even unhappy, without her. Sometimes he reached out a hand, patted her arm as she lay beside him on a towel or sun lounger, moved a foot so that it rested closer to hers when they were in bed. It was too hot to sleep or lie entwined with each other, but his need to bridge any distance that opened between them touched her. When he told her she was kind, or patient, he did it without mockery. With what might have been gratitude. They had more sex, often in the early mornings when the sun was up but before it had sucked the energy out of the day. Afterwards he would fall back asleep, arms still around her, so that now it was she who disentangled herself, moved away. But gently. Carefully.

'I don't want to lose you,' he said one morning, mouth close to her ear.

'You won't,' she said. 'Why would you?' Then, frightened that he would think that an invitation – to answer, to tell her something she didn't want to hear, she said, 'I'm going to make coffee. Do you want some?'

'No, you make horrible coffee,' he said, but with a laugh.

In the sun of his approval, she blossomed again, her whole self glowing with his goodwill so that her movements, now, seemed graceful and certain, not the clumsy misery of the recent days. Her skin – pale, pinkish – struck her again as something beautiful and she wore her large hats and careful drapery with pride.

'I'm better staying out of the sun,' she said, confident and clear as she chose shady seats in restaurants and cafés. 'I'll swim later, when the sun goes down,' at the beach, choosing a spot beneath a large rock, knowing Todd would join her wherever she chose to be.

Natasha he mostly ignored. When he had to speak to her, he did so with brevity, economy, barely looking at her face – 'Are you coming with us?'; 'Can you pass me that paper?' – then turned, with what seemed like relief, back to Jennifer, as though she were a welcome antidote to something that repelled him.

Where she had known, just a few days before, that when they got home she must break up with him, because the indifference of his regard for her was too much to be borne, now she knew, with joy, that she would not. That she would stay, because he needed her to, and because he seemed at last able to express that need.

At first Jennifer worried at the edges of what the transformation might mean – helped by Julie, who was determined to drop poisonous hints about the night out Jennifer had missed – but in the end set her face away from any of the explanations that presented themselves. What matters is now, she told herself. It doesn't matter how we got here. She tried to see them all – her, Todd, Natasha, Julie – as specks on a timeline, stretching back and forwards so that the events that had built them to where they were could assume the perspective she needed of them. Ten years from now, what will any of this mean? she told herself. It's simply a moment in time, no more.

It was a technique she had learned while studying for exams, a way of putting distance between herself and the source of stress in her life. She had tried communicating it to Natasha once, at the end of their first year. 'You put yourself as a tiny coloured dot on a piece of string, and then you make the string incredibly long, stretching in front of and behind your dot, into infinity. Then you start adding other dots, thousands of them, until your own dot can hardly be seen anymore.' She had been proud of her explanation, her ability to visualise it. Not that Natasha had seemed to find exams stressful, but perhaps she could find another use for it, Jennifer had thought. But Natasha had disliked the process.

'It's too passive,' she had said, shaking her head, when Jennifer had described the exercise.

'It's not passive, it's perspective,' Jennifer had argued.

'Too much perspective means exactly that – passivity,' Natasha said. 'After all, once you start with that, why ever bother doing anything at all? Why not just let Hitler kill all the Jews, or governments take away people's rights? When it all means nothing in the context of forever?'

'But it doesn't,' Jennifer tried to say. 'Hitler killed six million Jews. That's a lot of dots. Of course that means something.'

'Not if you're looking at one dot at a time. And allowing that dot to be swallowed up by history and the universe before you look at another dot.'

The conversation was becoming too metaphysical for Jennifer. 'It's a good way of caring less about the stressful things, when they happen,' she'd insisted.

'But you should care. You should care enough to find a way to do something about them. It's no good just sitting back and letting things happen. You have to try and help.'

'Help what?' Jennifer had been confused, even more so by Natasha's vehemence.

'Anything or anyone that needs to be helped.'

'I meant things you can't change – like exams, where you have to get on with it but you can't let it overwhelm you.' If Natasha was going to turn all crusading and knight-in-shining-armour on her, Jennifer didn't want to be relegated to whatever the opposite of that was. Someone who didn't care, who sat back while terrible things happened. 'I didn't mean not to care about *everything*,' she'd said.

She still thought the system was useful, and so she applied it now. 'Whatever happened, or didn't happen,' she told herself, 'it makes no difference unless I let it.' And because she didn't know anything, had no information about what might have gone on between Todd and Natasha, it was possible to put it out of her mind. Without images, there was nothing difficult in passing by the temptation to invent her own lurid scenarios, and allowing herself to open her arms to Todd.

She enjoyed the last days far more than the initial frenzy. Liked the way they all seemed to have burned themselves out and now drifted down like leaves in wind, to land gently and lightly. Liked, too, that Katherine seemed to confide in her more than the others about her romance with Dermot. As if Jennifer, with her relationship of several months' standing, was a tribal elder.

'He says he doesn't know where it's going, but that he wants to just follow it and see,' Katherine said one evening as they sat by the pool, watching the swallows skim the surface of the water, dipping then straightening in one fluid movement, like carousel rides. The others were indoors, napping, preparing dinner, or simply escaping after another day of conviviality. 'I don't know what will happen when we get home, but for now it's wonderful.' Her voice broke slightly, cracked through by the awed gratitude of discovering that the grandiose promises of fairytales were in fact true. Jennifer tried to say something wise and experienced – 'You have to be open to the possibility of love before it can happen' – but it came out sounding patronising and dim.

Natasha came out of the house then, walked towards them. She moved carefully, with a kind of brittle delicacy, like some long-legged bird picking its way through sodden marshland, lifting each leg high before placing it down precisely. As if the ground were treacherous, or her legs unequal to the task. Had she always seemed so fragile? Jennifer wondered. Or was that new? Then, recalling the nearness of death, the proximity of bereavement, she felt she understood.

'Natasha, come and sit with us,' she called. Natasha came over, sat on the edge of a chair beside Katherine. 'We were talking about love,' Jennifer said. 'How it can just hit you, when you don't expect it.' Natasha said nothing. And what, after all, Jennifer wondered, was there to say to a remark so clichéd? She squirmed a little, and tried to redeem herself by asking, 'Have you ever been in love? Properly?'

'No,' said Natasha. 'At least I don't think so. There's never been anyone I felt I couldn't live without. And no one has ever hurt me so badly that I couldn't get over it.' She said it defiantly.

'I'd say it's more the other way round with you,' Jennifer said. 'That if hearts are broken, you're the one doing the breaking.' She said it because she believed it, and because she wanted it to be true.

'Not really,' Natasha said. 'And, anyway, there's nothing to be proud of in breaking someone's heart. You'd be better off breaking their leg or their arm. It's a horrible thing to do.'

'Of course it is,' Jennifer said quickly. 'I didn't mean that it was something to boast about.'

'Well, lots of people do boast about it. And they shouldn't.'

'It's because they don't understand,' Katherine said, full of new-found joy, and the glorious self-importance of discovery. 'They don't know what it means to love someone, so they don't understand the pain of never being able to have them.'

'Or of having them and then losing them,' Natasha said, and Jennifer knew that she wasn't talking about a boyfriend.

Todd came outside then, some enquiry about the fish they were going to cook that he yelled across the empty patio with its discarded towels and bottles of sun cream, the debris of yet another day in the dogged pursuit of hedonism.

At the sound of his voice, Natasha flinched.

CHAPTER 13

Their few remaining days were quiet. As if the spirit of activity of the previous nights had spent them, they seemed content to stay at home. No more clubs and bars. Not even Julie suggested going out. Instead, they drifted, from pool to beach, and back to the villa for dinner, drinking, making plans that were rarely executed because of apathy. And certainly the currents around the villa were strange enough that there was no need to go in search of the peculiar or the fraught. It was all there in front of them, scratchy and rough, a grating combination of heat, exhaustion, accumulated hangovers and deflation.

Julie had obviously slept with Paul, and just as obviously regretted it. Natasha wondered had they waited until they had got back to the villa, or had they fashioned a spot at the beach club, behind a wall, in a toilet, in the sea. But if Paul thought the act might begin something for them, Julie was quick to disabuse him. She snapped and picked at him, contradicting everything he said and finding fault with all his plans, so that soon the rest of the group didn't know where to look.

'Give it a rest,' Natasha heard Katherine say quietly to Julie by the pool one afternoon when Paul suggested a game of poker and Julie had sighed and said, 'No one wants to play poker, Paul. We're all perfectly fine here, just doing what we're doing.' So that Dermot, clearly embarrassed, muttered 'I'll play,' and Paul had gone to get a pack of cards.

Julie turned then to Katherine, eyes round and hard, and said, 'Give what a rest, Katherine?', repeating it when Katherine didn't immediately answer. 'Give what a rest?' Katherine had looked down and said, 'Never mind.'

It was as if the Holiday of a Lifetime was slipping away from them, burning out like the sparklers that sometimes arrived in the silly cocktails they drank. Natasha was certain she wasn't the only one longing to leave, to get home. Only Katherine and Dermot were happy in each other's company, content to wander between beach and villa – a glass of wine, a plate of salted almonds – and draw around themselves the charm of their new love story, wearing it against the picking and small irritations of the rest of the group.

The pace of everything slowed with the new lethargy, so that even what had been unbearable in Natasha's mind became weighted down enough to at least stay still. She still didn't know what to call it, this thing with Todd that now lived front and centre of her thoughts. She had no place to put it, no way to process it, and so she began to bury it – digging deep the way she used to set out to 'dig to Australia' when she and Nancy were small, with spades and buckets of water to soften the hard mud – and buried it, deep down, thrusting it under, to join her grief about her father, her many regrets, and she left it there, all of it, trapped together. 'It's all I can do,' she decided. 'All I'm able to do with it. Later, when I'm stronger, I can dig it up and look at it again. *I won't always feel like this.*'

She had always known she was good in a crisis. It was something her mother used to say – 'Natasha is good in a crisis' – when there was blood, or a fall, some reason to run, fast, and get bandages, something for stings, cloths to mop up after a burst pipe – but Natasha had not realised how efficiently she could manage the crises of her own life. Squash them down, find a lid to put over them. 'Soon there will be so much stuffed down there, it will erupt like an angry volcano,' she told herself with a wry inner laugh. She imagined the bottom of her mind like one of the illegal rubbish dumps the Camorra operated in Naples, where they just poured so much waste into the beautiful canyons around the city that eventually it became impossible to squash down any more, and the filth fermented, grew hot and toxic, until at last it thrust its way up and out, irrepressible, a geyser of foulness.

Although she worked hard at being normal, playing her part in the poolside chats, the dinner-table debates, the shopping, drinking and horsing around, Natasha felt ever more removed from the group. Had there been nothing to hide, to fear, she might well have spent her last days visibly aloof, protected by a book. As it was, she didn't dare. The forced pace of social interaction kept her grounded and so she followed it, sought it out, obeyed it, but didn't like it. Her impatience with them all grew, her tolerance for what she considered the inanities of their chitchat dropped, so that, at times, she could barely conceal the sneer that sprang to her mouth as she heard them start up yet another discussion about the love life, or cellulite, or facial work, of some celebrity. A conversation about the best karaoke songs for bad singers took up nearly a whole afternoon.

"No Scrubs', TLC,' said Katherine.

'"Walk on the Wild Side," insisted Paul. 'It's hardly even singing.'

'Anything by Nancy Sinatra,' said Jennifer. 'She really couldn't sing.' And on it went: "I Love Rock 'n' Roll', Joan Jett'; "Yellow Submarine" – soon with demonstrations, poolside play-offs complete with extravagant posturing and bottles as microphones.

'Natasha, what do you think?' Jennifer was looking over, willing her to join in.

'Um, I don't know . . .' Natasha thought quickly. Something, anything. 'Um, Bruce Springsteen, 'I'm on Fire'? It's all on one note basically. And bonus points for being super creepy.'

'Good one,' they chorused.

'Come and sing it.' Julie held an empty bottle, proto-microphone, out to her with a smirk. And so Natasha sang, felt she had to, thanked God the song was short. Wished she could enjoy herself the way they were. Their hilarity oppressed her, even intimidated her, although she knew they didn't mean it. 'It's circumstantial, not personal,' she told herself when a sudden shriek of laughter made her wince. 'It's not malicious.'

But it seemed to her that every conversation was like Ariadne's thread. No matter where it started or how it progressed with twists and turns, it always lead inexorably back to the one spot – the intersection of their worlds: 'Didn't he go to St Paul's?', 'Oh, I know her brother', 'Her parents live at the top of the hill near me, don't they? The house with the huge garden?'

In every one of these conversations, Natasha knew herself to be an outsider. Not just an outsider, but someone without any hope of entry. Nothing she ever did would be a match for the years they had spent going to the same schools and youth discos, on holiday in the same spots, snogging each other, getting sick together, growing up in the same places, whose geographical boundaries, though narrow, were less restricted than the social ones.

It was like first year in college all over again, an impenetrable wall of people all knowing one another, all with the shorthand of shared years and carbon-copied outlook, from which only Jennifer's hand had been extended.

Julie, if Natasha was honest, slightly scared her. She had a way of looking between Natasha and Todd, her round, blue eyes narrowed and calculating, which seemed far from benign, and Natasha avoided her where possible.

In fact, Jennifer, who should have been tainted with Todd and what he had done, was the only one Natasha could really bear. And Martin, slow, unlikely to challenge, was soothing company. Behind his leaden wit was kindness, a desire to see them all happy, perhaps most of all to see her happy. She didn't encourage it, didn't dare, but the knowledge that it might be there comforted her. His admiration was an antidote to the desire and then despair that Todd had lit inside her.

'You're very well-read, aren't you?' Martin asked one morning, watching her as she laid down her copy of *Moby-Dick*. He said it with open admiration, without the shadow of mockery that Todd or Julie would have brought to such an observation.

'Well, that's for college,' she answered, then couldn't resist adding, 'though I have already read it. When I was fourteen. My father told me it was much too old for me, but I finished it, somehow, although I don't think I understood very much.' She remembered his pride when she came to the end, the way he had laughed and commented on her persistence – 'admirable persistence' he had called it – and said, 'Now you've got the sound of it, when you read it again, when you're older, you'll get the sense of it.' Sound first, sense later, she had thought. Is that the way to do it?

'You must have done nothing else as a kid except read?' Again, Martin sounded admiring, not teasing.

'We moved a lot and it was just the two of us, me and Nancy, so we read. We read together though, for company; in the same bed, or squashed into the same chair, sometimes sitting on the radiator behind the curtain, if we were in Ireland and it was cold. It felt like it was always cold in Ireland. We'd come back for summers and get sick immediately. My mother used to be furious with us. She'd have the whole house to clean and air after we'd been away for so long, and

Nancy and I would be in bed, with our books, demanding hot water bottles and lemon drinks. I think she thought we did it on purpose, but we just weren't used to the constant wet.'

'And now, are you used to it?' He sounded anxious on her behalf.

'Yes, I'm used to it, more's the pity.' She laughed. 'I guess you can get used to anything if you stick at it long enough.' With a sudden start, she realised just how true that might be.

A few more such conversations and Martin's kindness began to become necessary to her. More, in his company she could still laugh, and mean the laugh. His sense of humour, so ill-suited to the fast-paced back-and-forth of parties and nights out, was, over a longer distance, compelling. He had a knack for character analysis that she found unusual in a man, because it was detailed and absorbed, but without maliciousness.

'You're like a girl, the way you get so into this,' she'd said after one chat about Julie, in which he had described her as being 'constantly on the knife-edge of her own ambition'.

'It must be from talking so much to my sister,' he said. 'We used to spend hours dissecting the character of girls she went to school with. Some of them weren't very nice to her – in fact, my parents were going to move her at one stage, because she was so unhappy – but she and I got into the habit of talking about the worst of the girls, the "Queen Bitches" as she called them, and analysing what we knew about them and what it meant. We would put them into historical context – which ones were actually bad, like Bloody Mary, and which were just weak, or fools, like Marie Antoinette. It seemed to cheer her up a bit, and give her some perspective.'

'And did it help? Did she begin to get on better? If it had been me, I would have moved her straight away, like my parents did for me when I hated boarding school.'

'My parents thought it was character-forming for her to stick it out, for a while anyway, not to run at the first upset. I don't know if they were right.' He'd paused. 'It was awful watching her go through it. But she did make friends eventually. She found there were lots of other girls the Queen Bitches were nasty to as well, and so she banded together with them. She always says the character-assassination game helped too, that it gave her a frame to look at them which wasn't personal. But maybe she was just being kind.'

From the way he'd spoken, Natasha had begun to understand that Martin, unlike the other men she knew, wasn't repelled by vulnerability. That he had the rare instinct to protect where he saw weakness, rather than attack.

They had fun together, silly jokes and chatter that amused her, soothed her. Together they had discovered a love of sea stacks – or rather, he had, and she had played along because it meant they could disappear off together for hours, to beaches on the far side of the island where they had to scramble down steep, rocky paths, reddish earth sliding beneath their feet, to reach secluded coves where they'd swim and he'd tell her boring things about the formation of the sea stacks and cliff erosion that would keep her anchored to the telling.

She knew her need for him was simply a reaction, an illusion, but, nonetheless, in her wonky state, it grew on her until only in his company did she feel fully easy. She fought the feeling of panic that set in when he was elsewhere, but began making plans based on where he said he was going, what he said he would do. She knew that he had noticed, was gratified, and worried that he was making more of it than there should have been to make, but couldn't stop herself.

'I'll sort it out later,' she promised herself. 'When I can. Anyway, once we're back home, it'll sort itself out.'

'Back home', by then, had become a magical place, where all would once again be easy, comprehensible.

Todd was a puzzle, the way he behaved at once with constraint but indifference too. It was as if he didn't care about what he had done. Or rather, if she was honest, as if he didn't know. He still spoke to her, not as before, but with only a show of awkwardness at the start, something that soon faded entirely, so that he spoke to her as he spoke to any of the others. It was Jennifer who had his attention now, whose company he sought, whose opinions he asked for. He lay with her in the shade of a beach umbrella, the two of them chatting in low voices, laughing.

Only when Natasha was alone with Jennifer did he seem uneasy, seeking always to place them far from each other, keep them separate, to distract Jennifer when Natasha spoke to her for too long.

The last day came, the final morning of rushing, packing, saying farewell, exclaiming at how fast the days had gone. Then the airport, where, tacitly, they dispersed into smaller groups, preparing for the parting of ways that would come once they landed in Dublin. Already, in the rush for passport control, the plundering of Duty Free and grabbing of takeaway coffees, it was as if the Holiday of a Lifetime had never been.

PART TWO

CHAPTER 14

The bins were sprawled across the pavement, smooth lumps of grey and green plastic. Theirs were the last still out on the street where the binmen had left them. Jennifer pulled on a pair of Uggs over her bare feet, turning her mind away from the images that offered themselves like a little platter of horror – bacteria, sweat, dirt, trapped in the buoyant fleece of the sheepskin lining, now rubbing up against her naked skin – and ran downstairs. The road was still quiet. It was early, and this wasn't a street for early risers; cars vacated driveways between 8 am and 8.30 am, in regular procession, while doors opened and disgorged children in neat uniforms accompanied by South American au pairs in tight jeans and hoodies, their long, dark hair pulled up into thick ponytails that bounced behind them as they walked. Round here, there was never any confusion over who was a minder and who was a mother. The delineation was written in hair colour and body contours as much as in age.

She pulled the first bin back into the driveway and behind the wooden trellis constructed for the very purpose of hiding them, then went out for the second.

'I'm the last,' she said, smiling through the effort at a neighbour getting into her car.

The woman nodded forgivingly at Jennifer. 'Happens to us all,' she said sweetly, the lie standing up between them like the hackles of an angry dog.

Jennifer wondered had Todd noticed. It had been still dark when he left – Jennifer had heard him get up, move about in his dressing room and their bathroom, then the hiss of the coffee machine downstairs. She knew he had something big on that morning – a meeting with potential investors, or further meetings with existing investors; she was never very clear about the financial structure of what he did, although there seemed to be a lot of what he called 'wooing' involved.

Maybe he had been preoccupied, focused in that way he had when everything that wasn't the thing in front of him disappeared from his sight like land seen from a fast-moving boat. Maybe he hadn't seen the bins sprawled across the pavement. She considered the possibility for a moment, playing the dark, early morning in her mind, the relative discretion of the grey and green plastic, the searchlight of Todd's focus trained on the day ahead, then abandoned it. Of course he had seen them. And compared her failure to the neighbour's efficiency.

Back inside, the house was silent, with the muffled, well-behaved air of objects that knew their places and kept to them. Rosie was still asleep and, in her absence, even her toys – islands of cheerful anarchy in the ordered spectrum of grey and cream and oatmeal that subdued the house – weren't to be seen, hidden away behind the many smooth panels of fitted storage into which everything could be tidied, in which Jennifer sometimes thought she could sense a slow-brewing mutiny of things. Some days, she thought she could hear it, a building murmur of disgruntlement from glasses, plates, spare batteries, Sellotape, napkins, deadened by the wooden panels, soft carpets and thick, fringed curtains. She dreamed at times that the contents of these panelled cupboards would rise up and throw themselves out of their discreet confinement and at her, hurling their ferocity through the air, revealing the lie of all that order and carefully calmed space.

She still missed the busy, studious mornings – getting up, rushing to the library, trying to get there by the time it opened, because she believed that treating her thesis like a job was the only way to approach it. 'If I start letting myself make up my own hours, I'll never be finished,' she had said eagerly to Todd, who had nodded without answering, without really listening, Jennifer suspected. His interest in her academic life had always been limited; it was, he believed, a hobby, a way for her to fill up her days before something more serious came along, like playing house, or shop.

And then something more serious had come along – the pregnancy that had turned Jennifer away from her books and notes and plans, that had left her with nothing when it ended, abruptly, after just sixteen weeks and only the faintest show of blood.

She hadn't wanted to mention the blood; it had seemed so hysterical when it was so little, and she had been determined not to be one of those women – 'forever asking if there are eggs in things and making a big show of not eating blue cheese' as she had said to Katherine when she first found out she was pregnant – but Todd had insisted, telling her that the whole point of going private and spending so much money was so that she got the best possible care.

And so she had rung her doctor, a gravelly-voiced woman with deft hands, made an appointment, agreed with her that it was 'undoubtedly nothing', that 'a small amount of blood' was common, but better to be certain. She had gone in alone, telling Todd there was no point him taking time off work for something that would be nothing. He had been willing to be persuaded, and had, of course, meetings to attend.

And so Jennifer had gone by herself, sat in the waiting room with a folder of notes about Dante that she was trying to organise, had lain by herself, stomach exposed, covered in the cold viscosity of gel that felt like it had leaked out of her rather than been put on her, while the doctor moved the ultrasound nozzle up and down, across, down, then up again, over her stomach.

It took too long, the silence as it moved was too heavy and the press of the nozzle too deep, so that when her doctor finally said, 'I'm sorry, Jennifer . . .' Jennifer had known what was coming.

But she had not braced herself, because that would not have been possible. She was as open and soft as if she had never suspected a thing, and the pain had been more intense than she could have expected. A small, thin needle that punctured her entire world, that deflated it there on the narrow couch and left Jennifer to drag it along behind her for years, like a collapsed parachute.

It was odd, she thought later, that something you hadn't really wanted could, in the losing of it, prove so complete an annihilation. She hadn't wanted to be pregnant, although she perfectly knew that she hadn't worked hard enough not to be – had been foolishly imprecise about taking the pill – and when she had realised she was, had not been at all sure she wanted a baby.

It had been days before she'd told Todd, and even then she had told her mother first, over lunch, so that she had seen her mother's face – the flash of shock that could as easily have been horror, had heard the careful way her mother had asked for Jennifer's reaction before giving her own.

Todd had been pleased, something that had charmed Jennifer at the time. 'That's wonderful,' he had said immediately, hugging her. 'A baby will give you something real to do.' And Jennifer had stifled her annoyance at the fact that he didn't consider her thesis 'real' because, after all, she knew that already.

That had been six years ago, and the time in between, when she looked back at it, seemed like something viewed through the wrong end of a telescope. Tiny, squashed, hopelessly distant, her own doings in those years seemed the actions of a doll or animated figure, being jerked through days and weeks and months, without any more input than a tacit physical acquiescence.

She had put away her thesis, unable to concentrate, horrified by the solitary hours in the library that she had once adored, where time now seemed to tick past with malicious delay, jeering her inability to pace herself. Instead, she got a job, part-time, as communications manager for a mental-health charity, which largely consisted of issuing press releases.

She had done it, she sometimes thought, with rather less than half of herself. The other half she had put away almost without noticing, somewhere dark and quiet. She had lived with Todd, cooked for him, talked to him, moved house with him, had sex with him, occasionally even nodded and agreed when he had said that she needed to do something about herself. Had forgiven him for saying something so stupid because of the bond there now was between them of a baby that had been both theirs and was now dead.

She had met friends for walks and coffee and nights out, and had accepted her gradual slide to the corners of their lives, grateful that she did not slide right out, and all the while most of her had been elsewhere; dormant, she now knew, although at the time she had presumed dead too.

She had not thought much about another baby – had not dared after she had been so criminally careless with the first – and so it had been a surprise to discover she was pregnant again. At first she had not wanted to rush out to meet her own happiness, had held back, held herself aloof, although she had gone through all the motions very correctly. This time, she had been careful about raw eggs and blue cheese and lifting things, but from a distance of mind that she thought would never be bridged.

And then, once the sixteen weeks had passed, when she was woken night after night by sturdy kicks and punches, she had found herself responding. The half that had been put away in the dark was stirred up, kicked into being again, and Jennifer had begun to walk everywhere with her hands folded across her increasingly solid stomach. She'd spoken to her baby, placed her hand on the living wall between them in silent communication, made extravagant promises that could never be guaranteed – *I will protect you, I will take care of you, you will be safe* – but that had given her joy in the making of them.

Todd's joy had been less than his relief, she'd suspected, but somehow the bump, and then the baby – Rosie – had filled some of the gap between them. It hadn't brought them closer, but it had taken up some of the distance.

And it had certainly given Jennifer something 'real' to do, a never-ending list that frightened as much as delighted her. Should she wake Rosie up? she now wondered. It was nearly 8 am and she should have been up at 7am if she was to have her nap at 12.30 pm

Jennifer felt the anxiety of the schedule gnawing at her. Rosie had cried for nearly three hours during the night, howling in a pattern like waves, so that sometimes she'd dipped low to a smooth grumble that had Jennifer desperately projecting a lullaby of the mind, in case Rosie could somehow hear and slip fully into sleep, only for the child to go silent, then start crying again as she rolled once more onto the small, hard pea of her distress.

Each time, Jennifer's heart had made itself into a fist and struck at her, so that by the time Rosie finally cried herself silent, Jennifer had been left twitching with enough adrenalin to have seen her through miles of hostile terrain, unable to stand down from the state of high-alert into which Rosie's distress always threw her.

She knew that Todd didn't sleep through these episodes any more than she did, but that the quality of his wakefulness was different, his vigilance angled in a different direction.

Should she let the child sleep? she wondered now. Or wake her and try to catch up with the schedule? Maybe she could intercept it later in the day, like boarding a moving train, catch up before it left her entirely behind? She clenched her fingers over her thumb several times, flicking them rapidly up and down as if they were sticky and she had nowhere to wipe them, then decided that a tired Rosie would only be cranky and that it would be better to let her sleep, and hope to go through to the afternoon nap. These decisions exhausted her in a way nothing else did. Knowing what was at stake, how little and how much, knowing that she was the only one to make the decisions, knowing that no one else cared, but that Rosie's welfare depended on her getting these things right. The minutiae of time and opportunity wearied her, as if her day were a complicated recipe she had to follow with her finger even while mixing and whisking and stirring with the other hand.

If she was honest, the prospect of coffee now, alone and quiet, without Rosie, was too seductive to resist. She wondered did all mothers look forward so intensely to the times when their children were asleep, and understood that she would never ask any of the ones she'd got to know.

She made coffee and checked her email on the laptop Todd had given her, sleek and new and powerful, wasted on Jennifer and her smattering of communication – the emails from her brother, full of news of his life in London, sometimes with a hint of his someday return that Jennifer had learned to discard rather than cling to. The odd general mail from the mother-and-baby group she attended on Thursdays with Rosie, emails as long and complicated as the intersecting armour of an insect, with threads from various other mothers spooling off in all directions.

It had taken Jennifer a long time to work out the code – LD was 'Little Darling', meaning their babies, FB was firstborn, DH was Dear Husband – but she had never yet added anything of her own to the threads. She wondered what Todd would think about being called DH?

There was an email from Natasha, the first in several months. 'News', it said triumphantly. Jennifer opened it, wondering what tales of fabulous cities Natasha would tell her now. Her last email had been from Nashville and she had written about the strip full of Honky Tonk bars, where college kids in plaid shirts and plentiful tattoos danced to country music and drank tequila. She seemed to be constantly on the move, switching cities as quickly as a travel brochure. And everything she recounted seemed designed to keep Jennifer out: cheery missives about food she'd eaten, bars she'd visited, what the culture of the city was like. Nothing intimate, nothing to tell Jennifer who Natasha now was, all these years later. And through everything, the faint seam of a sneer: 'What have you done with your life?'

'Hey ya,' the email started. 'Guess what? I'm moving back to Dublin! The company is expanding the office and asked if I wanted to go over and manage my side of things there, and I said yes! So I'm back properly in August, but I need to come over before that and find somewhere to live and everything. It's great, right? We'll be in the same place again and can really catch up.'

Jennifer hit reply and typed quickly, letting her fingers run faster than her mind: 'That's amazing. Can't wait. You must come and stay while you look for somewhere to live.' She wrote before she lost the power to do it. Before the implications of Natasha coming back began to sink in and she found herself turning around and around in the too-small space of their friendship, the shriek of claustrophobia mounting within her.

She sent the email, then slammed the laptop shut. Even their emails were a lie – fake cheeriness, too many 'greats!', too many exclamation marks. She knew Natasha wouldn't come and stay – she hadn't even been to the house, although Jennifer had invited her each time she'd been back, preferring to meet in town, in coffee shops or bars.

The last time Jennifer had seen Natasha was at Dermot and Katherine's wedding the previous year; a marriage that was already in trouble. Natasha had flown in for two nights, staying at a B&B close by, whereas Jennifer, alone because Todd was working, had booked into the newly built country house, all shining marble and white columns, where the wedding was being held, so that they had seemed to somehow miss each other all weekend, coming and going at different times, seated at different tables – Jennifer with couples, Natasha at a far more exciting table of single people that included Martin, recently broken up with yet another girlfriend – promising to 'sit down and chat properly' but somehow never managing to.

Jennifer had been pregnant, and feeling remote from the partying around her, whereas Natasha was the soul of it, ordering rounds of sambucas, lamenting that the bar didn't stock tequila, and telling stories that Jennifer couldn't hear, but that left everyone around her in fits of laughter.

Jennifer, in contrast, had felt dull and rather depressed. She had sat with a woman she knew, also pregnant, and talked about back pain and how often they had to get up to go to the loo at night. They had been at a circular table draped with a heavy white cloth and the remains of dinner – dirty plates and abandoned cutlery – spread around them. A butter dish had red wine spilled in it, curls of creamy fat rising up out of the liquid like fish from a boiling red sea.

Katherine's father's speech – hesitant, too long – nonetheless had made her eyes prickle as she'd remembered that her own father had made just such a speech at her and Todd's wedding almost three years earlier.

Her father had told the small gathering what Jennifer had been like as a little girl, 'a kind heart that never could resist an honest appeal'. She hadn't cried, mostly because the twitch of Todd's leg pressed against hers had kept her pinned to the moment, holding her back from the kind of emotional flight her father's words should have conjured, and because she had wondered would her father say anything about welcoming Todd into the family – and, if so, how Todd would respond. He hadn't.

'Would you like some water?' the other pregnant woman had asked her.

'I'm fine, thanks. I've drunk enough water to drown.'

She'd gone outside for some air, and to escape the endless questions – 'When are you due? How are you feeling?' – from people who couldn't be bothered to listen to the answers. Natasha had been sitting alone on a bench, smoking, so Jennifer had sat down beside her. In front of them, a fountain lit pale fairy-green spurted water.

'Should I put it out?' Natasha had asked, moving the cigarette into her other hand, the one farthest from Jennifer.

'God, no. Smoke away,' Jennifer had said. 'I'm sick of being treated like a fat invalid.'

Natasha had laughed. 'Which is the bit you mostly don't like? The fat or the invalid?'

'Fat,' Jennifer had admitted. 'I started telling people almost immediately, way before I should have, because I couldn't bear the idea they might think I'd put on weight.'

'That's fucked up,' Natasha had said kindly, 'but I get it. Imagine Julie going around, wondering loudly if you're alright, because you don't look very well and has anyone noticed how *large* you've become . . .'

'She was one of the first I told,' Jennifer had admitted. 'Isn't that awful?'

'Awful,' Natasha agreed cheerfully. Then, 'Your mother must be delighted?' It had very obviously been a question, not a statement.

'Delighted,' Jennifer had agreed, wondering did the hesitation now in her own voice matched that of her mother's when she had responded to Jennifer's news. 'First grandchild. And, of course, Todd is delighted,' she'd said, because Natasha hadn't asked. 'It was his idea. I would have waited a while longer, but he said he didn't see the point, since we'd bought the house and finished doing it up and everything.'

'Right.' Silence, then, 'I like your hair. Big change.' Jennifer's hair was now short and blonde, a kind of pageboy bob that meant she had to go to the hairdressers every couple of weeks.

'I thought it was time I did something more grown-up with it,' Jennifer had said, defiantly, because Natasha hadn't sounded as if she meant it when she issued the compliment, and because Natasha's hair was exactly the same as it had always been, a thick mane of brown flecked with coppery lights, falling past her shoulders.

'Very right and proper,' Natasha had said, amused. 'We have to face up to being in our thirties now. No more unruly mops.' Jennifer had felt silly and embarrassed and started to say something about the terrible condition her hair had been in, the dry tufts that stuck up around her face like desert grass, but Natasha had said, 'Don't you think it's strange that we're all here together, like this?'

'No,' Jennifer had said, surprised. 'We're friends. Where else would we be?'

'Well, that's what I mean. Strange that we're still friends?'

'No. Why?'

'I don't know . . . maybe it's just that no other friends I've had have lasted. But somehow you guys have stuck . . . I think perhaps it's because of you.' She'd reached out and squeezed Jennifer's hand. Jennifer squeezed back.

'Silly. We like you. That's why we're still friends. Even though we don't see half enough of you.'

Martin had come out then and sat beside them.

'All on your own I see,' Jennifer had said to him. 'No plus-one this time?' She'd moved up to give him space.

'Nope. Just me.'

'What happened?' Jennifer had asked, adding 'Martin is about the most eligible bachelor left in Dublin', to Natasha.

'So I hear.'

'Not me,' Martin had said. 'I attract only lunatics and rebounders.'

'The last one was a bit of both, if I recall,' Jennifer had said.

'Well, maybe. I'm off girlfriends for now anyway. What about you, Natasha? Anyone?'

'Not here.' She'd smiled at him, deliberately sweetly.

Katherine had appeared in the double doors behind them, the fishtail of her ivory-coloured gown pooling gracefully around her, and had called out, 'There you are. The band's playing 'Sweet Home Alabama' and I want us all to dance.'

Jennifer had sat beside the dance floor, watching, as the others had flirted and laughed, dancing to all their favourite songs. She had felt remote and old. She had wondered then was Natasha right – was it strange that they were all there, together? Maybe it was more normal to drift apart? To move from group to group as life changed around you, instead of keeping such tight hold of people you had known almost since childhood. Then, as the music had changed to something slow and Martin had come over to encourage her to dance, very carefully, she had decided that, no, there was, after all, something wonderful about the reassurance of old ties.

She opened the laptop again and stared at the screen, puzzling the nature of friendship and trying to picture Natasha back in her life, into the new life with Todd and Rosie, when a loud wail and the frantic lights of the baby monitor, hurtling through green to red, made her jump. The sound, too sharp in that silent house, was an accusation.

CHAPTER 15

The smells of garlic frying in olive oil, of strange-shaped peppers cooking in heavy-bottomed casseroles, of petrol fumes and uncollected rubbish intoxicated Natasha. They hung heavy on the air, like birds locked into a warm upward current that needed no effort of wing.

Rome was busier, noisier even than she remembered it from an autumn spent there when she was sixteen, when her father had a teaching post at the university. She tried to capture some of that first time, but couldn't.

I used to live here, she thought. No, you didn't, the city said, indifferent, too old and grand to care.

Perhaps it was censorious, she thought. Angry that one who had known it as a place to marvel, should return wearing a plastic name-badge, fresh from a day at a conference in the air-conditioned business park on its outskirts, and in such unpromising company.

The guy from 'head office' was droning on and on, laying down the law about the way divorced parents should behave towards each other. 'Luke', he had said his name was, although it sounded more like 'Link' when he said it. He looked like a missing link too, Natasha had decided, something between a human and some kind of small, sinewy mammal with neat ears and tufts of wet fur that lay down flat but threatened to rise, spiky, if anyone disagreed with him.

'It has to be all about the children', he was saying pompously. 'They have to come first.' He looked around the table, daring them to disagree, challenging them, facing them down as if he was the first person ever to hold such a view rather than the last in a long, tired and often failed line. 'My ex-wife and I have a pleasant, amicable relationship. Because of our daughter,' he finished triumphantly. 'We put her first.'

Was it only Americans who behaved like this? Natasha wondered. As if they alone were privy to the secrets of the universe, when in fact they rarely seemed to get beyond the surface, harvesting only the most obvious truths, the ones thrust out to them, ripe and already falling.

Maybe it wasn't Americans, she decided. Maybe it was just people who did well in corporate environments, where stale ideas were recycled to cries of excitement and the genuinely innovative was mistrusted on principle. Maybe it was just people she met. Or maybe it was just the way she heard them. She sighed.

Natasha enjoyed her job – admin in a financial services company with offices in many countries – more than she had expected to when she had talked her way into it nearly ten years earlier. Her degree had been mediocre and all dreams of postgraduate work – a thesis, perhaps even a PhD, a book some day – had been dumped, fast, before they could begin to tear at her.

Instead, she had taken the first job she was offered, and shown herself to be good at it – 'You're psychologically astute,' her bosses had said with approval, and, indeed, Natasha was very good at working out who might be useful to them and how – so that she was promoted regularly, paid well, and flown, business class, to conferences and seminars in many of the cities she had first known as a child, trailing after her parents to galleries and churches. Now, she mostly sat in cool hotels and business centres that felt like a betrayal of her young self, of everything she had one day believed she would be.

'Link' had moved on now, from divorce to scientific research into deliberately manipulated virus mutation and why it was a good thing and could never go wrong. 'These guys know what they're doing,' he said. 'They don't make mistakes.' Quite as if he knew 'these guys' – all of them – and could vouch for them personally. Again, his eyes roved the table, daring them to challenge him. And although his complacency was unbearable, no one did. It was too hot.

Natasha's colleagues – financial analysts, administrators, guys who 'read' the markets and their back-up teams – listened politely, elbows on the table between still-half-full plates of pasta and grilled fish. It was too hot to fight and too hot to eat. Outside, where they had wanted to sit but had arrived too late, smells of food and hot cobbled streets mingled with something floral that could have been night jasmine, weaving in and around the sounds of car horns, movement and conversation, so that Natasha could have sat all evening, eating nothing, just listening and breathing, feeling the city pulse around her.

'These guys are the best there is. They don't do human error,' he was still droning on about the virus-manipulating scientists. 'The point is—'

'Hang on a sec,' Natasha said. 'You mean you're only getting to the point now? Everything up until now has been just random preamble, that you could have spared us?' She forced a smile, tried to take the blunt force from her words.

He looked startled. 'Well, I mean, I was setting the scene—'

'Procrastinating more like. So, what is your point?'

'Well, the point is . . .' But he was flustered, could no longer remember what he had been trying to say, and Natasha, who remembered perfectly well, didn't remind him. She changed the subject – 'Has anyone found time to visit any museums?' – trying to cloak the desire she had to lash out, at men with their ridiculous certainties, at life with its absurd reversals.

Luke looked hard at her, a considering look that rested so long on her face, she finally reached a hand up and rubbed it uneasily, as if his gaze might have left a mark. Or maybe there was already a mark, she thought, something only he and men like him could see, something that singled her out, made her visible to them in a way that other women weren't.

He smiled at her then, bearing needle teeth behind thin lips. Natasha forced herself to smile back. *Why is it so easy?* she thought with a sudden lurch of disgust.

Around her, Natasha's companions talked of the conference, of what they had learned, always with a reflexive enthusiasm that annoyed her. *Must everything be 'wonderful!', 'brilliant!', 'really super!'?* she wondered irritably. *What about just 'OK', or 'fine'?*

They were a mix of French, Dutch, Italian, although most were a certain type of clean-limbed Euro kid she was starting to get used to: mixed-nationality, bi- or trilingual, with mid-length dark-blond hair and smooth complexions, all speaking a very correct kind of English that they probably thought of as 'terribly Oxford', except that it was too good, too precise, showed too much deference to the laws of grammar and syntax. It lacked the hint of mockery or mild disrespect a native speaker would have brought. Also, no native speaker would be so damn keen on everything, she thought. They could have been dreamed up in a laboratory, perfect examples of a new world order, and as bloodless as machines.

Only Luke had any sense of restraint, and his pomposity and self-righteousness rendered that void. After a hiatus in which he was mercifully silent, attacking a plate of *spaghetti alle vongole* in a way that looked almost personal, so doggedly did he tear at the frilled shells, he started up again. This time it was tattoos on women which had him reaching for outrage.

'No matter how beautiful a girl, once I see a tattoo, she goes right down in my estimation,' he pronounced, emphasising the first syllable so that it came out '*esteem*ation', seeming delighted at the rigor of his own standards. 'For me, that's a tramp, right there.' A pretty girl called Cecelia, Dutch, with thin, straight, white-blonde hair and hectic pink cheeks, looked momentarily discomfited.

'Even if it is a very small tattoo? Something discreet, like, uh, just a rose, on the shoulder where the strap of a dress will cover it?' she asked.

Natasha almost burst out laughing, although she wished that Cecilia had simply pulled down her top to show them all the rose that was so clearly there, and told Luke to go fuck himself.

'It's not the size, or the location,' Luke went on. 'It's the idea that someone could mark their body like that. In fact,' he warmed up, 'the very small ones that can't easily be seen are the worst, because that person does not have the conviction to display what they have done.'

Cecilia looked crestfallen.

'Perhaps they haven't done it for display,' Natasha said. 'Perhaps they have done it, oh, because they like it, and not because they care who sees it or what they think? I mean, when I got mine done,' – she went on, deciding that if Cecilia wouldn't, she would; even though she didn't have a tattoo, she just wanted to see his face when he realised how crass he had been – 'it's a snake, coiled right across my back – I didn't care if anyone ever saw it. I just liked the snake. It's the serpent *Jörmungandr*, from Norse mythology. If I wear a low-cut top, you can see where the head meets the tail and it starts to eat itself.'

There was silence as they all looked at her, then finally, Luke spoke.

'You're joking, right?'

'I might be. But I might not,' she responded. 'And maybe you should think about that before being rude about something as common as a tattoo. I'd say half the table has one.'

'I do!' Cecilia squeaked, made bold by Natasha's stand. 'On my shoulder. A rose.' She pulled down the neck of her stripy Breton top to show them. The table murmured, faint appreciation of the tattoo or just excitement at being present at what, compared with their eagerness to find everything 'wonderful', must have seemed a major showdown.

'OK, OK, I'm sorry,' Luke said, holding his hands palms out in front of them, as if to ward off any more revelations. 'You're maybe right,' he said to Natasha, 'I didn't exactly think. Although I stand by what I said,' he added more quietly.

'You would,' she answered, but smiled to pretend there was no rancour. Later, he tried to persuade her to go on. 'Come and have a drink, there's a place close by I found. We can talk,' he said with a significant look.

'No thanks. I'd better go back and pack. I haven't yet,' Natasha said, determined for once to resist the short-term distraction of sex. Because sex was what he was suggesting, behind all that stuff about 'a drink' and 'talk'. When he failed to persuade her, Luke changed his own mind and said he would accompany her back to the hotel. When they arrived, he went to reception to ask something while Natasha lingered in the bar checking emails, so that they met again, by what was clearly not chance, in the narrow corridor outside her room.

'Are you really off to bed now?' he asked, blocking her path. He was barely taller than she was, and almost as thin, but he had, she conceded, presence, or something.

'Yes, it's an early start.'

'A drink in the bar?'

'No, thanks.' She tried to edge past him, but he didn't budge.

'You've led me along all week, so I've missed my chance with Cecilia and now you're going to turn me down,' he said angrily. 'You're a tease.' He had taken off his jacket, and close up, she could smell the sweat and frustration.

'I'm not. I haven't.' But she had. She had wanted him to want her and to show that he wanted her. 'Well, you could still go and make a play for Cecilia,' she said. 'You've got about nine hours. Surely that should be enough time for you?' Her voice rose sarcastically.

He gave her a dirty look. And, in an instant, she changed her mind. Decided not to bother resisting. Next time I will, she promised herself. Next time. It was what she said to herself every time, a solemn promise that she would stop doing what would only make her unhappy and ashamed the next day. Because she knew that the heat these men gave off was lust, not love, but found herself unable to resist because of the way the two things could be made to converge in her mind, directed into a semblance of each other by the urgency of her loneliness.

She missed being loved, missed it like a physical ache, and this was the only way she had found to answer that ache.

And so she shot Luke a different kind of look, and said, 'Or I guess you could come in here?', indicating the door to her room.

He looked hard at her, then said, 'OK. Let's go.' She unlocked the door with him standing close behind her, his breath hot on her neck. Once inside, he pushed her against the wall and began kissing her, hands knotted in her hair as she unbuttoned his shirt. Without the respectability of clothes, his torso was almost scrawny, all sharp ribs and clavicles, above a surprisingly round stomach. For a moment she wondered could she really be bothered to go through with it, but such was his eagerness – she could feel the hard outline of his dick pressing against her and his eyes when he pulled back for an instant, had the blind, set look of pure lust – that it conjured hers and she began to press back, pushing her

169

hips into his, hard and urgent. The room was small enough that he could lift her, turn and drop her straight onto the bed in one move, then pitch himself down beside her.

'I don't see any tattoo,' he said, as he took off her top.

'Oh, come on,' she muttered, pulling him towards her.

It was like being fucked by a ferret, she decided, as he thrust and twisted above her, face knotted in concentration. He kept asking her, or rather panting at her, breath hot and wet on her face or into her neck, 'Is this good? Do you like this?' so that she had to reply, 'Yes, yes, keep going', with a show of enthusiasm, even though she wished he would just hurry up and be done with it.

Afterwards, they lay silent, the slimy hotel bedspread tangled between them. After a while, Natasha nudged him.

'Time to go now,' she said.

'In a minute,' he mumbled.

'No, now,' she nudged again, sharply. She needed him to leave, fast; didn't want to see him in the vulnerability of sleep: unguarded, slack. This was why she usually opted to go back to their place – so she could order the moment of her departure. Another nudge. Reluctantly Luke gathered his clothes, dressed, then stood over where she lay.

'I'll see you in the morning,' he said, leaning down awkwardly to kiss her. Natasha turned her head so that he kissed her cheek.

'Sure,' she said, planning to do everything possible to avoid any such encounter. She wondered if she could leave early, make her own way to the airport. Check in before anyone else, so she would be seated alone. She resolved to set her alarm an hour earlier than she needed to.

CHAPTER 16

The door closed behind Luke, the dreary click of a hotel lock settling into place. Now that it was over, Natasha felt sick, just as she so often did. She lay flat on her back, unable to sink into rest or slumber. Why did she do these things? Each time, she resolved that she never would again. But too often, her resolve failed.

Because, each time, she fooled herself that it could have been the start of a big love story – after all, everything had to start somewhere, she reasoned. Except, of course, it never was, and in her heart she knew it never could be, because that was not how big love stories started.

It was partly the wanting them to want her, then being unable to say no. The feeling of power that came with being pursued, a feeling that, these days, lit her up like nothing else did, and that she then felt she had to pay for by honouring the silent promise. In part, too, it was the moments of obliteration that came with sex, the way her body and mind seemed at last to match. Although that now seemed like a charm that had been overused, one that was less and less reliable.

Mostly though, it was the way she could, in the now, control those acts as she had not been able to control the thing with Todd. Each time she had sex, it was an attempt to rub out what had happened; overlay that memory with newer, similar, better ones. It never worked.

The feeling of desire built and built in her imagination, then vanished like a startled bird almost as soon as the first kiss happened. And yet she went ahead anyway, because she didn't know how not to, and each time she felt worse. Once she got back to Dublin, she swore to herself, that would be the end. No more men. No more nights that meant nothing.

Her windows were open and Natasha could still make out the many smells of the city. Even this late, the streets were thronged with people, tourists and Romans, determined to stroll until the night cooled around them and made indoors bearable; bumping into one another, merging and separating like globules of oil in a lava lamp.

She considered the urgency with which she returned to these places that felt like the texture of her childhood. It wasn't that she had spent that much of her childhood in them, but somehow they lingered all the same, as a feeling, a smell of home, a memory she needed. Did she think her father would speak to her more clearly there? From the fish markets with their giant slabs of tuna and buckets of tiny shrimp, from the rancid gutters and stolid afternoon strolls where whole towns turned out and walked for the sheer pleasure of seeing, being seen.

Natasha knew she was broken, but she couldn't feel it. She could see it, in her face, in her eyes that met nothing for very long, flickering forwards or sideways, always looking for something else. Her skin was muddy, as if the blood that flowed through her veins was sluggish, the final marshy stretches of a tidal river. She could see it too in the way she behaved – so carelessly, subjecting herself to pain, almost with curiosity. Like the way she used to chew the inside of her cheek when the dentist gave her a numbing injection for a filling. Chewing and gnawing, trying to see could she feel anything through the muffling analgesic, until the sensation returned and she realised she'd bitten her cheek raw, the self-inflicted damage far worse than anything the dentist had done.

She barely read anymore, finding no comfort in books, where the problems and traumas weren't 'real' enough for her. And the smooth plausibility of her social self repulsed her.

All her yesterdays were milky and unreachable. She couldn't find or recognise herself in the past; had no feeling for the person she looked back on when each day was done. Often, she wondered who that dreadful stranger was, with her arch comments and clever put-downs. Someone from a book or a bad play? But she couldn't seem to stop playing this part she had assembled after the wreckage of Ibiza, an inferior degree, and the breach with Nancy and her mother that was no less definite for being unacknowledged, even denied. A breach that grew with time and each new, un-owned hurt.

'What are you *on* about, Natasha?' Nancy had asked, exasperated, the first time Natasha had forced herself to speak of it. 'You're making far too big a deal of this,' with a sneer, so that Natasha had felt herself put firmly in the wrong.

The part she played was that of someone full of resolve and energy, with a challenging wit and determined gaiety. It was a twisted version of the character Jennifer had once dreamed up for her. A part that other people responded to admiringly – 'Natasha's so funny', 'Isn't Natasha *brilliant*?'

It was tedious and tiring. Some days she felt it strangling her, choking the life out of her breath by breath so that soon, she thought, all that would be left would be this shallow husk into which other people poured their expectations: that she would amuse them, get drunk with them, suggest exciting plans to them, fuck them.

She was so tired of not being herself, of the effort required to sustain this other Natasha, whom she despised. How had she let this happen? Did other people's lives simply drift, the way hers had? she wondered. One thing leading to the next so that the joins were imperceptible and you didn't know that you had slipped from where you thought you were going, until you realised you were somewhere else entirely?

She could analyse where she had slipped and slid, even spell it out, but curiously, knowledge didn't help her. Part of the problem, maybe most of it, she believed, was all that grief, put away on the promise of 'later', but never exhumed. It had been stuffed carefully away because Nancy would not share it with her, and she didn't know how to share it with her mother. She was not, she knew, strong enough to look at it on her own. And so it had been left, and like all things stuffed out of sight, it had warped and changed and grown in odd ways.

Now, it was so intermingled with her recollections of that afternoon with Todd, that she could not untangle them. Could not be sure which, if either, or perhaps both, were responsible for the years of bad sex and the bad relationships, and the silence that had fallen between herself, her mother and her sister, broken these days only by inanities, to which they responded without interest or urgency. Her mother had taken to letting days go by before answering calls or messages, saying only 'but I know you are busy' when Natasha complained.

All of it made Natasha feel tired, a weariness that met her every morning and lay beneath every day. It could be dispelled momentarily by some new excitement, but it always came back again, dragging itself towards her like a dog with an old boot or blanket. And it made her feel lonely; a loneliness that was profound and physical, goaded by the knowledge that Nancy and her mother did not feel it. They had each other.

Sometimes, she felt as if there was another life, happening somewhere else at the same time as this one, where her father hadn't died. That if she could just get to the right place, knock on the right door, he would be there and everything would be alright. She even thought she could hear it sometimes – distant laughter that was the same as the laughter that had echoed through the house when he was alive, as much a part of it as the carved wood, the dust dancing in the streaks of light, the smell of all the years and all the people that had lived there. It was a particular kind of laughter, a kind she knew would never come again, that was like a wash of colour into every corner, rolling over all her and Nancy's obstructions of sullenness, the barriers put up by the opposite pull of friends and teenage life, their rows with each other and their mother. Nothing was proof against the flood of joy brought to her by the simple fact of his presence. In that life, there were still croissants and coffee for breakfast and hours spent around the table on Saturday mornings, making jokes, talking, teasing. She tried to feel, again, the rasp of his stubbled chin against her face and the way nothing else had ever made her feel so loved, but she couldn't reach it.

The protection he had offered her simply by being alive had clearly broken with his death. And into the void had come rushing all sorts of evil things. Things she couldn't clear from her path, that twisted around and clung to her like gnarled roots.

I need somebody to talk to about him, she thought. To set off the memories that will take me to where I can see him, hear his voice, follow the thread to where I can allow myself to begin to miss him. She was goaded by the idea that she had not deserved his life by failing to respond correctly to his death, that he might even now be in some kind of purgatory because her tears had been too few to set him free. It was a fear that hit her, like a bird smashing into a window, at unpredictable intervals.

But who was the person to do it? Her mother's memories irritated her. They sounded false, altered over time to be something they weren't but that suited the tale her mother wished to tell, their proper outlines worn away by the telling and retelling, until they were just stories, indiscriminate anecdotes that could have applied to anyone. Nancy had the right memories, and better recall than anyone, but still she would not talk about them to Natasha.

The row, when it had finally come, had been almost a relief, after the years of Nancy's insistences that Natasha was exaggerating and there was nothing wrong between them, so that Natasha, in asking the question yet again just over a year ago had expected the same kind of brush-off. She had been shocked when Nancy, instead of evading, had snapped, and yelled at her, 'Stop clawing at me, Natasha! You are like some kind of street beggar, with your skinny hand held out for more and more and more. I can't help you. I don't know what you want, and even if I did, I wouldn't give it.' When Natasha had said nothing, just stared at her in shock, Nancy had seemed emboldened. 'People have always given you what you want, given in to you. I used to think it was just because you were that kind of person, but now I see that it's because you're always asking, always taking, always looking for more.'

The angry words, thrown out in the sitting room at home, had brought their mother who had stood and watched as Nancy had screamed at Natasha, stayed silent as she finally ran from the room with a final 'just *go away*, Natasha', and had slammed the door behind her. When Natasha had turned to her mother, in desperation, asking, 'Why is she like this with me?', her mother had said only, 'It's her way, for now,' thereby taking Nancy's part and leaving Natasha with no one.

Soon after, Natasha had left again. And stayed away. And now she was going back. And in the meantime, distance had become more than physical, had become the tenor of their interactions. Her flight the next day, instead of returning her to the apartment in Brussels, was to Dublin. Back to her mother, and Nancy, and Jennifer. Back to Martin and Todd, and a life she thought she had left behind.

She wondered why she had said yes. Because it was a promotion and she was ambitious. Because she was curious. And because it was time. She had stayed away, feeling as she did, that it was impossible to be there. She needed distance from all of it, but especially from Nancy. It had been easier not to be there, not to witness the bad patches where she wore out the goodwill of those few who had stayed around her with a savage inability to rest or even repose. Pacing, muttering, jerking her shoulder forwards in a repeated hunch that served as both shrug-off and protection, somewhere to duck her face.

Natasha had been less and less good in these moments of crisis, not just because fear made her sharp and helplessness made her rough, but also because she came to believe her very presence – perhaps her very existence – was a source of frustration to Nancy.

'You are too much for her,' John had explained once, stiff as ever, but with a ring of truth to what he said that had persuaded Natasha. 'She thinks she has to fight you for the very air she breathes.'

'That's ridiculous,' Natasha had said, conscious that it was, and was not. And so she had followed her inclination and left, knowing that at the slightest lift of Nancy's hand, she would have stayed.

Now, though, it was time to go home. Time to see what changes the years had wrought, what more she could wring. Nancy seemed to have 'grown out of it', as her mother had once prophesied she would, settling to a more mellow approach to life that was a great relief after the years of soaring excitement and lurching defeat.

Jennifer, too, she was curious about. Their exchanges had become so desultory, dwindling from long, frank explorations of each other's lives, to short, overly cheery lines here and there. Natasha knew Jennifer had not been well after losing the baby – Katherine had told her, Dermot had told her, even Julie had told her, and she had seen it herself in the pallor of Jennifer's skin when they had met, the vagueness in her eyes and the funny twitch of her fingers, a kind of flicking motion she had made – but Natasha had never approached the subject directly with her, respecting the way in which she felt Jennifer had shrunk instinctively from the very idea of putting words on what she felt.

And because of Jennifer, she would see Todd. And then what? She had never worked out what had happened that afternoon – except that grief had made her do strange things, behave in strange ways. The guilt and dishonesty of her part made her cringe still, but what had been *his* part?

She no longer thought of him first when she woke, or last thing before she slept; the years had taken care of that. But it wasn't forgotten either. She had made a poisonous pearl of it, spun it over with many subduing layers so that it no longer caught her with its rough edges. It – whatever 'it' was – had blended in with the substance of her life as she knew it; no more remarkable than the ache across her shoulders when she worked late at night or the quick pang she felt when she saw fathers with their daughters, caught in the joyful acts of conversation or play.

Outside, the late-night noises – car alarms, the sharp wasp-like drone of scooters – were giving way to the rumbling rubbish trucks of early morning. A city in which some might sleep, but many more were ready to take up the baton so that quiet never reigned. She rolled over, determined to get a few hours' sleep before the alarm and her early flight to the airport, but sleep avoided her, slipping from her grasp.

CHAPTER 17

Jennifer hoped he would be late . . . would arrive in after she was asleep . . . would be content to let her stay asleep. Some nights, he did, moving noisily about the house as she tracked his movements, making himself coffee and sandwiches, turning the TV on loud to programmes where angry men shouted at each other, all driven by the belief that theirs must be the firmest, angriest voice.

Other times – more often – he came upstairs and woke her, shaking her shoulder, then tipping the contents of his mind out before her like a drawer full of odds and ends. Like one of the jars her mother kept on the kitchen windowsill, with pens, safety pins, string, charity pins, screws, maybe a tiny screwdriver.

But, Jennifer knew, the things that Todd tipped out, that he expected her to sort through with him, were not the whole contents of his mind. They were just the first drawer, the most obvious spot. There were other places where he was more reluctant to go, even some places, Jennifer thought, that he didn't have access to. She could dimly feel them, and only then at odd moments, but always had the impression that these places were even more oblique to him.

Sometimes, she wondered what was in those further reaches. Things to do with his childhood, she supposed, the things he had never told her; yet more plans for the future; maybe the carefree side of himself that he had put away and that she missed so much.

Those things he did tip into her lap, he expected her to analyse thoroughly, from all sorts of angles, in a process that was exhausting and loaded.

That night, she had read a few pages of *The Name of the Rose*, chosen because it reminded her of Dante and the thesis she had abandoned but might one day go back to, when Rosie was older. She didn't hear him come in, must have drifted off to sleep, because suddenly he was beside her.

'What do you think O'Keeffe means when he says he'll be in touch?' he asked, turning the bedside lamp on so that she found herself blinking under interrogation. 'He was impressed with the presentation, I could see he was, but all he said was that they would be in touch. What does that mean? Will they invest or not?'

She had fallen into a sleep so deep, it felt like a wave had washed her out to sea, then just as suddenly chucked her back up on the beach. She struggled for coherence, to sit up straight, smooth her hair. 'Maybe he just means what he said – that he'll be in touch?' She put a hand up to shield her eyes from the light.

But Todd insisted she try harder, look deeper, speculate more. 'He didn't ask a single question. Why not?' He smelled of sweat, cigarettes and coffee. She wondered if he'd eaten. Often, he didn't. The way he sat, he dragged the covers down so that her shoulders were left bare and cold. She tried to haul them back up again, but he didn't budge and so she couldn't. Neither could she wriggle down further under them. He liked her upright for these analysis sessions.

'He probably didn't know what to ask,' Jennifer tried, leaning to the side so the too-harsh light fell away from her face, because she worried that it was creased by her pillow, slackened by sleep.

'You're right. He didn't. I know far, far more about all this than any of those guys.' He leaned back, pulling off the covers even more. Her chest was cold now too. Todd could always be cheered by an appeal to his sense of superiority. In putting others down, he himself invariably rose. Sometimes, this would be enough to put him in a more cheerful mood and Jennifer would be left to go back to sleep. But more often he would worry and gnaw at the topic, sometimes for hours, keeping her awake and under sustained attack. What had someone meant? Why had they said what they'd said? And, most of all, did she think they would invest? His need for more money seemed greedy to Jennifer, who had been brought up to believe it the least of things to aspire to and knew that he had already been given over a million euro, but it seemed his dreams were bigger than hers, bigger than that.

She hoped he wouldn't wake Rosie. As if he read something in her thoughts, he said suddenly, 'You know I do this for you, and Rosie? Not for me. For you?'

Once she had reassured him about her grasp of his intentions, he went straight back to his obsession.

'They have no idea of the potential for interactive TV, here and right across the world. This is the new frontier, it's the Wild West all over again, and I am crossing it alone.' He took her hands in his, squeezed, then dropped them in order to make grand gestures with his own as he spoke, flinging them wide to show the breadth of his vision, his voice rising. 'These investors think they are pioneers, but they don't understand the model, they have no idea what to ask, and they're afraid of showing their ignorance.'

She knew he needed these night-time analyses, needed her to consider and analyse with him, adding her views, her faith, to his, for the weight of their agreement. Because, for all the fast-moving certainty of his daytime self, he too had moments of doubt brought on by the dark and solitude.

'I need more investors,' he said. 'More money, and from different sources. Right now, those guys think they own me because they are the only ones to buy in. So far,' he muttered, up now and pacing the side of the bed, turning right angles around it then back again. 'I need them to realise that they don't get the whole show. They don't get me, for that money.' He fell silent, shifting through his own thoughts. Then, 'You left the bins out this morning.'

She had been a fool to think even for a second he hadn't noticed.

'I'm thinking of giving a lunch party at the weekend,' she said, a diversion prepared in advance. She knew he would be pleased. He complained that she did too little, hid away too much. Only weeks ago, he had tried to persuade her to employ a nanny – a full-time, proper one, not the Brazilian student who baby-sat Rosie for odd hours here and there – he'd even come home with the name of an agency, got from someone he worked with, and had been angry when she'd refused. 'You need more free time,' he had insisted, so that she didn't dare say that she had nothing to do with her free time. Nothing she wanted to do. Instead, she had said that Rosie was too young and maybe in a while.

It was a battle Jennifer knew lay in her future. Sometimes she felt him reach for it, almost touch it, then pause and draw back. At those times, she was quick to offer a distraction – the state of the garden and how badly the grass was coming along, a faulty gutter, a stain. These ploys worked, because everything, now, was an extension of Todd. He saw his self-worth in the row of shining copper pots hanging at meticulous intervals on the rack above the pale blue Aga, as much as in the worth of his company or the number of times he was asked to appear on TV to talk about the digital economy; in the size of the alliums that bloomed in early spring along the low front wall, and the success of the shade of grey he had chosen from the paint chart.

His interest in these things wasn't creative. He cared nothing for the process, for growing or making, only for the perfection of the result.

'Good,' he said now. 'Who's coming?'

'It's for Natasha. She's just moved back to Dublin. I thought it would be nice to invite Martin, Katherine, Dermot, maybe Julie and her new boyfriend – the old guard, basically, and sort of reintroduce her. She's been gone so long, it's almost like she needs to start over. Like we all do.'

'Right.' Then, 'Are you sure that's a good idea?'

'Why wouldn't it be?' She sat up straighter, sleep banished.

'Well . . .' He paused. 'Just that it might underline how much your life has moved on, while hers hasn't. And she might not appreciate that.'

'I don't know what you mean.' But she did. She just wanted to hear him say it.

'Look, you're married, you have a baby, a house. You're settled. Established.' The word gave him a pleasant feeling; she could hear it in his voice, the way he rolled it round in his mouth. 'And she isn't.'

'She's very successful,' Jennifer allowed herself to play the other side for a moment.

'I agree she's done well. Far better than I would have expected. But really, what does she have? A job. Not much else.' Did he sound pleased? Jennifer wondered. And if so, was it the same way in which he enjoyed everyone's small failures, because they highlighted the relentless tramp of his own successes, or was it, with Natasha, more? And, if so, was that on Jennifer's behalf, or his own?

With Todd, she had discovered, nearly everything came back to him. She had once heard him say, 'I'm proud of you', to Martin, recently promoted, reaching a hand out to squeeze Martin's arm. The way in which Martin had recoiled and clenched his teeth over the idea of Todd being someone who had the right to be proud of him, had nearly made her laugh out loud.

Now, her head began to ache and she was tired again, with a gritty feeling behind her eyes, a thin layer of sandpaper between eyeball and socket that grated as though it lay between her and the world around her, and was too familiar. She snuck a look at the small brass clock on her bedside table. It would be time to get Rosie up in just a few hours.

'And Nancy,' she said. 'She'll have to come too. I suspect she's half the reason Natasha is moving back.'

'How so?'

'To keep an eye on her, or at least have a better look at her, close up.'

'Why?'

'I'm not really sure. I haven't seen Nancy in ages, but from a few things Natasha has said, I think she's worried. But you've seen her, haven't you? She does some work with the company, right?'

'A bit. I don't really see her. It isn't my side of things.' He rubbed his eyes, looking, she thought, like a sleepy lion. Where her own hair, beneath the careful mask of blonde, had faded to a peppery ginger, his still spun lights and golden depths. 'Are you looking forward to Natasha moving back?' he asked, with another of those leaps of intuition that sometimes unnerved her.

'I suppose so . . .' He waited, so that she had to continue. 'I mean, I am, but it's just that . . . well, I don't see how she's going to fit back into our lives.'

'As long as you don't feel you have to move your life up to make room for her.'

'But I do feel that.' She hadn't meant to say these things to him, knew how he might later return to them and in what different forms, but she was too tired to stay a step ahead. 'After all, I've known her practically forever.'

'Only since college.'

'It always feels as if I know her from school, because of the few months she was there. I know she doesn't think like that, but I do. I remember her arriving so clearly, and I feel bad that we didn't make more of an effort. I'm pretty certain she felt left out and a bit lonely, although she would never admit it.' And Jennifer would never admit how much she regretted being too scared, too uncertain of her own social position in the class, to have followed her heart and sought Natasha out.

'That's all ancient history.' Todd dismissed her reminisces with a wave of his hand. 'The point is, now she's coming back, and really there's no space for her in your life, not with Rosie, and she's going to expect there to be. You can't let that happen.'

She knew he was capable of going on and on about it, of extracting commitments and promises from her, so she tried to distract him, leaned forward and cupped his face in her hands. 'Do you want to, you know, quickly . . .?'

He looked at her for a moment and she tried to smile into his eyes; smile an invitation she didn't feel, a seduction she couldn't remember.

'No, thanks. I'm tired.' He stood up then, releasing the bedclothes so that she was able to pull them up over her shoulders, hiding the flush of shame that tinged the edges of her relief. At the door, he turned back, 'I need you to come to lunch on Friday. I'm meeting potential new investors, and I know they will like the idea of seeing more than what happens in the office. They want a sense of the home life of the person they choose to invest in, so you need to be ready for that. Jean has made a hair appointment for you that morning.'

CHAPTER 18

'So.'

'So.' Natasha looked uneasy, fiddling with coffee cup, phone, the strap of her bag. Jennifer remembered how much she disliked being at a disadvantage, disliked being the supplicant in any situation. Natasha liked to give – something she did generously, spontaneously, with much laughter: her time, her advice, clothes you might have admired. She wasn't good at receiving.

'You look very European,' Jennifer said, taking in the crisp white shirt, beautifully pressed grey trousers and pale-pink scarf. Of course there would be a scarf, she decided, and of course it would be knotted elegantly around Natasha's neck. Jennifer was wearing jeans and a T-shirt, neither of which fitted her very well. The T-shirt was too small, the jeans too big.

She smiled, trying to fill the gap between them with warmth and familiarity even as she carefully measured the changes to Natasha's face, marks made by time and life, and compared them with her own. The years suited Natasha, she decided. Where some beauty was fleeting, belonging more to an age than a person, Natasha's looks had grown, expanded and settled with her. She was stronger, more rounded than before, without the extreme slenderness of youth, but it worked for her. There was a flutter of faint lines around the corners of her eyes, and her skin was less translucent, Jennifer decided, disgusted at her own capacity to note those things, knowing too that there was a kind of magnetism that was in the very sinews of what Natasha was, her DNA, so that even when she didn't look great, she still drew eyes and attention in a way that she, Jennifer, did not.

'So. You're back.'

'I'm back,' Natasha agreed, the words flat and final.

'And what's it like?'

'It's funny.' Natasha wrinkled her nose. 'It's strange, and completely familiar. Half of me thinks I've never been away, that I dreamed all those years in Brussels, and that actually all I've done is move from my mother's house into my new apartment. The city feels smaller, like my feet might stick out the end of it into the sea. But I'm sure that will pass.' The duck of her head told Jennifer that she wasn't sure at all.

'What are you back here to do?'

Natasha's eyes flickered, meeting Jennifer's, then darting past them. 'The company has expanded the Dublin office. They say it's "strategically interesting", and I am now head of my side of it – all the support and admin stuff. So there's a bunch of analysts, who are mostly arrogant, spoiled children, and our job is to keep them that way so that they can carry on chucking toys around and sometimes making money.'

'Right,' said Jennifer, wondering what part of any of the things she knew about Natasha fitted her for such a career. 'And do you like it?'

'I like that they like me,' Natasha admitted. 'It's not my dream job. Never was. But . . . you know.' She shrugged. 'The money's good, I get to travel, I get my own PA to do the boring bits, and it's nice that they've basically given me my own office. Although I now have to set it up, so it's a bit of a poisoned chalice.' She smiled, deflecting attention from the truth of what she said.

'Right. Nice, though.' What might it be like, Jennifer wondered, to inhabit that brisk world? Where decisions were made and orders given, where Natasha, decisive and charming, must excel if she had been given a whole office of her own? And indeed, she was extremely effective, always had been. 'It comes of always making decisions for two of us, me and Nancy,' she had once explained. 'Of choosing what we did and where we went, which strange dogs you could pat and which we'd better leave alone. Nancy wouldn't decide, so I did.'

'What about you? Are you still thinking of going back to college?' Natasha asked now, with a brush of awkwardness that Jennifer recognised. It was the way people usually spoke to her about her lost years. Her lost baby.

Natasha, though, was better than most. She reached across the table now and grabbed Jennifer's hand abruptly, held it tightly.

'Jen,' she said, fast, 'I know you had a really, really bad time of it. Even though you never said a thing, and I'm sorry I wasn't here more. It wasn't a great time for me either' – she paused, mouth twitching slightly, then hurried on – 'but I wish I could have been more help.'

'There wasn't anything you could have done,' Jennifer said.

'No, but I could have sat with you in silence, or talked to you about the weather, or gone for walks, or whatever you wanted to do. And it wouldn't have been any good to you at all, I know that, but at least you would have known you weren't alone. Anyway, that's all hopeless and feeble, but I'm back now.'

'And I'm glad you're back. And it isn't hopeless, or feeble.'

'So, your thesis . . . will you ever go back to it?'

'I doubt it. It's been too long. And the bit of it I did is like a half-forgotten memory now. I haven't thought about it in years.' She tried to pretend there was casual indifference to communicate, in the way she sat, the way she picked up her cup and took a sip. But there wasn't.

Because it wasn't true. Painfully, piercingly, it wasn't true. Underneath the anxious pattern of her days, with their taut schedules and clinging domestic demands, it was an idea that wouldn't let her go; the fantasy that she could step back into the academic world, and that it would accept her as its own. Trust Natasha to spot that.

Maybe because of her years of fog and loss, those days of lectures and study shone brighter than anything else in Jennifer's life, except for Rosie. Freesia would forever mean exam time, she knew. Bonfires and the crunch of leaves underfoot would always make her think of the excitement of a new year. It was regret far more biting than simple nostalgia, sharpened by the so-conspicuous lack of any purpose or achievement beyond motherhood.

She had loved going back after the holidays in those days, loved the resumption of certainties that came with timetables, bells and days broken into forty-five minute periods. The orthodoxies of study, the camaraderie and jostling of groups with similar purpose and momentum. She missed it, in a way that dimly told her how much she had lost in life, and even though she knew Rosie was her purpose now. But Rosie would grow up – *was* growing almost visibly, like a stop-motion animation – and what then?

The best is now behind me. The thought haunted Jennifer, trailing her like a wet sleeve. It came to her unbidden, unwanted. As she walked home from the shops, pushing Rosie in her buggy, weighed down with bags full of food she had no interest in eating, wine she knew she would drink too much of. *The best is now behind me*. At such times, she tried to walk out of step with the words, away from them, feeling in them the betrayal of her daughter and herself. She tried to deny the significance of the phrase, make it just a collection of sounds that had put themselves together and stuck that way, but she knew that they beat out the same steady rhythm as the rest of her. *The best is now behind me.*

At first, she had agreed with Todd when he'd suggested she give up work, stay home and mind her child. It was what she'd wanted too, and had enjoyed a vision of the three of them doing family things together, in harmony. But Todd had never meant to be a continuous part of that vision. From the start, his appearances had been non-committal, irregular, brief, dictated by the rhythm of his working life, not the needs of his wife or daughter. When Jennifer had complained, or suggested something else, he had brushed her off. She was, he'd reminded her, lucky to have Rosie, to have money and the opportunity to stay at home with her, the way so many mothers wanted to and couldn't, so that Jennifer had felt guilty. And desperate. The years stretched ahead of her – Todd wanted a nanny, for status she suspected, as well as a wife at home, until Rosie started school, by which time Jennifer would be thirty-five. And useless. The idea filled her with panic, and the illusion of an alternative – the fantasy that she could do something different – had scared her. And so she had shut the door more firmly than ever.

'It was never much of a thesis anyway.'

'That's not true.' Natasha sounded indignant. 'I remember you telling me that your supervisor loved it, that he said you should think of it as a book.'

'I'm sure I exaggerated.' Jennifer didn't know quite why she was so keen to bat the idea away, only that she couldn't bear to let it build between them, knowing well Natasha's capacity for taking idle dreams and talking them into projects, possibilities; things that required action but that might, after all, succeed and become what you had hoped for. And how difficult that could be.

There was a pause that embarrassed Jennifer, because of the way it spoke of distance and awkwardness still between them, of having to reach far to find conversation and consider words carefully before they were said. Perhaps it was just the jolt of the unusual, she thought. And they could still find their way back to ease and intimacy.

'You know Martin is having a dinner for you on Saturday?' she blurted out. She had rung Martin that morning, having woken to find her plans tattered by the acid of doubt – in her ability and intentions – that had come to her after the conversation with Todd. Martin, bless him, had immediately said yes.

'I know. And he picked me up from the airport. Can't wait. Isn't it sweet of him?' The warmth of Natasha's voice made Jennifer miserable that she hadn't, after all, stuck to her plan. That she wasn't the one hosting the dinner.

'He's says he'll cook *osso buco*,' Natasha continued, 'and that he's inviting "everyone". God knows who that means any more. Nancy can't come, although he was sweet to say he would invite her when they hardly know each other.'

Saying Nancy's name had the same magic effect it ever did for Natasha, adding warmth to her voice, but Jennifer didn't ask how she was. She could see Natasha starting to fidget with her phone. Both their cups were empty and the untouched ham and cheese croissant that lay between them was now cold and greasy, so that she knew neither of them would pick it up. Outside, a seagull attacked a piece of bread with beady-eyed ferocity. Would they really leave each other without having done more than ripple the surface of their friendship?

But Natasha ducked her head under the table, fumbling with her bag. 'Here, I got this for Rosie.' She pushed a beautifully wrapped box across the table, pale-pink ribbons fluttering over the name of a famously expensive shop. 'I'm afraid Europeans like to dress babies in the fashion of little English aristocrats, so it's rather frilly and looks as if you'd need a dedicated nanny to starch and iron it.'

'Lovely. She's so fat now, she'll look like a little piglet in a wedding dress.'

Natasha burst out laughing and Jennifer thought then how she couldn't have said that to anyone else, wouldn't have dared.

'How is motherhood?' Natasha asked.

'Wonderful,' Jennifer said, as she always did, then added, as she usually never did, not even to her mother, 'and exhausting and frustrating and mostly I'm afraid that I'm doing it all wrong and she'll grow up and hate me.'

'No one could hate you. She'll grow up and realise she's the luckiest kid alive.'

'I'm so glad you're back,' Jennifer said then, knowing it was true, even as she wondered how they had come to this place of carefulness, where they couldn't quite speak what was in them, could only scatter clues like a trail of breadcrumbs.

'I'm glad too.' Natasha smiled. A proper smile, and her eyes held Jennifer's. 'I must go, I have so much to do. An office to set up, an apartment to move into.'

'Of course, me too,' Jennifer said promptly. 'I need to collect Rosie, and get dinner . . .' She trailed off, embarrassed at the contrast in their afternoons.

'Can you meet for lunch tomorrow?' Natasha wanted to know. 'Or come and see the apartment.'

'I can't really,' Jennifer said. 'I don't have any one to mind Rosie . . .'

'Oh, right. You could bring her . . .' But she sounded hesitant, so that Jennifer felt suddenly cross, and wished she hadn't said she was glad first.

Later, she wondered why she hadn't said she had to get her hair done, and shown Natasha that she had things in her life that needed good hair, not just baby things. Was it because Jean had made the appointment?

Jean was the skinny Asian girl who worked for Todd, 'Jean-of-all-trades', as he called her. She was something between personal assistant, office manager and geisha. She was fucking Todd, Jennifer was certain of it. Knew it from the way Jean spoke to her, the edge of familiarity that folded down the corners of their conversations, and from the sly amusement with which she approached the small personal tasks Todd delegated to her – Jennifer's hair appointments, facials, manicures, scheduled at regular intervals and paid for, Jennifer suspected, by the company. Jean should have resented these, any normal employee would have, and yet she seemed not to. Seemed even to embrace them, so that Jennifer could only imagine that she enjoyed an illicit feeling of familiarity with the texture of Jennifer's life.

Mostly, Jennifer knew it because of the way Todd behaved when she and Jean were both in his orbit together. 'You look wrecked,' he had said suddenly one afternoon recently, lifting his head from the newspaper in front of him and giving her a hard, appraising stare, like an art dealer in front of a painting of uncertain origin.

She had met him in his office for lunch, and had waited for ten minutes while he'd finished a call. Sitting in the next room while Jean had tapped at a keyboard beside her, watching him through the glass, she had seen uneasiness in his shoulders, in the way he'd hunched over the phone, scribbling on the pad in front of him and had darted glances between the two of them.

Later, when his uneasiness had turned to anger, she had been certain.

'It's just the light.' She had tried to laugh off his barb. 'Winter sun. So unforgiving.'

'You're thirty,' he'd snapped. 'Not fifty.'

Deciding not to confront him, Jennifer had simply said, 'I must be tired.'

'Then get more sleep. Shape up,' he'd said irritably, ducking his head again to the paper.

Jennifer had fought back her retort – that it was *their* daughter who was keeping her awake, in nightly screaming sessions that flayed her, stripping off layers of skin like clingfilm. That it was Todd who had condemned them to these sessions, with his mania for the routine he had chosen. 'She needs to learn,' he'd said, the conviction of the successful man making his words harder, surely, than he'd meant them to be. 'She needs a routine and to understand she won't be picked up every time she cries. Otherwise we'll have no peace.'

'We didn't have a baby for peace,' Jennifer had wanted to scream at him. But she didn't. She'd kept that cry inside her, along with the other things she hadn't said and all the things she hadn't done. And she had put her knowledge of Jean there too, believing that she would eventually work out what to do with it all.

She didn't really care about Jean – not as much as she should. Jean was not the first, and so the power to wound wasn't hers. It had dwindled in the procession that had gone before her. Always girls he worked with, so that Jennifer understood that it was a mechanical matter – they were there, he was there – rather than great passion. And she had allowed that to comfort her. These things did not, she decided, trouble the heart of his life with her and Rosie.

One day, she thought, she would confront him. Some day when his answer mattered more than it did now, and when she was strong enough to have her own answers to his answer. For the moment, she could only follow the same path she had travelled since the miscarriage, a path she couldn't see and could only pursue by putting one foot directly in front of the other, by breaking down her life into a series of small tasks: eat, change nappy, make food, go out . . . It was passive and subdued and meek, but it was the best she could do.

CHAPTER 19

Natasha stuck to her lines about being 'glad to be back and, yes, it is a bit strange but exciting too', for as long as she could but, within days, she was worn out with the effort of forcing cheerful enthusiasm and could no longer remember why she had agreed to return.

None of it felt familiar or comforting. There were new buildings everywhere she looked, new colours, new textures. The city even had a new sound – a busy, complacent roar of cars and cafés, faster transport and more shops. The old city, her city, was buried as if someone had scrubbed it out, badly, and drawn something new on top so that bits of the old picture still poked out but could not reach through to assert themselves.

People looked different and sounded different: rich and rude. And Natasha didn't know why she minded so much, except that the bits of herself that she had left behind seemed to have been rubbed out too.

Her apartment was across the road from her new office and was dominated by a wall of hostile green glass that reared up from the pavement as if it were trying to work loose from a trap. Inside, it felt unstable, too tall, slapped around by wind on all sides. The furniture was smugly contemporary.

'As if "contemporary" was a thing, and not just an absence of things,' she had complained to Martin. 'By which I mean an absence of any style, or wit, or imagination, so that all that's left is something so bland that it will blend with anything. If it was a blood group, it would be O-negative, the universal donor.' She was trying to be funny and sarcastic, to distract from the uneasy feeling that had settled across her, that she had made a mistake. Because for all that she had meant it when she told Jennifer that it was almost like she had never been away, there was another part of her that was already preparing to leave, a nagging feeling that it was time to go that tugged at her.

'Ignore the furniture. Look out the window,' Martin had said, pointing at the black water rippling like an oil slick below them. Natasha shuddered and pulled the blinds.

'I suppose it'll be nice by day,' she'd said. 'But imagine having to look at your own office all the time. I won't ever be able to call in sick. They could probably take my temperature from here.'

'You're the boss, you can do what you want,' he said, in a way that made her feel better, as if she was something after all. As if being the boss mattered.

Martin was the only one who seemed to feel that. Or who seemed truly glad at her return. 'About time too,' he had roared at the airport, crushing her in a swift, hard hug. 'You're at least five years late,' so that Natasha had felt tears prickle, hot and uncomfortable.

Her mother, when she'd phoned to say she had arrived, had said the same thing, but with a twist of sly aggression that had made Natasha think she had been right to delay the meeting for a couple of days.

'You are back,' her mother had said on the phone. 'Good. I think it is time.' She had said it with satisfaction, as if Natasha had been malingering.

And now Natasha was on her way – home, she supposed – although it felt more as if she was going to a terrifying party, something social and uncomfortable, where she would be judged and slyly criticised. She thought of all the songs and poems she knew about home, that tender concept that held itself out to people across continents and decades, when their lives were hard and terrible and the quiet joy it must be to them – thought of 'Sweet Home Alabama', and Robert Frost with his verdict that home was the place that, when you had to go there, they had to take you in – and then thought of her own home that was none of those things.

She looked down at her dress, neat and grey with white piping, and polished shoes, wishing she hadn't dressed so formally. What would Nancy be wearing, she wondered, for a dinner that should be casual, but couldn't be? She had chosen an expensive bottle of Spanish wine to bring with her, hoping the compliment would seem graceful, but now she wondered if bringing wine at all just made her seem more of an outsider.

At the garden gate, she paused, looking up at the house – the six stone steps up to the black door with the heavy brass knocker – and thought how very firmly shut it was. There were no lights in the front – this didn't surprise her, the rooms they used in the evening were at the back of the house – but the resistance of the façade bothered her. It looked indifferent, even hostile, as if it didn't recognise her.

There was no sign of welcome, no slight unbending or invitation. And yet, despite the forbidding exterior, and in the face of everything she knew to be true, Natasha couldn't stop herself from imagining that her father was inside, in the high-backed leather chair, reading, waiting for her visit. She imagined him standing up briskly when the doorbell went, calling, 'I'll get it', and walking quickly to the door, ready to fling it wide and pull her into a rough hug. Imagined herself walking into the house, that would smell of him – his shaving foam and soap, of newspapers and coffee cups left unattended on them, of old books and the yellow linseed oil he used for his golf clubs – and beginning to tell him everything she had been doing.

Her heart began to thump, a heavy tattoo of anticipation around what she would and would not find behind that door.

Her mother answered after the first ring, putting a hand out to Natasha and pulling her close for a kiss that managed to be both warm and formal. The embrace that went with it was brief.

'Nataasha.' Her mother smiled at her. If she felt the same awkwardness that Natasha did, she was much better at not showing it. 'Come in. Welcome.' Fury at being welcomed into her own home, like a stranger, like a junior diplomat at a formal reception, gripped Natasha, but she sidestepped it.

Maria took the wine without looking at it and Natasha suspected it would be put away immediately with whatever other bottles had been brought over the years and received in this way. She knew no one would ever realise she had chosen.

The house smelled of lilies – a giant bowl of them stood on the mahogany sideboard by the front door – and furniture polish.

'Is Nancy here?' she asked as they made their way down the hall. Everything looked the same, she noticed, but did not feel the same.

'She will be here soon.' Her mother tried to show her into the sitting room, saying 'we will eat soon', but Natasha refused. That, at least, she would not do.

'I'll come to the kitchen with you,' she said. 'Maybe I can help?'

'It is all done,' Maria said, but she shrugged and let Natasha follow her.

Where the rest of the house was the same, the kitchen was different. New. The old cream presses had been replaced by much smarter versions, in a pale blue-green and there were new tiles on the floor, ivory-coloured and very shiny.

'Goodness, this is lovely,' Natasha said, admiring the mega-watt extractor fan, the way cupboards had been rearranged at head height and a central island with high stools had replaced the old wooden table. 'It's much better. When did this happen?'

Her mother seemed relieved. 'Last year. You are sure that you like?' She waited, expectant.

'I like,' Natasha said firmly.

Clearly reassured, her mother began to tell her about more changes – a new skylight put in upstairs, the door of the bathroom, the one that used to stick when it got cold, and how she had changed it – and Natasha listened, imagining the difference each alteration had made to the house she had known, wondering would her mother offer to let her go upstairs and see. It was, she decided, as good a conversation as any.

Nancy arrived then, through the kitchen door so that Natasha saw her pushing her bike in through the garden gate and leaning it impatiently against the wall. She burst in – no bottles of wine for her, Natasha noticed. And she was wearing jeans and a flowered blouse that was pretty but so casual that Natasha felt stupid in her grey dress. Nancy kissed their mother casually, then turned to Natasha.

'Look at you. As prodigal a daughter as ever I did see.' She gave her a hug, complimented her hair and dress, then sat up on a high stool at right angles to Natasha. 'Lucky you're here,' she said.

'Why?' Natasha wondered was something up. 'Is everything OK?'

She knew she had asked too quickly. Knew it even more when Nancy said coolly: 'For your sake. I'd say you were weeks away from turning into one of those Euro-clones, with a khaki-coloured Puffa jacket and terrible flat shoes with gold buckles.'

In fact, Nancy was clearly well. Properly well. Natasha could see it immediately. Her voice was steady, without the warning note of shattered glass that had cut through it in the bad times. Her fingers were steady too – no telltale delicate tremor. She looked, Natasha thought, substantial, not that see-through feyness that hinted at sleepless nights and a feverish inquisition of herself. She said sternly to Natasha, 'It's great you're back, but don't think I'm going to help you move in and find your feet. I'm too busy.'

'I don't,' Natasha insisted. 'It's just lovely to know that we can see each other whenever we want.'

'Not whenever,' Nancy said. 'Only when it's convenient', so that Natasha felt like a cold caller.

'Of course,' she said stiffly. 'For both of us. I'll be busy too.'

Nancy, she knew, was busy. Was, to Natasha's secret surprise, successful. She had always assumed that she would be the one to make her mark, because of the early years of being braver, louder, but Nancy had found, or made, a role for herself, one at which, it seemed, she might excel.

'I turn companies into stories that people can understand', was how she explained it. 'People on the outside, but also people who work for the company, because often they haven't really got a clue what's going on there either. It's about taking the gibberish they come up with – awful stuff about "reaching out" and "shifting paradigms" – and turning it back into English, with a story, a quest even, to go with it.' Natasha, who was surrounded by people speaking in exactly those phrases, so that sometimes she wanted to scream 'what are you *on about*?' at them, could see how useful this might be, and how very good at it Nancy – with her gift for seeing stories everywhere and an obsessive need to tell them to herself – must be.

'We can eat,' Maria said, with a dish of baked chicory in her hands.

'We're not eating in the dining room, are we?' Nancy asked, looking around, noting the lack of cutlery.

'I thought it would be nice,' Maria said.

'Oh God, no. Let's eat here as usual,' Nancy said jumping down from her stool. 'I'll go get the stuff.'

Natasha wondered was Nancy doing this for her, to make it seem less as if she was a guest, someone to be managed carefully and treated politely, or was it to show her own ongoing familiarity with a house that was now almost strange to Natasha.

Dinner was roast duck, with the baked chicory and spinach done in butter and garlic. They talked about Natasha's job, the few lectures Maria had given at the Spanish Cultural Institute, whether Maria would get a cat. It was quiet, almost cosy, with the kitchen lighting subtly dimmed so that Natasha felt at ease, not under interrogation. Dessert was her favourite, a chocolate mousse laced with rum, and she wondered had her mother made it for her, or was it simply a happy accident, the roulette wheel of childhood recipes stopped in her favour.

'Nancy made it,' her mother said, when Natasha praised the mousse.

'To your recipe,' Nancy said.

'*No importa*,' Maria insisted, '*lo hiciste*,' and Nancy said something back that Natasha didn't understand but that made them both smile, so that Natasha felt left out and immensely conscious of the years, the many misunderstandings and failures between them. Failures of sympathy, of understanding, of kindness; a river full of submerged crocodile mouths, ready to rise and snap.

She cast around for conversation, something they could all talk about safely, felt relief when Nancy said, 'Oh, by the way, I got a new client.' But her relief then turned sour when Nancy carried on to say that the client was Todd.

'I'm doing some work for his company. One of his companies, I should say,' she amended. 'He has a couple now, related but separate.'

'Why him?' Natasha asked sharply. The unexpected introduction of his name had thrown her.

'Because he asked me. Because he's paying me. Because that's what I do.' Nancy, clearly, was irritated. 'He says I'm worth my weight in gold and that the work I've done so far has increased the value of the company.' She sounded smug. 'He's talking about starting something else, the two of us together, and giving me shares. He says that together we'll conquer the world.' She laughed, a hint of triumph.

'Seriously?' Natasha was floundering, unable to take in the picture Nancy was offering her.

'Well, ish,' Nancy back-tracked suddenly. 'He did once say that. Actually, I don't much see him. I don't work directly with him. He's too busy and grand.'

'What does John say about it?'

'What should John say?' Nancy was defensive. 'It's not his business who I work with.'

'Nancy, Todd's not a good person. I know it's a job, but try not to have too much to do with him.' The note of distress was plain to hear, at least to Natasha. But Nancy seemed not to catch it.

'But he's Jennifer's husband, and she's practically your best friend.'

'That's partly how I know he's not a good person.' She would never tell Nancy how she really knew.

'You know what they call Jennifer in the office?' Nancy veered off on a deliberate tangent.

'What?' Natasha felt the sly twist of disloyalty as she said it.

'The Straw Lady.'

'Why?'

'The way she looks. That stiff blonde helmet of hair. And the fact that she almost doesn't exist – like a Straw Man, you know.'

'That's horrible!'

'I suppose it is but, honestly, the way she drifts around, rigid and uneasy; that ghastly fake smile like she's biting glass. She's changed so much.'

'We all have.'

'Not like that.' Nancy said it with conviction. 'I certainly haven't.' She sounded complacent.

'I think she's unhappy,' Natasha said. 'Anyway, it's still horrible.

And if Todd employs the kind of people who would say that, who would feel that they have the liberty to say that, about his wife, the mother of his daughter, then that proves he really isn't a good person.' But Nancy wouldn't see it that way.

'"*A good person*",' Nancy mocked her. 'What does that even mean?' She was petulant now, as if she thought Natasha might be trying to take away something new and shiny that she wanted to keep. 'Natasha, you can be completely irritating, you know that? You can't give me a good reason. You just don't like him because he doesn't suck up to you the way all your other friends do.'

Natasha recalled the sudden defiance of which Nancy had always been capable. The veil of stubbornness she would lower over herself and the shut-lipped refusal to change her mind. As a child she had sometimes become so locked into her own cycle of 'No' that she had ended up terrified by the inflexibility of the limits she had set herself, screaming until she fell asleep, there on the floor of whatever corner she had barricaded herself into. At such times, it had been Natasha, not their parents, who was best at finding a door through which she could pass, helping her step outside the tightly woven, terrifying prison of her own defiance. She had always done it with soothing agreement first, as much as she could muster, before showing an escape hatch. So she tried that now, ignoring the barb about sucking up.

'I know, he's quite fascinating. All that energy and ambition. And he's smart and charming and can be really good fun. But, Nancy, he can be a creep too. You have to trust me on that.'

Nancy made a face, then turned away from Natasha to ask their mother something.

CHAPTER 20

'The *osso buco* is an experiment. I can't vouch for it.' Martin opened the door wearing a navy-and-white striped apron. He was the only one of Natasha's friends who seemed to know how to cook, apart from herself, and she didn't much bother.

'So this is the new house?' She said it airily, determined that he shouldn't know that she had stood at the bottom of the front garden for long moments, admiring the pretty red brick and the way wisteria trailed across the front, lit up by early evening sun so that the windows seemed to wink at her in a friendly way, and trying to compose herself as she wondered when – how – his life had surged so far ahead of hers. This was a country full of oak trees, she realised, where people put down deep, strong roots and stayed, moving only in order to root further. The world that she had been living in was a world of conifers, of shallow grip that clutched lightly at the soil, easily removed, easily planted elsewhere.

'It's far too fancy for a single man,' she joked now, secretly wondering how he, how anyone, could afford such a place.

'I may not be single forever,' he said, 'although I seem to be doing my best at that. And in the meantime, I have two appalling lodgers to help pay rent and make sure I don't enjoy myself too much.'

'Good, that'll stop you becoming one of the smug homeowners.' She laughed, adding, 'I'm early, I'm sorry. I don't have a whole lot to do on my days off yet, and my mother doesn't seem particularly grateful that I have made the great leap and come home. She told me she was busy today, so I didn't go and see her as I had planned.'

'I'm glad. That you're early, I mean, not about your mother.' Then, wisely, 'Give her a chance. People are funny when other people move back.'

'You're right,' she said thoughtfully. 'It isn't at all as I expected. It's like they don't trust me. As if I first insulted them by going, but now that I'm back, they're afraid I'm going to want to hang out of them. Even Jennifer . . . but never mind that. Who's coming?'

'Jennifer, Katherine and Dermot, Julie, Paul, some friends from work, in case you want to meet new people.' Work, for Martin, was the European headquarters of an international bank, where he clearly did very well.

'I hate new people,' she said. 'In Brussels, the rotation of troops was so constant that I long never to say the words "So where are you from?" to anyone ever again. Or hear someone launch into a cultural comparison beginning with "In my country, we . . .".' She laughed, then asked, 'What about Todd?', carefully busy with the camouflage of coat and bag. 'The coming man. Is he too grand to be seen with us now?'

'He's away, some kind of tech conference.'

'Right. And how is the *osso buco*?' she asked, relief making her giddy.

'Better than expected,' he answered. 'Things looked bad a few hours ago – a kind of orange fat appeared over the surface, like a kind of ectoplasm, as if the pot was haunted by my housemates' kebabs. I thought I'd have to abandon the dish. But I scraped it off and that seems to have worked.'

'Possibly too much information.' Natasha smiled. 'But I hope you kept the fat. You could put it in a bowl and serve it to anyone who gets really annoying. Now, what have you done with the housemates?'

'Sent them off for the night.'

'Like cats, put outside the back door.'

'Exactly and, like cats, they're probably no further than the back wall, sitting, watching us, their tails twitching.'

She helped set the table in the cosy, terracotta-coloured kitchen that gave onto a terrace paved in old, yellowy brick with the small, trim garden beyond. She was surprised at how elaborate Martin's culinary preparations were. He had made starters – strips of chargrilled red and yellow pepper in a balsamic dressing and was now chopping parsley to sprinkle over it – and there seemed to be several side dishes on the go, to accompany the *osso buco*.

'Saffron risotto and gremolata,' he said when she asked. 'It's traditional.'

'Oh well, if it's traditional . . .' She laughed, then added, 'You don't do things by half, do you?'

'What's the point?' he answered. 'Then they're only half-done.'

'Fair enough,' she said, accepting a large glass of white wine and thinking of all the things she did by half, or even quarter, and wondering if that was the secret of Martin's success? Perhaps success was simply steady, logical progression, not the something elusive and leaping she had always thought it? A thing visited suddenly upon the fortunate and just as suddenly removed? If so, she could see it would be a sure attender on Martin's rather plodding but logical nature, that seemed purposeful but without any flash of secret brilliance. Maybe brilliance is actually a bad thing, she thought. A kind of handicap; something to be got over, not something to be wished for?

'How's the office coming along?' he asked.

'It's fine. I start properly on Monday but I went in yesterday for a bit, before dinner at my mother's, to do all the boring stuff, like meeting the team and reassuring them that I'm not a psychopath, or planning to fire them all. We've got enough desks and computers, and fancy coffee machines in the kitchen. Two new analysts are starting on Monday, and that's it really.'

'Have you met them?'

'Not yet.'

'Will you enjoy it?' he asked, whisking together oil and some kind of vinegar with herbs in it.

'I guess so . . .'

'Meaning?'

'Meaning I do enjoy it. The pay is good, the days are busy, there's a good buzz when it's all going well and everyone is making money. But it's not what I ever saw myself doing, and I sometimes think I need a plan. You know, save for a couple of years then . . .'

'Then what?'

'Well, that's the problem. I don't know. Open a bookshop? Teach literacy to adults? Write a novel? I really have no idea.'

'You know that all you need to do is sit down and decide what you do actually want to do,' he said seriously. 'And you know I'll do that with you if you want?'

'I know,' Natasha squirmed a little. 'It's just not that easy.'

'It is,' he said with conviction. 'You could do anything you set your mind to. You are the brightest of the lot of us, Natasha. You always have been. At college, it was so obvious – you were like someone from a different planet.'

'Too much early promise,' she said sadly, but trying to sound casual. 'Which I never fulfilled. I may have had a bit of an edge at first, mainly because I was used to getting on with it and studying on my own, but by the time finals came round, you had all caught up and passed me out.'

'Not so,' he insisted. 'You didn't do as well as you should. But I'd say there were reasons for that.'

'I don't know about a reason, but I'm sure there's a rhyme,' she said quickly, desperate suddenly to switch him to another path, away from wherever it was he thought he was headed.

But he refused to be so quickly diverted.

'Very funny. Of course, you might have other reasons for taking time off in a few years. A family?'

'I doubt it.' But she said it too fast, with too much conviction, so that he looked surprised, as if he was going to question her. She changed tack quickly. 'So, Julie? I haven't seen her in at least a year. I had sort of forgotten about her. If it is possible to forget someone so determined to be the centre of the universe. But you seem quite friendly still?'

'Oh, she's not the worst. She rings me often enough,' he said. 'Now that she's going out with my boss.'

'He's not actually your boss, is he?'

'No, thank God. Just a more senior colleague.'

'A friend?'

'No.'

'That's good, otherwise you'd feel obliged to warn him.' She laughed.

'I wouldn't dare. Not after she so nearly got married – do you remember, Daniel, whose father owned the hotels?'

'That's right. They'd set a date and everything. What happened?'

'I'm not sure. He backed out, or they both did, but either way, she isn't about to let that happen again. Stuart was a dead man walking from the first date.' He laughed. 'Anyway, it's his lookout – he's older than us, been married once already. He should know what he's getting into. Although Julie is pretty good at keeping people guessing.'

'So she's the same old Julie?'

'She might be even worse these days,' Martin said, but he said it almost with affection, so that Natasha wondered again at the way in which proximity and longevity could force friendship in their wake. Was nothing else really required? No common ground of interests or personality? That, too, she supposed, was a consequence of deep roots. They tangled easily.

Julie, next to arrive, was indeed, if possible, worse. Perhaps because of the senior-colleague-boyfriend, perhaps just because it was the natural encroachment of her nature, she now behaved towards Martin with a kind of proprietorial familiarity that made Natasha ache to tip something thick, dark and sticky over the white lace top and skirt she was wearing. Treacle would do it, she thought viciously, or balsamic vinegar. Anything to wreck the affected purity of double doses of pristine white lace. She was carrying a boxy but undoubtedly very expensive handbag in a nasty shade of bottle green. It was the kind of thing that probably had a name, possibly even a passport. Overall she looked, to Natasha's eye, as if she were setting off for a royal garden party.

'Dress for the job you want, not the job you have, eh?' she teased, after Julie had offered her an unenthusiastic cheek to kiss and told her she was looking thin in a way that made it clear this wasn't to be taken as a compliment.

'What?' Julie looked confused.

'Nothing,' Natasha said, catching Martin's eye. He smiled, but downwards, in a way that suggested he was trying to hide the smile.

'Drink?' he asked.

'A glass of champagne if you have it,' Julie said.

'No champagne,' Martin said. 'Prosecco?'

'No. I don't drink Prosecco.' She laughed, a steely twinkle. 'Stu calls it "the lumpfish caviar" of wines.'

'Isn't he witty?' Natasha said. 'And original.' She kept her voice deliberately bland.

'I'll have a gin and tonic, thank you, Martin. With cucumber,' Julie said. She had clearly decided to ignore Natasha. 'I see you moved that painting,' she said firmly when Martin returned, glass in hand. 'Much better.' She made darting forays about the house then, coming back to pat Martin's arm and make little comments to show how very familiar she was with being there.

'That room is far nicer with curtains. I told you it would be,' and 'Oh, look, the alliums are up. I told you the aspect was perfect.'

Natasha wondered could she possibly have said such a thing, and since when had she become an expert in gardening? Soon she realised that Julie was now an expert, in her own eyes anyway, in anything that suited the new vision she had of herself. Homes, gardens, art, particularly the property market, were now all hers to pronounce upon.

'Stu and I are actively looking,' she said – as opposed to what, wondered Natasha, keeping their eyes closed and stabbing a map with a pin? – 'not around here, of course, although these houses are very sweet.' She smiled her gracious approval at Martin. 'But Stu prefers something with more Georgian proportions.' She laughed, as if 'Stu' and his delightfully eccentric foibles were a darling to be indulged.

Only then did Natasha notice the platinum band on her engagement finger with its three large princess-cut diamonds. They looked, she thought, the way she imagined the inside of Julie's mind – all hard surfaces and self-satisfied thrusting sparkle. And the ring looked like everyone else's. Every engagement ring that had been dangled before her eyes, and there were more every day, seemed identical in all but size. Some had hopeful little scraps of diamonds, others, like Julie's, were large enough to build into a supporting wall, but all were carefully modern and minimalist, lacking any kind of charm, set in platinum. Dull.

She thought of the beautiful ring her father had bought her mother, the soft reddish glow of the cluster of rubies in their old-gold filigree setting, and remembered the way the rubies caught the light, winking with a soft glow, like a candle in the window of a cottage. She remembered the cool, capable feeling of her mother's hands on her forehead when she had a temperature as a child, or stroking her hair when she couldn't sleep, and felt suddenly sad. She wished Jennifer would hurry up. Must she always be late?

Julie, by then, was questioning Martin, with deliberate intimacy, about what were clearly work things – 'Did the meeting go OK on Friday? I know Stu was concerned about it.' It was done with such a show of warmth that Natasha began to wonder: was it only for the sake of their shared knowledge of 'Stu', or could there be something else that prompted Julie's drive for such cosiness? She never used to be this nice to Martin, Natasha recalled, thinking back to Ibiza and how often Julie had rolled her eyes, silently inviting the rest of them to share her mockery, saying, 'You're so *sensible*, Martin', as if sensible were something despicable. Or 'Must you think about food all the time, Martin?' Back then, she was playing at being wasted, being daring, being wild. Now, she was playing at being grand.

She remembered how much Julie liked successful people. How quick she was to wash them over with all the cardinal virtues; as if being rich carried with it a natural entitlement to be presumed beautiful, intelligent, charming in the same way that others might assume that anyone who was blind, or lame, or disabled must also be brave, and patient, and good.

Well, Martin was all the good things already, but if Julie was forging intimacy with him so zealously, he must also now indeed be that very thing Natasha had suspected – properly successful. She sat silent, marvelling all over again at this place she had chosen to

211

come back to, where life was such a deeply competitive game, one publicly scored in acquisition and accumulation, until Julie began commenting flirtatiously on the preparations for dinner.

'What a beautifully set table, Martin. Hyacinths, how pretty! And what a lovely tablecloth. You're almost a gay man, Martin.' She laughed.

That was, finally, too much for Natasha.

'It's not the nineteen fifties, Julie,' she said. 'A "real" man doesn't have to drag home a bear carcass and live in it to prove himself, you know.'

'I never said he did.' Julie looked affronted.

'Not in so many words perhaps.'

'Oh, but Martin doesn't mind. He knows what I'm like.' She gave a little laugh. 'Don't you, Martin?'

Martin looked embarrassed, so that Natasha was glad when the doorbell went. He came back with Jennifer, Dermot and Katherine, and the awkwardness was swallowed up in a flurry of hellos, hugs and chatter. Bottles were handed over to Martin – 'It's cold but I'd say could do with another while in the fridge', 'open it now and it'll be perfect in half an hour' – and he reciprocated with requests for what they would drink – 'White wine, please', 'Whatever Julie's having, it looks delicious, but with lemon', 'Just water for now, I'm driving' – by which time the doorbell went again. Paul, followed by the work friends, so that it was many moments before Natasha got to do more than smile at Jennifer and hug her.

'You look well,' she said, although it wasn't strictly true. Jennifer had a cold sore starting at the corner of her mouth, and she looked tired. She dashed a hand under her eyes as Natasha spoke, as if she had a tic.

'Thanks, so do you.' Jennifer smiled at her. 'How is it all going?'

Natasha launched into her explanation of office life, feeling weary. Was she going to have this conversation forever? But she did her best, talking up the look of shock on the team's faces when she said she didn't expect them to have their phones on after 6 pm, and her 'team-building strategies'. 'I basically pretended to be Katharine Hepburn. Mid-period Katharine Hepburn. That's what I do when I don't have any better ideas,' she said. 'I become very grand indeed, and rather vague. It works, until they start asking me for specific instructions. Then I tell them they need to make their own decisions and that I am empowering them. That shuts them up pretty quick.' She carried on, deprecating wildly, although most of it was nonsense, and a large part of her wondered whether she should send herself up quite so much. Jennifer might actually believe that she had no idea what she was doing.

Katherine came close and listened too, laughing at the more outrageous arcs of Natasha's stories. Julie had gravitated towards the work friends and was using their natural good manners to spend longer than was fair talking about houses she'd seen and the compliments various estate agents had paid to her discernment. 'One of them told me I have a natural instinct for proportion,' she was saying. The work friends smiled patiently. Martin came in with two more bottles of Prosecco.

'Dinner in a minute,' he said. 'Who wants another drop of this first?'

'Actually,' Katherine said, flushing red and shifting a little on her feet, 'just before we sit down, I've got some news. I'm opening my own gallery – I'm done working for other people. I've found an amazing space, and I'm launching in just a few weeks.'

'I'm so happy for you,' Natasha said.

Then Julie came over, pushed past Natasha and grabbed Katherine's hand as if by rights.

'How exciting,' she gushed. 'And I have news of my own. Stu and I are engaged. We're getting married this time next year.'

213

'And you couldn't have saved the announcement for five more minutes?' Natasha asked.

'What?' Julie was honestly baffled, then ignored her. 'Jennifer, I need to talk to you about your interior designer. Whatever Stu and I buy, we will need to do work to it. I'm discovering that other people's ideas about "walk-in condition" simply aren't ours.' She flashed a look of steely triumph around at them. 'How did you find your person? She's done a good job, I must say – the photos in *Homes and Gardens* were lovely – but how was she to deal with?'

'I don't really know,' Jennifer admitted. 'I didn't have much to do with her. She and Todd decided things, and she did them, or supervised other people doing them. I left them all to it.'

'But you must have chosen materials?' Julie looked shocked. 'Tiles? Floorboards?'

'No.' Jennifer was embarrassed; Natasha could see it in the way she gripped the stem of her glass. 'I didn't see the point. Todd and the designer had so many ideas between them . . .'

'But what about putting your stamp on the house?' Julie asked, as if 'your stamp' were something sacred.

'I didn't much mind.'

'Well, *I* mind,' Julie announced, as if this must prove to all their satisfaction that she was the better person, then switched to flooding them with details of her wedding. 'I've already done so much research, on venues and dressmakers and wedding favours. Katherine, you must remember all these things from your own wedding. Isn't it fun? I've found the most stunning florist, just divine, does these bouquets that look exactly like they were picked in a meadow that very morning, but using hot-house varieties that last . . .'

Katherine looked first stunned, then a little alarmed. 'Well, I just used the local florist, who put some white roses into a bunch,' she said, stepping back, away from the intensity of Julie's onslaught, perhaps, too, unwilling to be reminded of her wedding.

Over dinner they talked about work, Katherine filling them in on the new gallery – 'It's tiny, but a great location, and I'm going to show work by new, young artists,' – while Paul told surprisingly funny stories about his life as a tabloid hack, for which, Natasha could see, his natural nosiness, coupled with a lack of emotional curiosity, fitted him perfectly.

They talked about Ibiza too, telling stories and asking many 'do you remembers?' that Natasha joined in with, reminding them of a trip to a mountain-top bar, and coming home in the dark, so drunk that the car had nearly fallen into a ravine – finding herself secretly shocked at the reckless way they had behaved. The work friends laughed dutifully, although she thought they seemed a bit shocked too.

Jennifer was quiet. With nothing obvious to contribute to the discussion beyond a few Ibiza reminiscences – no horrible boss stories, no anecdotes about professional triumph or humiliation – she barely seemed to be listening, her gaze turned inward and brooding. Natasha wondered was she thinking about her child; missing her perhaps, worrying about her. What must that be like? Was it the way she worried about Nancy? Or different?

'How is Todd?' Julie asked warmly. Clearly the magic cloak of success had fallen across him too, blotting out his more objectionable characteristics, Natasha thought, recalling Julie's once-upon-a-time annoyance at Todd's refusal to flatter her.

'He's good,' Jennifer said, starting a little. 'Working incredibly hard. I barely see him. What about Stu? He must work very hard too?'

'Of course he does,' Julie said sternly, as if Jennifer had accused her of complaining. 'It's what he has to do. This is the stage at which he has to consolidate everything he's done. Later, we'll have a chance to enjoy the success. Right now, my role is to support him.'

'She sounds like she's been reading a handbook for corporate wives,' Natasha whispered to Martin.

Julie must have heard her, or caught the sarcasm of her tone, because she turned then. 'So why are you back, Natasha?' She was careful to let a little bit of sarcasm drip onto "are", as if any reason Natasha might give was likely to be a lie.

'Because I missed you,' Natasha said sweetly, unwilling to go over the same ground – the office, the new team, the whatever – again. 'I couldn't keep away a second longer.'

'I must say, I never saw you working in finance,' Julie persisted.

'I didn't either.' Natasha was damned if she was going to admit to Julie that she was somewhat stranded in her career. 'But, you know, it's more interesting than the word makes it sound. I bet I can tell more about you from your financial choices than a psychologist could from an hour's session.'

'How so?' Julie sounded suspicious.

'The way people spend – and save – their money gives you huge insights into how they feel about themselves, their prospects, the world around them. That's how we predict things. It looks like we're analysing markets. Actually we're analysing people.'

'Give me some examples.' They were all listening now.

'OK. Well, the easiest is, do you have a pension?'

'Of course,' Julie said complacently.

'Right, well, it's pretty easy to extrapolate from that – you are someone who plans for the future, who believes in her ability to shape that future. You are considerate, not reckless. I would say, on balance, a pessimist rather than an optimist.'

'Realist,' Julie said.

'Maybe, but you're not leaving anything to chance, which means you're at the pessimistic end of realist.'

'Very clever, I'm sure,' Julie said.

'Natasha was always clever about psychology and motivation,' Martin said.

'Well, but everyone has a pension.' Julie was unwilling that praise should be let lie so easily.

'Trust me, they don't. The simple fact that you think that tells me even more about you,' Natasha said.

'Martin, you have a pension, right?' Julie was determined to be right.

'I do. But I also work for a bank. Which has taught me to be highly pessimistic, certainly about money. I'm almost not sure any more that it even exists.'

They all laughed, but Julie pursued her line. 'Katherine?'

'Yes, but my dad insisted I set it up. I probably wouldn't have.'

'Paul?'

'No, actually.' He looked embarrassed.

Julie pursed her lips, irritation that he had let her down rather than concern for his future.

'Jennifer?'

'I don't know. Todd does all that.' Jennifer looked even more embarrassed.

'You must have some idea,' Julie said.

'None.'

'Well, but you have the house, so you know you have some provision for the future.' That was Martin, trying to smooth things over.

'Actually, I think it's in some kind of trust. Or in the name of one of his companies, or something. I know it isn't straightforward. It's to pay less tax, I think.'

There was a silence, an awkward one, before Martin said, 'I'm sure he's done something very cunning,' and the talk moved on, to the latest financial scandal and what the fallout might be.

Natasha noticed that when Martin spoke, the work friends listened carefully to him, even deferred to his opinion, and that he spoke well, clearly and without exaggeration. Again, she was struck by how much they had all changed in ten years, but in such different ways. Some, like Martin, Julie, even Paul, seemed more themselves, a more definite outline and sure of what they wished to be. Others, herself and Jennifer, had blurred around the edges, bleeding into the world around them so it was hard to see who they were anymore. They both needed something to sharpen them up, bring them back into focus. She wished she could turn up the contrast, or whatever it was they did to photos, to concentrate both of them into something vibrant.

Jennifer looked almost ghostly these days, the blonde of her hair fading into the pallor of her skin as if she had been powdered. The rising-and-falling colour in her cheeks was gone, subdued beneath a thick layer of chalky foundation and what struck Natasha as a deliberate abstraction of her personality, as if she were metaphorically sitting on her hands, squashing herself down. Looking at her dusty features made Natasha think of the first shovelful of earth thrown across a coffin, and the way so little dirt could obscure so much. Only the smile was the same. Or almost. Even there, Natasha now saw a shadow, like tuberculosis on a lung.

She knew she looked better – the mirror told her that, men told her that – but the way Jennifer looked was the way she felt.

At least I don't have to live with him, Natasha thought then with a shudder. See him every day. Be subjected to him every day. She imagined Jennifer's house – a house that seemed to be universally greeted with admiration – as a cold and silent place, but with something moving in its depths. She took a slug of wine, wondering did she dare ask Martin for anything stronger.

Julie was holding forth again. 'It's stunning, simply stunning,' she said, about any number of perfectly ordinary things – the flowered wrap-dress Jennifer was wearing, the weekend she and 'Stu' had recently spent in Connemara, a dog her mother was thinking of buying. She waved her hands at them, flashing the huge diamonds

on her finger so that they gave the pleased glitter of financial approval
to everything she said.

Paul, beside Julie, listened in a way that suggested he was trying to
learn. The years since Ibiza had clearly forced him to accept that she
was never going to have him as a boyfriend, and so he had morphed
into, what? A familiar, Natasha decided, seeing how he backed her
up and cheered her on. A toad rather than a bat or a rat; a thing that
hopped after her, struggling to keep up, but with a concentrated
maliciousness that meant she would stop and wait for it at times.
Or perhaps a magpie, she decided later, listening to the competitive
jeering chatter as he and Julie outdid each other to be nasty about
various people they knew.

And still, after all these years, and despite their efforts to sound
knowledgeable and interested in politics, finance, books, in the end
they couldn't stay away from the same old litany, the comforting
recitation of names – friends from school, from college, from
'around' – who had married who, left whom, worked for who. Even
Jennifer, silent for so long by then, perked up, adding her nuggets
of information to the common store – 'They've just bought a house
down the road from ours', 'Someone told me she was having another
baby . . .'

Only Martin seemed uneasy, irritated by the ease with which those
well-worn paths were retrod, perhaps conscious that his workmates
couldn't slip into the same conjuring of people and places from the
past; that Natasha was fidgeting with a piece of bread, pinching it
into a pile of crumbs by the side of her plate.

Was it rudeness or smugness? she wondered. Did they realise
and not care? Or not realise? She couldn't make up her mind which
was worse.

Later, when most of the guests had left, Natasha wandered into
the garden where it was quiet. Something smelled sweet in the dark,

some flower that poured scent wastefully into the night where no passing pollinator would be spurred to usefulness by it. But maybe moths are pollinators, she thought, seeing a couple fluttering around the outdoor light. Maybe they did the job stealthily, under cover of night? But she couldn't imagine it.

They seemed so single-minded in comparison, say, with bees. Not for nothing was 'bumble' a way of describing the haphazard, clumsy way certain people went about things, she thought, thinking about the way bees seemed to just blunder from one flower to another, as if intoxicated by their smell and colour, unable to help themselves, buzzing happily with the joy of their work. Moths, with their silent whirl, seemed intent on their own destruction, caught in an addiction that gave them no pleasure, just the relief of a fixed purpose, a move towards light, any light, that could not be diverted.

Martin came out then, disturbing her reflections.

'I'm going soon,' she promised him. 'I must be the last.'

'Never with me,' he said, but without the edge of mock-gallantry that would have made it alright.

'That was a really fab party, Martin, thank you,' she said, to head him off. She was afraid of what he might say, what she might say in return. 'You always were good at entertaining, but you're even better now. And your house is perfect. I wish I lived somewhere this nice and knew I need never move again,' she said thoughtfully, the solemn darkness around her forcing her to be serious. 'It must be lovely to feel you have that security, that you're *settled*. Money behind you, a career in front of you. Respect. You're lucky. I don't mean that you've been lucky to get this, I know it's more than that,' she added hastily, 'just that you are lucky to be you. I wish I felt equally solid in my life,' she finished, feeling suddenly the chill of the dark night.

'If you ever wanted—' he began. But she cut him off.

'Martin, you know how much I like you, as a friend, but I don't think . . .'

'I said if you ever wanted. Don't answer now. Just think about it.' He said it firmly, with authority, and walked into the house, the light reaching out to surround him, welcome him, leaving Natasha invisible so that if he had looked back, he would have been unable to pick her out. He didn't look back. She could hear the voices of his housemates, returned, helping themselves to leftovers and wine with much loud approval.

CHAPTER 21

Showered and neatly dressed on her first day, Natasha swiped into the fishbowl office, cappuccino in one hand, bag in the other. She had banished the faint malaise that had greeted her that morning, a sharp prickle of uncertainty, back to wherever it lay and waited, and was looking forward to the day; to the chance to put forward a version of herself she always liked, because it was so uncomplicated – unshakable competence with a dash of charm and a hint of steel. Katharine Hepburn with the odd flash of Audrey. So easy. And effective.

She was deliberately early, to settle herself before anyone arrived. To pace and shape the space around herself so that it became hers, her ground on which to meet the new arrivals. But before she could compose herself fully, even as she was wondering why the lights were already on and could anything be done about the way they flickered, a body rose up from a chair, came towards her.

'Can I take something for you?' He reached a hand out for her bag, and she found herself handing it over, even as she wondered which of the two new guys this was – Maurice or Declan?

'Declan,' he said.

'Not Maurice then?'

'Not Maurice.'

'Natasha.' She swapped the cappuccino and held out her hand.

'I figured. Good to meet you.' He shook it well, brisk and hard. Had he spent time in America, she wondered, or just appropriated the twang and the confidence for his own ends? 'You sound English, but I bet you're not,' he said with a smile. His face was freckly and open, not handsome but appealing, with a corner of mischief somewhere that she liked.

'You're right, I'm not.' Let him work it out.

'Irish and French?'

'Irish and Spanish.'

'Damn! So close.'

'And yet so far. Only in this country would anyone think France and Spain were "so close".' She sounded wintry, and she knew it, but decided that was appropriate, even necessary, at this stage. Why was he here anyway, ambushing her in the pale morning sun? 'You're very early,' she said with a faint hint of accusation.

'I am. I like to be early. Life is too short for sleeping.' Normally Natasha hated people who said 'life is too short' for whatever it was they were going on about: too short to do a job you hate; too short for bearing grudges, stuffing mushrooms, whatever. Life, as far as she could see, was very long indeed, with plenty of time for all those things and more. But with Declan, she got the feeling he really meant it. There was an energy to him, a fizz, that didn't match with lazy mornings and endless flicks of the snooze button. 'So you've just joined?'

'I have. I was with Anderson O'Dowd in London until now.'

'Why move back?'

'A change of scene. A better job.' He shrugged. 'Sometimes, if you've started in a place, it's hard for others to accept a divergence in paths.' From which Natasha understood that, rightly or wrongly, he considered himself more dynamic than his co-workers, and therefore an object of resentment. From this, she would, later, put herself to puzzling out other aspects of his character: arrogance, possibly. Ambition, certainly. 'What about you? You're new too, or new here anyway.'

'New here. I've been working for Syndax for years, but based in Brussels. They offered me the chance to come back, take over the office here, expand it.'

'So it's the first day of school for both of us. I'm sure we can help each other adjust.'

And Natasha, who needed new friends because it was a new job, in a city that increasingly felt new too, dropped the frostiness.

'Let's start by road-testing the coffee machine,' she said.

Declan was younger than her by a couple of years, had been in London since his early twenties, and was just out of a relationship – 'We were together since college. She's a lovely girl, but we weren't connected any more. She's studying Montessori teaching and wants to buy a place and live together and plan a wedding, all that.' He made a dismissing motion with his hand. 'I don't. Not yet.' He said it with pride, as if braced to resist the pull of a rope-full of opposition with nothing on his side but the sense of his own rightness.

He was also, she soon discovered, clever at his job, quick and intuitive, with a grasp of figures that impressed her. 'I like things that do what I want and don't argue,' he said when she commented on this. 'That stay where I put them.'

He showed himself endlessly willing to help her – greeting her ideas with enthusiasm in the meetings with which the week seemed filled, cheering every suggestion she made and responding with alacrity to her directions, so that the rest of the team followed suit, and a transition that would have happened anyway, was made easier. Natasha found herself grateful for his back-up and her own speedy switch from newcomer to authority.

His was the kind of masculine presence that she understood and responded to, solid and unequivocal.

By the end of that first week, they had agreed to go for 'a quick drink after work' with the rest of the office. The quick drink became one more and then one more, so that they stayed on, alone together, after the others had left. They drank bottles of beer followed by tequila chasers in a bar that was deliberately, carefully sleazy – lit up by neon signs, with pinball machines decorated with cartoonish images of bikini-clad women – but full of clean-cut office workers.

'How are you finding being back?' she asked, genuinely curious, after the second tequila.

'I like it.' He clinked his glass against hers, downed it in one.

'Are your family pleased?'

'My mother has killed so many fatted calves, I'm worried about the national herd.'

Natasha laughed. 'You're the favourite, aren't you?' she asked.

'What makes you say that?'

'Just a feeling I get. The way you always assume everyone will be pleased to see you. The way everyone always is. And the fact that someone is clearly fussing over you – the well-ironed shirt, the smell of fabric softener. If it's not a girlfriend, I'm guessing mother.'

'Not bad.' He didn't confirm her guess, but he looked flattered. 'What about you? Is there a favourite in your family?'

'It used to be me.'

'And now?'

'And now it isn't.'

'What did you do?' He raised his eyebrows, ready, she suspected, to wink.

'Nothing. He died.'

'I'm sorry.' He looked as if he might really mean that.

'It's OK.' But it wasn't. Less and less every day. The squashing down didn't work any more. Running didn't work any more. Nothing worked. She had thought that coming home would make it easier to understand this thing, grief, that didn't go away and didn't get any less. That grew and spread so that it felt like the blood on Bluebeard's key, the key to the tiny room he told his bride not to go into. It had started as a spot, then, as she tried to scrub it off, spread and spread so that it covered everything.

'Complicated,' he said.

'I guess. All families are complicated.' But she didn't believe it. Not that they were as complicated as hers, anyway. Had her family always been so odd, and she had been too young, too much without comparison, to realise? Those years where her parents spoke but little to each other, while she and Nancy vied for their father's attention and approval. How had she not seen that their home was unlike the homes of the few friends she visited, where cohesion and harmony were things taken for granted, the disturbance of argument or bitter observation a deviation from a peaceful norm?

Nancy, she realised, must have understood this first. Or maybe she had just tired of the one-sided nature of the battle.

'Do you want to do a pill?'

She had been staring, unfocused, at her half-empty bottle of beer. His question cut across her abstraction.

'Huh?'

'Pills. Do you want one?' The music was louder now than when they had arrived, the clean-cut office workers more dishevelled. They were starting to pound the pinball machines more wildly; a couple of girls in pencil skirts were dancing.

'God, I haven't taken pills in years,' she said. But, 'why not?' was the thought through her mind. Everyone else she knew would be settling in for a cosy, domestic Friday night with their spouses, their houses, their babies upstairs or on the way. What else was she going to do? 'OK.'

'Great.'

She knew it was a mistake. Professionally, it was a very obvious mistake – one so glaring that it almost excused itself. But personally, it was foolish too. Declan was good fun, good at his job, exciting in a lurching, unpredictable kind of way. He was attractive, she could see that – his self-confidence and quick wit made sure of it – but he was also, for her, pointless and a distraction. For all the appeal of a new friend, what she really needed was to reconnect properly with her old friends. She didn't need to cheapen her work, or allow anyone in the office to have the kind of hold over her that she was granting him. She didn't want a boyfriend and, more than anything, she didn't need the complications of sex.

'Let's have one more quick drink here, then go on,' he said. 'There's another place I know, better than this. Open your mouth.'

She did as he told her, and he popped a pill into it in a quick, stealthy movement, then gave her his bottle of beer to wash it down, even though she had her own. She knew, as she took it, drank from it, swallowed the pill he had given her, that she was entering into a pact with him. That a deal had been struck, although she didn't know what, exactly, that deal was.

They went up to her apartment – she needed to change her shoes, it seemed churlish to make him wait downstairs, even though it also seemed foolish to invite him up so quickly – and he paced about, admiring the view, pulling books off the shelves and asking her did she really read that much, teasing her for the unpacked boxes everywhere, making himself at home on the chocolate-coloured leather sofa – 'Like sitting on a Labrador,' he said.

Then, they went to another bar, louder, smaller, as explosive as a night bus, where they stood close together as they drank, pressed up against each other. He made no effort to move or to make space, and neither did she.

The pill was doing its work, and Natasha began to regret saying yes. She had forgotten the disorientation, the sickening feeling of her heart thudding as her blood responded to the throb of music, the clatter and chatter around them, the pounding of his heart.

'It's OK,' he said, putting a hand on her bare arm. 'Give it a minute and it'll settle.' The jolt she felt when he touched her was so nearly physical, it took her by surprise. She felt suddenly like the Ugly Duckling seeing the swans for the first time – it wasn't the shock of their beauty, she realised, that had so awed the duckling, it was the simple shock of recognition: I am like you. You are like me.

Friends joined him – guys who spoke in loud voices about how much people were worth – 'Fifteen million, you can't argue with that' – and called each other 'good man' as they bought rounds of shots, the expensive kind, so that the barman had to reach high to get the bottles. They nudged Declan and grinned at him, inching their heads enquiringly towards Natasha so that he shook his, gently, discreetly.

Much later, he insisted on walking her home, and Natasha, by then unsteady, her hair flopping forward across her face, had to let him, but still knew enough, just, not to ask him up. To be grateful when he didn't suggest it.

'Will you be alright?' He leaned against the door as she fumbled with keys. He was chewing gum so that his jaw moved with an almost mesmerising evenness.

'Of course I will.' She worked hard to keep the words distinct and separate from each other.

'You're a blast,' he said then, kissing her cheek. 'See you later.'

Door open, sleepy, wasted, lonely, Natasha almost called him back, stopped herself only by an effort of will. Why not? she thought. Except that they didn't belong, and belonging was important.

CHAPTER 22

'Will you come to Todd's launch with me tonight?' Jennifer knew she sounded pathetic, and didn't care. And when Natasha said no, she pleaded shamelessly. 'I can't go on my own. Please?' So Natasha agreed, clearly reluctant and only because Jennifer had caught her on the hop, given her no time to invent an excuse. But Jennifer was too relieved to care.

'Try to be amusing,' Todd had said. 'Don't talk about books or the baby. No one wants to hear about that.'

Why did he make her go? she wondered. He rarely introduced her to anyone, expecting her to fend for herself and make 'interesting connections'. The people who worked for him mostly ignored her, and she never seemed to meet anyone he considered important, and yet he insisted on her being there. Once upon a time, she dimly recalled, she used to enjoy these nights – launch parties, receptions, openings; a chance to meet people, chat, amuse, be amused. Sometimes you would go on, she remembered; gather up a like-minded group and go for dinner or more drinks, gallantly refusing to think about work the next morning, telling yourself that you were seizing the day, and there would be time enough for early nights when you were old.

When had it all become so dreary? Was it getting pregnant that had taken the fun out of it? Or was it that Todd's ambitions had so quickly outpaced the kind of evening she had enjoyed? They had once enjoyed together?

For years now, as Todd had scaled up his expectations, she had spent most of her time at these things alone, chatting desperately to people on the periphery, those who, like her, didn't know anyone. Wives of colleagues or competitors, mostly, some pleasant, many as secretly bored by Jennifer as she was by them, but needing the social camouflage of conversation because to stand alone was even worse.

It would be great to have Natasha. Jennifer was surprised by how much, after all, she enjoyed having her back. She had forgotten what it was like to have a friend. A real friend, one who knew you, cared for you, carried with her the idea that what you said would be interesting, amusing. A friend such as Natasha, who saw the parts of you that no one else seemed to believe in any more.

That evening, Jennifer arrived alone – a bar so new and brash that the many layers of gold paint seemed scarcely dry, while the crystals tacked to every surface still winked wetly as if they would be soft to the touch, like turtle shells before the air has hardened them. The place was packed, with all the people whose opinions Todd cared for: journalists, heads of PR companies, successful business people, even a junior minister. For energy? Jennifer thought. Or was it enterprise?

The roar was that of a finely tuned engine – crowds of people excited to be in one another's company, all convinced that they were just one connection, one introduction, away from the big time. She grabbed a drink, something pale blue and heavily alcoholic, and made her way over to a knot of Todd's office staff. Jean gave her a small smile before turning away to a thin man who Jennifer recognised as one of the original investors. She still wondered why they had put up so much money. Was it because they understood and wanted in, or because they hadn't a clue, and were therefore afraid a rich ship might sail without them? Her impression of the grey men who constituted the fund was that they were simply gamblers, without any kind of flamboyance. They didn't really 'believe' the way Todd wanted them to believe; they were hedging their bets in case he was everything he said he was. In case 'new media' was what he said it was. If it wasn't, they would walk away from him as if they had just dropped something into a bin.

Someone introduced her to a girl whose name sounded like Moppet but surely couldn't have been, Jennifer thought. The girl proudly explained that she was the new receptionist and admin assistant, then said, 'Oh my goodness', and put her hands up to her mouth, squeaking, 'I'm so excited to meet you', through them when Jennifer said she was Todd's wife.

Clearly no one has told her how little I count, Jennifer thought wryly, scanning the crowd for Natasha.

'What's it like living with him?' the girl asked.

'It's not that exciting,' Jennifer said. 'Just breakfast, laundry, shopping lists, you know.' Wishing it were, indeed, just those things. 'How are you finding the job?' she asked politely.

'It's like a dream,' the girl said. 'My last job was with a firm of solicitors and they were horrible to me.' Her nose twitched, some small nocturnal mammal in distress. 'Most of them couldn't remember my name, and there was no way any of them would ever have thought I was capable of more than answering the phone and taking messages. Todd' – she said his name as if it was holy – 'says I can learn everything I need to know, inside and out, from the ground up, and that this is the car manufacturing of the future, an industry that will be the backbone of every successful country's economy. And he says he's going to give us all shares so that we are the original founders and have an emotional investment in everything that happens . . .' On she went, eyes shining with gratitude at being rescued from the indifference of the corporate world.

Jennifer half-listened, wondering at the way in which Todd could inspire such devotion in those who worked for him, knowing just how little he reciprocated. She could see him now, over at the bar, leaning close to a tall, thin girl with black hair piled on top of her head who swayed towards him as she whispered something into his ear. Todd laughed, then caught sight of Jennifer and waved. The girl turned, half-waved too, then turned firmly away. It was Nancy.

The girl who couldn't have been called Moppet moved off, with what could have been relief, and Jennifer felt invisible, as if she could have stripped naked and walked with impunity through the room. If only she was back home with Rosie, where the child's easy laughter could create a charmed circle around the two of them. And where was Natasha?

Jennifer was pointed out by a few people – as what, she didn't know: Todd's wife? The mother of his child? The draggy woman who hung out of him and clearly wasn't good enough for him anymore? – but very few made any effort to speak to her. One man stayed long enough to figure out that Jennifer had nothing actually to do with the company, then turned on his heel and stalked off, as if he felt she had been trying to deliberately mislead him.

Another, younger, man, a boy really, chatted about his own media dreams. 'I have this idea for advertising screens in public loos, in restaurants, or bars that will show ads specifically tailored for each person who walks in. It's revolutionary. No more wasted ads!' He said it as if it were something glorious, like an end to world hunger.

'But how will the screens know what people like?' she asked.

'There will be something to scan them and upload their likes in an instant.'

'But what will the things scan?' She was honestly bewildered.

'A barcode maybe, like a tattoo.' He sounded vague then, and slightly irritated at her questioning.

'So you'd have to choose to get a tattoo, which could then be scanned by a machine, and tell everyone that you bought Persil instead of Bold? Why would anyone do that?'

'Rewards,' he said, even more vaguely, and shortly afterwards terminated the conversation by asking what she wanted from the bar, and disappeared for good.

Finally realising that he wasn't coming back – she spotted him on the other side of the room in conversation with a lady in a tight electric blue dress; he was holding his hands up in the shape of the screen, thumb and index fingers at alternate right angles, presumably to show the size of his revolutionary personalised advertising hoardings – Jennifer went to get her own drink.

Natasha was at the bar, sitting between two young guys wearing V-neck jumpers and suit jackets. She jumped down when she saw Jennifer, ignoring one of the guys' attempts to take her number – 'In case I ever come across that film you were talking about. I bet you can get it reissued on DVD now, no matter how old it is' – and whispered, 'Thank goodness! I looked everywhere for you. This place is packed.'

Jennifer hugged her. 'You seem to have made friends.' She indicated the guys.

'God, I can't take another minute of the get-rich-quick schemes. Everyone here seems to believe they are on the cusp of becoming a billionaire. They've all "invented" something "revolutionary", and I don't understand any of it.' She laughed, flicking her hair over her shoulders.

'I hate these things,' Jennifer said, wondering where Todd was now. 'I've become so terrible at remembering people's names. It puts me into a panic. I didn't used to be. I didn't even realise it was a thing you had to do. I just knew who people were automatically.'

She sounded confused, plaintive. 'Now I'm terrified I'll bump into someone I've met through Todd, someone he thinks is important, and I won't have a clue who they are.' She did, indeed, look terrified, blinking hard in distress at the idea.

'It's because you're thinking too much about yourself, not enough about them,' Natasha said, as if it were simple. 'My dad taught me that when I was a kid. You have to let them make an impression on you, by stopping thinking about the impression you're making on them, and then it's easy.'

It was true, Jennifer supposed. She did think too much about what kind of impression she made – what people thought of her, how she compared to their expectations of her, what they thought of her in relation to Todd – but when had that happened? Surely she didn't used to be like that? 'Did you see Nancy?' she asked.

'Nancy?' Natasha looked astonished.

'Yes, she was here. I don't see her anymore.' Jennifer scanned the room again.

'Right.' Natasha paused. 'I forgot she did some work for him. Or,' she corrected herself, 'for one of his companies. But she said she hardly ever sees him, just his team.'

'Yes, he said. It's very nice and supportive of her to come along.'

'Isn't it?' Natasha said. She sounded, Jennifer thought, annoyed. Perhaps she didn't like that Nancy hadn't told her? 'I'm going to see if I can find her. Wait here, I'll be back.'

CHAPTER 23

Natasha scanned the room urgently, pushing past people and walking to the far end, but found no sign of her sister. She had turned, ready to push back again to Jennifer, when she saw Todd, moving in her direction. He hadn't seen her. Was glad-handing people as he went, moving effortlessly because a path seemed to form in front of him as the crowds stood back, ready to clap him on the shoulder as he passed and call out encouraging words. He looked, Natasha thought, taller than she remembered, although that was surely impossible, and more golden. His shoulders were broad and strong, with a faint forward thrust, like a bull, that spoke of power and impatience. Far from the monster of her imagination, he was still, she saw, a remarkably good-looking man. In that room of achievers, young men with plans and dreams and determination, he stood out. It wasn't just that it was his night; it would, she thought bitterly, always be his night.

Instinctively, Natasha turned in towards the wall, flattening herself, eyes on the ground lest their gaze, drawn to him, should alert him to her presence. She was desperate for him to pass without seeing her, then she stopped herself, forced her head up. It was, she decided, time.

She could no longer skulk through this city where they both lived, scared to meet him, speak to him, be spoken to by him.

Heart hammering, she planted herself directly in his path. And Todd, to her astonishment, greeted her with the same enthusiasm she saw him dispense everywhere.

'Natasha.' He gave her a hug, indifferent to how stiffly she stood, waving over her shoulder at someone, holding up two fingers – *two minutes!* 'I heard you were back. How are you finding it?'

'Fine.' She had planned this for so long – how she would stand, what she would say, the way she would be, to show him that she had not forgotten, but that he could no longer touch her. Now the moment had come, she couldn't muster any of it, just stayed there, gauche and at a loss as people swirled past them, curious, momentarily, as to who she was. '*You* seem to have done well.' The words came out in the absence of anything else, and she hated herself for saying them, for being someone else who sucked up to him. And instantly he expanded, physically settling back onto the balls of his feet and rolling his shoulders.

'I've been very fortunate,' he said seriously, nodding. 'It's been exciting.' She had noticed many times the way successful men never said they were 'lucky,' because 'lucky' might imply that some part of their achievements had nothing at all to do with them. 'Fortunate,' it seemed, was the chosen phrase – modest, but not unassuming. 'Good to see you,' he said then, already in motion towards someone else, 'We must catch up.' He said it to the air above her head, and he was gone, leaving Natasha with a head that spun sickeningly at the smell of him, the feel of his body so close to hers, two memories vying with each other in a way that made her want to run away from both – the memory of how much she had once wanted him, the way she had once dissolved into the heat that surrounded him – and the other memory. His hand on the back of her neck, holding her down, crushing her. His arm around her waist, pulling her towards him as if she had been no more than a creature made of sand or snow; something lifeless created by his hands. As easily smashed by them.

She fought her way back to Jennifer, who was still at the bar, grabbed two small glasses of something amber-coloured that smelled of aniseed and knocked them back, one after another. Jennifer began telling her something about what Rosie had done that day, but Natasha barely listened. 'We need to get out of here,' she said.

'God, yes,' Jennifer agreed instantly. 'Let me find Todd and tell him I'm going. There's Jean, she'll know.'

Jean did know. 'He's gone,' she said impatiently.

'Gone where?' Jennifer looked around, surprised.

'Some of the venture capitalists he invited wanted to go for dinner, to talk more. So they've gone. They'll get more business done that way. This was just an introduction. I'm off to join them now.'

Jennifer, Natasha saw, couldn't bring herself to ask where they had gone, or to suggest that she also join them. Instead, she tried to smile, look as if she was in possession, already, of these facts; make them not shattering, but ordinary.

'Of course,' she said. 'I had forgotten. Well, have fun.'

Jean gave her a pitying look and left.

'They sound like vulture capitalists,' she said then to Natasha. 'Circling, high in the sky, looking to make a kill.'

'Or find an already-rotting carcass,' Natasha agreed absently. Then, 'Come on, let's go for dinner ourselves. There's no reason to stay here anymore.'

'Come back to mine,' Jennifer said. 'It's still early. We can order takeaway. Rosie might still be up.' She said it with sudden excitement.

The house was, Natasha saw immediately, exactly the sort of thing people raved about and took photographs of. Endless shades of cream and grey dovetailing into each other, like living in the pleats of a tablecloth. Hard, shiny tiles stretching in all directions, and carefully recessed lighting. No signs of actual life.

'Where do you keep everything?'

'In the walls, basically,' Jennifer said. 'It's all an optical illusion. Behind those smooth surfaces are crammed hordes of things, all trying to get out.'

'It's like an interior design version of that H.P. Lovecraft story, 'The Rats in the Walls',' Natasha said.

'Exactly,' Jennifer said approvingly. 'Except it's not rats, it's pens and phone chargers and batteries and things. If it wasn't for Rosie's toys, I'd think I was living in an after-hours airport or corporate law firm. Let me see if she's awake.' She ran upstairs, eagerness in every swift step, to where the Brazilian babysitter was getting Rosie ready for bed, and brought her down, clean and pink from her bath, in yellow pyjamas.

'What a little duck,' Natasha said, holding her arms out. Jennifer gave Rosie to her, then took her back almost immediately, seeming unable to be apart from her. She was so gentle, so loving with the little girl that Natasha felt almost like a voyeur, watching scenes that weren't meant for her. Jennifer bent low to her daughter, talking, cuddling, kissing her over and over again.

And there it was. All the passion and energy, the enormous capacity for love, and the excitement of love, that Natasha remembered from Jennifer, that she had thought was gone from her. The girl who had turned cartwheels, flame-coloured hair streaming in the breeze, chattering about the things she wanted to do, people she had met who interested her – the girl Natasha thought had disappeared beneath the weight of being a grown-up, married, a mother, miserable – was after all not so very far away.

She had wondered what it would be like, meeting Todd's daughter, only to realise immediately and with relief that the little girl wasn't his – she was Jennifer's, she was her own.

Jennifer took the child back upstairs, and Natasha sank back on Todd's tightly upholstered, cream-coloured sofa to think back over her meeting with him that night. The thing that she had anticipated, dreaded, for so long. The real reason she had said yes to Jennifer – because she needed the moment to be behind her, rather than in front, where it wavered like a heat haze, making her sick and keeping the future from taking firm shape. Seeing Todd, speaking to him, had been so unremarkable – a hand clasping hers, a formal hug, a few bland words – that it should have been an anticlimax. And yet it wasn't. Because behind the indifferent formality, something had stirred that Natasha suspected was better left alone.

They had dinner once Rosie had gone to bed, eating Thai takeout off elegant plates and drinking red wine from glasses so bulbous, with such slender stems, that Natasha said it was like being a flower fairy and trying to sip from a tulip.

'Todd won't be home for hours,' Jennifer said. 'Not if there's a whiff of investment to be had off those vultures.' So they talked about Natasha's job, about Declan.

'I'm looking forward to meeting him,' Jennifer said with a smile, so that Natasha responded, 'It's not like that,' and changed the subject.

'What do your parents think of the house?'

'I'm not sure. They don't come up that much.'

'But you go down?' Natasha was curious, had long wondered what Mary thought of Todd. Of Jennifer's life.

'I do. They love us visiting.'

'Does Todd go with you?'

'Not normally. He doesn't like staying there. He says the mattresses creep him out because they're old. But' – she giggled a bit – 'when he does, he sleeps all the time. First he complains about the unhygienic mattresses, and then he barely gets out of bed. He's tired, I know.'

'What about his family?' Natasha asked. 'Do they come over?'

'We hardly see them at all. His dad doesn't go out much, and the brother, I don't know . . . they're not close.'

'His mother died, right?'

'Yes, when Todd was thirteen. I often wonder if that . . .'

'You can't make excuses for people based on what happened to them as children,' Natasha said firmly. 'Not at this age.'

Later, she realised she would have done far better to stay quiet and discover what else Jennifer had been going to say.

They moved to the sitting room then and Jennifer switched on the fire, although it wasn't cold, because it was so quick and easy and made the room less impersonal.

'The benefits of it being fake,' Jennifer said, 'although a real fire is so much nicer, but Todd didn't want the hassle of dealing with ashes and cleaning chimneys.' Then, 'Did you even see him at the launch?'

'Briefly,' Natasha admitted.

'Good. He was asking about you.'

'Why?'

'He's impressed with you; he always has been.'

Natasha felt sick. 'He's not, that's just the way you hear it.'

'No, he's always had a thing for you,' Jennifer continued, with what tried to be a gay and understanding smile. 'Remember that summer we were in Ibiza? He definitely had the hots for you then.'

Feeling even more sick, Natasha said, 'Jen, that's ten years ago. I can barely remember back that far. Now that he's married to you, with Rosie, how can you even begin to think about that?'

'I don't much,' Jennifer said, then blurted out, 'He cheats.' It was the closest she had yet come to whispering that all was not well in the picture-perfect house where she lived, and it was a confidence Natasha didn't want, or know what to do with.

'How do you know?' Natasha forced herself to ask, for the sake of friendship. For the sake of appearances.

'I just know. He is so unreadable in so many ways, but that, I can always tell. He doesn't look very far – girls he works with. Jean.'

'The skinny Asian one we met earlier?'

'Yes. At the moment. They don't last very long. Actually, I think he might be moving on from Jean.' Jean had been hostile and impatient with Jennifer recently, no longer sneeringly pleased about doing small jobs for her.

'Well, but, what are you going to do about it?'

'Nothing. What can I do?'

'You could say something to him? Or leave him? Or at least threaten to.'

'The thing is, I've thought about it. I don't want to leave him – there isn't anywhere to go, and I wouldn't know how to begin arranging for there to be somewhere. And so there's no point saying anything to him. He'll be furious, and deny it, and I have no proof. He stays out late, but he works hard. Sometimes, he stays out all night, but he has a pullout bed in his office, and I know he does stay there, at least sometimes, so there isn't anything I can say that he won't dismiss. And he'll just be furious.'

She looked, Natasha thought, like someone who had seen Todd angry, who didn't wish to see it again.

'Anyway,' Jennifer continued, staring at her hands, 'it's kind of my fault as well. We don't, well, since Rosie, we haven't really had sex much . . .' She trailed off, then blurted out, even as Natasha was about to say something about a small child making you tired, 'Even before Rosie, we had more or less stopped.'

'Why?'

'I don't really know. At first, after the miscarriage, I just couldn't . . . then later, he was always at work, and when he did come home he'd rant for hours about investors and finance structure and models and things until I was exhausted. And when we did, it was just, I don't know, so functional. Not romantic or loving. He always seemed angry. With me, with everybody. Sometimes, we'd have sex and it would be as if he hated me. Or as if he didn't really know who I was.'

Natasha knew she needed to change the subject. 'How is he with Rosie?'

'He's not a bad father.' Jennifer sounded thoughtful. 'He's a bit distant – there are loads of days he doesn't see her at all, because he's at work, but he always asks questions about her and what she's been doing and eating. And I've seen him play with her and cuddle her and bury his face in her neck. And he loves when he makes her laugh.' Her voice became warm and rounded as she described the ways in which Todd was no more proof against the magic of those fat hands and soft cheeks than she herself was. 'But I still never see the same interest or excitement in him as he gets when his plans and projects are going well. Nothing else fires him up like that. And he won't let me go to her at night, when she cries.'

Natasha looked at her, shocked. 'Why ever not?'

'He says she needs to be in a routine and not to learn that we'll pick her up every time she cries. Sometimes, she cries for hours, and I can't even sneak in to her because I know he's awake, although he doesn't say anything, and that he'll stop me.'

Jennifer was clearly far more upset about this, Natasha thought, than about the affairs.

'Jen, she's your daughter. Couldn't you stand up to him?' Natasha asked, but she asked it kindly. She could well imagine that standing up to Todd would be hard, especially when you had so many years of learning not to stand up to him.

'Maybe . . .' Jennifer clearly didn't mean it.

'After all, it's not good for Rosie to grow up with such a controlling father.' Natasha wondered would the direct appeal to Rosie's welfare stir any spirit of defiance.

But again, 'Maybe . . .' was all Jennifer said.

So Todd cheated, Natasha thought later. And probably had no shortage of willing partners. She'd seen the way girls had looked at him at the party – some quite openly flirting, as if Jennifer being there couldn't have any importance. Did they not smell the danger off him? Probably they did, and liked it. Because they had no idea what it actually meant.

CHAPTER 24

Much later, Todd returned home full of energy and excitement. 'They get it,' he said, pacing the bedroom. 'They really get it. For the first time, I am with people who understand what's possible here.'

He didn't mention walking out on Jennifer, and so she didn't either, afraid to bring it up and shatter his good mood. Afraid to admit to herself how upset she had been. He began to quiz her on who she had spoken to, what connections she had made. When she said she couldn't remember names, and didn't manage to describe a single person he recognised, except the guy with the personal advertising screens whom he dismissed as 'a moron', he was annoyed.

'I'm sorry,' she tried to say. 'They're just not my sort of people.'

'What does that even mean?' he demanded. 'Who are "your sort"? Country doctors and solicitors? Academics with dandruff on their shoulders and confused ideas about the importance of literature?'

'Something like that,' she answered, trying to keep her voice low and steady.

'Well, these are "my sort" now,' he said. 'And so they'd better be yours.'

'I see you're giving the employees shares now?' she said, to change the subject.

'Who said that?'

'A girl called Moppet. At least it sounded like Moppet. Receptionist or something.'

'Marrit, not Moppet.'

'Marrit. That's nice of you.'

'Don't be silly.' He sounded amused by her naivety. 'The intellectual property is held in a separate company, so the value is all in that. The shares I've issued are just window-dressing, a bit of flag-waving,' he said as if he expected to be congratulated for his cleverness. 'Ownership of the valuable company will be reserved for investors. And Jean. She's worth keeping.'

Because she's as ruthless as you, Jennifer thought suddenly, then tried to push the thought away.

'But that's horrible,' she said. 'You're like the British and French carving up Africa.' He looked baffled. 'It means you're basically cheating the staff. They think they're getting something they're not.'

At that, he looked annoyed. 'They are getting as much as they deserve. Why the hell should they get their hands on my company when all they're doing is typing and filing and phoning people? It's my vision, and the investors' money. We're who matter. The rest can be replaced, twenty times over, in the morning.'

'But that's what you offered them,' she tried to explain. 'They never even expected it. It was you who brought it up and offered it.'

'Because it ensures their loyalty, their buy-in.' 'Buy-in' was one of the words Todd liked to use these days. More and more, he used words that Jennifer didn't understand, in a way she didn't understand.

'But it's a lie. Don't you see?'

'It's not a lie. It's business,' he said, lip curling at her childish sentimentality. 'If they don't understand the way companies are structured, that's hardly my fault. *Caveat emptor*,' he pronounced with the authority of indifference.

'But they're not buying; you're giving, or you said you were,' Jennifer said wearily. She was so tired of these conversations, conversations in which she was always behind, trying to catch up, or resigning herself to knowing she never could. Struggling to see things his way, to understand the way his mind worked, while he forged ahead without any reciprocal interest in the workings of her mind.

She didn't tell Natasha how much Todd hated any displays of affection between Jennifer and her parents, his profound irritation at what he called their 'pathetic co-dependency', and even greater disgust at the way her parents doted on Rosie. 'They spoil her and indulge her,' he would say angrily 'It's ridiculous. And she's already playing them up.'

Evidence of the love of her family repelled Todd. He preferred to believe that the distance he put between his widower father, younger brother and himself, was 'normal', that her family were dysfunctional. 'We're grown-ups,' he would say. 'I've left home, I don't need to constantly go back, looking to be babied and reassured.'

'Why did you marry me?' She didn't know why she asked, except that it was late and she was half-asleep and the question popped up and took her so much by surprise that she blurted it out. He answered with more ease than she had expected.

'Because we're good together. And you have the kind of background I need. Your people may be stuck in a sad time-warp where good manners and an arts degree are all you need to get on in the world' – he said it cheerfully, almost admiringly – 'but until this country finally shakes itself up and admits it has lost the race, your type still have credibility. I doubt there is a politician or high-court judge in the land your mother couldn't get on the phone in half an hour through that network of "girls" she went to school with, or through various cousins who married various other people's cousins; the whole damn cat's cradle of connection and influence this wretched country is made up of.' He sounded amused, but bitter too. 'I didn't have that. Not yet. So I married it.' He said it as though expecting her approval.

'Me.'

'What?'

'Me, not "it". You married me.'

'Yes, I married you.' He sounded no more than curious, then shrugged and went downstairs. She heard him at his laptop, tapping at the keyboard with a sound that reminded Jennifer of the way the thrushes at home would knock snails against tree trunks to break their shells.

Jennifer wished then that she'd had more training at this, at people being cruel to her. But she hadn't. Had only thirty years of kindness behind her, years that now seemed useless, because they hadn't prepared her for what the world was really like. Hers was the defencelessness of a happy childhood.

There had been a girl at college, someone of whom it was whispered that she was a prostitute. The whispers were prurient, disapproving, but Jennifer had been fascinated. The girl, Marie, was small, crop-haired, with a shut little face. The same age as Jennifer, she was the mother of a five-year-old who, the rumours went, she raised alone and provided for by sleeping with men for money.

Jennifer had searched the girl's face for clues, keen to see something that would explain the hows and whats of her setup. Where did she work? How often? What did her face look like when she greeted men? she wondered. What did it look like when she greeted her child after men?

For all the squalor, the smell of need like a small coal fire, Jennifer saw glamour too. She wondered what it would be like to be so hard that you could do that, let men you didn't know breathe and paw over you, stay smiling and responsive as they came inside you, or on you. Or perhaps not smile, not respond, allow your disdain to be the challenge they had to meet to acquire you, use you? What would it be like for the world to have no more power over you? This girl, Marie, she felt certain, must have built up a protective layer like old leather, whereas she, Jennifer, felt newly flayed, forever wincing at the salt of each casually cruel word. She could no more shrug off Todd's cruelties than she could ignore Rosie's desperate night-time crying. She thought she had become adept at letting his words slide off her, glancing blows without the power to sink deep, but she wondered now. Perhaps each blow left something, a faint trace that met and fused with more, so that in the end there was damage, deep and cumulative, that must rise to the surface like a bruise, showing first blue and red, then yellow and green as it passed up and out.

CHAPTER 25

In an effort to make being back something that counted, Natasha said yes to Sunday lunch at her mother's the first time she was asked, instead of playing for time the way she wanted to. She would have preferred something more casual, but understood they would all deal better with the formality of a proper arrangement, rather than the awkwardness of apparent spontaneity.

The three of them being always together, always alone, like handmaidens without a sacred duty, bothered her, but she stuck with it, because she needed to. She imagined herself slowly drawing closer to her mother at last, finding a way through the years of silence and muffled intent, thanks to a shared diligence – time spent chopping or cooking together that would allow them to speak without the terrible stiffness that had gripped them both for so long.

I'm sorry, Natasha wanted to say. Sorry I was mean. Sorry I let him use me to hurt you. Sorry I hurt you too, willingly, when I thought it would please him. But she hadn't said any of it, because the opportunities, the cracks in her mother's careful exterior, had not yet come. Her carefully maintained indifference, buffed and touched-up like a professional manicure, kept all intimacies safely at bay. They had spoken of him, but only briefly and with specific purpose – a dish he had liked, a restaurant they had visited together – so that there never opened up the kind of meandering pathways Natasha needed to begin the difficult business of emptying her heart, and discovering what was in her mother's.

Perhaps it is too late, she thought. Perhaps sometimes things are too late. A moment passes without heralding its passing, and that's that.

Nancy arrived and they set the table together – dining room, not kitchen, because it was Sunday and their mother insisted. So they laid out three lots of silver cutlery, china and crystal glasses.

'Is John coming?' Natasha asked Nancy, wanting to understand what to expect.

'No. He has lunch with his parents on a Sunday.'

'You don't do much together, as a couple, do you?'

'We do enough.'

After lunch, the three of them walked on the beach, across the corrugated strand that rippled towards a pale horizon while plump sea birds scattered before them like washing on a windy day. Maria complained about dogs and dog owners, so that Natasha said to Nancy, when they had pulled slightly ahead, 'Why does she moan so much?'

'It's cultural,' Nancy said with a laugh.

'Don't be ridiculous. That's not cultural. It's a bad habit, learned over too many years with servants and languages she didn't speak very well. Remember how awful she used to be in Mauritius? Shouting at the help in Catalan, even though she knew they couldn't speak it.'

'It was pretty awful alright.' Again, Nancy seemed amused.

'I wonder why has she never remarried? She could easily if she wanted to. She looks amazing.' They both turned to look at their mother behind them, still slim and elegant, dark hair blowing across her face.

'She sees herself as Penelope, forever waiting for Ulysses.'

'But he isn't coming back.'

'That isn't the point. The point is the waiting.'

'But they fought all the time when he was alive. They didn't love each other.'

'Don't be ridiculous, Natasha. Can you really not see that they did?'

'But the way they were together . . .'

'There are many different types of love.' Nancy sounded wise. 'I suppose you think that because you were the favourite, Daddy's Little Girl, that she was nothing?'

'I . . .' and because she had indeed thought that, Natasha stayed silent. 'I miss him so much,' she said after a while, voice barely audible against the brisk slap of the wind.

'Of course you do.'

'No one will ever understand me like that again.'

'Oh God, you're selfish!' Nancy snapped. 'Is that really what you think? It's all about what you lost. What about what I lost? What about what she lost? All the things she had already lost before he died, because of you?'

'What do you mean, that she lost before he died? And how because of me?'

'She wasn't first in her own house. You were. And that's humiliating.'

'That wasn't my fault.'

'Yes, it was, as well as his. He might have encouraged you, but the impetus was all yours. You're like a small aggressive nation, constantly trying to gain more territory by pushing out its borders. You always had to come first. You always do.'

'I do not! It wasn't like that. I loved him. He loved me.'

'I know you did.' Nancy's voice was softer. 'But we all did. And he shouldn't have put you first. Or rather, let you put yourself first.' Walking ahead then, farther out towards the sea that was ever in retreat, Natasha began to realise that she didn't see nearly as clearly as she had always believed. That her perceptions were cloudy, even distorted, and the procession of tiny figures in her past behaved very differently when others looked at them. She also realised that the vague feeling of guilt she had felt for so long towards Nancy, was no more than Nancy expected of her.

Later, after tea, Nancy said she was going; she clearly expected Natasha to go with her, and even looked a little cross when Natasha said she would stay and clean up.

Why had she stayed? Natasha wondered, as her mother complained about the produce in the local shop and the rudeness of the man who served her there because he wouldn't carry her groceries out to the car. 'He says he is busy,' her mother sniffed. 'I don't see him busy.' There were more complaints, specific and general, that Natasha stopped listening to, allowed them to become merely a base coat as she pondered Nancy's earlier comments, and forced herself to pursue the things they had opened up.

She interrupted the flow of minor recriminations by asking, 'Why did Dad never become an ambassador?'

Maria drew herself up proudly and said, 'I would not help him. That is why.'

'But how could you have stopped him?' Natasha worked hard not to put any particular or insulting emphasis on the 'you'.

'Ambassadors need ambassadors' wives, and this I would not be.'

'Why not? He would have been brilliant. It's what his whole life was aimed towards.' Natasha was furious, ready to say more, ready to say that it was no wonder he had preferred his daughter to accompany him in public, rather than his sullen, resistant wife, when Maria continued on.

'And I did this for you. You think those women wearing their sacrifices like a badge were good? Their children with no homes and only little bits of family, squeezed in around receptions and national days? Always an anecdote to keep conversation moving along, always the praise for the dishes of the country, the wine, even when it is terrible. Always with the eye on other people, never on their families and their children. These women who have confused duty with love or don't understand there is any difference, who make no sound when they fall over because they are rotten right through.'

As usual her mother's descriptions, though not precise, were vivid, like cave drawings, full of significance and hostility, and Natasha was astonished – at the vehemence, and the suggestion of strategy, rather than inadequacy, to her actions. She had always presumed that her mother's failures were inherent, things to be despised and pitied. Now she saw that there was more to it.

'But what difference would it have really made?' she asked. 'I mean, we moved all the time anyway. Why would his becoming an ambassador have made that worse?'

'It wasn't just moving,' her mother said. 'That we could all do together, as a family, and when he was not there, I was always there. In an embassy, as ambassador, that would have changed. I would have been gone, like he was, and then you and Nancy would have been sent to some school somewhere, like that Mary *Immaculata*' – she gave the word its full Spanish pronunciation – 'with those so snob girls, like your Jennifer.' Maria had never seen beyond Jennifer's awkwardness, to her sweetness and charm.

'Jennifer wasn't like that, but I suppose others were,' Natasha admitted.

'I knew he wanted to be an ambassador, but he wanted to be a father too, even if sometimes he was not a very good one, and because he could not choose, I chose for him. That was my power and my gift.'

'He was a good father,' Natasha said, but automatically, because she was considering what her mother had said.

'Sometimes. To you. Not to Nancy. And so look at Nancy now – with that man, John, who she stays with because he is nothing, and she thinks she deserves nothing.'

'Why not to Nancy?' Natasha didn't bother to deny it anymore.

'I don't know.' Her mother sounded sad and confused. 'I understand that we cannot always decide where our heart gives itself. I know that when you were born, his eyes looked into your eyes, and that was it. But he did not need to make it so obvious.'

No, Natasha thought, he didn't. She remembered a thousand incidents, carefully recast by her so that she didn't have to acknowledge the fundamental unfairness of what he did; times when he chose her, spoke to her, laughed with her, forever leaving Nancy and his wife on the outside of the tiny circle of two he had tightened around himself and his eldest daughter. The inside of it had been a wonderful place, but the outside, she saw, must have been awful. She thought of Nancy, her mother, prowling around, looking for a way in, forever rebuffed, and felt, for the first time, pity that outweighed a grief that now seemed almost selfish.

Later, alone again, she rang Martin, to see would he come over; better still, if she could go to his. Sometimes she did on a Sunday – they watched TV together and had mugs of tea. It took the edge off her loneliness, which now seemed more needled after lunch with her mother and Nancy.

When Martin didn't answer, she rang Declan. 'Meet me for a drink?' He said yes, as she knew he would. They had become close by then, in a way that felt pleasantly easy-going – a drink after work, coffee on the narrow balcony outside the boardroom, him smoking as they chatted about colleagues and office stuff – but with a potential edge; a kind of phony war, one that might after all never be declared.

He worked out at the gym close to her house, at odd hours –

very early or very late – and would often buzz for her afterwards so that she had got into the habit of grabbing coffee with him in the mornings, then walking over to the office together. She suspected there was sly gossip already which could not have been helped by his wet hair. But he was good at his job – quick and confident, thriving on the adrenalin of busy days and long evenings – and popular in the office, which meant the whispers were faint, even approving.

There had been exchanges of confidence between them that Natasha had found herself powerless to resist. He told her that he liked sex in public places. They had been drinking, steadily that time, had reached the stage of the evening that seemed to demand some kind of intimacy. 'It's the hint of danger,' he explained. 'And the way it feels far more dangerous than it actually is. I mean, what's the worst that can happen – someone might see you and take a photo, or you might get done for acts of indecency? – but somehow, the stakes feel higher. And I like that. We live in such a safe and boring world most of the time.' He sighed, mock-theatrically. Natasha wondered if it was a sly kind of come-on; he could have no idea how little any element of sexual danger thrilled her.

They did drugs together. Sometimes a line or two before a night out, other times staying in, watching TV, listening to music, smoking, snorting, talking, hours passing like salt through her fingers so that she would see the sun coming up, realise it was nearly morning and that she hadn't slept, had spent the night in conversations as meaningless as the prophecies of an eight-ball; solemn idiocies like 'You may rely on it' or 'Very doubtful', floating to the surface of the dark liquid in which they seemed suspended at those times.

His friends rang and texted him constantly, but he mostly kept Natasha to himself. She had introduced him briefly around – to Nancy, Jennifer, Martin – but wasn't keen on anyone getting too cosy. She wasn't at all sure what the point of her friendship with Declan was.

'I feel as if I'm walking through spider's webs and I keep ripping them, but without meaning to,' she complained now to him. They sat close together at a small table in the same pinball bar they always went to. It was empty, Sunday-ish, with just one indolent waitress, her cropped T-shirt showed a flat stomach with pierced navel. 'Everyone is so complicated.'

'People are as complicated as you let them be.' He took a long swig of his beer.

'Surely they are as complicated as they are?'

'Nope. As you let them be.' His worldview, she had discovered, was simplistic and self-reliant – 'You get out what you put in', 'If it's worth doing, it's worth doing well' – shading into motivational – 'When you feel like quitting, think about why you started'. Natasha laughed at his certainty, the conviction with which he believed in himself, and especially at the motivational one-liners. But she found it appealing too, so completely did it differ from her own way, which was to choose a more wavering view of everything, indulge in a constant reckoning process; her plans and understanding changing as new information was calibrated – an alteration in the weather, a change in dinner plans, no matter how slight – like waves coming in and out, scrubbing the sand clean each time.

'So who's making things complicated now, apart from your family?'

'Well, obviously they're doing most of it, but my friends seem to be pretty complicated too. One of them, Katherine, got married barely two years ago and is already talking about divorce. She says she and her husband had fallen out of love even before the wedding, but weren't able to face the fact, so they just went ahead. Now she's opening a gallery and I think it's a prelude to leaving him – you know, finding herself, reclaiming her independence, that kind of thing.'

'That's just life,' he said. 'Not particularly complicated.'

'And then there's Jennifer and Todd.'

'Todd?'

'Her husband. They have a child, but he works all the time and is kind of horrible, even though he's really successful.'

'Wait, is this Todd Beatty? The tech guy?'

'Yes. Why, do you know him?'

'I used to. So he's married to your friend, Jennifer, the one I met, with the baby?'

'Yes. How do you know him?'

'We worked together, briefly, in London, years ago. I was just out of college. Todd was older, more senior, and a total prick.' Natasha stayed encouragingly quiet and, sure enough, he went on. 'He made all our lives miserable – the new guys – in every way he could. Like, he actually went out of his way to be horrible.'

'How?'

'Putting us down, sneering. At meetings, he had this trick of asking what you thought about something, so that you had to say, and then he'd sigh as if you were beyond a joke, and say something despising about what you'd said. Bullying, basically, I suppose. It was like being back at school and some older kid decides to make life hell. I left the company because of him.' His voice had gone quiet and Natasha knew how much it had cost him to admit how badly Todd had affected him.

'I'm sorry. That doesn't surprise me. He can be . . .' She trailed off, uncertain what else to say.

'Well, it's all long over with now.' Declan swung into action to cheer himself up. 'I got on, and did well, and it hardly matters now.' Natasha didn't believe that for a second. 'Another drink?'

'OK.' Her phone rang. Martin. 'Do you mind?' She gestured at it.

'Nope, go ahead.' She went outside, with Declan following her. 'I'll have a cigarette while I'm waiting.'

'Hey,' Martin said. 'Sorry I missed you. Shall I come and pick you up? *Primal Scream* is on at half nine.' He had such a nice voice, Natasha thought, growly, like a bear.

'Shit, I'd love to, but I'm out now . . .' She felt embarrassed, didn't want to say she was with Declan. She knew she didn't have to, because she had walked away from him so that he wouldn't hear her being evasive.

'No problem. How was lunch?'

'Ugh. Fine. A pain.' She told him about Nancy saying her mother was Penelope and, sure enough, he laughed.

'It certainly suits her far better than playing The Merry Widow would. She's more tragedy than comedy.' But he said it kindly. He liked Maria, whom he had met often over the years, once describing her as 'sweet', a word Natasha would never have associated with her mother.

'Coffee during the week?' Natasha asked.

'Definitely. See you then.'

She walked back to Declan, half-trying out excuses in her mind – 'That was my mother; I need to go', or 'That was Jennifer; she wants to talk to me' – in case it was possible to back-track on her evening with him, and still make it to Martin's in time for *Primal Scream*.

A homeless man, with a black plastic bag, was standing talking to Declan. He was a man Natasha knew by sight, young and bearded, with fingernails that always gave her a queer feeling in her stomach because they were as hard and stained and gnarled as the nails of toes.

'I can see ye do. I'm not a fuckin eejit', the guy was saying as Natasha approached. 'They're in yer pocket. Give us one and I'll be gone.'

'I told you, I don't have any cigarettes. Now fuck off.' Declan, consciously or not, was enunciating like a man striking bells, knocking each word clearly and precisely. For authority? Natasha wondered. Or to emphasise the vast distance between the two of them?

'You fuck off. Ye fuckin shite.' The man stood there, unmoving. Seemed willing, for the sake of pride, or drama, or because he had nowhere better to go, to continue the altercation indefinitely.

Declan clearly wasn't. 'I said *fuck off*,' he said, leaning forward on his toes, a threatening inch closer to the man.

The man stepped back, but again, held his ground, neither advancing nor retreating. 'Ye fuckin shite,' he said again.

Natasha was about to intervene, placate, when Declan lunged forward and grabbed the man's plastic bag from his hand.

'That's mine,' the man yelled, reaching for it. Declan held it out of his grasp so that the man lunged again, yelling, 'That's me stuff. Give it back.' The way he said 'stuff', pouring into it everything he didn't have, would never have, made Natasha wince.

'Give it back,' she said. 'Declan, give it back to him.'

'What's in it?' Declan asked, opening the neck of the bag for a peek even as he manoeuvered himself around so that his shoulder came between the man and what he sought, blocking him. 'A stinking sleeping bag. Anything else?'

'It's me stuff. Give it back.'

'Declan' – Natasha was yelling now – 'give it back!'

'There you go.' Declan chucked the bag insolently towards the man, who grabbed it desperately. 'Now, piss off before I throw it in the water.'

The man muttered 'fuckin' cunt' under his breath and walked away. Natasha ran after him.

'Wait,' she called. 'Wait. Here.' The only money she could find was a tenner. She thrust it at him. 'I'm really sorry. I don't know why he did that.'

'*You're* alright,' the man said, stuffing the note deep into his jeans pocket. 'But yer boyfriend is a shite.'

'He's not my boyfriend,' Natasha said, but the man was already moving off, indifferent now that the moment had passed. The indifference told Natasha what she already knew – he had seen worse, been party to worse. She went slowly back to Declan, who was waiting at the door of the bar for her, holding it open.

'What did you do that for?' She felt sick at what she'd seen, disturbed by the casual cruelty of it.

'It was only a bit of banter,' he said.

'It wasn't. It was horrible. It may just be a stinking sleeping bag to you, but that's probably all he's got. That's his tiny store of respectability, just about the only thing that anchors him here. His "stuff" means something to him, in the same way yours does to you.'

'OK, OK. I'm sorry. He wouldn't go away, just kept asking for cigarettes.'

'That's no excuse! And it's not me you need to say sorry to, it's him. You could have just given him a cigarette.'

'I had given him one.' He sounded apologetic now. 'He wanted a second. Anyway, I'm sorry. Forget it. Let's have another drink.'

'No, I'm going home.'

'Ah, don't be like that. I said I'm sorry.'

'No, you've ruined the night. I'm going.' And she did.

But she also took his call later and allowed him to say sorry again, and ended the conversation by saying, 'OK, fine, forget it,' grudgingly. The fact that she did sickened her, but she didn't know what else to do.

CHAPTER 26

By the time of Katherine's gallery opening, Natasha had begun to feel that perhaps, after all, it was only a matter of time. She was settling down, just like everyone had promised her, feeling less like something unearthed and exposed. It wasn't anything as corny as the guy in the café remembering how she liked her coffee – that had happened almost instantly, lattes and decaf cappuccinos being the currency of false intimacy – it was a feeling that she recognised the view outside her window in all weathers, had seen the water and sky through the rotation of their changes and felt easy with their many tricks of light and shade and surface. It was in the air and the way it smelled familiar, of things she could almost name. Even her mother had begun to stay longer on the phone, not easing herself out of conversations with a brusque 'I have to go. I have things to do.'

Walking through town to Katherine's gallery opening, Natasha felt a glow of excitement that may have been only the reliable effect of the weather on her spirits, but which she chose to feel as something more. These were the warm nights of late summer, long and slow-moving, always with a hint of something in the future that could have been anything – excitement, opportunity, love,

I have the freedom of my city, she thought then. Because she had learned that it wasn't Rome, or Madrid, or Brussels after all. It was right here, in this city of brief flashes where neither weather nor mood lasted, but where the odd little bit of good, of magic, was stronger than anywhere else she knew. She couldn't wait to tell Martin about her sudden revelation, the recognition of belonging. Then she remembered that Declan was coming too.

Katherine had invited him, from politeness or genuine regard Natasha didn't know, and he had said 'love to', with all the certainty of his usual welcome for himself. Dammit, she thought, wishing he wasn't. They had seen each other at work, of course, since the last night out and his show of temper, and they had carried on as if nothing had happened, but something had. Natasha had seen a different side to him that she couldn't forget. And, she thought, she'd have to keep talking to him, because he didn't really know anyone else, and she wanted to talk to other people. Maybe Nancy would talk to Declan. They had seemed to get on well, the few times they had met.

'She's very intense,' he said, after their first encounter, afternoon coffee, in a dwindling sliver of sun downstairs from their office. Nancy had been passing by, had texted, 'See you in five? For five?'

Nancy had treated him to her usual machine-gun rapid-fire of questions, but with more than her usual archness: 'Where did you grow up?'; 'What's your favourite thing to do?'; 'And if you weren't doing that, what would you do?' veering even into the personal: 'Why are you only wearing a T-shirt when it's chilly?'

'She is,' Natasha agreed.

'A bit mad?' he asked, but matter-of-fact, not curious, or mean.

'Not mad,' Natasha said, 'but definitely delicate. She has bad days.'

'So she has good days too?'

'Yes. I guess.'

'And what was that? Good or bad day?'

'God, good, no question. If it was bad, you'd know all about it. We all would.'

'She's gorgeous, right?' He made it a question, although it shouldn't have been, so that Natasha understood that he wasn't so much asking about Nancy's looks, but whether Natasha minded him saying it, and what her minding, or not, might mean.

'Yes,' Natasha said firmly.

'You're funny together, you and Nancy,' he said then.

'In what way?'

'You both want a lot from each other, don't you?'

'I suppose we do,' Natasha said, struck. 'But isn't that normal, in families?'

'Not in mine,' he said. 'We mostly leave one another alone. Although we'd kill for each other.'

'People always say that.'

'We mean it.' He had the unreflecting confidence of certainty.

'You sound like my mother. She says things like that. Except more blood-thirsty, and with a Spanish accent.'

He laughed. 'That's family, right. If someone hurts you, you'd like to think your family would get them back.'

'I suppose . . .' she hesitated, unsure how much more she wanted to say. 'I've never really thought like that . . . I guess I always felt that I was the one who would be doing the avenging and protecting, if it was needed.'

'Give them a chance. Nancy looked well capable of a bit of avenging.'

She could see what he meant. Nancy, over the coffee and a huge slice of carrot cake, which she'd pronounced 'dry and sweet, the worst kind', had questioned Natasha too.

'Are you enjoying the job? Is it what you really want to do?'

And then Natasha had said, 'Yes, I enjoy it very much. It's interesting, rewarding. And I can see what you're doing, you know. You're turning your corporate-story-telling tricks onto me.'

Nancy had responded sternly with, 'I worry about you. I think you might be wasting your talents, like the guy in the Bible. You've buried them all, and now you're waiting for someone else to come along and dig them up.'

Natasha, through her astonishment at this rapid turning of tables, had seen Declan laughing.

The gallery was empty when she arrived, early, and Katherine was in a flap.

'Thank goodness you're here,' she said, taking hold of Natasha's arm. She was flushed and flustered, eyes darting. 'The glasses haven't arrived, I have to dash out and get some. You need to hold the fort until I get back.'

'Hold it how?' Natasha asked. 'What if people start arriving?'

'They won't,' Katherine said. 'It's very early still, even the artist isn't here yet, and I'll be straight back. Just stay, give the place a lived-in look, and if anyone does come, say hello and smile and let them look around.'

'OK,' Natasha said. 'I guess I can do that.' Waiting, she looked around, walking from one painting to the next – seascapes in sombre oils, heavy blues and greens and purples pierced with the odd bright ray, that reminded her of childhood holidays on sullen Irish beaches, where the promise of a gleam of sun kept them far beyond the span of their enjoyment. No wonder we have fairy stories full of a magical land beyond the waves, she thought. There's always a lying patch of light out at sea that looks as if it will blossom into a brilliant day, and never does. She was so lost in this thought that she didn't notice that a man and woman had come into the gallery, and were standing almost beside her.

'Hi,' she said, recovering. 'Can I help you?'

'Where were these painted?' the man asked.

'The West,' Natasha answered. 'Would you like me to show you around?' And she did, walking them from one painting to the next, talking about the use of light and shade and colour, the layering of strokes and the effect of distance as against proximity. So absorbed was she, and enjoying herself so much, that she barely noticed Katherine return, now with a lady wearing a long black dress, blonde hair hanging in two straight hanks on either side of her face.

When Natasha had finished with the couple, delivered them to the table where bottles of wine and now glasses were laid out, Katherine came over. 'This is Lucinda, the artist,' she said.

'How nice to meet you,' Natasha said, putting out a hand. 'What beautiful work.'

'And how beautifully you explain it,' the artist said with a smile. 'You do a better job than I would have.'

'Or me,' said Katherine. 'But Natasha has always been brilliant about art. I remember going to the National Gallery with you when we were in college . . .' She began a story about a trip to see the Turner watercolours, then broke off as more people started to arrive, 'I'd better go,' she said, 'and, Lucinda, you'd better come with me. Natasha, I'll talk to you later.'

Left alone, Natasha watched the room fill up, thinking how incompatible were the demands of lighting paintings and lighting people. The small, square room was bright, the rather stark light reflecting off white walls, against which Lucinda's paintings appeared to rise up and throw themselves at the viewers. But the same light that so favoured the natural drama picked out in oils was too much for the faces of those gathered, seeming to deliberately fall on certain features – a large nose, uneven lips, yellow teeth – and hold them out to inspire revulsion. As the crowd swelled, as people moved around, laughing, chatting, drinking, largely ignoring the paintings, Natasha thought how grotesque they all looked, like caricatures of deadly sins.

'Greed' was clearly a fat man in a shapeless suit, the pockets of which bulged, as if he were a child with bags of penny sweets. 'Lust', another man leering into the face of a dark woman with tired eyes. 'Envy', a thin woman in a fringed crimson shawl flung over one shoulder, a piece of clothing so affected that Natasha would have been tempted to dislike her even if she hadn't cast such avid glances around, upper lip twitching over prominent teeth like a hare, head raised to scent the air for something someone else had that she didn't.

Declan came over to her then, his buoyant physical confidence causing her to wonder what deadly sin might be his. Pride? Or Anger?

'There you are.' He leaned in to kiss her. 'I was just thinking I'd have to leave before anyone asked me what I thought of the pictures. I don't know if art is my thing.' He laughed as if the very idea that he might have thoughts on the paintings were a ridiculous one.

'Well, what *do* you think of them?' Natasha asked. 'They're pictures. You must have some impression when you look at them?'

'They're nice?' he offered.

'OK, and what else? What do they make you think of?'

'Well, they make me think of the beach when I was a kid,' Declan said, drawing the words out as if they were forming slowly in his mind as he spoke, each word appearing then fading as the next came up behind it, like road signs on a dark night. The effect was like an act of creation, Natasha thought, a vision of a mind in action.

'Right. Me too.'

He looked pleased. Encouraged, he asked 'Really? That's all it is? Just thinking about what the pictures make you feel like?'

'Pretty much. Obviously there's all sorts of stuff about tradition and influence and artistic symbols' – he looked wary again, as if she might be trying to bore him – 'but basically, it's about what a painting communicates to you. How it makes you feel.'

He looked even more delighted then, at being what he now saw as 'right', and when Nancy joined them, a few moments later, he immediately set forth his views with conviction. 'It's like when you're at the beach as a kid, and it's freezing but you don't want to go home, because it's the beach. It's a day out. And that's better than being at home.'

'I see what you mean,' said Nancy, with a little teasing sideways flick of her eyes. 'Sometimes anything's better than being at home. I guess that's why I'm here.' She laughed then and Declan laughed too.

Nancy looked well, Natasha thought; skin glowing, wearing a black jumpsuit that accentuated her height and slimness, hid the sharp angles of shoulders and collarbones.

'Jennifer was in the office today,' she said. 'Flapping around like a great big bat in a long black coat. Todd made her wait nearly half an hour while he finished a meeting. She just sat there, staring at her hands. I don't know how she can bear to wait for him like that.' Something in the way she said it gave Natasha pause. This was cruel beyond the usual run of bitchy sneering.

'Stop being horrible,' she said.

'Oh, lighten up,' Nancy said. 'You've always been silly about Jennifer, ever since college. As if she's something rare and precious that has to be minded.'

'She is,' Natasha insisted, wondering did she mean 'was'.

'Look, isn't that her now?' Declan said.

Natasha watched Jennifer approach through the large front windows of the gallery. She appeared, Natasha thought, defeated. Her mind shied away from the cruelty of the word, then reverted. Defeated.

Jennifer was burdened with plastic bags that banged against her legs as she walked, and moved with her head down, barely looking up to cross the road in front of the gallery or to hold back the straggle of dusty hair that blew into her face.

'Shopping,' she said, plonking the bags down beside them once in the door. 'I'm sure I look like a bag lady. But where was I supposed to leave them?' She looked worried, as if she had missed a trick, been too dim to see an obvious solution.

'It's OK,' Natasha said, 'I'll put them in the back. Katherine has a little office. You can get them later.'

'Thanks.' Jennifer smiled with too much gratitude. 'I'll get some wine so. Wine for everyone? I can carry four I'd say.' They all said yes and Natasha picked up the bags, making for the back office.

Natasha dumped the bags, then couldn't resist peeping inside to see what Jennifer and Todd ate; curious to get some unfiltered insight into their domestic lives. To see the story, not as Jennifer told it, but as the humdrum details revealed it to be.

Inside the bags, along with jars of baby food, were various bright plastic tubs. Shepherd's Pie. Lasagne. Chili Con Carne. Some of them said 'Hand-made' or 'Authentic', although there was no possibility of that being the truth. A jumble of ready meals. Even the bright images couldn't disguise the creepiness of the mince, chunks of carrot that suggested the end of a bad night out, rather than a delicious dinner.

She felt depressed by the sight, as if the meals revealed, not two people busy, perhaps uninterested in food except as fuel, but rather two people who had severed all warmth between them, whose life together was but a glancing blow.

She met Katherine in the office doorway, face lit up with a broad smile. 'They've bought two paintings, the couple you were showing around,' Katherine said. 'And they want Lucinda to take on a specific project for them. It's so wonderful, and I feel it's thanks to you, Natasha. They both said how much they enjoyed talking to you.'

'Good!' Natasha said. 'And you don't even have to give me commission.'

'I'll buy you a drink!'

Elated, Natasha walked back out into the crowd, to where Declan, Nancy and Jennifer were standing, except that now Todd stood with them. As ever, the effect of his physical presence caused everything around him to shrink a little, so that he seemed a trick of perspective, a clever use of some kind of artistic device that enabled him, always, to be the foreground of the scene. Declan, she saw, was looking wary.

'Natasha.' Todd leaned in to kiss her cheek. 'How nice. We've just been talking about you.' There was nothing in his tone beyond the casual, even superficial; a piece of polite social chatter, but she felt her heart beat faster with the anxiety his presence brought to the surface as surely as rain brought worms.

'Oh?' she said.

'Yes. Nancy has been telling us about your time out with the Iveagh hunt. How you drank too much home-made sloe gin before you started, and fell off.'

'She couldn't walk for a week.' Nancy laughed. She was standing beside Todd, looking up at him with bright eyes. 'She landed right on her hip flask. It still has a dent in it, the shape of her hip bone.'

'Like a fossil,' Todd said. 'A negative image of Natasha's hip, in silver.' The way he said 'Natasha's hip' made her want to retch.

'Not silver,' Nancy corrected him, 'pewter. Or something. A base metal.' The emphasis was on 'base'.

'Nancy is making it sound far more exciting than it actually was,' Natasha said.

'Don't be silly, Natasha,' Nancy said, stung by what she perceived as Natasha's rejection of her story. 'You know that's what happened. You said you were so drunk you couldn't tell if your horse was going forwards or backwards.'

Jennifer, Natasha noticed, was smiling with agreement at everything that was being said, head moving from one side to the other depending on who was talking, like someone watching a tennis match, or a nodding figurine in the back of a car.

'Todd, do you know Declan?' Nancy said, taking Todd's arm.

'We haven't met,' Todd held out a hand.

'We have,' Declan said.

Todd looked more closely at him, did a big blank face that could easily have been a lie, Natasha thought, and said, 'Sorry, memory must be going . . .'

'It was years ago,' Declan said, almost with relief, Natasha thought.

'Well, nice to see you again.' Todd sounded bored. He turned away towards Nancy and dropped his shoulder so that they were manoeuvred into intimacy, cut off together. Nancy, Natasha saw, gazed up at him as though mesmerised, and all over again she remembered his power to fascinate, the mix of provocation and concern, the way he made you feel as if he had draped a scarf around both your necks so that you stood together, close, warm, protected. Until he snatched the scarf back and pushed you out into a cold wind.

'I'm going to get more wine,' Natasha said, needing to get away.

Declan walked with her to the wine table. He gave her a curious look. 'So what is it with you two?'

'Me and Nancy? We're sisters, that's all. Sisters nark at each other sometimes.'

'Not Nancy. Todd.'

'What do you mean?'

'There's a way you have of talking to each other . . .' He broke off, not having the words to do justice to what he had discerned.

'Oh, he's just so pompous sometimes, it annoys me. It's nothing.' She brushed off his question, although she guessed he would have loved to hear her say something disparaging about Todd. She caught sight of Martin then, chatting to Katherine, and couldn't bear to talk to him with Declan beside her.

'Would you go and see if Nancy wants a glass of water? I'm going to get one from the back.'

'Sure.' He was, as usual, happy to oblige. Maybe happy too to have an excuse to talk to Nancy. Quickly, Natasha made her way to Martin.

She wanted to tell him her news before anyone else joined them, wanted him to be the first, perhaps the only one, to hear.

'Guess what?' she asked.

'I don't know. Something good? You look happy.' He sounded generous, approving, but she saw his eyes flick momentarily to where Declan was standing beside Nancy, and she wanted to put a hand on his arm, clutch him, say urgently, 'It's nothing. He's nothing', except that she didn't yet know what it was, whether it was, indeed 'nothing'.

'A couple bought two paintings, and Katherine says it's thanks to me.' The flick of his eyes had taken some of the joy out of her, but now his reaction restored it.

'That's great!'

'Isn't it?' His determination to see her happy, to think the best of her, were the sure things in a shifting world.

Declan arrived at her side. 'Nancy doesn't want anything, she says she's heading off. Todd's leaving too.'

'OK.' Natasha felt tired, as if the evening were moving too quickly for her, whirling past like the house in *The Wizard of Oz*, off on its own crazy path. 'You know Martin, right?'

'I do. Martin.' Declan held out his hand, shook Martin's hard so that Natasha thought she saw Martin wince slightly. Declan had the gaudy aggression of a magpie, Natasha decided, lots of chest and front and a disarming brightness. Martin excused himself almost at once and Declan looked pleased, as if he had won something. Perhaps he had, Natasha thought. But what?

Julie came over then, simpering, 'Stu and I have bought a painting. I thought it was only fair, to support Katherine. It's such a brave venture. And I don't suppose she'll sell many.'

She sounded so satisfied that Natasha couldn't resist. 'She sold two almost as soon as the exhibition opened,' she said, before adding maliciously, 'The two best.'

Julie, predictably, looked furious.

* * *

Later, she and Declan went for something to eat, because it was still early and she didn't want to go home, and because everyone else had simply drifted away. Katherine, clearing up glasses, had said she might join them, but she looked tired and Natasha knew she wouldn't.

They ate plates of shrimp in garlic, fried chorizo and tiny battered fish at a tapas place, and discussed the launch.

'It's going to be hard to make it work,' Declan said. He might not be much good on art, but on the commercial prospects of the gallery he was, she knew, pretty accurate.

'Art is always going to be hard.'

'That's why I stick to money.' He smiled. 'So, Julie? What's her deal? She seems nice.' Declan, Natasha had discovered, was something of a gossip, although he would have outright rejected the word, convinced that only girls were capable of that kind of prurient interest in other people's doings. But he liked knowing her impressions of the people she introduced him to, and all the details of who had once gone out with whom, had made a pass or a fool of themselves, who might be a cheat or a success.

'Does she?' Natasha asked. 'Maybe to you.'

'Go on.' He settled back comfortably, and Natasha found herself telling him as many bitchy things about Julie as she could remember, because he so clearly enjoyed hearing them. 'And Todd?' he asked, eagerly, when she had finished with Julie, just as she had known he would, but even knowing how receptive her audience was, Natasha couldn't turn Todd into a character, a series of entertaining anecdotes about a two-dimensional tycoon. She got the feeling that, were she to try, the corrosive parts of Todd's personality would burn right through her feeble attempts, like sun through clouds.

'I hardly know him anymore,' she said.

'But you must know about him,' he insisted, clearly determined to hear something of Todd.

'Well, he's the most financially successful of all of us, obviously. Soon I imagine he'll be so grand, he'll be one of those guys who lives his life on private planes. Jennifer says there's some big deal in America in the pipeline.' Declan, as well as disliking Todd, was jealous of him, she could see that. It was professional – he would have been of any man as obviously successful; about whom the eddies and currents of excitement rippled – but intensely personal too. It wasn't just the early history between them, it was more. Both he and Todd were chest-thumpers and swaggerers, but Todd was taller, broader, with just a little more of whatever it was that made them both demand admiration and achievement. And perhaps it was that, the consciousness of competition between them, which made him say: 'And him and Nancy?'

'What do you mean him and Nancy?'

'Well, you know . . .'

'What?' But she did know, had guessed it even as Todd had looked at her, and couldn't hide the claw of fear that grabbed her throat. She put a hand over her mouth to stop the flood of words, accusations that would sound wild, incoherent phrases and snatches of foulness, watched him silently, waiting for him to say something that would take it all back, make it all not so. He didn't.

'I'm right, amn't I? It wasn't hard to spot. They're hardly discreet. Are you going to tell Jennifer?' There was more than a hint of satisfaction in the way he said it.

'I'm not sure.' Secretly she wondered did Jennifer already know. 'This is really not good. Really not, not good.'

'Well, obviously not. He's married. She has a boyfriend, but it happens.' He shrugged, a man of the world. Reasonable.

'No, you don't understand. I know it happens, but this can't happen. Todd is too brutal for Nancy. She's delicate, like I said. He crushes things, breaks things, and she's much too easily crushed.' Her voice gave away enough that he looked more carefully at her.

And then, to his evident satisfaction, she did tell stories about Todd, but careful stories, calculated, where menace was allowed to edge through discreetly without spotlight or telltale fanfare. Stories that could be nothing, but that could also lay a fragile lattice, a foundation to build on later.

Thus encouraged, Declan told stories too – the ways in which Todd had worked to humiliate him, the pleasure he evidently took from it, so that Natasha understood this was no clash of personality – two aggressive men jostling for supremacy – but a pattern, one Todd had evidently found pleasure in.

She could not, yet, tell Declan why and how she was so quick to catch the spark he struck, but she encouraged him, leading him to say more, dare more, speculate more, about Todd, his motives and objectives. Every step closer to anger that Declan took was a step that Natasha helped him to take.

'You know a lot about him,' Declan said at last.

'I know more than I could ever want to know about anyone,' she said, then switched away from herself before he could ask. She talked about Nancy and her fragility, Jennifer and the terrible years she had had, and Todd's malign hold on both. And each word, she could see, had a profound effect on Declan.

'He has already all-but destroyed Jennifer,' she said. 'I can't seem to stop that. But I can't let him do the same to Nancy – it would be so pathetically easy. She gets so confused. She sees patterns that aren't there and signs in the most everyday occurrences. A broken doorbell or an empty crisp-packet can be "a sign" to Nancy sometimes. You have no idea how hard it has been for her to come this far; to be this well. I can't let him take that.'

'He won't,' Declan promised, maybe just as she had wanted him to.

CHAPTER 27

Nancy seemed more inclined to push food around her plate than consume it. She was moving a chunk of lamb shank back and forth between fork and knife, like someone with an ice hockey puck, taking large slugs of her white wine.

Natasha had ordered a salad and a glass of sparkling water. She had to go back to the office after this, and wanted a clear head for what needed to be done. She knew Nancy would be furious – bitter, resentful, defensive – and she was. Natasha laid the accusation out without preamble, because she chose to believe they could discuss it fairly.

'You're having an affair with Todd, aren't you?'

Nancy went instantly on the attack. 'For fuck's sakes, Natasha, you are the smuggest person alive. Trust you to ambush me with the offer of lunch and then throw accusations at me.' She was doing her best to reach outrage and anger fast, but Natasha could see she was rattled.

'This isn't about me,' she said.

'Yes it is. You are so full of judgement. "*You're sleeping with Todd, aren't you?*"' Nancy mimicked.

'So you are?'

'Yes, and what of it?'

The defiance was a poor mask for her embarrassment, and Natasha tried to be gentle.'I just don't think it's a very good idea, that's all. He has form. Jennifer says he has affairs all the time, with girls who work for him, and they don't last.' It was cruel, and she knew it, but knew too that she needed to work quickly and thoroughly. Sure enough, Nancy looked distressed, but she righted herself adroitly, like a skater might change the angle of their weight to hold balance.

'Maybe, but this isn't like that.'

'What else is it like, Nancy? It's an affair. He's married, has a kid. You have John. It won't go anywhere, and you'll end up hurt. Don't do it, please. Everything is going so well for you. This can only wreck all that.'

'It won't. He loves me.'

Natasha flinched at the word. Had not been expecting it. It was like hearing that Hades was in love with Persephone, she thought. Grotesque and terrifying.

'Well, what about John?' she asked. 'I thought you two were happy?'

'We are, but, well . . .'

'And he's been so good to you. All those years where you weren't great and he cared for you.'

'Mmm,' Nancy said. 'All that caring and minding . . .' She trailed off. Didn't need to finish.

'I see,' Natasha said. She did. Saw that the roles of friend, minder, lover were neither compatible nor complementary.

'And Todd is exciting,' Nancy said.

'I can see that.' Again, she could. After all, she had once, briefly, seen it to the exclusion of anything else.

'This could really be something,' Nancy continued, appealing now to Natasha to enter into the story the way she saw it – something beautiful and new. 'I know it's not perfect, but honestly, I love him, and I'm certain he loves me. I'm sorry, for Jennifer's sake, but you said yourself she's not happy. He says they've barely slept together in years. I don't see the point of them staying together.'

'Has he actually said anything about leaving her?' Natasha was scared. There was so much more here than she had expected and it was unspooling so fast, the thread getting wound around and about and lost so that she didn't know how to find her way back to the conversation where she succeeded in persuading Nancy to end something that was thrilling and full of exhilaration, but ultimately just a distraction that she could be brought to relinquish.

'He has. And not in that vague way men do when they don't mean it. We've talked about it, in detail.' Nancy sounded proud.

'Nancy, you can't do this! You really can't. Todd is dangerous and unpredictable. He's not like you or me or any of the rest of us.'

'Meaning?' The hostility was like a scouring pad.

'You know the way when certain men are very drunk, and you know they could do just about anything? Anything at all? That they would have no inhibitions, no inner voice to stop them, and that afterwards they wouldn't even remember they'd done it?'

Nancy nodded but looked angry. She was clearly moments away from scooping up her bag and walking out.

'Well,' Natasha continued desperately, 'Todd, I sometimes think, is like that even when he's sober. All the time. Like there's nothing he wouldn't do. Which is probably great in one way, and why he's so successful, but worrying and scary too.'

There was a silence then, one in which Natasha yearned to feel her words sinking in somewhere that Nancy might hear them, feel them, then and later. Instead, Nancy threw them off with fury.

'Todd knows all about you.'

'What does that mean?' Natasha's heart began to beat too fast, a lurching, three-legged race.

'We've talked about you.' Nancy said. 'I told him about you when we were younger, because he was interested.' She sounded defensive; she knew well that what she had done was wrong.

'I see. What did you tell him?' The idea of being some kind of pillow talk for Nancy and Todd was disgusting.

'Oh, about you always wanting to be the best at everything, going off with Dad, thinking you were so wonderful, and him thinking you were so wonderful too. Todd was interested in all that. And he told me something about you, too.'

'What!'

'He told me what happened in Ibiza,' Nancy said, shifting backwards in her chair, farther from the table. Farther from Natasha.

'*What?*' On the other side of the room, their waiter looked up, head jerked back on a string, at the loudness of Natasha's voice. She dropped it to a hiss. 'What did he tell you, Nancy? What?'

'That you had a thing together, once, when Jennifer was in bed with sunstroke, but that, afterwards, he felt really guilty and went back to Jennifer. That neither of you ever told her, which means that you all still meet up, but that he feels awkward when you do. And that you must feel just as bad because you're really weird with him. And I saw what you were like at the gallery the other night, sort of intense and hostile, so I think he must have a point.'

'He told you that?'

'Yes.' She was proud. 'He trusts me. He tells me things.'

'That's not always a sign of trust,' Natasha said. 'Sometimes it's a way to control. And it isn't true, what he said. He's lying. That isn't the way any of it happened.' She knew she was floundering, trying to understand her way too fast, without pointers.

'Whatever,' Nancy said, the snap of finality in her voice. 'I'm not sure how many shades of grey there are, when you cheat on your best friend with her boyfriend. And, yes, I know it's a bit creepy to fall in love with him when you've been with him already, but I am going to try and forget all that, and I think you should too. I love him, Natasha, and I'm going to be with him.' She got up to go, gathering her bag and coat. The waiter moved forwards to help her and Natasha knew that she had moments only, and unless she moved with the momentum that was before her, she would never be able to come to this point again.

'Nancy,' her voice rising to a squawk. 'Wait. I have to tell you something. And you have to sit down and hear it.'

Nancy ostentatiously checked her watch so that Natasha wanted to scream, but she sat down. The waiter drifted away again.

'What? You've got three minutes. I have to be somewhere.'

Natasha made the three minutes work for her. She told Nancy everything. All that happened that hot afternoon on the white island. Told it the way she remembered it, the way she believed it to have happened. Took out all the details she has so carefully packed away – the slimy green lizard bikini, the click of the cicadas, the intense, rolling heat of the day – and laid them out for Nancy to look at.

'It started the way he said it did – there was something between us, an attraction, a strong one, which is why I can see that you feel it too. And it built up and up. Partly I think it was the heat, and the proximity, and me being so miserable . . . I couldn't get away from him. Everywhere I turned, he was there, beside me, and we were always wasted, so there didn't seem to be any difference between what was "real" and "not real" – everything was part of the same dreamy sequence. Especially that day – remember the day you came to the villa? Even *that* felt like a dream. And then in the afternoon I was so hungover, and still a bit high, and everything felt a bit floaty. And then, everyone went out and it was just me and Todd at last, and I wanted him, I know I did. But not like that.' She shuddered. 'It all went wrong suddenly. And the moment it actually happened, when he was having sex with me, all the silly, fantasy, dreamy stuff stopped and I realised where I was, what I was doing. What he was doing to me . . . I led him on, I know I did, but in the end, he went too far. He did something terrible, Nancy.'

Still Nancy said nothing, instead making rivers and roads in a mound of sugar she had poured onto the table, intersections and dead ends, doubling-backs and highways, in tiny white crystals.

And so Natasha fell silent too. Even now that she had finished, she still didn't know exactly what she had told her sister. Bits of a story without beginning or end, a sequence of events without a defining purpose or organising principle. A random heap of images that had little shape themselves, but that warped all that lay before and behind them. It took Nancy, with her gift for understanding stories, her training at this stuff, to give it the form that would hold it all together.

'Wait – you're saying he raped you?' She said it with blunt incredulity. The word Natasha had denied herself for ten years, Nancy managed to spit out in that one instant.

'Yes,' Natasha said, forcing herself to accept the word at last. To keep her mind from framing it as a question any longer.

'After you leading him on for days?'

'Yes.'

'Did you tell him to stop?'

'No. It was too quick. Too sudden. I didn't know what to do, and then it was over . . .' Natasha hated that she was justifying herself like this, to Nancy of all people, who should have leapt to believe her. 'You have to believe me.'

'Why do I?'

'Because I swear to you I'm telling the truth.'

And Nancy was silent again, until she swept the sugar roads and paths off the table with a vicious swipe and said, 'I hate you, Natasha. I hate you.' There were other things she didn't say but that Natasha saw in her eyes. Things about their childhood, their separateness and their togetherness, the resentments of youth, untended, grown old and cold.

Nancy grabbed her bag and stood up then, the chair shooting out behind her. Natasha tried to say 'wait' or 'stop' or 'please', but Nancy left, on a surge of mad desire, the way a bee does when it has been bumping against a window for too long.

CHAPTER 28

Jennifer knew she should have been taking Rosie to the park –
indeed, when Todd asked her later, as he surely would, what she
had done with her day, she planned to tell him that that was where
they had been: park, playground, home. But she couldn't face it.
Nowhere did the loneliness of her life hit her harder than tootling
round that windy expanse of green, with Rosie indifferent to the
notions of fresh air that had forced Jennifer there, more likely to be
screaming in her buggy than smiling around her.

The playground was worse. Rosie was still too young, Jennifer
thought, to have much interest in being pushed on swings or slid
down slides, and the presence of the other mothers made Jennifer
more conscious than ever of the ways in which they fitted in, and
she did not.

They all seemed to know one another, or, if they didn't, they had
the habit of easy conversation and familiarity that enabled them to
fall into chat about their children, their routines, their lives, in a
way that Jennifer never could. They stood around, takeout coffees in
their hands, looking smart in their cashmere sweaters and neat jeans

under expensive quilted coats. Often they had more than one child, and seemed to find no difficulty in managing two, even three, with an easygoing efficiency that made Jennifer painfully aware of her own struggles with just one.

They seemed effortless in their ability to handle babies, buggies and bags, chatting, making plans to go to one another's houses or meet up at yoga, pilates, toddler play groups, so that Jennifer felt deliberately excluded, although she knew it couldn't be that really. That if only she were better at being friendly in that casual kind of way that said you could take or leave an acquaintanceship, they would invite her too. But she couldn't. It meant too much to her. She tried too hard, and not hard enough. Her questions came out eager, needy, so that she sounded as if she was trying to quiz these stylish women with their plans and play dates, and saw them recoil politely, instinctively from her.

It wasn't just that she questioned them too earnestly. It was also that she then didn't know how to behave when they reciprocated with polite questions of their own. She weighed up what she said much too carefully. Should she admit that Rosie didn't sleep through the night? And, if so, that they were trying 'controlled crying'? What did this say about her? she wondered. About Todd? Would they judge her? Judge Rosie?

After one such exchange with a woman wearing a very smart navy trench coat, during which the woman had said that she thought controlled crying was tantamount to child abuse 'because of the way in which it stunts a child's emotional development', Jennifer had gone home almost in tears, and had spent hours online, futilely trying to discover was there any possibility that the woman was right. Had she allowed Todd to damage their daughter by not standing up to him? She had found nothing to support the woman's claim, or rather, no more to support that than the opposite – that the ability to self-soothe was a valuable life skill that all children should quickly acquire – but the experience left her more than ever unmoored, uncertain of her direction, conscious of how vulnerable she was to every crosswind.

After that, Jennifer avoided the playground. And so she found herself heading for town instead. She would take the bus, with Rosie, and wander around shops, into galleries and cafés, all the places she used to visit when she was young and visiting them was no big deal, just what she did – pop into the National Gallery for an hour, stop quickly for lunch or coffee in whatever place she and her friends favoured at the time, dash into a shop and try on a few things, maybe buy something cheap for the next big night out, all between lectures or appointments or on her lunch hour.

Now, her going was an event in a way she didn't want it to be. Wherever she went, she was wearily aware of the fact that she didn't need to rush. Had hours to kill, with nothing except Rosie's tea, bath and bedtime to hurry her home. Before, the places were exciting because they were fleeting. Now, settled into some coffee shop, a cappuccino and maybe a muffin in front of her, Jennifer had to try and stop herself from checking her watch or any visible clock, knowing that not enough time would have passed for the exercise to be anything other than demoralising: *Still another four hours until bedtime . . . another two hours before I can go home and turn on the TV . . .*

Around her, groups of younger women seemed to be living her life, or at least had slotted themselves into the space she and her friends used to occupy. She would watch them silently, under cover of a magazine or newspaper, noting what was so obvious to her now – the ephemeral nature of what they thought was permanent. Jennifer could tell by the way they moved, spoke, ordered food and drinks that they thought they were at the beginning of something – that life had opened up before them and they had started down a long and exciting road.

Instead, she knew, they were at the end of something. This was the golden finale of their lives thus far, a final burst of glory before the next stage moved in and cut them off from what they thought they knew was theirs.

She remembered herself, Natasha, Katherine, Martin, even Julie, back at that stage – expansive, confident with the glow of youth and successful achievement. She remembered how it had felt – like they had made it. Out of school, through college, into the real world, where they were to be greeted with cheers and cries of welcome, and which would continue to open up before them, unfolding layer after layer of new and lovely and enticing things.

Instead, within just a couple of years, it seemed to Jennifer, the promise had been revoked, the welcomes shut down and the layers packed away. The path life had given her had turned out to be narrow, straight and hard, not full of delightful curves and windings after all.

And so she watched these women, the new Jennifers, Julies, Natashas, who were so unaware of what lay ahead, and she pitied them and was intrigued by them. They were the ghosts of her former self, the life she had once had, running parallel with her new life and mocking her from it.

The Julie of each group was instantly easy to spot – she was the one who called over the waiter with a peremptory wave of her hand, who ordered decisively and said, 'Let's all have something different, so we can share' or 'Cocktails to start, I think'. And the others, Jennifer saw, did what she and Katherine and Natasha had always done – agreed, demurred, shot each other silent eye-rolls that were nonetheless indulgent too, allowing her claim on them.

The Katherine of the group was easy to spot, too – quieter, gentler, the compromiser. 'I don't mind, whatever you all think,' she would say, to the demand that they all have another drink, dessert, two starters.

But when it came to herself and Natasha, Jennifer often became confused. First, she would spot a particular girl, vivid, laughing, and decide that was Natasha, only to see the girl do something or say something in a certain way that made her think that no, the girl was actually herself. Often, it was in the way someone else reacted to this girl, the response she elicited from those around her, that swapped Jennifer's impressions around.

It was a confusion and a confluence that fascinated her, because of the way in which it showed up something she had never realised – that, on the outside, she and Natasha had been far more alike than she had ever noticed. That they had provoked a similar warmth and regard in those around them, and that she – so dazzled by what she thought of as Natasha's sophistication – had never noticed.

That afternoon, Rosie was asleep in her buggy, and the day warm enough that the foregone trip to the park mocked Jennifer more than usual, with its seductive, lying images of herself and Rosie serene on a blanket in a patch of sunshine, or splashing water in the tiny ornamental fountain.

She walked aimlessly, telling herself that she was having a pleasant stroll, and it was only when she heard Katherine calling her that she realised she was walking right past the gallery, probably deliberately, she realised.

'Jen. What are you doing here?' Katherine sounded so delighted that Jennifer forgave herself the subterfuge, wondered why she hadn't just called to the gallery openly, marched up with Rosie and asked if Katherine had time for a coffee.

'Just wandering about,' she said. 'I thought I might do a bit of shopping, but I haven't got round to it yet.'

'Pop in here. I'm waiting for an artist to come and see me, so I can't leave, but I'll make you coffee on my fancy new machine.'

'Thanks,' Jennifer said, angling the buggy through the narrow doorway.

'Lucky you, being able to do whatever you want on such a lovely day. We won't get many more of them. I wish I could be out in it.'

Katherine made a face, even though Jennifer could see she was still too excited over the gallery and its possibilities to really mean the regret.

'I'm sure it looks better than it is,' Jennifer said in response, unwilling suddenly to pretend to a satisfaction she didn't feel.

'Most things do,' Katherine agreed. 'But still – no money worries, an amazing house, all the free time you want, Rosie – it sounds pretty nice to me.'

'Loads of free time isn't necessarily such a great thing,' Jennifer replied; 'not when you don't have anything you want to do with it.'

'But you have Rosie?' Katherine sounded shocked, but tried to hide it.

'I know I do, and I adore her, and I love that I get to be with her so much, but God, Katherine, the days are so long. We tootle round at home for what seems like hours and hours, and Rosie cries and plays and cries again, and I think it must be time to give her lunch, and then I find that it's barely eleven o'clock, and I have no idea how we're going to get through the rest of that day. And none of you guys have kids, and I don't know anyone who does whom I like, and there isn't ever anything to do. You know, last week she had to get her jabs, and I was actually almost excited, because it was something to do with the day, and I went to the chemist after the doctor and got some Paracetamol in case she came down with a temperature, and we had a chat, the chemist and I, about whether I should get ibuprofen as well, just in case, and I really enjoyed it and didn't want to stop chatting, even though I could see she was done with the whole thing and ready to move on to the next person . . .' Jennifer was crying by now, slow, hopeless sobs that seemed to bring her no release.

'Jesus, Jen . . .'

Katherine, clearly, had no idea what to say, and the obviousness of this made Jennifer wave her hands and say, 'It's fine, honestly, it's fine. I just . . . sometimes, the days just seem so long, and lonely. I don't see anyone from morning till night except Rosie, and I love her so much, but it isn't always enough.'

'What about Todd?'

'He works such long hours. He's often gone before I get up, and by the time he's home, I'm in bed, or so tired that I don't want to talk about his business and his plans, and if he asks questions about what I've been doing with Rosie, I can't ever answer them as fully as he wants me to. It's like there isn't enough in our days to convince him that we "do" anything, and so he accuses me of hanging around uselessly. He'd like us to be going to baby yoga and massage and toddler groups and things, with all the other mothers, but I hate those and I never know what to say, and Rosie is so young it hardly seems worth it when she's just as happy, or unhappy, at home.'

'And does he never take Rosie and let you go off and do something?'

'It's not how it works with us,' Jennifer said. 'Or rather, it's not how it works with him. He doesn't have time and, anyway, he doesn't think that's how it should be.'

'Well, then he should pay for a nanny,' Katherine said.

'He'd love to. That's exactly what he wants, but until I know what I could do with my time, I don't dare say yes, because the idea of having more time to fill, and nothing to fill it with, terrifies me. We don't communicate very well anyway, me and Todd. And I know he thinks I'm too passive and sort of lazy, but I'm not. It's just that I have got into the habit of drifting along and I can't seem to get out of it. It annoys Todd – I annoy Todd – but I can't stop myself. Recently, I feel like he's comparing me with someone, and that I always come off worse in the comparison – more boring, dowdier, less fun, less exciting. But I don't know who the someone is because he doesn't actually say anything specific.'

'Go on.'

'Every time I try and tell myself to snap out of myself and make some proper decisions, I get overwhelmed about where to begin and what order to do things – should I get a nanny and then find something to do, or find something to do and then get a nanny? But then, what if Rosie doesn't like the nanny and I can't leave her? All the things that could go wrong or hold me back seem to crowd in and stop me from taking any of the steps I think of . . .'

'OK, but Jennifer, this is awful.' Katherine was rallying herself, swinging into responsive action. 'You're unhappy and unfulfilled, and why shouldn't you be? You weren't brought up to stay at home with a baby. You are smart, and well educated. You need a job.'

'I don't want a job. I hated the one I had, and I don't know how to go about getting a better one. And, anyway, I don't want to leave Rosie for too long. But I would love to go back and finish my thesis.' She said it wistfully, like something that could never happen.

'Well, do that then. Or, better still, do something new. Maybe that thesis is finished for you now. It was a long time ago. I think trying to recapture it might be hard. And maybe it isn't exactly what you need. Maybe it belongs to a different time . . .' Katherine trailed off, embarrassed, knowing she was referring, however obliquely, to things Jennifer didn't like to talk about.

'I suppose I could go back and study something new . . .'

'Of course you could. Something completely different. You could do psychology. Or sociology. Or shipbuilding. You could do anything you want.' Katherine was trying to bring Jennifer along with her, fill her with enthusiasm and resolve. And it began to work.

'I've always wanted to learn more about medieval literature. *The Decameron, The Song of Roland* . . .'

'So, do it. I bet I can find something online for you right now.' She opened her laptop, tapped briskly at the keys and within moments was saying, 'See here. The perfect course. All you need to do is send off for an application form. Do you want to do that now?'

'No.' Jennifer sounded almost scared. 'But it does look perfect.' She leaned over Katherine's shoulder. 'I need to think a bit more about it.'

'No you don't. You have to send away for the form and fill it out, and you can think about it then.'

'OK. I will. Not now – Rosie's waking up, I need to feed her – but I will do it.'

'OK, well, I'm sending you the link, and you have to promise me.'

'I promise.' Jennifer began to sound excited. 'I really will. I'll read it properly, and I'll do it.'

CHAPTER 29

In the days that followed, Natasha tried to ring Nancy, but Nancy never answered. Natasha texted but got no reply. When Nancy finally did answer, Natasha knew immediately that it was bad.

'I knew you'd ring now,' she said, her voice shivering with anxiety, as if disturbed by tiny, choppy waves. 'I can see a pattern to your calls.' Natasha felt a lurch of alarm. In her bad moments, Nancy saw patterns in everything. She could look at a bird hopping on a branch, and its light aimless flutterings would show her a pattern as surely as though it had string attached to its feet and were weaving a tapestry behind it as it went. The path through city streets to a shop or bar could become a cat's cradle, held in her hand, signifying something that only she could see and understand.

'Something terrible has happened,' Nancy continued, voice rising in panic.

'What?' Natasha was scared, wondered if she had confronted Todd, what he had said. Or done.

'I caught a blackbird.'

'What are you talking about?'

'In a trap. I put the trap out because John saw a rat in the back garden, and I baited it with peanut butter, and this morning I saw something in the trap and I was glad, because I hate rats and I was glad one was dead. But when I went down with my coffee and looked properly, it wasn't a rat, it was a blackbird. The blackbird's neck was broken and twisted, and there was blood on the feathers. And the feathers themselves were heavy and greasy, not light or airy anymore. Its eye was still open, staring at me. It's a sign.'

'A sign of what?' Natasha asked. She knew it was no good telling Nancy in such moods that the signs and symbols she saw were nothing of the sort, just a random collection of objects and events that she had washed over with the fever of her mind. Instead, she tried to allow Nancy to talk herself round to the more sensible point of view. It didn't often work.

'I don't know of what, but something terrible. To kill a songbird, a blackbird, in a trap. Bad will come of it.'

'It wasn't on purpose.'

'That won't matter.' She said it scornfully, as if Natasha were a child, trying with pathetic earnestness to get herself out of trouble.

'What does John say?'

'That I'm getting into a state about nothing. He says blackbirds are territorial birds and another one will come along to replace this one as soon as it realises that the territory is unclaimed. But I know I'm right. Blackbirds mean power and finding it in yourself, and awakening to the mystery of who you are.'

Natasha groaned inwardly. Nancy's gift for stories could be a bad as well as good thing.

'Nancy, it's just a bird. It's horrible, I know, but it's not your fault.' Again Nancy ignored her.

'Remember that Beatles song about the blackbird singing at night?'

'Yes,' Natasha was almost reluctant to agree, could see too well where this was going.

'There's a line about taking broken wings and learning to fly,' Nancy said, in a high, wobbly voice. 'And waiting to arise . . .' There was silence as Natasha searched for something to say that would take away even a few of the branches heaped around Nancy's burning pyre.

'It doesn't mean anything—' She tried to begin, but Nancy cut her off.

'Yes it does. It means something bad.' Then, just as Natasha was wondering would she even mention Todd, she said, pitiful: 'Why did you tell me, Natasha? About Todd?'

'I never wanted to tell anybody. I thought I would never have to.'

'Well, then, you should have stuck by that and taken it all the way to the grave. You shouldn't have told me.' She said it so that Natasha began to believe that she was right. 'I don't even know whether to believe you, because I don't understand what I know. I know what you say, and I know what my heart says, and I can't make any sense of either of them. I don't know if I hate you or feel broken for you, and I don't have what it takes to hold these two things inside me. I don't understand why you told me, now, after all these years, when you could have told me at any other time and I only would have felt pity for you, and love for you.'

There was nothing at all that Natasha could say, no point in trying to share the loneliness of her own path in those years, because Nancy would not have been comforted. No point in saying that Nancy herself had created the 'why' by falling in love with Todd. So she asked the question she needed to know the answer to: 'Have you seen him?'

'No, I can't see him. I don't know how to. And I can't talk to him. I can't ask him if you are telling the truth, because then he will tell me something and there will be another voice – another version –

in my head and I can't take what is there already. I can't, Natasha. I don't know what to do with it.' She was bewildered, the way she had been as a child when their parents fought and Natasha shut their bedroom door and tried to distract Nancy with songs and games so they would not to hear the distant thunder of the gods throwing rocks at each other.

'It will be OK, Nancy.' It was all she could say. Nancy hadn't once asked her how she was, so that she couldn't say, *I will be OK, Nancy.*

'No, it won't.' Nancy put the phone down then and didn't pick up when Natasha tried to call back.

The days that passed then were the worst Natasha had known for many years. She believed she could feel the plates of Nancy's mind grinding and clashing against one another, trying to soak in what Natasha had told her, trying to make that fit with what she already knew, had hoped, and planned.

Then John called. 'Nancy checked herself into St Canice's,' he said, voice flat, without emotion or, as Natasha sometimes now suspected, kept deliberately so, levelled by years of dashed hopes.

'What?'

'She checked herself in. She said she had to.'

'But didn't you try and stop her? Why didn't you call me?'

'She was right; she had to. Natasha, she spent the afternoon carving her arms up so that by the time I came back and found her, she looked like she had been washing in blood, or tried to kill herself, but she said she hadn't, had just been trying to get free of the feeling inside her. She kept going on about that blackbird, and something about The Beatles. She said she tried screaming but it didn't work, that blood worked better.'

He might have been delivering a lecture, one he had given a thousand times before, to a bunch of unappreciative students.

'Why didn't she ring me?'

'I don't know, Natasha. The cuts were very neat, regular', like that was important to record, as if the neatness proved something, or disproved something else. 'The blood had mostly dried by the time I got home, although there was a whole lot of it and she hadn't tried to clean any of it away. She rang a doctor she sees sometimes, and he arranged St Canice's. I took her there and settled her in. She was quiet when I left. They'd given her a sedative, a strong one.'

'Can I ring her there?'

'No. Not tonight.'

'Tomorrow?'

'She said not to.'

CHAPTER 30

Natasha thought about calling Todd, arranging to see him. Saw herself warning him off her sister, her friend. Saw him duck his head in shame and promise to stay away.

But she knew it was all nonsense. Todd would never allow her to behave in that masterful, precise way. As soon as she saw him, her heart would do the horrible hammering thing that made her feel faint, and her words would tumble out, incoherent, vague, indirect. She would be unable to name what it was she wanted of him, what she was accusing him of, and so he would laugh at her, misunderstand her, try to force her into saying something clear and stark that he could deny, and she would not manage to say any of the things she felt. She would go away humiliated, beaten again.

So Natasha decided to do something different, because she had to do something. The buzz in her head was like a bees' nest about to swarm, thoughts rising and spiralling in intensity until she felt they must burst the confines of her skull. With an effort, she subdued them enough to feel her way forward towards some kind of resolution, moved more by instinct by than anything else; that and the feeling that, finally, all the space around her had dwindled to nothing, that nothing more could be taken from her. With her plans finally made, determined not to look too closely at them but simply to act, Natasha suggested a drink after work to Declan, who cheerily countered with: 'What about dinner instead? Then I can go to the gym beforehand.'

'Can't. I have to go to Jennifer's for a few hours. I think Todd is really getting her down,' Natasha carefully confided.

'Oh, what now?' She had known that would intrigue him. He sat on the corner of her desk, leaning back at his ease. She saw her PA start towards them, then veer off once she caught sight of Declan, took in the casual intimacy of his posture.

'Actually, he's getting us all down. Worse than usual.'

'Really, how?'

'He's worse to Jennifer. Even beyond the cheating. Now he bullies her too. Once or twice, with me, recently even, he's been a bit, I don't know . . . odd?'

'Well, you know I didn't like the way he was at the gallery opening. But odd how?' Declan leaned in, enjoying himself thoroughly.

'It's hard to say. Just standing a bit close and saying things that make me feel uncomfortable.'

'Like what?'

'Compliments, but sort of intimate ones, like saying I have nice knickers. I mean, not that exactly, but that sort of thing.'

Declan looked confused, but alert. 'Do you think he's coming on to you now?'

'I don't know. I'm sure he's not.' She put a deliberate brightness into her voice. 'I've never given him any reason to think I like him.' She squashed down the memory of herself and Todd in the sea in Ibiza, the water sparkling and dancing around them as they swam, sliding her wet body along the full length of him as she dived from his shoulders, sun beating down as though it smiled upon them.

Instead, she put Nancy's face, Nancy's bleeding arms, into the space, and closed it off. 'And anyway, he knows I'm seeing a lot of you these days.' She ducked her head, looking up through her lashes.

'That's true,' he said. 'You are.' He was pleased, must feel that the weeks of slow approach were leading him somewhere at last. That was what she needed him to feel.

Natasha is good in a crisis. She remembered her mother saying it, and knew now that her mother had been right.

Natasha didn't go to Jennifer's. Had never intended to. Instead, she walked for an hour to allow enough time to pass. She moved aimlessly, allowing her feet to lead, largely indifferent to where they took her, although she stayed on the broad and well-lit streets, the streets with people and traffic and noise on them. In her head, she replayed the terrible scenes again and again, allowing herself to look at them, dwell upon them, recall them as never before, adding new to old until she nearly choked on the relentless layering and the way each piece of the picture fitted so neatly with the others. Finally, with her mind sufficiently filled, and cold beyond the merely damp summer evening, she rang Declan. 'Can you come to mine?' Her voice quivered, with fear, with the enormity of what had once happened . . . what might now happen.

'Of course.' He was a man to enjoy a direct appeal. 'Are you alright?'

'I'm OK, I think.' Her voice shook. She had spent too long dwelling in best-forgotten places.

'I'll be right there. You can tell me then.'

He was as good as his word, waiting at the front door of her apartment when she arrived, so that she ran the last few steps and into his arms. Not crying then would have been much harder than crying.

He led her upstairs, face buried in his shoulder, half tucked under his arm as he got her key and fumbled with the lock. She cried and cried, the kind of tearing sobs that hurt, brought on by all those memories finally revisited. It was a kind of crying she rarely did, without purpose or any end in sight, just the logic of its own momentum, each heave releasing another one so that it felt almost like retching, not sobbing. Declan said nothing, just sat with her on the sofa as she gasped and fought for breath. Instead of fussing with silly bits of tissue, he got her a towel from the bathroom and she buried her face in it, tears and snot streaming. He asked her nothing.

'I'm sorry,' she said at last, and she was. Although a small part of her wondered why women always apologised for their tears. Why 'sorry' was the inevitable codicil to a display of strong emotion. Except for her mother, who never apologised, and whose bouts of weeping could tear apart a house.

'Don't be sorry,' he said. Tell me.'

She started, wondering still how much to tell him. 'Todd,' she began, then could go no further for a while.

Again, Declan sat patiently. She could see that he had sunk into crisis mode and that nothing, now, would be allowed to faze him until he had the story, a story he believed to be full, and he had worked out a response. She faced first one, then another, of the pictures in her mind, alternative versions of the scene she was about to play out, trying to chose. The older picture was hard and yellowed, like the ceiling of a country pub stained with decades of cigarette smoke and despair. The newer picture was soft and pliant, wavering at the edges, ready to be created. Which to pick. Uneasy, she made her choice.

'You know I went to Jennifer's this evening? Well, Todd came in after we'd been there a while and I chatted to him, to be polite, you know, because I think Jennifer knows I don't really like him and I don't want her to feel awkward about it.' She stopped again, trying to find the words for the next bit, wondering what the next bit would be. Her breath still coming in gasps so that she had to double-up at the top of each inhalation, sending a second attempt at enough air after the first. 'After a while he sent Jen out for some wine, even though we didn't really want any, but he insisted and she went, and she was gone for ages because there aren't any off-licences near them . . .' She allowed the minutiae of detail to take over for a moment, to slow down the delivery of actual information with a facsimile of it; the illusion without the content.

'After Jen went out, he tried to kiss me. As if he thought I would want to kiss him. And when I pushed him away, he got annoyed and said not to pretend I hadn't been coming on to him, and I hadn't, I swear I hadn't. I never would. I don't like him. He gives me the creeps. And then he said I was wasting my time hanging around with you.' She felt Declan stiffen beside her, as she had known he would.

'Oh yeah?'

'Yes, and I said that I liked being with you, and what about Nancy, and he said never mind about Nancy, and then he tried to kiss me again, and when I pushed him away he grabbed me, really hard.' She paused, breath ragged, then resumed. 'He pushed me back in my chair against the wall and started tearing at my clothes. He put his hand up my top and grabbed at the button on my jeans but they're a bit too tight, and he couldn't manage the button with me pushing back at him so he pulled my hair really hard, at the back.' She put a hand up to her head and winced. 'I thought he was going to slap me.' Her voice wobbled again, as if she were on a bad phone line somewhere else. 'But we heard Jen's key in the lock so he let go and moved away, and I grabbed my bag and ran out as she came in.'

'Why didn't you leave? As soon as he tried to kiss you, why didn't you just leave?'

Why indeed? She had known he would ask. All she could offer as explanation was something close to the truth, as she had known it.

'It took me so much by surprise. One minute, I thought it was just all going to be embarrassing and would I tell Jennifer or not, or even Nancy, then next he had me against a wall and was grabbing at me. It was so horrible . . .' She buried her face in the towel again, and took refuge in the most effective weapon she had: 'I'm so sorry. I'm so sorry.' He tightened his arm around her, said nothing, so that she knew her 'sorry' had worked.

Neither of them mentioned the police. Declan asked more questions, not many, and Natasha answered them as best she could, making the truth, old and faint as it was, do duty among the lies. The tears and choking sobs calmed at last and she drank a glass of brandy.

'I'm OK now,' she said. 'Thank you. You were the only person I could think of calling.' He sat back a little at that. 'It could have been much worse,' she added valiantly. 'Mostly, it's Jen I'm sorry for. He is such a creep. And you.' She squeezed his hand. 'He was rude about you. He said you were a loser and that I could do so much better.'

'It's alright,' he said. 'It's alright.' And he poured her another measure of brandy. He sat, arm close around her, for long enough that the brandy did its work.

'I'm tired,' she said at last, weighed down with the aftermath of what she had just done.

'You should go to sleep,' he agreed. 'I'll wait until you're in bed and asleep, so you know I'm here. Then I'll let myself out.'

She did as he said, got into bed, took the hot water bottle he made for her, and lay shivering until he left, faking sleep when he put his head around the door one last time to check on her. She felt like Salome, beguiling Herod so he would ask her to dance, then slyly suggesting that John the Baptist's head would look good on a plate.

The lies didn't disturb her, because the substance was true, but her own vengefulness did. Worse even, was the excitement she felt about what might happen next. She slept then in short uneasy bursts, waking often and with a lurch. She dreamed in equally uneasy bursts, nothing that meant anything, nothing she could recall in any detail, but dreams that left her confused and sweaty. At last, unable to go face going back to sleep yet again, she turned on the light, tried to read, but the words slipped off the page and left no impression. So she lay, and allowed the accumulating thoughts to pass through her as she had once read she was supposed to, when they were thoughts that were hard or unwelcome. She tried to see herself as a smooth, shiny surface off which the unwanted things could slide, falling to nothing below her.

She thought of Nancy, of her selfishness and neuroses, of the way in which she was the base note of Natasha's life; the constant throb that ran through and under everything else, and the way that Nancy would not, could not, reciprocate with any kind of approximate care.

She thought of Jennifer, away now at her parents' with Rosie for a few days, and how she used to be *the world's knight in shining armour*, as Natasha had once joked, having seen Jennifer battle to find the best in a girl they both probably disliked, certainly avoided. 'I always think what her mother would feel, if she could see how much we steer clear of her. How hurt she would be,' Jennifer had said. It had the effect of making Natasha try, for a short while, to be nicer to the girl.

In the midst of the three of them, she saw Todd, the careless way he grabbed and lashed out, the things he took and the things he rejected.

He didn't love Nancy, not the way Nancy might love him, Natasha was certain of it. And he wouldn't leave Jennifer and Rosie for her. She was a girl in a long procession of girls – a diversion Todd believed he owed himself – but, in the background, he would continue to want a wife, a family, a perfect house, all of which would show him to advantage in the only place that mattered to him – his work.

She knew what she had just done was terrible, but she told herself that it was necessary, a first step without which no other steps could be taken. Nancy and Jennifer must never know, but because of what Natasha had dared and done, their lives could be better – would be better.

CHAPTER 31

The invitation for Julie's engagement party had arrived weeks earlier, rather to Natasha's surprise, and had been standing, alone, above the never-used fireplace ever since.

'It should be keeping company with others of its kind,' she had joked to Jennifer. 'Cards for race meetings and lunches and garden parties. Instead, it's up there beside a couple of takeaway flyers.'

As she got dressed for the party, she watched the lights of early evening bounce off the water, black and flat as a stone. The waterfront was quiet, without the stop-motion rush of daytime or the tumbling raucousness of night. Outside, she walked the few metres to the main road, breathing deeply, loving the way the city smelled in early autumn. Of wood and coal and more ancient fuels, as if the chimneys themselves breathed out the old odours soaked into their brickwork.

First, she went to Katherine's, even though it wasn't on the way, because Katherine had asked her stop by, and Natasha, knowing of the trouble in her marriage, had said yes.

'Everything OK?' She hugged Katherine and they went into the kitchen, tacked on 'like an afterthought', as Katherine said, to the end of the little red-brick cottage.

'Just about,' Katherine answered. 'Fine, really. Just, you know . . .'

'Any change in anything?'

'Not really. Dermot's staying with friends for a few days. We're talking about living separately for a while.'

'Oh, Katherine, I'm sorry.'

'It's OK. Or it will be, somehow . . . Anyway, meantime, I've been trying to think about the good things in my life, the gallery mainly, and what I need to do to make that successful and, Natasha, I need a partner, someone to come in with me and help to manage it. I can't do it all on my own.'

Katherine was looking expectantly at her, so Natasha said, 'OK . . .?'

'Well, what I was wondering, was, would you be interested?'

'In what?'

'Running the gallery with me? Becoming a partner. Fifty-fifty, You and me? Natasha, you'd be so good at it. Your understanding of paintings is amazing, and you're so good with people. I know it's a big gamble, and you might not want to, and the money would be less than you're on now, at least in the beginning, but will you think about it? Together, I think we could really do something amazing.'

As Katherine spoke, Natasha saw exactly how it might be – herself running the gallery the way she ran the office: efficiently, smoothly, cleverly, except this time it would be aimed at art, which she loved, rather than money, which she didn't. It seemed as if the very thing she had been searching for might have found her.

'Oh, I will most certainly think about it!' she said. 'Katherine, what an amazing suggestion. I'm already thinking, and I like what I'm thinking . . .'

They had a drink to celebrate, then called a taxi and headed off to collect Martin on the way to Julie's.

'Well, how bad are we expecting this to be?' Natasha greeted Martin.

'Oh, bad,' he replied. 'Presumably a full staging of the next act of Julie-the-Magnificent.'

'World Domination Stage Three?'

'At least.'

'So, any inside info? Anything we should be prepared for?'

'I only know boring things – stuff about flowers I couldn't block out. There's going to be a string quartet, and Julie has told them to play classical music, although they usually do classical-sounding covers of pop songs, because she thinks it's more elegant.'

'Sounds lively,' Katherine said. 'What else?'

'Well, I know who the caterers are, and who recommended them, and can guess how much they cost.'

'She's probably calculated how much each of us will eat, and what that will cost, and has weighed up whether we're worth it. I suppose I should be flattered to have been invited,' Natasha said.

'Except that she's calculated that you won't eat anything, so basically you're a free guest.'

'Ha! She doesn't know how much I'm going to drink!' Natasha laughed.

'You look great,' he said, after a minute.

'Thanks. It's not new, but I've never worn it.' She indicated her dress, striped black and pink like a stick of rock.

'It's not that, it's you. Yourself. You look so energetic or something. Happy, maybe?'

'Maybe.'

'That's good.' He took her hand, and she let him. He had nice hands, she thought. Large and strong and warm. They sat in silence, Katherine too, as the taxi lurched slowly forwards, stopping and starting its way through traffic, dropping them at last outside a big red-brick house, three-storey-over-basement, with a deep bay window and a flight of steps up to a navy front door, on either side of which stood tall metal planters with neatly clipped cone-shaped box trees pointing towards the upper windows in proud flourish.

'Jesus. Really?' Natasha asked, looking up.

'Yes. Stu's, of course. Bought with his last bonus.'

'Right.' Then, 'Do you get those kinds of bonuses?'

'I will in a couple of years,' he said, 'if I'm still there.' Natasha said nothing, felt again the sick-making swoop that time seemed to have performed, the weird action by which it had carried some of them so far forwards, while leaving her on what felt like a small and arid patch of land.

'Come on,' she said, 'let's go.' Then, catching hold of the door knocker, a chunky lion head, brass ring held between snarling teeth, added, 'Abandon hope all ye who enter here!'

The party was everything Natasha had expected. Large, showy, uneasy. Light bounced off hard, shiny surfaces – mirrors, chandeliers, highly polished rosewood and mahogany tables – and pooled on the faces of the guests, many of whom Natasha had never seen before. Those she did know, she was surprised to see. They were people from college that Julie hadn't much liked at the time, but she clearly liked what they had become, or the person they had married.

The women were mostly blonde, wearing small, tight dresses in cream and peach, and shoes so high, with clumpy platform heels, that their legs looked like fully extended construction cranes trying to lift something heavy. Julie herself was in the deluxe version of the uniform, a peach bandage dress so tight it cut into her middle as if it would snap her off in half, and send the two halves running around separately, with platform shoes in an anodyne colour Natasha knew was called 'nude' and that looked, disconcertingly, just that. As if Julie's feet were blunt-edged, with no toes, like hooves, or pig's trotters. Her hair was so done it hardly moved, held in a brittle helmet, and shining harshly like fibreglass. She looked a decade older, Natasha thought, and, with Stu beside her, large and laughing in a navy velvet jacket, as smug as a cat lying in a patch of warm sun.

Natasha took a drink from a passing tray held by a black-and-white-suited waiter, and went to say hello.

'Congratulations.' She smiled and leaned forward to kiss Julie.

'Why, thank you.' Julie inclined her head graciously. 'Are you here alone?'

'I am.' Natasha held the smile in place with an effort. 'Although I shared a taxi with Katherine and Martin.'

'Ah, Martin.' Julie's smile deepened to something close to authentic. 'Where is he now?'

'He went to put our coats somewhere.' Natasha put a tiny extra inflection on 'our'; why, she did not know, except perhaps to annoy Julie. And sure enough, Julie caught it, held it in her mind for an instant, then gave Natasha an appraising look. 'Well,' she said, 'tell him I'm looking forward to continuing our chat. We had such a good discussion about switching investments to gold.'

'I will,' Natasha promised, moving off so that Julie could squeal at the woman behind her.

Martin and Katherine had found drinks and a quiet spot, so Natasha joined them.

'Julie wants to keep talking to you about gold,' she said to Martin.

'Oh Lord,' he said. 'Not again.'

'What it is to be the chosen one,' Natasha joked, rolling her eyes at Katherine.

'It's all about precious stones and metals with Julie, right?' said Katherine. 'She keeps wanting to talk to me about diamonds. Carats and settings and stuff. She's like King Midas.'

'Or that girl in the fairytale who every time she opened her mouth, jewels and pearls fell out,' said Natasha.

'Not pearls,' said Martin, laughing. 'They're a terrible investment. The Chinese are producing them really cheaply, and flooding the market. Apparently Stu suggested getting her a pearl necklace, and she said no chance.'

'The very idea!' said Katherine in mock-horror. 'Luckily our Julie is nobody's fool.'

'Yes. Except that she's so busy being nobody's fool that she can't ever see what's going on around her. Too busy peering suspiciously at everything to make sure it's not a scam,' Natasha said.

Around them, the room was now full to bursting. Natasha caught sight of Paul, his small eyes screwed up cunningly as he muttered, side-on, to a tall man in a black suit. Julie came towards them, laid a proprietorial hand on Martin's arm, and led him to the centre of the room, where Natasha saw her introduce him to a blonde girl in an aggressively tailored jacket, who smiled, showing large teeth.

'Well, that's him sorted for the evening,' Katherine said. 'Julie will have lined up a battalion of blondes. She's determined that one of her new friends will marry Martin. Keep him in the family.'

'They seem pretty willing,' Natasha said, seeing the toothy blonde throw back her head and laugh at something Martin had said. She tried to catch his eye, hoped that he would look over, desperate to be rescued, but he didn't.

'I'm not sure *he* is,' Katherine said. 'I suspect he has different ideas', and she gave Natasha a sly smile that brought with it a warm feeling.

The warm feeling made Natasha look around the party with new eyes. Yes, the majority of them were still dreadful, but, here and there, she caught sight of an interesting face, a pair of bright, expressive eyes or a kindly expression. A guy she remembered from college who had studied law in the year above her, with an absurd, almost surreal, sense of humour she had liked. Two girls from Martin's office she had met over drinks once, who had been enthusiastic and funny. The sea of faces around her no longer seemed homogenous and hostile, but just a collection of people – some decent, some not – to be discovered and appraised on their individual merits.

Looking around again, her gaze tangled with Martin's. The toothy blonde was still beside him, mouth moving in animated chat, but he was staring at Natasha. Their eyes caught, held, so that she couldn't look away, waited for him to pull his gaze from hers but he didn't, not until the toothy blonde laid a hand upon his arm, dragging his attention back to her so that he gave a tiny start. She shot an irritable look in Natasha's direction, then steered Martin around, gesticulating at something on the other side of the room, so that his back was to Natasha. Natasha smiled. It didn't matter what the girl did, because she knew what was in Martin's mind, and was ready, at last, to show him what was in hers.

She thought of Declan briefly, and what must happen there to extricate herself, but it would, she realised, be easy. After all, there was nothing much between them. No solid promises, no ties, just the hours they had spent together, that could be lessened, could dwindle to nothing without scenes or showdowns. A few kindly memories, his arm around her shoulder when she had needed it, the comforting up-and-down of his breath when she leaned her head against his chest. She felt a wave of relief that she had stayed clear of any physical entanglement, and any moral obligation. She had played her hand, made her dubious disclosure, and he had not, after all, responded. Nothing had happened. There had come no answering deployment. And although she was surprised that her hold on him was less than she had thought, that her understanding of his psychology less neat than she had believed, she was glad. Moving to the gallery and the next stage of her life could now be clean and final. The bait had been thrown out in what she now saw had been a moment of intense madness. How lucky that he had not, after all, taken it.

Trays of food – bite-sized things on crackers with scraps of green herbs topping them – went around, then trays of champagne were passed around, and Katherine nudged her. 'Speeches,' she said. 'I wonder if Julie will speak.'

The room settled into expectancy, conversation dying down while heads turned to where Stu and Julie stood, arms around each other, in the open double-doorway between the two reception rooms. As silence fell, Stu stepped forwards, a smile on his broad face.

'He looks like he's ready to deliver a financial report,' Martin said in a low voice to Natasha. She turned, smiled, grateful that he was back beside her and leaned into him a little. His body remained solid, steady, to her pressure.

'It's the only language Julie understands,' she whispered back.

Just as Stu opened his mouth to speak, the farthest door was flung open and Jennifer appeared, looking left and right, head moving in wide arcs. A long, black raincoat flapped around her and her hair stood up around her head in a frizzy halo. Clearly disconcerted to have collided so neatly with the speeches, Jennifer stood and scanned the faces in front of her anxiously, while Stu, ignoring the interruption, made some kind of joke about 'pay day, I mean the Big Day . . .' Catching sight of Natasha and Katherine, Jennifer made her way around the edge of the room towards them.

'She looks like a mole,' Natasha whispered, 'feeling her way forward by touch.'

Katherine shot her an odd look. 'She looks upset,' she said.

Natasha looked again and realised that Jennifer did indeed look upset. Her eyes were screwed up, as if in pain, and her face was paler than usual. She reached them at last, sidestepping an older man in pinstripes who ignored her whispered, 'Excuse me'.

'Can we go outside?' she hissed. 'I have to talk to you both.'

'Of course.' Natasha nodded, seeing Julie take centre stage after Stu.

Out in the back garden, far larger than a garden in the city had any right to be, Natasha decided, Jennifer plonked herself down on an iron chair.

'What's up?' Katherine asked.

'I wondered if you were coming,' Natasha said. 'I thought maybe you had stayed on at your parents.'

'I came back this evening,' Jennifer said. 'I was worried about Todd. He didn't ring at all, but he often doesn't, yet he wasn't answering his phone either. So I rang his office and they said he hadn't been in, hadn't been in touch. They thought he might be away and hadn't told them, but I knew he wasn't, so I came straight back. I went to the house and he was there – and someone's beaten the shit out of him.'

'What!'

'Someone beat him up really badly.' Her voice broke. 'Surprised him and hit him with something. A bat, or a bar. Todd didn't say very much about what happened.'

'Jesus! Is he OK?' Katherine sounded shocked.

'No, he seemed awful. His face is a bloody pulp. It looks like a giant ball of plasticine that someone has squished up, into different, horrible colours. Some bits are brown, some are red, lots are purple. And it's wobbly and squashy, like it's all liquid beneath the surface.'

The image was so violent that Natasha flinched, saw Katherine do the same.

'When? Where?' Natasha wanted to know, needed to know.

'Has he been to hospital?'

Jennifer took Katherine's question first. 'No. He won't go. He says there's no point, that he knows nothing's broken, except ribs maybe, and there's nothing that can be done about that anyway. And he doesn't need stitches, he says, although his lip looked so bad to me that I'm not sure he's right. He can hardly talk, and a couple of his teeth are broken. It's terrifying. He doesn't look anything like himself; he's like some kind of animal, crouched down because he can't stand straight, mumbling and grunting in pain. He told me to get out because I kept crying, so I came here, to find you guys.'

'When?' Natasha asked again. 'Where?' Her voice sounded deadened to her own ears, like trying to talk through the muffling numbness of a dentist's anaesthetic, but Jennifer and Katherine seemed to notice nothing wrong.

'Monday, but he didn't tell me till I got back this evening. On his way home from work. He stayed late, as he often does, and so it was after eleven when he left, and he says someone just set on him, that bit along the towpath where no one goes much. It's a shortcut to the main road so he uses it, even though it's obviously dangerous. The guy took him completely by surprise so Todd didn't have a chance to defend himself.'

'Why?' Katherine asked.

'I don't know. The guy didn't even take anything, not that Todd had much, but not even his phone. I think he just beat him up, and left him lying on the path, but he won't tell me anything much. He says I'm hysterical and make things worse.' She started to cry, choking sobs that sounded out her shock as much as her upset.

Katherine and Natasha put arms around her, patted her head, waiting until the sobbing had subsided a little.

'I'll get you a drink,' Natasha said. 'The speeches should be over by now. And you need something stronger than wine. I'll see if I can score some whiskey.' She needed to get away, from Jennifer and her choking sobs, her wet face and desperate sniffing because her nose was running and she had no tissue. Away from this talk of a face that was now a 'bloody pulp'. Away from the thoughts that went off like pop art explosions in her head, violent speech bubbles with words like 'Wham!' and 'Thump!' 'I'll get tissues too,' she said, as an afterthought. Jennifer gave her a grateful look.

Inside, she found Martin, told him what had happened, then asked him to get whiskey. 'You've a much better chance than me. If I ask Julie, she'll just give me that round-eyed stare, like an outraged doll.'

Natasha was shaking, with fear and anticipation. She found her bag, a scrap of black leather with thick chain handles, and went to the loo. She knew she had a tiny bit of coke left over from one of the binge nights with Declan, and scrabbled desperately through the lipsticks and coins until she found the wrap. There was barely any, enough for one small line, but it was so much better than nothing, might calm her nerves. Because she didn't know what to do with what Jennifer had told her. Didn't know how far ahead to race in trying to join the dots. Didn't know how to look at the picture that might emerge.

Because what if she had done this? Or rather, set it in motion? What then? She wondered did she feel shame? Regret? Realised that she didn't, only fear of being found out and, somewhere, a deep satisfaction. Weirdly exhilarated, like Queen Elizabeth I, issuing death warrants without ever signing or saying a word.

She knew being beaten wouldn't hurt Todd for more than a few days. It certainly wouldn't teach him anything – he would never know that Natasha had any hand in it. It wouldn't stop him from becoming glitteringly successful, or spare a single other girl from going through what she had been through, what Nancy had been through but, still, it evened the score slightly. Now, every time she thought of what Todd had done, she would also think of what she had done, or what Declan had done for her, and maybe that would balance out the tilt of her life.

She bent over the thin line of coke with a rolled up twenty and snorted her way along its path. As she straightened up, throwing her head back, feeling the coke hit the back of her throat with a tinny wetness, the door, which she had forgotten to lock, opened.

Julie looked at Natasha, at the rolled-up note in her hand, the credit card lying on the top of the toilet cistern and said, 'Get out. Now.'

'What's the problem?' Natasha asked. 'It's just a line.'

'I don't care if it's a bucketful, just get out.'

'But it's just coke.' Natasha was honestly bewildered. 'You used to do this stuff too.'

'Maybe, a long time ago, but I certainly don't now, and neither do any of my friends, and I don't intend to let you come along and trash everything with your disgusting values.' She said it as if the moral high ground were an actual place, somewhere she had hoisted herself onto and planted a flag.

'Fine,' Natasha said. 'Can I at least get my coat, and tell Jennifer and Martin I'm leaving?'

'Leave Martin alone,' Julie said. 'You don't want him, and there are plenty who do.'

'Well, they can't have him,' Natasha said. 'He's not the offer of a cup of tea to be passed around.'

'Exactly,' said Julie in thin tones. Natasha left, strangely buoyant, whether from the coke or the secret thud of satisfaction, she didn't know. She felt miserable about Jennifer, who was clearly suffering, but she could not deny the triumph she felt too, and knew she needed to remove herself quickly before her secret pulse of excitement was spotted.

She itched to ring Declan, to suggest a drink, more drugs, but knew she had better not, knew too well where their unacknowledged but shared sense of triumph might lead. She longed to ring Martin too but couldn't. Julie, she knew, would have told him some nasty version of why she needed to be chucked out, but it was more than that. She couldn't ring him, not with what had just happened, so much a part of what else had happened, because these were the things that kept her from him. Kept her from speaking, and from letting him speak. Once they were resolved, she could, at long last stop blocking the path for both of them. Because now, the chapter was closed, book-ended by two appalling acts of violence that, she believed, could cancel each other out.

So she went home, giddy with new knowledge and the emerging drumbeat of her triumph in which the world felt her own once more.

If this were one of Nancy's stories, then Natasha had slain the beast, or at least dealt it a blow and, in so doing, had rescued them all.

Nancy, she told herself, would get better, would forgive her in time, because she had to. She would never know what Natasha had done. But Natasha would know that she had done it for both of them.

And Martin would not know either, but he would know there was a difference in her, a new possibility within her.

CHAPTER 32

Todd, Jennifer realised, was much nicer when he was sick. Gentle and grateful for her care.

'Bring Rosie in here,' he said, except 'Rosie' came out 'Roshie' through his damaged teeth. 'I can watch her while you cook.' He was in bed, had continued to refuse any doctor or hospital, saying that he just needed a few more days for the bruising to go down. He had made Jennifer tell Jean that he was in the States and not to contact him. He was, she could see, embarrassed by what had happened. Shamed by the mortifying evidence of his human frailty. Jennifer had promised to cook chicken broth, and he had agreed, with something so close to gratitude that she felt a swell of happiness; that he needed her, that he could show it.

'I'll leave the baby monitor with you, so you can call if you want anything, or if Rosie starts being too difficult to manage.'

In the kitchen, as she chopped carrots, celery and leeks, then sweated them gently in butter, she could hear him talking to Rosie, laughing at her nonsense replies. Could hear the love in his voice that was stronger even than the pain. For once, Rosie was his only focus and, as Jennifer heard him chatting to her, reciting snatches of nursery rhyme or making funny animal noises, she was happy in a way she knew she hadn't been in years.

By the time she had come home from Julie's the previous evening, Todd had been in a high fever, sweating and shaking, and apologising through chattering teeth for having been so rude earlier, for pushing her away and snapping at the evidence of her concern.

'I'm sorry,' he kept saying, as if he was a kid. 'I'm sorry. I behaved very badly. I felt awful and I wanted you to go but I shouldn't have.' He had heaped the blankets round himself so that he sat as if in a sweat lodge, cross-legged against the head of the bed. Jennifer had coaxed him to lie down, and dosed him with painkillers and pills to bring down his temperature. All night, she had lain beside him while he had tossed and muttered in his sleep, sometimes starting upright, still muttering, warding off invisible attackers with his hands, so that she had to soothe and reassure him before he would lie down again.

When Rosie woke and cried towards morning, Jennifer got up quietly and brought her into bed with them, keeping the little girl on her side, away from Todd, where she quickly fell back asleep again.

Now, Jennifer was exhausted, but without the usual prickling sensation that being tired brought her. She felt calm and capable as she made soup, pureed some of it for Rosie and carried a bowl up to Todd. Even the house felt friendly and warm, the kind of place a family might live, rather than the cheerless setting for magazine spreads and other people's envy.

'How are you feeling?' She balanced the soup bowl on the bedside table and reached down to take Rosie from him.

'A bit better. I'll get up later.' She suspected that bravado was behind his determination to get up, rather than any improvement.

'Will you really not go to the police? See a doctor?'

'No. I'll be fine.'

'But the guy might do it to someone else. This might be the way he operates; not taking anything, just beating people up. And you could help the police catch him.'

'I don't think it's like that.' He paused. Jennifer put Rosie down and gently moved the soup closer to him, ready to feed him when he was ready. 'It was weird.'

'It was awful,' she said with ready sympathy.

'No, I mean weird – something odd about it.'

'What?'

'Something . . . never mind. I'll be fine.'

'Would you like me to tell your father or Gerard?' she asked tentatively. Usually, talk of his family irritated him, even more than Jennifer talking about her own family.

'No need.'

'But don't you think they'd like to know?' She felt her way forward, ready to leap back if he snapped. He said nothing. 'I'd like to know, if it was my brother. So would my parents.'

'Yes, but your family is different.'

She waited, uncertain whether to agree, and admit she was lucky, or insist – feebly – on all the ways in which her family was a mess too.

Then he carried on. 'My family – we don't really know much about one another. That's why I don't go home. There isn't any home, just three people who don't know what to say to the others, who have spent so long not saying things that there isn't any way back from that.'

'Is that since your mother died?'

'Yes. We stood back from each other then, I suppose, because no one knew what to say, and it became a habit.'

Todd almost never spoke about his mother, once rounding furiously on her when she had tried to suggest that maybe he found emotional intimacy difficult because of losing her when he was so young.

'Don't try your amateur psychoanalysing on me,' he had snapped. 'Your pathetic Psychology 101. I'm perfectly capable of doing that for myself, because I've read just as much, or as little I should say, as you have. You think my mother's death is the reason why I don't trust relationships, why I have to "push people away" and "dominate" . . .' He had expertly proffered a complete reading of his personality and behaviour in the light of early tragedy and the severing of a primal bond, so that Jennifer had nodded, despite herself, excited at the idea that he had insights beyond what she knew of him. But when his analysis was finished, he had looked at her and laughed bitterly. 'You're wrong. You're so duped by that stuff that you have no idea of the real reasons people do things.'

Now, though, he said, 'After she died, we all retired to our separate corners of the house. We almost never ate dinner at the table together again. That's why I hate going to your parents' so much. All the sitting around together, talking, taking an interest in one another. It's alien to me. I don't know how to do it, or how to behave when you all do it.' In all their years together, it was, Jennifer thought, the biggest admission he had made.

'Why didn't you say?' She could have cried. 'We could have eaten in front of the TV. I wouldn't have cared. They wouldn't either.' If anything, she thought, they would have been relieved not to sit through another demonstration of the hostility with which Todd evidently covered up his discomfort. 'It was cancer, right?' she said then, wanting to keep open this startling conversation. 'Your mother?'

'I always tell people that.' Todd said. 'It's easier. Actually, she killed herself.' Into the silence that followed, Jennifer placed a silent vow; that she would earn this confidence. That she would try to care for Todd better. That she would never again allow so much cold and empty space to open between them. That she would stop being scared of him – and of herself – and do better by all of them, especially Rosie. He might never thank her, or even acknowledge the change in her, but for all their sakes she would be stronger, more fit for the purpose she had chosen.

She opened her mouth to speak, but Todd forestalled her. 'Don't,' he said, putting up a bruised hand. 'Don't start crying and telling me how sorry you are.' But he said it without his usual edge. 'I know you are, Jen. That's why I married you. Your kindness, your ability to forgive even where forgiveness isn't deserved. You don't weigh what you give, you just give it, with both hands. Now, bring me up my laptop. I'm going to do some work. That's quite enough domestic psychological excursions for one day. I don't even know why I told you. It changes nothing.'

But it did, Jennifer knew. It changed everything. She took Rosie and went downstairs. The future that had been so long obscure to her was limpid again. This was her life, after all, not something she had wandered mistakenly into, and she was conscious, for the first time in what felt like forever, of wanting it, but also of wanting to make changes in it.

The funny thing was, she thought, that she was conscious that she loved him less – far less – than she had. The hero-worship of their college days which had given way to a kind of desperate, one-sided wanting, had, in turn, given way, to something equivocal, that carried conditions on her side. He too needed to be better – a better husband and father – and Jennifer knew that loving him less blindly might mean she could finally demand that of him.

The doorbell went, startling her. Theirs wasn't a house that people called to uninvited.

It was Natasha, looking tense.

Jennifer remembered that she was annoyed with her. 'Where did you disappear to last night?' she asked, hostile. She had been wondering why Natasha had simply upped and left, right when she needed her.

'I'm sorry,' Natasha said. 'Julie found me doing a line in the bathroom and chucked me out. She wouldn't let me pass Go, so I couldn't come and tell any of you. I didn't text because you never check your phone. So I just went home. Why? What did she tell you?'

'A version of that . . . that she'd found you doing coke in the loo, and that you'd said to tell us you were off to a party with Declan.' Jennifer felt cheerful.

'She's good, isn't she?' Natasha said. 'Always works with what she has.' Then, 'I thought I'd drop by, see how you were. How Todd is. Is that OK?'

'Of course, come in. He's still lying down, but I think he should get up. He's still refusing to go to hospital or the police. But seeing you might cheer him up a bit.'

She brought Natasha upstairs, tapped on the bedroom door and then, to a muffled sound that could have meant anything, opened it. The room was dimly lit, curtains pulled against the daylight, and stuffy; strong masculine odours of sweat and worse.

'Maybe he would feel more comfortable in the sitting room,' Natasha whispered. 'More of a neutral space.'

'I think you're right.' Jennifer gave her a grateful look, impressed by her tact. 'I'll get him up.'

After some moments, she brought Todd shuffling downstairs and to the sitting room. He leaned on her and his steps were slow, slower even than they had been that morning, Jennifer noticed, wondering was he exaggerating, just a little, for Natasha's benefit. Well, she decided, she didn't blame him. He was entitled to every jot of sympathy.

She eased him into an armchair while Natasha looked on silently. She looked more shocked than Jennifer had expected.

'Todd.'

'Natasha.'

The silence then was awkward, and Jennifer could see how much Todd hated being at such a disadvantage. Hated being the weak one, the broken one, in front of Natasha. She was about to say something, suggest that she and Natasha have tea in the kitchen and look in on Todd later, when he said, 'Jen, could you go to the chemist and get me more of the strong painkillers? I've used them all, and the other ones are useless.'

Jennifer jumped up from where she had been sitting, protective, beside him. 'Of course. I'll be right back. Rosie's asleep.'

She left, on a wave of solicitude and excitement.

Todd stared at Natasha.

CHAPTER 33

When Jennifer had suggested going into Todd's room, Natasha had known she couldn't. That she would start to scream if she had to sit in the intimacy of those smells that hung like sheets of cobweb.

She had wanted to see him – to see his bruised face and broken teeth. Remembering the sound of Nancy's voice, the cold slide of Todd's flesh inside her, like a fish unexpectedly disturbed and moving quickly, she had wanted him to be worse even than Jennifer had described him. And yet, watching him come downstairs, seeing his ankles sticking bare from the bottom of his tracksuit, she had felt a sudden stab of pity. Then, her gaze moving to the ugliness of his toes and toenails, she felt revulsion take over. To her relief. Now was not the time to allow pity in, letting it eat away at her anger. Only when Jennifer had left could she look straight at him, appraising. His beauty was ruined, for now anyway. His broad flat nose, like a lion, was broken and slightly off centre, the bridge swollen and discoloured. The scattering of freckles, a join-the-dots game that had added charm to the symmetry of his features, were lost now in the puffy skin still with traces of blood that hadn't been washed off. One eye was nearly closed, the other looked out from a bloody circle and, overall, there was too much blue and red in the usual palette of gold and bronze. She could almost see the imprint of Declan's hands, fists, feet in Todd's face and form the pattern of his intent, and she shuddered. And yet, behind the human instinct to comfort someone so obviously hurt, to bathe the dried blood from his face and put a soothing something on his bruises, she found herself admiring the thoroughness of Declan's work. The way retribution was so clearly picked out on the soft tissue in front of her.

'You look terrible.' She tried to issue the words with shock and sympathy, but knew a sly note of satisfaction was there too. The way he looked at her, from out of the bloody circle, warned her that he had picked it up.

'I feel worse,' he said. He put his hand up to his mouth as he spoke, to hide whatever was inside it, and in his voice was a slur, a sliding of words into each other.

'So why not go to a doctor?'

'No point. There's nothing a doctor can do much about. It'll all heal with time.'

'You might have a few scars,' she said, in defiance of his ability to brush this off.

'Natasha,' he said, 'what's going on?' It came out 'what'sh goin' on'. She could hear the damage to his teeth in each word.

'What do you mean?'

'It was that friend of yours, Declan, who hit me.'

'What?'

'I saw him. And heard him.'

'Heard what?'

'"That's for Natasha", whispered in my ear, somewhere in between him breaking my nose and kicking me in the stomach.' He was trying to sound hard, indifferent, but Natasha suspected he might be trying not to cry. She set her mind away from pity for him.

So it had indeed been Declan. She had known it, and yet not known it, unwilling quite to admit her own part in whatever he might have done. But now she knew – it had been him, for reasons that were his own as much as they had been hers. She felt grateful that he had chosen to take the bait she had offered, but irritated too. What an idiot he was, she thought. He couldn't resist letting his revenge be known, letting himself be known. She sighed. Couldn't he have taken Todd's wallet? His phone? Just for form's sake? He had been an instrument, but a very blunt one.

'Why would Declan want to hurt you?' She was playing for time. Had no idea what came next. This wasn't any part of her script – she had imagined vengeance falling anonymous; swift and sharp like a stiletto knife, then raised and removed as fast as it sliced; sheathed once more and hidden away.

'I don't know,' he said. 'Although I do recognise him. I recognised him at Katherine's gallery, but I couldn't be bothered to say so. I worked with him in London years ago. He was a kid, useless, wanted to be minded and babied, and I probably wasn't very nice to him, but why would that make him attack me now? Anyway, he said it was for you? For you, why? What's going on?'

'You know why.' She had not expected or even wanted to be there, but now that she was, she decided that she would enjoy telling him that his pain matched hers, his humiliation came from hers, his wretchedness was only a fraction of hers.

'I really don't.' He looked at her for a long time then and she stayed silent; she wanted to force his acknowledgement without prompting it. 'Ibiza?' he said at last.

'You know what you did.'

'I know what we did.' His mouth barely moved, the one open eye in its circle of blood was so fixed, the face so swollen, stiff and fantastically coloured, that it was as if a totem or oracle spoke through him.

'Not we. You. What you did. To me.'

'What *I* did?' He said it very slowly. She could see it hurt him to move and tried to be glad.

'Yes, what you did. What you did that got you this.' Her hand made a fist as she spoke and looking down at it, imagining it used the way in which Declan had used his fists, Natasha suddenly wanted to be gone. Todd's battered face made her feel sick, and the instinct to pity still gnawed at her. She wasn't enjoying this at all. Confronting the reality of her revenge had been a mistake. She should have left it in Jennifer's telling, in her own imagination. The smell of his unwashed body, the fear and pain that must have dried on it, disgusted her. But it was the disgust of shame. She no longer feared him – the failure of his flesh to withstand blows, the clear evidence of his mortality made sure of that, but she wanted to be away from him. She began to stand, but he spoke again.

'I always did wonder,' he said slowly. 'Not at the time. At the time, I thought we did what we did together but, afterwards, I wondered. You were so odd. I realised something had gone wrong. But, Natasha, I swear, I didn't realise. I know I'm not always good at understanding what's going on with people. But I thought maybe you just felt guilty, because of Jennifer.'

'I felt guilty alright,' Natasha said, 'but far more than that, I felt disgust, at myself, mostly at you.' She wondered why she was talking to him. She hadn't meant to. Maybe it was because he had opened a possibility that she couldn't resist. 'You say you don't know what you did? Well, I'll tell you. You raped me.' Into the silence that followed, Natasha refused to let the scene pour into her mind once more. She was done with it, she decided. Finally done. 'That's what you do, Todd. You break things. You break people. Me. Jennifer. Nancy.'

At the mention of Nancy's name, he looked up sharply, winced at his own sudden movement, but said nothing, so she went on.

'That catches up eventually, and this is what you get.' She waved her hand, taking in the bruises, the swollen eye, the broken teeth. 'And I am so glad you finally know what it's like to have someone hold you down and hurt you.'

Again a silence. He was the one to break it.

'All this time,' he said. 'You went away, and I forgot all about Ibiza, about you, and what happened. And all this time, you've been thinking about it, believing what I did was rape? Natasha, I don't know why you think it, but I'm sorry that you do. It's not what I intended.'

And Natasha couldn't bear it. Confusion that was almost more terrible than certainty. She decided that if she could get out of that room before Jennifer came back, if she could take the sound of his voice saying 'sorry' and leave all the rest, she would be OK. And so she almost ran. Took her bag, wrenched open the sitting room door. The sound of Rosie wailing from upstairs fell into all that serene oatmeal-coloured perfection like a cascade of water.

He said nothing, watched her go from the bloody circle of his eye. On the doorstep she met Jennifer with the painkillers.

'Oh, don't go,' Jennifer said, taking her arm cosily. 'I'm sorry I was ages. The first chemist didn't have them. Come in. You haven't had tea or anything.'

'I must go,' Natasha said. Then, 'Rosie's crying', which made Jennifer drop her offers of tea and dart quickly into the house.

CHAPTER 34

Natasha walked for miles while she thought, or tried to think. What had Todd said, exactly, and what did it mean? She turned the possibilities over in her mind while her feet found a path to the strand where she sometimes used to walk with Nancy and her mother. Led her, sure and inexorable, to those whorls and undulations of wet sand that reached outwards for a pale-grey sky.

There was more of winter than of autumn in the air, a change in just a matter of days, as if autumn had suddenly realised it was going to be late, had gathered up its bits and pieces and left in a hurry.

Natasha felt alone and stranded, a bird late to the migratory flock and left behind; sacrifice for the bitterness of winter's wind and snow, something to speed the others on their way. She walked and walked, using her feet to beat out the puzzle that perplexed her. Tentatively, she cast her mind back, past all the points where, until now, she had forced it to stop, to the moment itself. This wasn't the way she had told it to Nancy – that had been a skimming of the surface, a joining of specific dots to create the picture she expected to see. This was a deeper, more thorough, analysis.

She knew that the years of squashing what had happened out of sight, her refusal to ever dissect the details, coupled with the contents of that day itself – the heat, her hangover, the drugs still pulsing in her veins that gave a layer of unreality to everything – had meant that she had no very clear idea of any of it. She had had so many bad dreams – terrible dreams, where she tried to escape and failed, from which she woke, heart pounding, to a room she expected to be full of angry noise, only to find the silence more frightening again – that she understood that she no longer knew exactly what had happened. She had a flesh memory only. All she knew were sensations, the limp, acquiescent heat of lust, the sudden jarring of his hand on her neck, the smooth coldness of him inside her. The way she hadn't been able to breathe for those moments, and the way, afterwards, breathing had seemed like something she needed to remind herself to do.

She recalled the days following that day, and the way she had had to plot the sequence of all her actions, how even walking had been a question of establishing the order of effort: lift leg, pick up foot, lean forward, place down, repeat with other foot, so that she worried she muttered these things aloud, audible to those around her.

And maybe it had all been for nothing. Or not nothing, exactly, because the ambiguous brusqueness of Todd's actions, the anger he had brought with him to her, could never be washed over, but if his intent, his purpose, had been other than she understood it – what then? How much did his intent matter?

If Todd was right and she was wrong, what then? Did the fact that he didn't know what he was doing change what he had done? Could there, after all, be a way back to that moment, and a way of making it new?

As she walked, the rhythm of her feet brought her the answer, a feeling of lightness that came from the ground up. Yes, there was a way to change this. His intent mattered. Mattered more than anything. If Todd was telling the truth – that, for all his aggressive acquisitiveness, his purpose had not been as she thought it – then everything was different.

Her humiliation, carried with her, cupped between her two hands so that she had no freedom of movement, was changed. Shame at what she had done to Jennifer remained, shame at the way in which she had let excitement and grief build together into something she couldn't control also remained, but the most searing shame, of what Todd did to her, the way he had used and treated her, were not the same.

He had still done it, it had still been ugly and clumsy and angry, nothing could change that, and she still knew that she hated him – but he had not done what she thought he had done. He had not raped her. She had not been raped.

And if that was so, all those things could become smaller in time, in a way the misery lurking within her never had.

She allowed herself to remember the sound of his voice saying 'Sorry', and understood that to be the thing she had wanted more, even more than she had wanted revenge. Because for a new version of that day to exist, she had to be willing to accept it. And she was. More than anything, now, she was.

A profound and disorienting relief gripped her then, making her mind into the speed and shape of an arrow, flying fast and true across the miles of shiny wet sand. She felt she could fly forever. Except that she held back, forced herself to think about the mess that still lay at her feet, the rubble of plans and schemes, set in motion and executed, trapping her even now.

Todd's battered face came to her as surely as the sound of his voice wrapped around that word 'sorry'. The imprint of Declan's fists on his face, the sound of Nancy asking, 'Why?' All these things she had to deal with and somehow make better.

But, still, the excitement of her relief, and determination to hold onto it, made her giddy, told her that all would be well and everything could be resolved. And she listened, too grateful to say no. Todd was beaten, but he would heal. A few more days and the marks would fade. She was determined to obey the limits of her regret. She would keep it simple. Declan and Nancy were both complicated – Declan, she saw now, she had picked up as if he was a pin or bit of string, because he might be useful later. And he had been useful; her calculation had been correct. And unforgivable.

But Nancy was more urgent. Because Nancy's breakdown was now her fault, not Todd's. She needed to talk to her, even though she had no idea what she could say.

She rang John.

'How's Nancy? Any news? Can I visit today?'

'No.' He paused. 'She didn't ring you?'

'No. Why?'

'She's gone to your mother's. They were willing to discharge her into care and your mother went and got her.'

'When's she back at yours?'

'I'm not sure.' He paused again. 'I think she's going to stay a while.'

'Stay?'

'Yes. She said she needed to get away, that she couldn't be here anymore.' Behind the usual stiffness in his voice, the way he braced himself against any emotion, he sounded unhappy.

So Natasha, realising how close she was to her mother's house, amazed to see where her feet had carried her, went home too, to the house where lunch was being prepared, where Nancy was slouched in an armchair, wearing a top with sleeves that fell past her wrists, reading one of their father's old hardbacked books that smelled of damp and endeavour. The light behind her was as sharp as a question mark.

'I didn't know you were coming back here?' Natasha sat beside her on a footstool that wobbled and forced her to look up at Nancy.

'I didn't either.' Nancy's head stayed bent over her book.

'Are you OK?' What she really wanted was for Nancy to ask her the same question. Nancy, of course, did not.

'I'm fine.' Her response was a door slammed by a brisk wind.

'I mean, you know you can tell me if you need to talk?' Natasha tried again, to open that door sufficiently to step through.

'I know.' Again, Nancy shut her down.

'Do you want to go for a walk?'

'No thanks. I'm just going to read. And lunch will be ready soon. It would be rude.'

'She wouldn't mind.' Too often, Natasha still referred to her mother as 'she', unable to give her the power of being anything more intimate.

'Of course she'll mind,' said Nancy. 'She's been cooking for hours, then you just turn up without a word, so now she's having to make more so that there's enough.'

Natasha had seen Nancy like this before – blank, stonewalling – but never to her, only to others, people whose questions she considered dumb or impertinent.

'It's my house too. My mother, too,' Natasha said stiffly.

'You can't have it both ways. Either they are, and you take more interest, or they aren't, and you don't.' Nancy angled her head to move the hair away from where it cast a shadow across the page in front of her, but still didn't look up. 'Once a week for Sunday lunch and some boring conversation about your job doesn't entitle you to anything.'

'That's unfair,' Natasha said. 'It's you and her that keep things like that. I would love for there to be more.'

'Poor Natasha, always waiting for an invitation.'

'What do you mean?'

'You know, she came every day when I was in St Canice's. You never came once.'

'I would have come. I would have moved in there with you,'

Natasha said, stung by an injustice that seemed deliberate, a careful catch-22 that Nancy had planned. 'You wouldn't let me.'

'I told her not to as well, but she came anyway. Sometimes, I wouldn't even see her, but she still came. She didn't wait to be asked, like it was a *party*.' Nancy dripped sarcasm onto the word. 'She didn't make it all about her.'

Understanding that to remain was useless, Natasha left the room. There was nothing, then, that she could say to Nancy. Nothing she dared to say. She took pains to close the door carefully so that no sudden bang or click might further disturb the air or jolt more bitter accusations from the walls and floors. The house felt more empty than ever before, more empty even than the day they had returned to it from the funeral, their ears full of those promises of 'anything we can do, anything at all, just ask' that are so easy to make, so difficult to translate into action.

What did 'anything' mean? Was it an offer of practical support? A lift to the shops? To the garage? Or was it a more metaphysical thing? A shoulder to lean on, cry on? A calm voice and steady arm in time of heartbreak? In fact, none of the offers had come to anything, because they had never taken them up, preferring first to huddle together, then to stand awkwardly away from each other, allowing the space between them to broaden.

She made her way to the garden, bypassing the kitchen where she could have asked for a job – something to clean or chop – that would have given her focus. Outside it was blustery, with a damp chill. Tree branches, still heavy with late leaves, bent low to the ground, pressed hard by the wind and by a sense of the inevitability of winter. The wrought-iron table and chairs, where she had sat smoking with Jennifer after the unhappy family meal of so many years ago, were still outside, in case of a few final good days.

She sat down, ignoring the wet, and tried to listen to the sounds around her. But nothing reached her ears except the roar of the wind. No birdsong, no hum of insects, no delicate distinction of leaves rustling according to their own position and balance, just the blanket whoosh of wind.

So she went into the kitchen, where her mother was halfway through a soup with chickpeas in it.

'I'm sorry,' Natasha said, 'I think I can't stay for lunch after all.' Her mother shrugged, as if the news were no surprise to her, so that Natasha added, 'I would have liked to, but I think Nancy is better without me for the moment.'

It was the kind of remark her mother usually greeted with silence; a silence that, to Natasha, spoke of loyalty to Nancy, dislike of Natasha. This time, her mother broke it. 'And you are just going to leave her like that?'

'What else can I do?'

'You can do something, Natasha. To leave is pathetic. She doesn't want you to, you know that? She wants you to force her to let you stay.'

'But how do you know that?'

'I know,' her mother said, then added, 'I'm sorry you never learned Spanish.'

'What?' Natasha was surprised.

'Your father did not think it was worth the while for you, but I am sorry.'

'Why?'

'Because if you had, I think you would understand many things better. I know you would understand Nancy better. Me, too,' her mother finished sadly.

Was it true? Natasha wondered. Was this simply a language barrier? 'I don't believe in revenge,' she remembered saying to Jennifer once, so long ago that it seemed a different life, with a different set of rules. She was, she now knew, far more like her mother than she had known, and knew that the realisation must bring them closer.

'Well, I can still learn it,' she said.

'You can.' Her mother smiled. 'Your mind was always quick. Now, go and talk with Nancy.'

And so Natasha did. Burst back into that room where Nancy still sat, hostile, in the old armchair, and instead of being polite and cautious and deferential to Nancy and her problems and her sensitivities, Natasha was none of those things. She took the astonishing feeling of freedom she had found with Todd's apology and rushed forward with it.

'Right, so you hate me and feel hard done by because you think you had the raw edge of our childhood.'

'I don't think, I know.'

'OK, you know. But the thing is Nancy, he's dead.' She spoke to herself as much as to her sister. 'There's just the three of us now. Whatever he did, or didn't do, whatever I did or should have done, or any of it, there's only you, me and Maria now, and none of us is doing terribly well on our own.'

'I can't. Not unless you admit it,' Nancy muttered.

'Admit what?'

'That it was unfair.'

'I do admit it, Nancy. It *was* unfair. Very unfair. He shouldn't have, and I shouldn't have let him. I loved him, so much, but I should have seen that it wasn't right. I should have listened when Maria tried to tell me it wasn't right, but I didn't want to.'

'Parading you around the place like some kind of superstar,' Nancy said bitterly.

'He did a bit, I know. I liked it,' Natasha said, wry, 'but I should have realised how bad it was.'

'Bad,' Nancy agreed.

'Very bad,' Natasha said.

'I loved him too. But anything I ever got from him felt like it was accidental, or because you weren't around. Do you have any idea how that makes someone feel?'

'I can imagine.'

'You can't,' Nancy said, 'but maybe you can begin to.'

Maria came in shortly afterwards to tell them lunch was ready, and burst into sudden tears to see her daughters sitting squashed up together in the armchair, talking to each other in voices that were kind, not sharp. Seeing her mother's tears, allowing herself to be moved, not angered by them, Natasha cried too then, and Nancy, who didn't, patted both their shoulders.

Wiping her nose, Natasha realised that the grief she had formed the habit of not looking at was out now, released. It lay in front of her. And, she saw immediately, it was less than she had supposed. Only by a little, but it was less. There was, after all, a limit to it. Edges, places where it tapered off instead of continuing into a terrifying infinity. She saw that she could start to plan at those edges. They all could.

CHAPTER 35

The sound of the phone in the dark and silent apartment was hysterical, and Natasha woke, heart thumping. It took a moment to realise that the screams, for once, came from something other than herself. She found the phone, answered it, frantic.

'Hello?' The number was unfamiliar. *Nancy. It must be Nancy.*

'It's me.' Jennifer. 'I'm ringing from the hospital.' She was crying. 'Todd's taken a turn. A bad one. He fainted and they think he's bleeding internally and they don't know how bad it is.' The crying got worse. 'I knew he should have seen a doctor, but he wouldn't, and I didn't force him, and now he might die.'

'He's not going to die,' Natasha said, but with frightened need only, not conviction. 'He'll be OK. Where are you?'

'The Royal Hospital. I'm in A&E. They're finding a bed for him.'

'OK, I'll come now. It'll be fine, Jen. He'll be OK.' But would he? she wondered frantically as she dressed, trying to think calmly about what she would need. About what Jennifer might need. She threw a few books into her bag, a large blue pashmina in case they were sitting on chairs all night, cold, tired, unable to sleep. Would he be

336

alright? And what if he wasn't? She saw his face again as she had seen it that afternoon; bruised blue and yellowish, swollen, as if a toad was sitting under his skin.

What if he died? What then? She tried the idea on, allowed her mind to turn it this way and that, watching as the light of her attention caught it. She saw his coffin, Jennifer weeping, Rosie in her arms. If Todd died, Jennifer would never know what she had done. But if he died, what about Declan? What, then, was he? A killer? And for what? For whom? Because if Todd died, it would be for no reason; not retribution, but murder.

Natasha ran to the loo and vomited.

She found Jennifer, face grey with exhaustion and fear, in the waiting room. Around her was the lethargy of people sunk in their own misery, natural curiosity subdued by their own cares. Some bled, some slumped, some clutched the bits of themselves that hurt. A woman complained about the wait, but to herself, the words 'disgrace' drifting from the corner of her mouth as she tucked her head into the collar of her dirty raincoat. The hard, white lights flickered overhead, interrupted by what seemed to be the regular plucking of ghostly fingers. An empty chair beside Jennifer was badly bolted to its frame, the beige plastic seat jerking back as Natasha sat on it, as if trying to tip her onto the floor.

'Any news?' She took Jennifer's arm, hugged it to her hard.

'Not really. They found him a bed and hooked him up to heaps of drips and things. They've given him various injections and he's asleep now. I'll go back in a minute. I came down to wait for you, and get something to eat. I think I might faint as well.' She gave a wobbly smile.

'And there probably aren't any spare drips for you.' Natasha forced herself to smile back. Jennifer did indeed look ready to pass out. But it was more than the exhaustion of worry and the late-night vigil.

'Where's Rosie?'

'I had to ask one of the neighbours to help because it would have taken the babysitter far too long to get over. The woman next-door. I've almost never spoken to her, except about bins and car parking,' Jennifer said, adding in wonderment, 'she was really nice. Said not to worry, to go with Todd and she would be delighted to help.'

They shot coins into vending machines and armed themselves with coffees, milky and sweet, and chocolate bars. The momentary giddiness of sugar brought relief.

'How did the doctors seem? You can always tell a lot from them,' Natasha said wisely.

'I don't know. Calm, but sort of urgent.' Jennifer broke off, gulped. 'The nurses were great. They made a few jokes, but nice jokes, not horrid ones. They wanted to know why he hadn't seen anyone earlier, and I said he refused to and they just nodded, as if that was almost normal and not stupid and crazy of him. I should have forced him, Natasha. I was going to ring my dad even and ask him, but Todd wouldn't let me. He made me swear I wouldn't, but I shouldn't have listened. It's my fault.'

'It's not your fault, Jen. Don't be ridiculous. You can't have this – this is Todd's drama, not yours.' Worry made her harsher than she meant to be. Jennifer looked hurt. 'I'm sorry, that sounded awful. But you know what I mean – this isn't about you "not making" him. You couldn't have made him. You've never been able to make him do anything. And even if you had rung your dad, what was he going to say over the phone, without seeing Todd? Tell you to make sure he goes to a doctor? Which you couldn't have done. So forget it. It's going to be fine, and it's not your fault.'

'Do you really think it'll be OK?'

'It will,' Natasha said stoutly, desperately. In truth, she thought nothing, except that he had to be fine.

'He was in so much pain,' Jennifer said. 'Before he fainted. He was in agony and his stomach was swollen and he was so scared. He didn't know what to do then either. Even though he always knows what to do. And suddenly I did know. I called an ambulance. I took control.' She sounded amazed at herself.

'You see, you did exactly the right thing.'

'Maybe I did.'

They went in then, to a small room where Todd lay, eyes closed, arms arranged neatly outside the blue hospital blanket, palms upwards, while lines and tubes gathered and delivered various liquids to and from his body. He looked serene; even the battered bits of his face no longer struck Natasha as grotesque. They had assimilated, found space for themselves. Or maybe it was just that, eyes closed, the body didn't have Todd's personality.

And yet, his form had something more, by far, than a body without life. Even though both lay in repose with shut eyes, the instantly discernible difference had nothing to do with the movement of breath, the gentle rise and fall of a chest. It was a thing in essence. Inside, Todd's body lay the impetus of self, ready to uncoil. A dead body, Natasha knew too well, had nothing, was simple an absence, a black hole into which you could fall forever. He'll be OK, she thought.

They stood, watching, in silence, Jennifer holding Natasha's hand, until a nurse came in. 'You can't be here,' she told Natasha. 'Only one.'

'Is he going to be alright?' Jennifer asked.

'The doctor will talk to you later. He's on his rounds. We'll have a clearer picture in the morning.'

'Please tell me,' Jennifer begged. 'Will he live?'

'The bleeding is under control,' the nurse said gently. 'He needs

339

to be monitored. He won't wake up for a good while. You don't need to stay here. We'll look after him. Get some rest, or a cup of tea.'

'She's not going to tell us any more,' Natasha whispered, and felt the painful squeeze of Jennifer's hand in hers. 'She can't. There's a café close by that stays open late. Let's go there. You need proper food. Or as proper as they have.'

Jennifer allowed herself to be led away and out, where the cold night air with its tang of fog was like a whoop of good cheer after the hospital fug. The café was empty and ugly, too-bright lights, too-yellow surfaces, smells of old grease and grubby newspapers, but the man behind the counter said he would bring them fried eggs and potato waffles.

'And tea,' Natasha said.

'You shouldn't have any more caffeine,' Jennifer said. 'You should go home and get some sleep.'

'No chance,' Natasha said. 'I'm staying with you. Though he'll probably be out for hours. Are you sure you don't want to get some sleep? I can stay here.' It was the least, the very least, she could do.

'I want to stay,' Jennifer said. 'He might wake up and need something. If he does, he'll be frightened.'

They poured cups of tea, into which they heaped teaspoons of sugar, and sat eating greasy bits of waffle and talking gently, while the night stayed muffled and dark around them. Jennifer rang her parents, who said they would come and mind Rosie the following morning. She stood up to go to the loo, but blood began to gush from her nose, the way it used to when she was small; fast and hard so that it seemed every bit of her would liquify and pour out through her nostrils.

'Oh shit. Sit down,' Natasha said, grabbing at napkins, signalling the café owner to bring more. 'Head back?' she asked.

'Head forward,' muttered Jennifer thickly, through the stream of blood that ran around and past her mouth, leaning forward and pinching the bridge of her nose. 'Get ice.'

Natasha got ice, wrapped in a tea towel, which Jennifer applied carefully to the bit where her nose met her forehead. Most of the mess was on her clothes but sticky spots around her feet showed like a sprinkling of shiny sequins thrown over her and come to rest on the floor.

The café owner came over. 'You need a doctor?' he asked.

He must be itching to get a mop and bucket and bleach, Natasha thought. And who could blame him.

'No, I'll be fine in a minute,' Jennifer managed. He hovered for a while, then moved back behind the counter.

Gingerly, Jennifer leaned back. The bleeding seemed to have reduced to an intermittent spotting but she knew from experience that a false move – too fast, in the wrong direction – could set her off again.

'Jesus,' said Natasha, 'There's nothing vague about a nosebleed is there?'

'No,' Jennifer agreed gallantly, although she looked very white. 'I used to quite like them as a kid. Best attention-getters ever.'

'And no describing the pain,' Natasha agreed. 'No need to say where it is, like with a headache, and if it's sickness too or just sore. A nosebleed pretty much announces itself.'

'I think I'm out of the habit though,' Jennifer said. 'I don't remember there being this much blood.'

'Just take it easy there,' Natasha said. 'Keep your head still. No sudden movements.'

'I'm going back to college next year,' Jennifer said after a while in which they sat quietly, with the low hum of the café radio in the background, playing old songs interspersed with rambling chat from the DJ. 'I decided this afternoon.'

'That's a great idea,' Natasha said. 'Will you finish your thesis?'

'I'm not sure. I can't honestly remember what I wanted to do with it. It all feels very long ago. I think I'll start something new – I'm

going to study medieval literature – and see what happens. In a way,'
she admitted, 'I don't much care what I do. The idea of getting out of
the house more, of having deadlines and classes, is just . . .' She made
an expansive motion with her arms, curtailed by the necessity of not
moving her head, but Natasha could see what she meant. Freedom.
Choice. Things to do.

'And Rosie?'

'Soon she can go to playschool in the mornings. Todd's been on
at me to get a full-time nanny for ages, and I might now. I didn't
want to before, because I didn't know what on earth I would do
with myself, but now . . .' The mention of Todd made them both fall
silent again, aware of just why they were sitting in that harshly lit
café in the dark watches of the night.

'He was so sweet today,' Jennifer said after a while. 'So unlike
himself.' She gave a wonky laugh. 'That sounds terrible, but what I
mean is, he was gentle, because he was vulnerable. He isn't normally
gentle.'

'Most people are far nicer in their weak moments than when
they're on top of the world,' Natasha said.

She wondered would Todd tell anyone what she had done, what
Declan had done. And if so, what then? Would he tell Jennifer?
What then would Natasha say to explain herself? The enormity of it
all threatened to crush her, so many things, jostling and thrusting,
all determined to be first, jeering at her because she didn't know how
to handle them; how to order and subdue them.

Todd will be OK, she told herself. He will get out of hospital
tomorrow, with just some bruises and, bit by bit, I will put all
this right. She saw herself lining up the dominoes of her duty and
knocking them over one by one. More than anything, she wanted
the world around her to reset itself. Back to zero. Back to a time
before all this. So that she could get on with her own life at last.

Jennifer's phone rang and she pounced on it.

'Yes. Yes. OK. Yes' she finished the call, stood up too fast and swayed, clutching the edge of the table. 'I have to go. That was the hospital. They want to scan Todd's brain. They are concerned there might be some trauma.' In the eye of an emergency, Jennifer was strangely calm, and so Natasha imitated her.

'OK,' she said. 'Will I come with you?

'There's no point,' Jennifer insisted. 'You should go home.'

'No chance.'

'Then wait here. It's less awful than the waiting room.'

'OK. Leave your bag and coat; you can come back for them. Call me if you need me. Call me anyway. I'll be right here,' she repeated it urgently, needed Jennifer to know that she would go nowhere, that she would keep vigil at their table, now covered with crumbs and the odd splash of blood.

Jennifer left and Natasha watched her through the window until the fog swallowed her. She set herself to cleaning up the bits of blood with a paper napkin dipped in water, scrubbing until the table was clean.

It was so late by then that 'tomorrow' felt conditional; too remote a place to ever arrive. And perhaps it wouldn't, she thought. Perhaps she could sit here forever in this moment and keep everything at bay.

'More tea?' the owner asked. Natasha wondered how many dramas and tragedies he had surveyed from the peripheries, how many cups of tea he had dispensed into desperate voids. She nodded, not because she wanted any more but in order to buy herself time and space at his table. Then she rang Martin. And although it was early, or late, or whatever it was, and although she told him nothing except, 'I need to see you, I'm at the hospital. Beside the hospital,' he said he would come. He asked first did she want to go to him, and when she said no, said, 'Stay there, then. I'll be right over.'

'Beside the hospital,' she repeated, knowing he had grasped the essentials already. 'A café with a green awning.'

She pulled one of the books she had brought out of her bag but couldn't read. The words sat on the page in stodgy isolation, refusing to come together into sentences. So she killed the time waiting for Martin by pouring sugar onto the table and making roads in it like Nancy had done, a complex infrastructure in specks of white.

'So?' And there he was, beside the table. Of course he had found the place immediately. She liked that he hadn't rushed in, frantic, with questions, loud whats? and whys? driven by sly curiosity as much as by a desire to help.

'Martin.' She smiled at him, at the familiar set of his shoulders in a grey jumper, the broad chest and neatly cut hair. 'You always look so clean.'

'What's going on?' he asked, sitting. 'Why hospital?'

'Long story.' Now that he was here, she was reluctant to begin. Didn't have the energy to say it all, didn't know what shape she wanted the words to take, so she traced a few more roads in the sugar. 'Will you order something?'

'Yes, tea. Natasha, why are we here?'

'Todd's in hospital, next door. He fainted, internal bleeding. From the beating. Jennifer's there now.'

'Is he going to be alright?'

'I'm not sure. Jennifer is signing forms for a brain scan. They think there might be trauma.' She said the word slowly, questioningly, unsure what exactly 'trauma' might mean in this context, forced herself to ask, 'What would that mean exactly?'

'Some kind of brain damage.'

'Right.' She accepted the weight of the words, their judgement on her. She had made Declan a criminal, sent Nancy mad, and, possibly destroyed Todd. Destroyed his life. Jennifer's life. Rosie's life. She played out scenes in her mind where Jennifer helped Todd to dress, to eat, brought him out for walks, showed him how to play simple games on the laptop. Rosie was beside Jennifer in these pictures. At first, still a baby, she was another care and duty for Jennifer. Later, as a child, Rosie resented her father and the amount of time and care he took up, the drain he was upon her mother's energy and happiness. Later again, a grown up, Rosie helped Jennifer. She too cared for a fumbling, halting version of Todd, grown old without ever reaching his full self; called 'father' without fulfilling the thousand loving duties that would have earned him the name.

'I'm sure it's precautionary,' Martin said. 'They have to do these things. It's routine.'

'But he was fine,' Natasha said. 'I saw him today, yesterday I mean, and he was fine.' As if saying might make it so. But had he been? she wondered. All that unaccustomed reflection and humility. The same things Jennifer had seen in him. Was that just a fading reaction to being scared, or was it some kind of strange manifestation of damage?

'It can take a while for trauma to show up. But I'm sure he'll be fine. He pretty much lives in his own movie most of the time anyway.' He sounded faintly amused.

'And what if he's not?' Natasha asked, as if he had, indeed, any answers.

'We'll deal with it then.'

She clung to that word 'we', and the knowledge that he meant it. Did not dare think much beyond the comfort of his solidarity.

'I'm thinking of moving back to Brussels,' she said then, trying out the idea. And indeed her instinct was to flee; if Todd should prove to be damaged by her hand, she could see no way other than further exile.

'Why?' Martin sounded almost as if he had expected this.

'Well, no one seems all that pleased that I'm back.' She waited an instant to see would he disagree. He said nothing. 'And I don't really feel at home here, any more than I did there.' It was a lie, but a useful one.' And so . . .' She was deliberately vague, deciding to let silence do the rest of the work. It was the desperate part of the night when darkness is at its most profound, where words fall without resonance into a flat black pool and make no echo.

'What about Katherine's gallery?'

'I don't know . . .' She didn't finish. Couldn't make herself say, 'I don't know anything anymore. Until I hear about Todd, I cannot know anything.'

'Can I tell you what I think?' Martin said at last.

'Yes.' She felt scared.

'I think you should wait it out. I think you've made a mess. Of something. I'm not sure what, although I might have some idea. And now you're frightened, and feel bad, and so you're thinking of running away. Again.'

'And if you're right' – it was as close as she could come to admitting that he was – 'then what should I do?'

'Stay, try and set things right. Tell me.'

'I can't. I don't dare.'

'Natasha, just tell me.'

And even though Martin, of everyone, had the power to take her bitter mistakes, her misunderstandings and violent retributions, and make them alright by the very fact of his knowing them, she wouldn't. Because he alone, now, could say 'I forgive you'. And because of that, she couldn't let him. She couldn't allow herself the comfort of disclosure. Not for her the clean slate, the fresh start that comes with a full confession and forgiveness. That, she understood, was to be her penance. She needed to forgive herself, not wait for others to do it.

Instead, she told him about Nancy and her mother, about the new and better understanding and where she believed it could lead.

And when she had finished, Martin only said, 'It's funny how often things aren't what we think.' Which to Natasha meant nothing, at least nothing useful. She had hoped he would say he loved her, that everything would be OK and he would mind her, but he didn't. 'My head hurts,' she said.

'You need some sleep.'

'I'm not leaving.'

'Sleep here then.'

So Natasha wrapped herself in the blue pashmina and leaned her head against Martin's chest, his arm around her. She slept, a blacking-out of senses that was so complete, she didn't know where she was when she woke and sat up, confused and alarmed, to find that Martin was in the same position, and it was morning.

'Any news?' she asked immediately. For all the comforting and solid heat of his body, her neck was stiff and her head ached. The café owner was gone, replaced by a young woman with dirty hair, and, around them, tables were filling up.

Outside, the street was busy. People passed by, takeout coffees in hand, texting and chatting and starting their days with an energy that astounded her. Filled with purpose and what looked, to her, like joy. There was an honesty and humility to their flow that she wished for. The way they went about what was simply business, without rancour or grandeur. That was what she wanted to do – day-to-day things, in a day-to-day way, with a simplicity that was precious.

'Not yet.'

She felt then that she had woken to another of her nightmares, but one where she was not victim but wrongdoer.

CHAPTER 36

Declan was shifty, and Natasha knew why. The news was all over the city, or so it seemed – excitable missives that travelled faster than details: 'Todd Beatty's been beaten so badly he'll never walk again'; 'He's been left a vegetable, unable to talk or feed himself'. The telling was quick and giddy, news hopping from person to person like a bird on a branch, a sharp undercurrent of excitement outweighing the careful protestations of sympathy, so that by the time Natasha made it to the café below their office, she knew Declan would have heard many versions, each more lurid than the last.

She was first to arrive, still under-slept, so that her eyes itched and her skin felt thin, translucent as tracing paper, as if the bright day might shine right through it. She had called in sick as soon as she'd woken, hardly able to believe that there was a place where normal life was going on, where her colleagues would be assembling in the glass-walled office for a normal day.

She had rung Jennifer as soon as she'd woken up, looking for any late scrap of news she might have missed.

'The investors were on to me first thing,' Jennifer said. 'Distinctly nervous. I'd say ready to move against Todd and take control of the companies if they feel they need to. I think Jean must have tipped them off, out of spite or in the spirit of a rat on a sinking ship.'

'Or both,' Natasha said. 'Did you get any sleep yet?'

'Not really. My parents are here now, minding Rosie, but I feel like I'm fizzing. It's like an electric current is running through me. As soon as I stop moving, I start to twitch. It's horrible.'

'You're still in shock,' Natasha said. 'It's just a reaction. You're overtired, overwhelmed. You'll be fine.' She didn't know where the soothing words were coming from, some place of instinct or automatic reassurance, because she felt no connection with them as they emerged. Too tired, too shocked herself to understand or feel them fully. When she closed her eyes, she saw flashes of red – blood streaming from Jennifer's nose – cut through with flashes of green – the awning of the café – and Todd's swollen and battered face, a map of things bruised, bloodied, broken, all pulsing horribly in and out of each other. So she kept her eyes open.

'How are your parents?' Natasha asked.

'You can't imagine how lovely it is having them here,' Jennifer said. 'The first thing my mother did was move the furniture around so that the kitchen and sitting room actually feel cosy. It's funny. All she had to do was move a few chairs and a lamp or two, and the place feels completely different. And the way she took Rosie, as if she understood and loved her, when I feel they have barely seen her, barely know her, was so incredible.' And she burst into tears; crying then in the way she hadn't dared to all the long night before.

'It's going to be OK,' Natasha said, weary but still unable to stand down from her place of high alert. 'It's all fine now.'

And it was. Because Todd was going to be OK – Jennifer had announced it to her and Martin early that morning, bursting into the café, by then filled with steam and the smell of bacon, to where they sat, still huddled in their corner, like two people marooned on a tiny, dirty, plastic island.

'It's alright,' Jennifer had said. 'I've just seen the consultant. He'll be fine.'

'Hey.' Declan drew up a chair then, smiled, but she could see he was uneasy. His eyes darted to her face and away from it, flickering like a lizard's tongue. It was a look, a flicker, that Natasha recognised, one that spoke of too many thoughts and schemes, self-justifications and doctored explanations delivered to an invisible cast of accusers. She felt, all over again, the outrage of her intrusion into his life, the vicious seeds she had planted and the way she had tended them, then led him to harvest them.

'Why aren't you in?' he asked.

'I called in sick, although I'm not actually sick. I spent most of the night in hospital, with Jennifer. Todd took a really bad turn.'

'I heard that. How is he?' She could hear him choking on the words, desperation for an answer driven under by fear at what the answer might be.

'He's going to be fine,' she said, then rushed on before either of them could betray themselves, because she wanted so much to get clean away from this conversation, leave no splinter of acknowledgement between them that could fester or multiply. 'He got beaten up' – she had to look at the table as she spoke – 'and the worry was that there were complications, but there aren't and he's fine.'

'Lucky.'

'Yes, lucky.' Lucky Todd. Lucky him. Lucky her. 'Very.'

He sat back a little then.

'He's a shit,' she continued, desperate to slide some kind of message below the partition between them, because part of walking away was to leave nothing behind; no debt of honour or obligation. 'I'm sure he deserved to be beaten up, but I'm glad it isn't worse.'

'Me too.' He reached a hand across the table, clasped hers with a warmth and familiarity that shocked her. 'Let's have a drink? You're not going into the office anyway, and I've got a fairly easy afternoon.'

'Can't.' She disentangled her hand gently. 'I need to go to bed. I'm wrecked.'

'Grand. I'm off to London for a few days tomorrow, but soon.' He must have booked the trip that morning, she thought, perhaps as soon as he heard – whatever it was he had heard . . . *Todd's dead. He's dying. He's brain-damaged* . . . His instinct, like hers, was to flee. But he was resilient, she knew; as ready to rise up as yeast. Soon, no doubt, fright forgotten, he would tell himself that Todd deserved it, that he had acted correctly, even admirably.

'I booked last week,' Declan was saying, 'my ex has been on to me for ages. She wants to meet and talk.'

Why was he bothering with the elaborate explanation? she wondered, before deciding that it really didn't matter.

'So will Todd go to the police?' he asked.

'I'm not sure. At first, he said he wouldn't, but after everything that's happened, maybe he'll change his mind. Jennifer wants him to.' She needed to move carefully; enough signals to be useful, not enough to be an admission. 'She says the attacker might do the same thing to someone else. I told her I didn't think that was likely . . .' She looked at him, but not properly, focusing her attention on a point very slightly past his face.

'Anyway, it doesn't matter,' she went on. 'It happened the night we went to the cinema together, right?' It was as close as she would ever come – to admitting her part, to promising her protection. But he refused both, as she had secretly hoped he would.

'We've never been to the cinema together.' Then, with a smile, 'Why would we bother? There are far more interesting things to do.'

So she gave it up, sat through another few minutes of chat – what had happened in the office that morning, a race through bog and rivers that he was planning to do when he came back from London

– before excusing herself with the plea, 'I'm fading rapidly. I feel like the Wicked Witch of the West, melting. Soon I'll be a puddle all over the table.'

He walked her back to her apartment, hugged her hard at the door. 'Mind yourself. I'll see you later.'

Natasha went upstairs, to bed, to sleep that welcomed her like a friend.

'He seems to have completely forgotten how frightened he was,' Jennifer said wonderingly.

It was the next day and they were walking briskly, takeout coffees in hand, along the seafront after Natasha's working day had ended.

'As if it never happened. If I hadn't seen him myself, I wouldn't believe it now. But I did see him. He was terrified. I know he was. You know what I was most frightened of? That Todd wouldn't recover – and then what would happen to me and Rosie? I realised that I don't know anything about his business, or where he keeps anything important. I don't know where the deeds of the house are, or if there are any savings or anything.'

'Jennifer, don't you have a joint bank account?'

'No. If I need money, Todd gives it to me.'

'Jesus. That's not very smart.'

'No.' Jennifer stayed silent a moment, then said, 'Isn't it awful that my first thought was for me and Rosie, not for him?'

'No, it isn't. It's called survival instinct, and you could probably do with a bit more of it.'

'I think you might be right. Do you remember you once joked that I was like Lady Lazarus, in the Sylvia Plath poem?'

'I do.' It was a lifetime ago, in a different country and a different time, but she remembered.

'Well, I think maybe I need to try a bit harder to be like her. I need to rise out of the ash, of myself mostly.'

'And how might you rise?'

'I have some ideas,' Jennifer said. 'You know, I saw things clearly for the first time in years, the day at home with Todd, before you called over. Even more so the night at the hospital. I saw myself, mostly – a ghost in my own life. I saw how bad it must be for Rosie to have a mother who is barely there, and for Todd to have a wife who never says no to him, never checks the reach of his ambition, never asks for anything at all. Todd, of all people, needs someone to stand up to him a bit. Once he was down, even for those few days, I saw that. And that I need to do more things for myself. Those damn baby books are right – happy mummy, happy baby – and I haven't been. It was like that film *It's A Wonderful Life*, except in reverse. I saw myself removed from my own life, and how small the dent my going would make.'

'That's not true, Jennifer.'

'It is, at the moment, but I'm not going to let it be any longer.'

Maria, glowing with the joy of better understanding, decided to have a party. 'So many anniversaries and birthdays that have not been celebrated,' she said firmly. 'It is time.' They were ordered home to help, ordered to invite friends, to show themselves bright and willing.

It was, Maria said, to be the party they had never had since he died. A party that was ten years too late, 'but better than never'. To celebrate everything that had been allowed to slip by untended, to celebrate for the sake of celebrating, and because it had been so long since any of them had seen the house lit up and full, of people, food, music, fun.

Natasha stayed over for the week, in her old room. She had given notice at work, ready to make a success of the gallery with Katherine, and had duly taken the 'gardening leave' she had expected to be offered. She stayed, she said, because it was easier than coming and going, and meant she could help more, but really, they all knew, she was there because it felt better. 'Nicer,' she said to Nancy one night as they read quietly together. 'It's like being on holiday.'

'On holiday to your own childhood,' Nancy joked. She seemed her old self again, but with perhaps another layer of wariness. Nancy had so many by now, the veils and curtains that hung between her inner self and the world, that protected her but also shrouded her. The marks on her arms had almost all healed to scratches – only the worst still showed any heat – and she was making plans to take up work again where she had left off.

It was that which had finally forced Natasha's reluctance to talk about Todd. She had considered saying nothing, leaving Nancy to believe whatever she wanted, but the strong feeling that they needed to have no more secrets between them made her speak.

Also, if Nancy went back to work, that might mean going back to Todd, at least seeing him, and what might he now do or say, freed up from moral decency as he now was by knowledge of her clumsy, violent actions?

Nancy sat in the same chair, with the same light behind her, as she had the day she had accused Natasha of waiting for an invitation to visit her in St Canice's, and Natasha seized the moment of her stillness.

'I need to talk to you.'

'Really, Natasha, you don't, it's all OK now.'

'Well. I do and I have to. It's about Todd.' She told Nancy she had been right, that Todd had not, after all, done what she had said he had done. Her voice was hoarse with the enormity of what she told.

Nancy let her falter through the telling, before she said, 'It doesn't really matter if it's true or not.'

'Of course it matters.'

'No it doesn't.' The idea that it might matter to Natasha, very much, had obviously not occurred to her, or if it had, she had chosen not to mention it. 'Todd doesn't want to see me anymore.'

'Jesus, Nancy, whatever about you and him, it still matters. Maybe matters more than ever.'

'Not to me.'

'I see. So what did he say?'

'Not much. He said he's going to try harder with Jennifer, because of Rosie, and that, anyway, he didn't think it could have worked between us. He said we're too alike.'

For a moment Natasha wondered what similarities Todd saw with her sister, who was capricious and childish, with all the reflexive, touching selfishness of the perennially discontented. But maybe that wasn't how he saw her.

'So will you go back to John?' she asked.

'It's over with John too. A few weeks ago I had two boyfriends, now I have none. Thanks to you.' But she was nearly laughing, and Natasha decided to let that be enough.

The night of the party, the house looked beautiful. Its high ceilings and spacious rooms were the same, but the week of hard work, the fact that they had all slept under its roof together, eaten together, made toast late at night, had given it a warm feeling of bustle, of cosy things happening in corners and little jokes to be laughed over that took the chill out of its imperiousness.

Halloween was in the air by then; the crisp, apple-y smell of autumn and the sharp inhalation of cold moonlit nights. So they lit braziers in the garden, burning logs that gave off a deep glow and sweet-smelling smoke, and strung lanterns shaped like pumpkins through the half-naked trees so that when guests arrived they were drawn straight outside, to stand chatting and laughing, moving in and out of the light like moths.

Natasha didn't know if the party was the end of something, or the beginning, but both, she decided, were good. For the first time in so many years, she felt as if she had context, a place that was hers. The whirling weightlessness felt fastened down at last, by what, she wasn't sure; the profound heaviness of relief maybe? The knowledge of possibility? All the things that she would now do, could do, gathered in front of her, in a joyous line, stretching far into a future that caused her no unease.

The house filled like a bath. Nearly all those they had invited appeared, friends from all the walks of their lives, as if they had simply been waiting for the summons. Natasha saw her mother, face flushed with effort and excitement, offering drinks, taking coats, finding vases for flowers, and laughing as she hadn't seen her laugh in years.

'She looks so beautiful when she's happy,' Jennifer said.

'Everyone does,' Natasha agreed.

Jennifer was alone, but said Todd would look in later, after work. Natasha had not specifically invited him. Had wondered would he come – surely not, she thought, with both her and Nancy there, but she had been wrong apparently.

'So he's back at work already?' she asked.

'God, yes. Almost immediately. He had a hell of a battle keeping control of the companies.'

'But he managed?'

'He did, and he loved every minute of it. That, more than anything, convinced me he really is OK.' He was, she said, just as he had ever been – 'working on three laptops at once, busily conquering America' – but that he was making more effort to get home in the evenings to see Rosie, and they had begun to talk about having another child.

'I don't want one, not until I'm properly established in college again, but he doesn't need to know that.'

There was laughter and talk reaching into every corner of the house, but Natasha couldn't settle to any conversation. Couldn't respond to the excited queries about the gallery and her new job there, compliments on how well her mother was looking, how happy Nancy seemed. The two gin and tonics she had drunk only made her twitchy, not light and gay as she had hoped.

On her way to the kitchen for more white wine, she found Julie looking critical as she appraised the African masks on the wall. 'I suppose ethnic art is making a comeback,' she said as Natasha passed by.

'I can't wait to tell my mother. She'll be so excited,' Natasha said. Then, 'Is Stu here?'

'No.' Julie paused, and Natasha expected some detail of the important conference Stu was attending, or his urgent requirement at work. Instead Julie said, 'I heard about you and Katherine and the gallery. You must be delighted. I suppose it will all work out for you and Martin now too?'

'Maybe.' Natasha had no idea if what she said was true or not, did not dare consider it too closely. 'And you're furious because you don't get to annex him for one of your friends?'

'That has nothing to do with it.'

'What then?'

'I once thought there might be a chance for me and Martin,' Julie said stiffly. 'That's all. But with you back, I suppose that was never going to happen.'

All the hating Julie and sneering at her disappeared then, like snow falling in a heap from a furry winter branch, under the knowledge that she, too, had hidden chambers in her heart, places where she buried regret, and disappointments that didn't ease over.

'And if you ever say that to anyone, I will finish you,' Julie said.

'Gotcha.' Just because Julie had a heart, didn't mean it was a large or generous one.

Natasha had known the moment with Todd would come at last and, sure enough, she saw him, in close conversation with a friend of her father's who was now special adviser to someone in government. The two were standing close enough to have put their arms around each other, talking thoughtfully in that way Todd did when he needed to shrink the age and experience gap between himself and someone he considered important.

Knowing she couldn't be in the same house as him without some kind of confrontation, Natasha went over, touching his arm lightly, said, 'Sorry to intrude, may I have a second?'

The special adviser said of course, told her how well she was looking, and wandered off to refill his glass.

Todd, Natasha thought, looked like a slowly ripening fruit. The bloom of bruises on his cheekbones had softened and blurred, the colours faded down to a gentle array of greens and yellows. His bloodied eye was clear once more, though the puffiness around it hadn't yet fully subsided. She wanted to say something that would be significant, and final, to draw a line between them, but could think what it might be.

'What is it, Natasha?'

Whatever softness had been in him the day at the house was gone. He listened to her stammered apologies with barely concealed impatience, then dismissed them with a flip of his hand – 'forget it' – as if she were being boring. She could see him looking over her shoulder, clocking the movements of the special adviser. But she wouldn't be silenced, not until she had taken her fuller share of wrongdoing.

'Declan would never have done it if I hadn't prompted him,' she said in a low voice. She could see Jennifer looking over from the other side of the room, could sense Nancy waiting to interrupt.

'Declan?' He seemed almost surprised at the mention of his name. He really did live in his own movie, Natasha thought, so much so that nothing existed unless he chose for it to exist.

'Yes. Declan. I know what he did was unforgivable, but the fault is still mine.'

Todd listened, with what almost seemed like incredulity, then said, in a way that could almost have been fond had it not been for the tinny sound of mockery, the smile that lifted those still-swollen lips. 'Dear Natasha, always so willing to believe the best of everyone.'

It was, she thought, a curious remark. What did he mean? For a second, the old desire to scrape and worry at his words came upon her, to scatter them like bones in a voodoo ceremony, the better to see them from all angles, and try to understand them. But she shook her head, and stepped away.

She had spent too long talking to Todd. She needed to find Martin. In a sudden panic that he might have come and gone, she went from room to room, through the laughing groups, ignoring her mother beckoning her to meet someone, Katherine smiling and inviting her to sit on the sofa. Nowhere could she see Martin. In the kitchen, people were making cocktails with fresh lime and crushed ice and dancing to Donna Summer.

She went into the garden, standing in the shadow of the house, back from the chatting groups around the braziers, preferring to watch for a moment. And in the darkness that was betrayed by shifting patches of light, she caught sight of Martin at last, standing on his own. She did not know if she could go to him. There was too much hope in her. Too much fear. Because if he still said nothing, or if he said no to the two of them, then she knew she couldn't bear it.

So she stood and watched him for a moment, until he lifted his head and saw her. He walked over. 'There you are.'

'Here I am,' she agreed. 'At last.' And before he could respond, she wrapped her arms around him and reached up to kiss him. They stood like that for a moment, in which she breathed in the smell of him, mixed with the smell of burning logs and night air. Ducking her head to his neck, Natasha buried it close into him, with all relief that she now knew lay at the heart of love.

Around them, drawn close by the braziers, tiny moths fluttered among the sparks, willing to risk life for love. They looked, Natasha thought, like a miniature, mobile constellation of stars, the lights of their own world, dancing to a secret tune.

ACKNOWLEDGEMENTS

Everybody who told me second novels were hard, was right. They are hard. Less time, more pressure, more expectation and more self-doubt than with a first. But, to balance that, the knowledge that now you are a 'real' writer. After all, one could be fluke, two – that's a pattern . . .

This book wouldn't have made it out of the starting blocks without the help of a few good people. They are, in no particular order: My brother Liam Francis, because he read an early draft and was kind. My sister Bridget, who read an early draft and was horrible. Domini Kemp who read a later draft and was enthusiastic. Val Kemp, who provided one of my favourite lines in the book (even though I later took it out and am keeping it for better), and because sometimes, distance gives enough perspective to realise when someone is really remarkable. Justin Callaghan, who helped with astute financial plot advice. Paula Ryan, who gave me time and space to write the last chapter. Susan Morley, who found me somewhere beautiful to work (I'll take you up on it next time!), and Eimer Philbin Bowman, for the years of friendship. Brendan O'Connor who has launched two books for me, and is a wise sounding-board on many things.

These are just the tip of the iceberg. There are so many more, friends, neighbours, colleagues and kind acquaintances who make life not just possible, but wonderful. I can't name you all, although I hope you know who you are, but trust me – you are a source of inspiration, comfort and fun.

Among you, I count my 'cancer friends,' some of whom I have never met, because you kept me afloat through bad times, out of the sheer goodness of your hearts, and your own hard-won understanding of the misery of that experience. Thank you.

My agent Jonathan Williams, who treads a perfect line between encouraging and exacting. Ciara Doorley, who is not just a pleasure to hang out with, but also a remarkably sharp, and perspicacious editor, with an instinctive understanding of what a book wants to be. Breda Purdue, Joanna Smyth and all at Hachette, who are such a joy to work with. Rachel Pierce, whose edit was superb, and just the right side of tough.

My husband David, who thinks all the characters are based on him. My children, who bring me more delight every day. My brothers and sisters, the best and funniest people I know, and my mother, who is the gold standard in everything I do.